KILLING BLUE EYES

KILLING BLUE EYES

A Alex Come'

ARPress

ILLUMINATING IDEAS.
EMPOWERING VOICES

ARPress
45 Dan Road Suite 5
Canton MA 02021
Hotline: 1(888) 821-0229
Fax: 1(508) 545-7580

Ordering Information:
Quantity sales. Special discounts are available on quantity purchases by corporations, associations, and others. For details, contact the publisher at the address above.

Printed in the United States of America.

ISBN-13:   Softcover   979-8-89330-854-9
            Hardcover   979-8-89330-855-6
            eBook   979-8-89330-856-3

Library of Congress Control Number: 2024903364

Dedicated to our parents:

Clayton and Pauline & Eddie and Leti

For we do not wrestle against flesh and blood, but against principalities, against powers, against the rulers of the darkness of this age, against spiritual hosts of wickedness in the heavenly places.

EPHESIANS 6:12

"For God did not send His Son into the world to condemn the world, but that the world through Him might be saved. He who believes in Him is not condemned; but he who does not believe is condemned already, because he has not believed in the name of the only begotten Son of God. And this is the condemnation, that the light has come into the world, and men loved darkness rather than light, because their deeds were evil. For everyone practicing evil hates the light and does not come to the light, lest his deeds should be exposed. But he who does the truth comes to the light, that his deeds may be clearly seen, that they have been done in God."

JOHN 3:17-21

CONTENTS

CHAPTER ONE

MAY 2, FISHER'S POINT WOODS, BROOKE, INDIANA

THE TURN-OFF TO FISHER'S Point was less than twenty minutes away. Clayton Cooper's 1998 extended-cab Dodge Ram pickup skirted easily through the layered shadows of an unusually cold midnight.

The black asphalt road lay dark and deserted, and it pleased him, for he did not wish to come upon a speeder or a weaver and have to pull them over. All he wanted was to get to Fisher's Point, take care of business, and return home.

Storm clouds concealed the Hoosier stars and full moon glowered amid the darkened sky. It hovered just over the trees to his left, and Clay glanced up into its mocking face. Black-gray eyes watched the moving truck, taunting, as if to say, "I witnessed everything and I'm not telling."

Five minutes from his turn-off, Clay gave thought to the reason he'd been called to Fisher's Point. What awaited him was not something he was anxious to see. Deputy Carl Brown had called by cellular, rousting him from the amorous arms of his wife, Nancy. Recalling his last vision of her lying in bed snuggled beneath the flower-patterned comforter, naked, Clay let his mind linger on the sight. A smile showered at the corners of his mouth.

Clay considered himself especially fortunate. Nance was a terrific wife, the perfect companion, his true soul mate. And the Beta HCG test taken last month, informing them she was two weeks pregnant, had only enriched their love. Even now, as he was on his way out, Nancy had ordered him to hurry back, saying that she was far from finished with him. The thought caused him to blush, but the feeling was short lived. His thoughts shifted back to what lay ahead.

There were two bodies, Brown had told him, one male and one female. Both were nude and hanging from the same tree limb, and both were very dead. The female hung upside down by her feet and the male upright by the neck; facing one another, their fingers were interlocked, as if holding hands. And there was something else, Brown had said, something bizarre, something sick, something Clay would just have to see for himself when he arrived.

He slowed to forty-five miles per hour. The road here was exceptionally winding and required cautious navigation. On both sides of the highway, shadows crept out from the woods, their bizarre shapes kindred to the peculiarly cold night air. Shivering, he turned up the heater. Actually, it felt more like the later days of fall than the early budding of spring. Indiana had just come out of a harsh winter, and now it seemed those cold, bitter days had found their way back.

Oblivious to the increase of the blower motor's soft whir, Clay sighed, thankful for the additional warmth. Leaning over the steering wheel, he glanced up into the dark sky. Treetops swayed to the force of an intense wind, the same cold creature that howled at his windows and occasionally rocked the heavy vehicle with fierce vengeance.

Clay pressed the brake and the truck's rear window light kicked on. Soft crimson showered the bed. Turning onto a one-lane drive, he prepared himself for a bumpy ride. The road onto which he turned was narrow with low hanging branches and tall grass sprouting between age-worn tire tracks.

Laden with washed-out holes, the road wound through a forest of thick trees. But he knew the way to the edge of the Iroquois River. Originally a thoroughfare worn down by fishermen with four-wheel drive pickups, it was seldom used now, except for teenagers seeking a safe haven for pot smoking or a little backseat Macarena.

The truck bounced and twisted over holes impossible to avoid. Tree branches scraped the roof and sides, and the narrow pathway cut by the headlights provided barely enough light by which to see.

Clay made a final turn to the left and entered into a small clearing. After driving another hundred yards through tall grass, he came to a stop beside the department's year-old Crown Victoria Cruiser. Its red and blue lights still turning, it sat slightly angled with its trunk to the riverbank and its headlights shining into a section of the dark woods.

Clay sat silent a second, scanning the area. He then zipped up his green Carhart jacket, placed a Denver Broncos ballcap on his head, stuck two pairs of surgical gloves in his coat pocket, grabbed his long-handled flashlight, and stepped out. Wind pushed fiercely against the door, but his six-foot, two hundred twenty-four-pound frame held it at bay.

Deputy Brown, holding his campaign hat tight to his head, stepped around the truck to greet him. Clay nodded with a thin smile and let the vehicle door slam shut. Turning then, he glanced momentarily out over the Iroquois river. Cold moonlight reflected off the water's choppy surface.

Brown spoke, his voice edge with excitement and nearly a shout to be heard above the wind. Clay turned to face him and hear what he had to say.

"Man, you're not going to believe what the hell is in those woods! Son of a bitch, I've never seen anything like it before. God almighty, Clay, it gives me the creeps."

Clay nodded and spoke loudly: "Show me."

They moved to the front of the patrol car and stepped into the long stretch of headlight beams shooting off toward the woods. Putting its bright glare to their backs, they moved toward the front row of trees where the light began breaking up. A sudden strong gust of wind came up and Clay had to grab quickly to keep from losing his ballcap.

Once inside the tree line, the moonlight was of little use, as were the car's headlights. Darkness, it seemed, came upon them almost instantly. Clay switched on his flashlight and, using it along with the one Brown carried, they were able to light the pathway well enough to lessen the chance of tripping or being struck with a low-hanging branch.

Despite the thick barrier of trees, the wind continued to blow and howl around them. Limbs swayed and weeds on the forest floor danced with unruly zeal.

Carl, leading the way, yelled back each time he moved a branch out of the way with his hand. The wind never ceased, and the fluttering weeds slapped incessantly against their legs.

Clay had already ordered Carl to notify the State Police, Sheriff's Department, and Coroner. He had also told him to request the Fire Department to bring their rescue truck with portable lighting. As far as he was concerned, he wanted this over with as soon as possible.

The approaching storm's first rumble of thunder sounded, followed by a brief streak of lightning that lit the woods. All traces of the car's headlights had vanished and the flashlights they held were their sole sources of light. Though not truly deep into the woods, the solid darkness placed them in an alienated world; although it was morbid, Clay had to admit that this was the perfect location for a killing.

Then suddenly they were there. Two dark forms, naked and lifeless, hung in the black abyss, swaying to the push of a cold and unforgiving wind. Lightning flashed again, and though only for a second, it highlighted the killer's grotesque and senseless work. Shaking his head, Clay asked himself the million-dollar question: Why?

CHAPTER TWO

THE FLASHLIGHTS OFFERED LIMITED light and vision, but it was just as Carl had told him. There was one male and one female, both totally nude, with the male hanging by the neck and the female upside-down by her feet.

Tucking the flashlight beneath his arm, Clay pulled on a jar of latex gloves, careful not to tear them (although he had the extra pair, should that happen). Both bodies hung by the same rope, half-inch yellow nylon swung over the same thick limbs.

Focusing first on the male victim, Clay shined his light around the neck. He noted significant bruising and guessed he probably died of slow suffocation rather than a fractured cervical. The killer had probably pulled him up slowly just above the ground, then watched as he struggled.

Off in the distance they could hear the wail of sirens. In less than five minutes, state and county officers would be on the scene, and soon to follow would be the Fire Department with the lighting they so desperately needed.

Kneeling, Clay examined the female's head and face. Her mouth was fastened around the male's penis. Though difficult to tell how much, there was significant blood covering her face and matted in her hair. The hair had a crusty feel, resembling too much hairspray. Its stiffness told him they had been dead several hours.

The inside of the male's thighs were stained with blood as well. Carefully Clay put a finger to the female's lips, noticing they would not part. He guessed they had been super-glued around the penis. A quick check showed her nostrils were also glued closed. No doubt she too had died fighting for air, and in her desperate attempt to breathe her teeth had caused notable trauma to the male organ, probably while he was still alive. Clay looked up at Carl and yelled above the wind.

"Hell of a way to go. Had to hurt!"

Further investigation showed the hands of the victims had been glued together with fingers interlaced like lovers. A pool of blood had soaked the ground beneath both bodies.

Rising to his feet, Clay moved around the hanging corpses, looking for other obvious wounds; none were found. He also made a quick search about the immediate area. But with the wind blowing the grass and trees and only flashlights by which to see, it was all a waste of time. In agreement, Clay and the others decided to return to the vehicles and wait for the Fire Department.

In less than thirty seconds from the time they cleared the woods, a state police car made the last turn into the clearing and bounced its way across the open field. The vehicle came to stop just to the right of Carl's cruiser, with its headlights also shining into the woods.

Sergeant Ron Parks stepped out. A stocky five-foot eleven-inch trooper with brown, crew cut hair, he was eleven-year veteran sixteen days away from his thirty-third birthday.

It was no secret than Ron was Clay's closest friend. Having known one another since seventh grade, their relationship was more like that of brothers. They had shared their first cigar, prayed side by side to the porcelain God, and lost their virginity the same day to thirty-six-year-old Rosy Rossmussen at age thirteen. Clay had gone first and never let Ron forget it. Ron Parks was a welcome sight on this cold and unpleasant night.

Overhead, thunder rumbled again. Far across the river, a bolt of lightning tore through the darkness. Clay glanced out over the choppy water once again, then up into the heavens.

The stars were still missing, and except for the moonlight seeping through thin-wispy clouds, a cold blackness mantled the earth. He was pleased to be where he was, far below, wrapped inside the warmth of his old Carhart jacket.

When Ron reached Clay and Carl, the three shook hands, and then Clay explained what they had. Out on the highway, more sirens could be heard, and he knew the lighting was soon to arrive. For the sake of preserving the crime scene, they decided to wait, and all go in together.

Fifteen minutes passed by the time Fire Department personnel arrived and unloaded their portable generator with six tripod quartz halogen lights. Also, a sheriff's deputy and the coroner had checked in.

At 2:08 an assembled team of four law enforcement officers, one coroner and four fire-fighters entered into the dark woods toward the crime scene.

Lighting was set up in a circular pattern, two facing toward and four away from the bodies, as an aid to illuminating a larger portion of the crime scene area. Ron and Carl both took photographs and videotape for their department files. When that was completed, Clay and Carl assisted the coroner while Ron and the others diligently combed the grounds. The coroner was thorough in his duties.

It was estimated that the victims had been dead ten to twelve hours, placing the murders somewhere between 3:00 and 5:00 p.m. the female's age was guessed to be around nineteen or twenty, and the male was placed in the early thirties.

The coroner saw everything Clay had already noted. The blood pooled below the victims on the ground had all come from the male genitalia. Close observation revealed the penis had been nearly severed and now hung by only a few threads of skin, the female having bitten it horribly while fighting for air. The blood covering her face and crusted in her hair had come from the male as well.

Bill "Zig" ZigCoskey was both a good coroner and personal friend. While respected by almost everyone, Zig was notorious for speaking his mind and possessing a sense of humor not always considered tasteful or appropriate – but like so many in the business of pain and death, Zig dealt with it in his own way. Clay never judged him.

Without removing his eyes from his work, Zig spoke loud enough to be heard above the wind as he moved about the victims. His conversation was just that, conversation, and was not truly necessary. "You guys have any idea why anyone would do such a thing to these poor people?"

"No," Clay yelled back, "but we have every intention of finding out."

Zig began a thorough check of the female's feet, then slowly began moving down her body in systematic fashion, not missing an inch. "It could be, too," he went on, yelling above the wind, "a satanic thing. Hell, thousands disappear every year without a trace…men, women, and children. You guys know the statistics."

When he reached the woman's private area he began thumbing through the pubic hair. Although no explanation was necessary, he told Clay and Carl, "This isn't foreplay, guys, so don't think I'm just another sick coroner working up a woody. I'm searching for signs of foul play. Things like blood, tears, abrasions, cum gobs, and the like."

Then he gave a short whistle and said, "Well, holy private parts, what do we have hidden here in this cold little cavern?" Zig tuck the small maglight he'd been using between his teeth to free up both hands. Spreading the vaginal lips apart, he meticulously began working something out of the vaginal canal.

"What the hell is it, Zig?" Clay asked.

"Yeah, what in the world is that?" Carl echoed, moving closer for a better look.

Thunder rumbled somewhere to the north. Zig worked carefully, taking great pains to maneuver it safely out. Whatever it was, it appeared round, pliable, and cylindrical in shape. Diligently, his fingers worked it up to the opening. Lightning streaked through the woods. When he finally pulled it free, he raised it to the maglight's beam and examined it slowly, turning and squeezing it gingerly.

Finally, satisfied with his examination, he nodded to himself and placed it in Clay's gloved hand. "Now this," he said, removing the maglight from his mouth, "is something you don't find everyday in a dead woman's vagina."

Clay looked from Zig to the object he now held. It was a small, tightly rolled sheet of heavy parchment tied in place with a piece of blue ribbon. The ribbon was fastened in a neat little bow and came undone easily. Working against the wind trying to tear it from his hands, Clay unraveled it carefully. On it were written six words, words he mumbled to himself, words that left him stunned.

Without warning thunder exploded directly over their heads. The three jumped and, although he did not suffer from Tourette's Syndrome, Zig spontaneously yelled out loud, "Fuck Me, You Thunder Boomer!"

Everyone searching the grounds stopped to look at him. Embarrassed, Zig forced a smile and waved, yelling above the wind. "It's okay everybody, I'm fine, thanks." As he turned to face Clay and Carl, a streak of lightning again tore through the woods, lighting it brightly. As though its power had ripped a hole in the sky, drops of rain began falling. They were soft at first, but within seconds the speed increased, becoming a wild downpour. Thunder rumbled angrily and another flash of lightning followed.

The small parchment in Clayton Cooper's hand was difficult to hold against the attacking wind, but he maintained a firm grip, staring at the paper as if mesmerized. Carl removed his campaign hat and held it over the paper in an attempt to keep it dry. After throwing a puzzled glance toward Zig, Carl looked back to Clay, yelling, "Clay!"

Startled, he looked up. But his expression told Carl he was a thousand miles away. Swiping at the rain streaming down his face, Carl asked, "Well, what does it say?"

Clay stared at him a few seconds, then as if waking from a dream, told him. "You're not going to believe it."

"Try me!" Carl shouted.

Lowering his eyes, Cooper read just loud enough to be heard above the deafening squall now thrashing their world.

TO CLAYTON COOPER
INESCAPABLE COLLABORATOR
BELIAL

There, in the hammering rain, Zig and Carl stood silent, their faces showing the same shock and disbelief Clay was expressing. Seconds passed with no one saying anything. The wind howled at their sober mood and the relentless downpour sent streams of water cascading down their faces. Then, over the choppy Iroquois river, lightning sparked an extravagant network of brilliant flashes that brought them back to reality.

Quickly, Clay placed the scroll under his jacket and ordered Carl to the cruiser for an evidence bag. Upon his return, he packaged it, then called Ron over and surrendered it to him.

With that done, Zig resumed his examination of the bodies but turned up nothing further, as was the case with the crime scene search. Based on worsening weather, it was agreed that they'd call it a night.

Clay, Carl, Ron, and the sheriff's deputy met briefly while the Fire Department took down the bodies and wrapped them in sheets. Glued together as they were, the remains would not fit into a traditional body bag. Therefore, enfolded only in sheets, they were carried to Zig's old 1974 Cadillac Hearse and transported to the morgue.

By the time the Fire Department pulled out to return to the station, the meeting had been adjourned. It was decided that divers would come at morning light and search the river.

It was nearly 3:00 a.m. when they caravanned out of Fisher's Point. All the way home, Clay's thoughts focused on two questions: why was his name on that scroll, and who the hell was Belial?

CHAPTER THREE

MINDFUL OF NOT WAKING Nancy, Clay switched off his headlights prior to pulling into the drive. Exiting the truck, he made a speedy dash for the porch, hoping haste would limit much of the torrential downpour. It didn't. When a flash of lightning silhouetted his scurrying form grotesquely across the garage door, he shrieked. His mind had been on the bodies and the sudden flash startled him. "Way to go, Cooper," he berated himself. "I can see the headlines now: *Brooke Town Marshall dies from fright – sees his own shadow.*"

Beneath the protection of the porch, he sputtered away a procession of water trying to flow into his mouth. Cold fingers unlocked the front door, and, except for the sound of pounding rain, he slipped in quietly. The small end table lamp was lit, and it bathed the couch in soft, shadowy light. Nancy was sitting there, waiting. Rising to her feet, she smiled, and for Clay it was holistic medicine, welcome warmth that, at least for a few seconds, chased away the harsh chill settling in his bones.

She approached and he took her in his arms, holding her a long time. Despite his wet clothing, she remained in his embrace until he was ready to let go. Nancy was always there for him, mindful of the traumatic responsibility his job often demanded. It was because of this nurturing insight he had long ago nicknamed her his Little Lifesaver- and this was the perfect example. Once again, her hand held the tether, gently pulling him back to safety and away from yet another round of incongruous insanity.

When he finally released her, she shivered, and he realized he had soaked her nightclothes. Repentantly, he apologized. "Sorry sweetheart, I didn't even think about getting you wet."

Nancy smiled thoughtfully and squeezed his hand. "I know, it's okay. Listen, I just made a fresh pot of coffee. How about a cup?"

"Sounds great."

She winked, releasing his hand. "Thought it would."

When she left for the kitchen, Clay pulled off his wet coat and hat and hung them on the coat rack near the door, then removed his boots and damp socks. Tiredly, he walked barefoot to the couch and plopped down, throwing back his head and closing his eyes. There was no erasing the sight of the hanging bodies, or the incriminating words on the scroll.

Thunder boomed above the town and lightning bathed the little community in a second-long flash of piercing light. *How could anyone do such a thing? He wondered. How did the Dahmers, Gaceys and Bundys live with themselves? What kind of thinking went on inside their minds to enable them to kill innocent people, stealing away precious human life, and, sickeningly, find enjoyment in it? And why in the hell was his name on that scroll?*

Clay sighed. He wanted this killer! Wanted him badly. Wanted answers and wanted the feel of his hands around this madman's throat. And he wanted the pleasure of beating him within an inch of his life before reading him his rights and putting him in a pair of extra-tight cuffs.

"Coffee's here."

Clay opened his eyes and sat up. The coffee was hot, and the acrylic carafe steamed as Nancy set the tray on the coffee table. Sitting, she poured a cup and handed it to Clay. It was just what he needed. Even the warmth of the rising mist was a welcome sensation. After pouring a cup for herself, Nancy sat back and glanced into Clay's face. It was strained. "Bad out there, uh?" she asked.

Clay nodded, taking his first sip. "It wasn't pretty."

"Want to talk about it?"

He looked at her admiringly. His Lifesaver understood him so well. Perhaps it was unfair and created an unwanted burden on her, but she so perceptibly understood his needs to talk following unpleasant investigations. Taking another sip, he told her, "We found two bodies in the woods at Fisher's Point."

"Homicide?"

"Yep."

"Shot?"

"No, both hung."

"Yikes. Any clues?"

"Possibly," he said. "The bodies go in for autopsy today, and we found a scroll on one of the victims. Hopefully, it will turn up a print."

"A scroll?" she asked questioningly. "You mean a scroll like in ancient times, as in the Dead Sea Scrolls?"

Clay gave a nod. "Well, yeah, but not exactly. I mean, it looked authentic, but this one was small and had very little writing on it."

He took another sip of coffee, mentally re-visualizing Zig pulling the parchment from the victim's vagina. It was difficult, if not impossible, for him to understand how anyone could desecrate a human body in such a way. Shifting his thoughts to whoever the killer might be, one word stuck in his head: Deranged. He recalled the sight of the two naked forms hanging in the cold woods. They had died so horribly. Who ever the murderer was, he was one sick S.O.B.

"Well?"

The word brought Clay back to reality and he turned to his wife. "Sorry, what?"

"What did it say?" she asked. "What was written on the scroll?"

Clay stared blanky at her while refocusing his thoughts. "Belial," he told her. "The word 'Belial' was written on it."

Clay did not tell the whole truth, that his own name had been included in its inscription. There was no need to worry her-not right now, anyway.

Nancy's brow wrinkled thoughtfully. "You know, Clay, I've heard that word before." She repeated it several times aloud. "Belial, Belial… *Belial*." Then she nodded. "Yes, in the Bible! I think that at least it has something to do with the Bible, or something to do with religious beliefs. I think it was something bad, though, something evil." Nancy continued to work her mind, searching for the information she wanted.

A sudden crash of thunder exploded over the house, rattling doors, and windows. Rain continued its hammering. A headache was forming in Clay's temples; closing his eyes, Clay laid his head back again and took in a deep breath.

What he needed was to forget about everything, go upstairs, relax, and sleep-but he knew that wasn't going to happen. Somewhere inside stirred a disquieting feeling, one unlike anything he'd ever experienced.

Things were far from over, and they were going to get worse…a good deal worse. Perhaps it was intuition, or just plain gut instinct. Exactly what it was, he did not know, but it was there, strong, and very real; something was not right, something was wrong…very wrong.

Suddenly, behind his closed eyes, there was an explosion of light, and a vision formed as if he sat in a theatre looking upon a big screen. He saw himself standing alone in the yard looking upon his own house, and there before him, oblivious to the hammering rain, an army of dark football-sized creatures were scaling the sides of his house and roof, thousands in number, like ants on a sand-hill. His heart raced, for he knew what they were doing: searching for a way in.

Their voices shrill, the flurry of creatures were chanting something amid the harsh downpour, but their cries were a garbled mass of inaudible non-sense. Cooper stood behind them, motionless, watching the assemblage of crawling things envelop the building beneath their increasing numbers. Straining, he struggled to make sense of the mantra they chanted.

Then Clay watched himself advance a step closer to the house; although only observing, he could feel his other self's fear. Clay paused, closed his eyes, and took a deep breath, then opened them again and moved forward one step at a time. At last, he stood so close that his shaking hand reached out and touched one of the strange things with his fingertips. Gnawing madly through the vinyl siding, the creature paused and stiffened. The thing was layered in hair, and every strand bristled.

Slowly it rose, turning to look at him squarely in the eyes. Pointy ears towered above its flat, snakelike head; small marble eyes with yellow, elliptical pupils widened. Then it opened its mouth, a mouth stretched beyond the limits of its face. Pointed teeth, sharp and jagged, appeared; Clay waxed white with terror, fearing it was perching to bite. Its eyes grew tense, and drool seeped from yellow-brown gums onto its teeth. A scream rose within Clay's chest, but the creature's gargantuan jaws closed, and slowly, methodically, its head moved toward him until they stood face to face. Its breath was horrid. In a low guttural tone, it said two words… "Kill Him!"

"Shit!" Clay shouted the word aloud, jerking open his eyes and bolting to his feet.

Startled, Nancy turned. "My God, Clay, are you alright?"

Taking in a deep breath, Clay then let it out shakily, sitting back down, not realizing he had spilled the remainder of his coffee.

Nancy asked again: "Clay, are you alright?"

Looking toward her, he forced a grin. "Yeah, I'm fine. Just tired. It was a bad dream, that's all. I'm okay, really."

He set his empty cup down, hiding the shaking of his hand.

Concern remained on Nancy's face. "Why don't you go upstairs and get cleaned up, and try to get some rest? You need to get those wet clothes off, anyway."

As an attempt to appease her, he agreed.

In the bedroom, he stripped down and took a long, hot shower. By the time he had finished and come out, Nancy had the bed ready. He climbed in and she pulled the covers over him, smiling warmly. "You get some sleep. When you wake up, I'll fix you something to eat."

"Can't sleep that long," he told her. "I've got to meet Ron and the others at the crime scene by 10:00. Make sure I'm up by 9:15."

She promised, then kissed him and left, turning off the light on the way out. In the calm, shadowy darkness of the upstairs, he lay staring at the ceiling. Slowly his eyes grew heavy and closed. He opened them harshly, not wanting to sleep, wanting to remain awake and mull over all that had been happening. This killer had to be caught and put behind bars. He yawned and his eyelids lowered again, slowly. It felt good.

Visions of color, things good and bad, past and present, leaped through his thoughts. Clay's eyes darted fiercely beneath their thin, closed lids. Within seconds he had become hopelessly lost in deep sleep, and a nightmare began.

Nancy screamed. His eyes opened. Her voice was heavy with panic, calling his name, crying out for help. Wildly, he bolted from the bed, grabbing his 9-millimeter lying on the dresser.

On the run, he left the bedroom and entered the hallway leading to the stairs. He heard himself shouting into the darkness of the house, "I'm coming, Nance!" to him it felt as though he moved in slow motion. God, why wouldn't his legs move faster? Nancy's screams grew louder. They were agonizing screams, wails that rose from the horror of excruciating pain. He felt tears sting his eyes. They streaked down his cheeks, and he tasted salt in his mouth.

He was at the top of the stairs now. They stretched long before him, ending far below in a thick mass of darkness. Pausing, he shouted out Nancy's name She did not reply.

He bolted down the stairs. His heavy weight caused the steps to creak as he bounded toward the waiting abyss. Halfway down he stumbled, falling hard, slamming into the carpeted steps, tumbling like a giant boulder of flesh and blood. As he rolled, he once again heard the tormenting cries of his wife, but it was bittersweet; she was alive and for that he thanked God, but now her cries were weak and distant, strange in their sound, muffled, as if she were being drug down a long, hollow tunnel.

At some point during his somersaulting, the gun he held tight in his hand came free and flew through the air, landing with a thud somewhere in the same blackness that imprisoned his wife.

It was a fall that seemed never to end, but when it did, his stop was sudden. He rose quickly and placed a hand over his left side, for at some point during the plummet he had injured his ribs. Now, motionless, he stood listening. Blackness wrapped around him like a cavernous fog.

There was silence throughout the house, a deathly quiet that rippled through him in a wave of fear. Not for himself, but for his wife. No longer was she calling for him, no more did she cry; his beloved Lifesaver had fallen quiet. Raising his head toward Heaven he screamed his rage, then plunged into the darkness.

He could not see. Where his gun had landed, he had no idea, but he wished it were in his hand. He called out to Nancy, but there was no reply. Then his body bumped into the couch and felt only soft, empty cushions. Anxious hands fumbled for the lamp and found it, but it would not work: the bulb had been removed. He cursed.

Like a blind man, he stumbled through the room, feeling and groping in a desperate search. Where was she? Where was his love? "Cry, Nancy," he mumbled, "Say something, anything, moan, please, just give me a sign you're alive!"

Clay found himself at the kitchen door. Somewhere in the darkness ahead he could hear the soft hum of the refrigerator. There were no other sounds. *The refrigerator!* If it was running, he reasoned, then there was power. His hand groped for the kitchen's light switch. Nothing. He cursed again.

Maybe, he thought, just maybe, the killer forgot the light inside the refrigerator. Sliding his hand down the wall, he felt the long countertop that would lead him to the humming appliance. Hurriedly, he followed it, moving swiftly through the dark.

Then he was there. Grabbing the handle, he abruptly pulled open the door. The kitchen exploded into light… Thank God! He whirled about, his eyes taking in the room. No one! Nothing! A cry of anger welled up in his throat, but a mere second before its release, he turned back to the refrigerator and his eye caught a piece of paper hanging from one of the refrigerator shelves. It was a note, and he knew it was for him.

A single word had been finger painted in blood.

GARAGE?

From behind, a hand touched his shoulder and he whirled to deliver a striking blow.

"Clay!"

Nancy's yell startled him awake and he bolted straight up. He was bathed in sweat. Although groggy, Clay quickly realized he had been dreaming and fell back onto his pillow.

Looking at Nancy he closed his eyes then opened them again.

"Sorry."

She sat beside him, letting her breath out slowly. "I'm glad you stopped yourself in time. That must have been some dream!"

"No, nightmare," he told her.

She stared at him empathetically. "Look at you," she said, forcing a smile to help ease the tenseness. "You're drenched. You need another shower." Rising to her feet, she added, "Why don't you grab a quickie? I'll fix you something to eat."

Clay looked up from where he lay and let his own smile show. "A quickie, huh, now that's something that just might help."

Smiling back, she pointed a finger. "Not that kind. Now get in the shower." Nancy left, shaking her head. Clay climbed out of bed and headed for the bathroom. The shower felt wonderful and revitalized him, but it did little in preventing his dream from haunting him the rest of the day.

The entire morning and early afternoon were spent tediously searching the crime scene. Rain had continued to fall in a steady, endless mist so that everything remained wet, making the job uncomfortable, but the worst of it was that their efforts had turned up nothing. Even the dive team had come up empty-handed.

Just before 2:00 pm, the storm began to dissipate, and a warm sun began drying things out. At 2:10, disappointment but satisfied with their efforts, the team called it quits.

On the way home, Clay remained lost in thought. This killer was good. No evidence, no mistakes… at least not yet. And whoever he was, he was one sick individual, a pure psycho. He loved killing, enjoyed making it a game and obviously delighted in making it personal. And the more Cooper thought about it, the more it became fine with him. For although he felt strangely uneasy about the whole thing, he didn't want it to be over; he wanted to capture this psychopathic bastard, but he needed more time for that to happen.

Besides, they still had the autopsy and scroll to go on. But more importantly, he was confident this killer was going to contact him again, this time directly. He wasn't sure exactly how, only that he would.

Clay hadn't mentioned it to Nancy, but from the moment of discovering the bodies, in addition to his eerie vision and unsettling nightmare, a little voice had found its way into his head and had remained there, repeating the oddest message again and again.

It made no sense, and he hadn't even the smallest idea where it was coming from, or why it was there. But the little voice had whispered the words so often that he had begun to repeat them to himself. Even now, under his breath, he mumbled their words… *"Pray, Clayton Cooper, pray and don't stop."*

CHAPTER FOUR

MONDAY MORNING, DESPITE BEING eager to get to work and check on clue results, Clay was an hour late thanks to the seductive ploys of his wife. She had been in the mood-and who was he to argue? After all, it was his obligation as her husband to put a smile on her face. Of course, by the time he walked through the office door at 9:06, his own smile had just begun to fade.

On his desk lay a note to call the State Police Post, extension 422. He recognized the number immediately; it was Ron, hopefully with good news. Anxious to get things in motion, he dialed the moment he was seated.

The phone rang twice.

"Parks."

"It's me."

"Clay old buddy. You want the good news or the crapola?"

Closing his eyes, Clay grinned at his best friend's eagerness to agitate. But cutting to the quick was Ron's way, and he had come to accept it as something special between them. The ola first."

"No prints on the scroll. Clean. We took it to Purdue for carbon testing and get this. The note is original papyrus, almost two thousand years old. Damn well preserved, too, I might add. We don't have a clue where the killer got it. We're checking museums statewide for B and E's over the past five years. Also contacted Interpol for overseas hoists, but nothing yet. That's the ola. Ready for the good?"

Clay nodded even though Ron could not see. "I could use some. Go."

"Zig worked over the weekend without Doc on the autopsy. Got a copy of the results here for you, along with ID on the victims. I'll fax them over in a second. We don't have the lab test back yet, but it's on rush. My guess is late today or early tomorrow." Ron paused, then added, "There's one more thing, and it's definitely not good news."

"Let me have it," Clay told him.

"OK buddy. You're gonna have a visitor today."

"Visitor? Who?"

"Name's Bob Lemus from the Bureau, flying from the New York field office. I'm to tell you to cooperate and under no circumstances to discuss the case with anyone, not even Carl."

Clay frowned. "What the hell is going on, Ron? I got a double homicide, but… the Feds?"

"That's because they were contacted by our department late last night. Turns out we'd gotten a memo from them a few years ago, requesting notification of any homicide, suicide or threat notes involving the word Belial. Hell, it wasn't ten minutes before they called back and said Lemus would be arriving today. He wants badly to talk to you, since your name was on the scroll. Anyway, my boss wants me to stay with the case even though the Feds made it clear they will handle everything themselves. I guess as far as they're concerned, the state's essentially out of the picture."

Agitated, Clay told him, "Not as far as I'm concerned. If they want my cooperation, you'll be right here beside me."

"Well, that's good, buddy, because I'll be picking Lemus up at the Purdue Airport and driving him to your office for a pow-wow. He's supposed to land around 10:40. It should put us at your office about noonish, give or take."

"What do you guys know about Lemus?" Clay asked.

"Heard he's a no-bullshit guy, a top specialist in serial killings. Written tons of papers on the subject, lectures around the world and heads up nearly all the serious investigations for the Bureau. Rumor has it the man has no friends and hates kids, kittens, bunny rabbits and TV comedy. And if that's not enough, his favorite hobbies are stepping on toes and throwing his weight around."

"Great." Clay frowned.

Ron envisioned Clay's exasperation and smiled to himself. "I knew you'd be thrilled, meeting someone famous and all."

"Well," Clay told him, "If everything you say is true, it rates an honest ten on the ola scale. But, because you're more muscle than brain and full of it yourself, I have to downgrade it to a five. So, see you around noon… and send me my fax!"

Clay hung up and sat in silence for a moment. Lemus would not be coming if the murder did not tie into an existing case, one involving Belial. But more than anything Clay wondered, as did Lemus he was sure, why the killer implicated him personally. Why Indiana, and why the insignificant little town of Brooke?

He gave thought to recent arrests, tickets, and drug busts. He could think of no one he had pissed off lately that would have the cold-heartedness to do something so horrific, and he was not aware of any hard cases he's put behind bars being released or having escaped. None of it made sense.

As with many town marshals in Indiana, Clay's office constituted a room within a single building housing all of Public Safety and City Hall. He and Carl made up the town's paid Police Department while the Fire and Ambulances services were made up of dedicated volunteers. Also, for six hours a day, sixty-two-year-old town clerk Gertrude Goffry sat in the office next to his, tending to public needs such as water payments, parking tickets, complaints and so on.

Every morning, without failure, Gertrude came in at 7:30 sharp, unlocked the building, and made coffee in the kitchen just off the large, open conference room. Today had been no exception. Clay rose from his chair to retrieve a cup of coffee. On his way out, he stuck his head in her office and asked if she'd like one, too. When she declined, he smiled and walked down the long rectangular room toward the kitchen, where he could smell the fresh coffee brewing.

Gertrude had been town clerk for nearly twenty years, never calling in sick, and on every July first through the fifteenth, taking her vacation. Reputed to always know what was going on in Brooke, she had earned the alias Gertrude Gossip, but too often her information came from an ear placed to the thin wall between their offices. Because of her snooping and eavesdropping, Clay had learned to be cautious, but thought the world of her.

However, Gertrude Gossip also picked up tidbits of information on Saturday night excursions to the local tavern. On the good side, from a town Marshall's perspective, Gertrude always had the answer or seemed able to get it, even in situations relating to him. Her uncanny talent had aided him more than once in leading to an arrest that otherwise would have never come to be.

From the cupboard above the sink, Clay pulled out his favorite personal cup, an off-white ceramic mug displaying a faded black police badge across its face. Old, it possessed a serious crack just above the handle. It was the first gift he had ever received from Nancy, and he found it impossible to part with. In addition to the cracked handle and well-worn insignia, there was good-sized chip along the rim on the side from which he drank. Therefore, when using it, he had grown accustomed to not picking it up by the handle. Although a sentimental keepsake to him, its unsightliness prompted Nancy to encourage him to leave it at work.

After filling it three-quarters full, a requirement to keep it from leaking, Clay returned to his office, setting the cup on the desk. He walked to the filing cabinet and pulled a few files. The remainder of the morning would be spent combing through them, looking for possible suspects. He was confident that the search would prove a waste of time, but nearly three hours remained before Ron and Lemus would arrive. Besides, he had learned early on that the obvious often held the key.

He was barely through the first file when the fax machine kicked on. It sat on the wall near the door, so he rose and anxiously retrieved a total of six sheets. Upon returning to his desk and taking a sip of coffee, he sat and began rifling through the material, beginning with the information on the female.

She was or rather, had been twenty-one-year-old Carol Careen Waldron, a fourth-year college student at the University of Miami, majoring in Theatrics, born April 20, 2000, in Albany, New York. She had just celebrated her twenty-second birthday at home and was returning to campus when she was apparently abducted. Her 2021 Yellow Corvette had been found abandoned at the Chitanango Service Plaza, New York State Thruway, on April 24th. No prints other than family and those other wise accounted for were found in the vehicle. She was five-six, 110 pounds, blue-eyed and Catholic. The cause of death was noted as suffocation; that was certainly the right call, Clay thought. The coroner's report stated she had been both raped and sodomized. There was no skin, blood, or other traceable DNA under her nails nor from semen found in all 3 orafices.

The male victim had been identified as William Henry Roget, a soldier on active military duty, Special Forces, six-foot, 219 pounds, sandy blond hair, and blue eyes. Age thirty-four, he had been born in Charleston, South Carolina, on December 24, 1988. He had apparently been abducted from his current duty station area at Washington, DC. The cause of death had been suffocation and severe hemorrhaging. Like the young woman, he too had been sodomized. Clay shook his head.

Aside from the obvious, Zig had also reported a couple of odd findings. There were traces of dust inside the lungs of both victims, possibly the result of a ride in the trunk of the killer's car. Also, on the back of Roget's neck, he had discovered a small pinhole just below the hairline.

Clay took another sip of coffee while reasoning; there was a good chance the puncture came from a syringe, or tranquilizer dart. Roget was a trained fighter and, according to the report, other than the neck, groin and wrist area, , there were no other notable bruises or injury sites on his body. Also, like the girl, there was no trace of skin, hair, or other substances beneath his nails; therefore, there were no obvious signs of a fight. He had to have been taken without a struggle.

Leaning back in his chair, Clay sighed, placing his hands behind his head. All that remained now was the toxicology results, and maybe, hopefully, the big bonanza: personal contact from the killer.

It was 12:38 when Ron and Company walked through Clay's office door. Clay rose from his chair. Ron led the way with two men in suits trailing behind. Introductions were made by importance; therefore, Bob Lemus was first.

A short, African American man in his mid-fourties or so, Lemus stood approximately five eight. Though nearly bald except for a horseshoe of short, neatly barbered salt and pepper hair, he wore a gray, three-piece suit that accentuated his broad, powerful shoulders. A prominent square jaw and compelling dark eyes gave him a look of both authority and knowledge. Lemus's handshake was strong and accompanied with a silent nod. Clay's first impression was that of a politically empowered man lacking personality and social graces. "Pompous ass" was actually the name he believed was most suitable.

The agent with him was Doctor Brian Spulder, a specialist in criminal psychology. Tall and lanky, he was much younger, perhaps thirty or so his handshake was gentler and came with a friendly smile. Unlike Lemus, Spulder wore glasses, the round-lens type that hooked behind the ears. Vivid red hair, cut per Bureau regulation, covered his head, his skin was fair, almost milky-white. Clay sensed confidence, but not arrogance.

As soon as they were seated, Clay asked if they'd like coffee. Spulder and Ron said yes while Lemus declined. Excusing himself, Clay left for the kitchen. In his absence, Lemus's eyes wandered around the room.

The stockpile of files on the desk told him that Town Marshall Clayton Cooper was a thinker, already looking ahead. The old coffee cup sitting on his desk told of his love for the profession and belief in the system. Lemus secretly considered those notable traits.

Overall, the office was neat, tidy, clean, and well organized; that impressed him, too. Also, there were no weapons, keys, or police equipment out in the open. Other than stack of files, there were no papers lying about that could be glanced upon by unprivileged eyes. Lemus gave him a high mark for a first impression.

As soon as Clay returned and handed out the coffee, he sat behind his desk and began the meeting. "So, what is it I can do for you, Agent Lemus?"

Lemus made immediate eye contact with a confident, self-assured stare. He held it a moment, then said, "Well, first off, let me ask you this: has your secretary been to lunch?"

Clay was taken aback at first, but quickly remembered the thin walls. He was impressed. Without leaving his chair, Clay glanced toward the wall dividing their offices and slightly above voice level said, "Gertrude, please go to lunch." There was a moment of silence, then the slamming of her office door.

Lemus began. "Marshall, we believe the bodies you found in the woods are the work of a serial killer we call 'The Blue Eyes Killer'."

"Obviously a very bad man, I take it?" Clay asked.

"Yes, very much so. We've been tracking him now for several years. He's good…inventive. To date he's killed nearly as many as John Wayne Gacy; that's thirty-three victims, in case you're not up to par. But unlike Gacy, his victims are not little boys. He prefers young people, yes, but in their late teens to early thirties, male or female. And as you already know, he sometimes chooses to kill both at the same time. We're here hoping to high heaven for a capture."

"I'll help any way I can," Clay assured him.

"Great. Then are you aware of any soured arrests, pissed off people, DUI's, speeding tickets, parolees, unhappy house arrests?"

Clay shook his head. "No, I've already been over all that." He made a sweeping motion with his hand. "That's what all these files are. Nothing!"

Lemus pulled a pack of cigarettes from his suit pocket, and telling more than asking said, "Mind?" He lit one, not waiting for a reply.

Clay threw a glance toward Ron, raised his eyebrows, then looked back to Lemus. While he himself did not smoke; he respected the right of those who did. Reaching into his desk drawer, he pulled out a small, red plastic ashtray and extended it to Lemus.

"Here," he told him, "I keep it on hand for self centered, boldly presumptuous smokers." Lemus paused before taking it, staring a few seconds into Clay's eyes. Then Clay added, "But you can use it, too."

For the first time since their meeting, Lemus smiled, although it was brief. With a nod he took the ashtray from Cooper's hand. The town Marshall had brass. Lemus gave Clay another high mark.

Following a deep draw from the cigarette, Lemus exhaled the smoke toward the ceiling. Like a drug, it seemed to relax him, and he settled back in his chair. Crossing his legs for comfort, he told Cooper, "Blue Eyes is a cold son of a bitch, Marshall. He's professional, incredibly elusive." Reaching into his pocket he pulled out the little evidence bag housing the scroll, tossing it on the desk in front of Clay. "Your name being on this is the best lead we've had in a long, long while. For some reason our killer has made personal contact with you, and let you live."

Clay picked up the bag and stared at it. Then looked back to Lemus. "Why me?"

"We think it's because his MO has reached the final stage: four."

Clay's expression told Lemus of his lack of understanding. "I'll let Doctor Spulder explain."

Everyone turned to the Doctor with the red hair and round glasses. Perhaps feeling a bit uneasy, the lanky man rose from his chair and walked to the wall. There, he put his back against it and drew in a deep breath. Folding his arms across his chest, he paused a moment, gathering his thoughts, then spoke directly to Clay.

"Serial killers, Mr. Cooper, fall into one of two categories: organized or disorganized. 'Blue Eyes' is most certainly organized. His Modus Operandi has been, for the most part, incredibly routine."

"How so?" Clay asked.

"Well, he is religiously premeditative and plans every step to the letter, even to what 'tools' to use. He inspects the spots where he will place the bodies and insures, they are found easily. Almost always his victims, male or female, have blue eyes, are perfect physical specimens and are young, between the ages of eighteen and thirty. He used cunning to lure his victims. We believe he himself to be young, perhaps thirty or so, but not much more. We also believe he is handsome, probably with blue eyes, and intelligent. He's educated, charming, and if our guess is correct, very wealthy. All of these things help him to blend in with any crowd and that gives him a big edge."

"What is this stage four?"

"The organized serial killer proceeds through four stages with each victim. It is during the fourth stage that law enforcement will usually apprehend him, if they're lucky, or if the killer so desires. In stage one he chooses his victims, usually very carefully. The killer watches them, stalks them to the point of recognizing their vulnerabilities and by so doing, will use that information to his advantage. The killers hunting arena has no bounds; they love the geographic mobility, especially our Blue Eyes Killer. We've tied him into thirteen overseas killings…six in Europe, four in the Orient and four more in the Middle East. The remaining sixteen were here in the U.S."

Ron counted in his head and spoke out loud in a question. "Thirty victims?"

Spulder glanced his way. "Yes, Trooper Parks, that is correct. Actually, thirty-two, now."

The doctor looked back to Clay, unfolding his arms, and sticking his hands into his pockets.

"Stage two is the thrill of pursuit, to include the capture and torture of the victim or victims. The killer will have in his possession, or waiting at the torture site, the tools I mentioned earlier…instruments of choice, which he will use on his victims. These can be anything: knives, scalpels, drills, saws, baseball bats, drugs…the list is limited only by the killer's imagination. I might add, too, that in this stage, if authorities interrupt the killer, he will immediately murder his victim, thus postponing his need for gratification. There will be no leaving the victim alive."

Tired of standing, Spulder returned to his chair. "In stage three we can have variations. Sometimes the killer places or buries bodies at a specific location or leaves them in the open as a means of teasing those tracking him. Blue Eyes always leaves them to be found in the open or informs us of their location."

Leaning forward, Spulder rested his arms on his legs, interlacing his fingers. "Now for stage four, the one we call the 'stage of hope'. Here we often learn important things about the killer, things about his personality, sense of humor and level of confidence. Sometimes he will actually call the police and offer hints or leave obvious clues at the scene. Blue Eyes does all of these, and always leaves a scroll dedicating his victims to Belial; our killer enjoys watching investigators struggle and grow frustrated in their pursuit. He believes he will never be caught- that is, never unless he wants to be. Which leads us to you. We are hopeful that his contact with you means that he has had enough and is beginning his grand finale, the final stage four. Because your name is on that scroll, Marshall Cooper, we think-hope-this is the case: that Blue Eyes wants to be caught and, for whatever reason, is making you the key element to his capture."

Spulder leaned back in his chair. "He's going to contact you, Marshall Cooper. He's going to contact you and we need to be there. We can't afford for anything to go wrong."

Lemus jumped in. "Starting now, Mr. Cooper, you're the sugar and we're the flies. Every move you make, we'll be there. We're going to tap your phones and maintain a twenty-four-hour surveillance."

Clay took a sip of coffee, nodding his agreement. Then he asked, "Who is Belial?"

Lemus twisted his cigarette out in the ashtray, explaining, "Belial is a demon, Marshall Cooper. According to Hebrew scripture, he is by far the most evil of all. He was the angel, created right after Lucifer. So, if you believe in God and the Devil, then you can appreciate how powerful this Belial character is. His job here on earth is to create wickedness and guilt among humans through perversion, fornication, and lust. And if that's not bad enough, the Hebrews say he is married to a female demon Lilith, the demon queen of lust. A mom-and-pop operation, as it were." Lemus laughed lightly at his humor and lit up another cigarette as he talked. "It is said he is an incredibly beautiful angel, that he alone commands eighty legions of demons with 6,666 per legion. Do the math-that's one hell of a lot of little scary fuckers, pardon my French."

Clay recalled his vision of demons clinging to his house, but he kept it to himself.

Lemus went on. "Blue Eyes is of the belief he is working-killing-for Belial. He believes each victim must die differently, uniquely, and be sent into death only after being defiled."

"The coroner's report," Clay injected, "stated that both the male and female victim had been sodomized. Is that how he defiles?"

"That is correct," Lemus told him. "He sodomizes every victim, male or female."

Clay made a face.

Lemus went on. "Historically, Blue Eyes has always left leads and clues that get us close, inches away, but never there. This is the first time he has implemented someone specifically. We are hoping, as Doctor Spulder pointed out, that he has had enough killing and wants to come in." Lemus took a draw from his cigarette and sat back in his chair. "Bottom line, Marshall Cooper: you are the man of the hour, the FBI's greatest hope."

CHAPTER FIVE

QUINTEN CHRISTENSON, ALIAS BLUE Eyes, understudy to the demon known as Belial, removed his expensive Italian loafers. He then unbuttoned his long-sleeved blue denim shirt, slowly pulling it out from beneath his belt and letting the wrinkled tails fall to the side.

The full-length mirror he stared into portrayed a muscular, mildly hairy chest with superbly developed pecks and washboard abs. pleased with what he saw, he totally removed the shirt and carefully draped it over the foot of his four-poster oak bed.

Next, he removed his belt, closing his eyes while unbuckling, finding the soft jungle erotic, powerful. He could feel his penis begin to stir. One at a time, he pulled his legs free of his dark-brown khaki pants and laid them neatly beside his shirt. Since he wasn't wearing socks, his bright-red bikini underwear followed. Blue was by far his favorite color, but he loved red, too; it was so…puissant.

Completely naked now, he stared admiringly at the six-foot-two, model-handsome man in the mirror. The long, shoulder length, blond hair, the superbly developed muscular body, and the brilliant blue eyes made him irresistible to women, and to many men as well. They all found him desirable, perfect in every way. But it was the unique hugeness of his penis that over-shadowed it all: when erect, its towering beauty always left his lovers in awe.

From the bed, he retrieved the glossy eight-by-ten photo of the attractive, bikini-clad blond standing at the shore of Lake Michigan.

After tearing off a strip of scotch tape from the roller, he taped the picture to the mirror at eye level. While fastening the photo, he spoke softly to the smiling creature.

"You do not realize it yet, but fate has shown you great favor. Master Belial has chosen you. Soon you will belong to him, become one of his own, and live in a world where darkness is the light, and the cries of pain and fear are music to the ear. You'll walk where the darkened souls of men and women are sent for falling short of His mark. You'll abide in that giant, unhallowed abyss where the great Master rules, that paradise of evil where you will be treated as a queen and experience sexual pleasure you could never imagine. For you, and soon myself as well, these pleasures will be for all eternity."

Studying the woman in the photo, he wrapped his hand gently around his enlarging penis. He loved feeling it grow in his closed palm. Slowly he began to stroke, each stroke soft and long, sending exquisite waves of pleasure through his body.

He envisioned the woman in the photograph on her knees, smiling in admiration, reaching out and gripping him, beaming. He imagined the tender softness of her feminine caress, her long, silky strokes. And in her eyes, her lovely blue eyes, he could see the wanting, the desire. He imagined her other hand joining the first and the stroking-tempo building into a mind-bending crescendo.

Oh, how he loved serving his master, choosing those who were perfect gifts, always ensuring they were ready and sent to him in unique and inventive ways. Because the master required they be defiled, their preparation was always pleasant and exciting. Life was good; as good as it could be, living within a flesh and blood body amid feeble and prejudiced humans.

But soon that would end. The day was close when he would take his rightful place at the left hand of Master Belial, ruling with the saints of darkness such as Asmodeus and Lilith. And as Belial had promised he would be made Chief Incubus.

"Yes," he yelled aloud with panting breath, his strokes now wild and frantic, "My pleasure is for your exultation, oh Lord of the Abyss!"

Then the world exploded in his brain and exquisite pleasure surged through his veins as semen shot out, splattering the giant mirror. Cries of ecstasy fluttered from his throat like screeching bats flying from the mouth of a dark cave.

After cleaning the mirror, he showered, dressing in a charcoal linen crepe three button single-breasted suit. He chose a black-and-white-checkered linen banded-collar shirt, light brown socks, and black boots by Mongerson Wunderlich. It was a last-minute decision, but he chose not to wear underwear on this auspicious occasion; it was important he look, and feel, just right tonight.

Chanel would be dining with him. This time, the body attached to that beautiful smile would be sitting across the table, not kept within the confines of an eight-by-ten glossy photograph taped to a mirror.

Quinten had been watching her religiously for nearly three weeks. He had captured her splendid magnificence on thirty-five-millimeter film, unbeknownst to her. He knew where she lived, what she liked to eat, and where she preferred to lay when bathing in the sun and sand.

The topless bar where she danced had been the perfect setting. It was dimly lit, and crowded with a sea of faceless men, providing easy pickings for someone with money and pristine looks.

Pausing for a quick check in the mirror, he smiled, then turned and descended the stairs to the kitchen. Chanel would love the shrimp with tomato and feta; for dessert, there would be shortcake with walnuts. Then, after dinner, the soft, smooth taste of a bottle of aging French Chablis would surely please her. The two would make love, filled with the wine's mellowed warmth, then pillow talk until the arrival of peaceful slumber. The evening would be perfect.

However, it would be the special surprise that awaited her upon waking that truly excited him. It was a surprise she would never guess in a million lightless years. He giggled, giddy at the thought of seeing her face when she discovered it. Then he frowned. Waiting was such agony.

The kitchen smelled just the way he had hoped, and with a less then forty-minute drive round trip to pick up his lovely date, the scrumptious odor would linger perfectly in the air.

Placing a lid over the still steaming feta, he turned the oven down to a low sixty degrees just enough to keep it warm without overcooking. His stunning blue eyes glanced at the time; he had to go. Grabbing the keys to his 1963 sky-blue Corvette convertible, he hurried past the table set for two and down the steps of his little country house.

She had done just as he had instructed. Chanel had taken the bus to the corner of 19th and Washington and waited. When he pulled up, she smiled joyfully. Traffic was thin and the buildings aglow with dazzling radiance; a perfect full moon lingered, and the stars hung romantically.

He loved the Windy City, especially the unbridled nightlife. There were always parties and crowded dance clubs with sweaty bodies and pulse-pounding music. He applauded the throng who lived for its neon darkness, its addictive stimulation and ever-present seduction of hope, mystery, and fear.

Quinten exited the car and walked around to open Chanel's door, giving her a gentle kiss on the cheek. Once seated, he closed the door, then slid back behind the wheel and looked into her eyes. "Chanel," he told her warmly, "you are absolutely stunning."

She leaned close to him, breathing deeply. "And you smell maddeningly delicious. What is that?"

Quinten grinned boyishly. "It's called, Obsession for Men."

Chanel pouted teasingly. "I was hoping your obsession would be for women."

The tiniest flush reddened his cheeks. "Oh, it is. At least for tonight, for you."

They stared a long while before Quinten spoke again. "I have a delicious dinner planned. Hungry?"

Chanel grinned. "Very. So hungry, in fact, I could eat you."

Throwing the Corvette in gear, he pulled onto the street then glanced her way with a smile. "Well, if that's the case, we had better get you to my place quickly."

In just under twenty minutes, they were pulling onto the long, secluded drive leading back to his house. The lane was one of gravel and stone, a half mile long, with woods and brush thick on both sides. When they entered into the moon-bathed open yard, Chanel sighed. "Quinten, it's beautiful."

She saw a smaller, two-story log cabin house with a matching two-car garage. An expertly manicured lawn encircled the premises, and to the left of the house grew a beautiful flower garden. Her heart was beating quickly; she loved flower gardens. Maybe, probably, definitely, she smiled to herself; a stroll would be on the agenda first thing after breakfast.

An oval drive circled past the front door; that's where Quinten pulled to a stop. Not waiting for him to come around, Chanel climbed out and swept the surroundings with eyes full of possibility, breathing in the country freshness.

Chanel looked up into the bright, starry sky. Could all this signal the promise of romance? She felt like a smitten schoolgirl.

CHAPTER SIX

DINNER WAS FINISHED, AND now the two sat at the table sipping wine. Chanel gazed amiably at Quinten across the top of her glass. "So, Quinten, what is it you do for a living?"

Pausing thoughtfully, the man with the beautiful blue eyes smiled. "Let's play a game, Chanel." His tone was soft but challenging. "A game of detective, if you will. Feel free to look about the house, be a snoop. See if you can determine my profession by simple deduction, based upon the things you observe."

With a wide grin, she accepted. Titillated, she gracefully rose from her chair, leaving the table. This was going to be fun!

"However…," he added as an afterthought.

Stopping, Chanel turned to look at him.

"The basement is off limits. It's the door behind the staircase. The contents of that room would make your quest, less challenging. I do promise, however, to show it to you later. Fair?"

"Fair enough." She chimed cheerfully.

Her first stop was a beautiful black baby grand piano. Glancing his way she asked, "You play, I assume?"

He nodded, with a tender smile. Chanel could not believe her luck. This man was too good to be true.

Atop the piano were a series of photos. But she took time to scrutinize only two. The first was the picture of a smiling gray-haired couple sitting behind a desk, with the woman snuggled on the man's lap. On the wall behind them hung a large medical diploma from the Indiana University school of medicine. She could not make out the name on the diploma. The other photo was that of an adorable little boy with beautiful blue eyes standing in front of an ambulance.

Satisfied, Chanel left the piano and slowly sauntered around the room. A huge stone fireplace with white marbled mantle held a large-scale model of an old wooden galleon and three wood carved figurines: a flying dragon, a bearded wizard, and a sexy, practically nude female warrior holding her sword triumphantly above her head. There were also two globe bookends, housing four books: *Encyclopedia of Men's Health, L. Ron Hubbard's Dianetics, The Republic and Other Works by Plato, and The Complete Kama Sutra.* Chanel tapped that book with her finger and grinned sheepishly.

The remainder of the downstairs house held no further clues. Finding herself at the foot of a spiral staircase leading up to an open loft, she paused and smiled at Quinten. "May I?"

Quinten returned the smile. "Please."

The upstairs revealed no particular clues as to his profession. But she did discover a couple of interesting things. In the bathroom just off the master bedroom, resting beside his toothbrush on the sink, she found a second brush identical to it. A blue ribbon had been tied in a bow around it, and her name had been eloquently written on the ribbon. She smiled warmly. That was enough for her. She had seen enough.

On her way out she passed the full-length mirror at the foot of the poster bed. Pausing momentarily to ensure she looked her best before going downstairs, her blue eyes spotted a small, filmy streak midway down the glass. It surprised her; everything else had been so clean and perfect. How did this man, Mr. Clean, ever miss such a noticeable stain? Bending, she wet her finger and rubbed the spot until it was nearly vanished from the glass. With a little of it remaining, she wet her finger one more time and finished wiping, then polished the spot with the sleeve of her cardigan sweater.

This would be her secret. If he'd known such a blemish existed, he would have been mortified. The last thing in the world she wanted to do was embarrassed him. Quinten Christenson was just too sweet and gentle for that.

CHAPTER SEVEN

BACK AT THE TABLE CHANEL sat down, smiling jubilantly. "You're a physician. And your father was a physician."

Raising his eyebrows, Quinten let the slightest smile show at the corners of his mouth. "And what clues brought you to this conclusion?"

Proud of her Sherlock Homes savvy, Chanel shifted her expression to a pleased, stare. "First, the photos on the piano. That is, you as a little boy standing by the ambulance. And the picture of the older couple: in the photo, there is a medical degree hanging on the wall behind them. I'm willing to bet that the man and woman are your parents. Your father was a physician and as a little boy you were infatuated with him, wanted to grow up and be just like him. So, you did."

He stared at her, amused by her findings.

Chanel took a deep breath. "And over there," her head nodded toward the lamp, but her eyes never left his, "the lamp's body is the staff of life, the insignia used in the medical world."

Quinten smiled a little wider. "Well done. But…"

Chanel cut him off. "That's not all. Your house is so clean and well-kept, and so are you. I'm going to step out on a limb here. I'm going to say that not only you are a physician, you're a specialist, a surgeon."

Finally finished, Chanel sat back in her chair with folded arms. She was beaming. "Well, am I correct?" she asked.

Smiling, Quinten walked to her side and refilled their wineglasses. He then pulled her to her feet. After handing Chanel her glass, he tapped the rim of it with his and proposed a toast. "To Chanel, my loveliest guest ever, whose name is as charming as the wine we sip, who is as sweet as she is beautiful. And who, like no other, can make my head swim with nearly unmanageable desire. May you forever grace the master with your charms."

After taking a sip of her wine, Chanel removed Quinten's glass from his hand and set it on the table along with her own. Eyes fixed upon his, she told him, "That was so sweet." Her fingertips stroked his cheeks tenderly. "Is that extra toothbrush upstairs meant for me?"

Quinten nodded. "Yes. If you'll have it."

Chanel smiled. "Of course. In fact, I'd like to see it again. Why don't we go upstairs?" They stared into one another's eyes for some time, as though poised in a vacuum. Nothing else around them existed; longing fueled their desire until passion exploded. Like magnets, pulled together irresistibly, their mouths clashed in heated rush and their tongues danced with fire. Quinten swept her into his arms and carried her easily up the winding staircase.

Setting her on the edge of the poster bed, he tore free the Cardigan sweater and black satin, trimmed bra beneath. Chanel caught her breath. Her skin was smooth and silky, her breasts more beautiful than he remembered, the perfect fit for his gentle, powerful hands.

On his knees before her, Quinten kissed her nipples, suckling them with closed eyes. They grew like rose buds in a soft spring rain. She moaned, hands gripping his blond hair. Then he pulled away, and slowly, one piece at a time, removed her shoes, white Capri pants and laced panties. Beautiful and naked now she sat before him, wanting, burning like the fire of Dante's Inferno. Passionately, he kissed her one last time, then withdrew and rose to his feet.

Standing before her, he felt powerful. She was so feminine, so small and vulnerable. Slowly, for her enjoyment, he began to strip, leaving his trousers for last. Chanel marveled at his magnificent build, his rounded well-developed chest, perfectly sculpted shoulders, and flat rippled stomach. She grew increasingly wet, anxious to see his manhood, to feel it in her hand...to feel it inside her.

Slowly Quinten unbuckled his belt and undid the waist button, then teasingly lowered his zipper. When the metallic sound ended, he released his hold and the trousers dropped. With grace he stepped out of them and stood naked, poised with confidence.

Yearning for him, desirous of giving the greatest of pleasure, Chanel lowered herself to her knees. Reaching out she took him into her hand, amazed at his size and still yet amazed that he continued to grow as she stroked. She had never been with a man so large. This was going to be a night to remember, a night she wanted to last forever, a night she would carry into eternity.

When Chanel awoke, she told herself that she was dreaming. She was no longer in the upstairs bedroom in Quinten's arms, but rather, in a darkened room lighted only by burning torches. Her arms were stretched out by chains with iron clamps tightened around her wrists. Her ankles had been bound in the same fashion; legs pulled apart. She was naked and it was cold and dreary. She tried making sense of what was going on. Pulling against the chains, she fought a wave of panic as the iron links rattled. Her mind was groggy. Had she drunk too much wine last night? Was she drugged, or was it all a dream, a terrible nightmare?

Again, she told herself to wake up, but she did not. Desperately she tried pulling her tiny hands through the heavy iron clamps, but it was no use, there was no give, and it only caused her pain. With eyes fading in and out of blurriness, she looked around the room, shaking her head and blinking as a means of maintaining vision. She felt light-headed and from time to time fought painful waves of nausea. She had to have been drugged, she thought.

The walls around her consisted of large stones fastened with thick mortar. Antique medieval torture equipment made of iron and wood filled the shadowy room. She recognized some of it...a stretching rack, a narrow, wrought iron starvation cage hanging from the ceiling, a huge wooden vice used to cause crushing injuries, another cage with long spikes fastened to the door. And there were several others, most of which she did not recognize, but had added fear to her already panic-stricken mind.

Although remaining in a mild state of confusion, her head had cleared enough to realize that if this were some kind of joke, it was not funny. *"God,"* she screamed aloud, *"What the hell is going on?"*

She cried out for Quinten, but there was no response. Tears formed in her eyes. Again, she pulled against the chains, this time wildly, like a madwoman. They rattled noisily in the empty chamber but did not give. Chanel broke into a hard cry, her tears a mixture of anger and fear. Mostly fear.

She screamed, struggling against the heavy chains a long while, pulling and prying, trying in desperation to squeeze her hands through the tightened wristlocks. Laboriously, she fought to free herself. Time passed in long, agonizing segments, minutes turning into hours.

Chanel cried until there were no more tears, struggled until there was no more strength, screamed until there was no more voice. Hoarsely she whimpered time and again for Quinten to come and unchain her, to let her go home.

In time, exhausted from her efforts and having come to grips with fate, Chanel's naked body hung slumped, suspended by the iron chains, her head too heavy to lift. Weak but alive, in the cold dark stillness of the stone prison, she asked herself again and again. Why?

CHAPTER EIGHT

THURSDAY MORNING, CLAYTON COOPER sat south of Brooke, tracking with radar. Several speeders had gone by well over the limit, but he let them pass; his thoughts were more on the Blue Eyes Killer than speeding offenders. To be specific, he was thinking of the killer and his own wife.

Perhaps by not telling Nancy the whole truth, he was placing her in danger. Whoever this person was, he was cold-blooded and had no respect for human life. His victims were always young and blue-eyed. Nancy qualified in both areas. Even the newest rookie understood the surest way to get to someone was through a loved one. Not knowing the killer's agenda worried him.

Turning, he stared out the window to watch the flight of a hawk. It circled against the blue sky, making three loops above a small island of trees in the middle of a field. Then it dove, disappearing into the grove. Within seconds it reappeared, but it was empty-handed.

Maybe Clay was blowing it all out of proportion. The fact that his name had shown up on the scroll could have been nothing more than a slam met for Lemus. The killer was probably far away by now, doing mayhem on someone else's turf. "Yeah," Clay told himself aloud, "he's moved on, far away."

A gray Chevy Nova shot past doing eleven miles an hour over the limit. Clay reached up and adjusted the tracking unit even though he did not need it. A minute passed before the next vehicle, an old Dodge Dart zoomed by, but it slowed as soon as the driver spotted him. At least someone in the world still showed respect, he thought.

Clay glanced at his watch. In twenty minutes, he'd break for lunch.

While he disliked the politics that came with the job, he understood its evil necessity. The board of trustees required he write a certain ticket quota per month, and since they signed his paycheck, he respected their wishes. But because the month's end was still far off, he was in no rush to meet the obligation just yet. Besides, he disliked writing tickets just for the sake of writing tickets.

For a twelve-minute stretch, the highway remained abandoned. Bored, he sat tapping restless fingers against the steering wheel. Inactivity had always been the most difficult part of his job. Warm rays filtered through the window, but the cruiser's air conditioner kept the interior cool.

At 11:32, a long string of vehicles passed. "When it rains it pours," he told himself. One of the vehicles had been a white church bus filled with singing children. He could not hear them, but he could see their mouths moving and hands clapping happily. "The joys of youth," he smiled warmly.

The sight of the bus triggered a long-buried childhood memory. He recalled sitting at a small table as a six-year-old, during one of his Sunday school sessions. The day's lesson had been the secret of becoming a brave and daring crusader for Jesus. His smile widened.

"God's great Knights," the teacher had told the group of boys and girls quietly, "have to be brave and learn to be still in their hearts so they can hear the whispers of God, for that's the way He talks to you, soft and gentle within your heart."

Clay could still picture her looking about the room dramatically, as if insuring no one was close enough to hear what she was about to add. "The Lord's secret crusaders, The Knights of the Holy Table," she had said in a whisper that leaned them forward in their chairs, "wear a very special suit of armor. Only God can see it, but it's the brightest of armor, made of silver and gold. And most important of all, God's Knights, people just like you, carry the most powerful sword ever made, and it has a name, The Sword of RESISTANCE."

Clayton Cooper still envisioned her raising a finger for emphasis, "But beware, the Devil also carries a powerful sword...The Sword of TEMPTATION. And these two swords are always clashing and clanging in battle...the devil trying to tempt you with his sword, and you as a brave crusader fighting to resist him with yours. Temptation," she had explained, "is when the Devil tries to trick you into doing something wrong, and making it feel as though it were right."

Clay remembered she had read them Webster's definition of temptation that day. It had been interesting, but not a single kid had even the smallest inkling of what the dictionary was saying. Now, well over twenty years later, he was curious about those words she had read. Reaching into his briefcase lying on the seat next to him, he pulled out a small dictionary. Vigilantly, he turned through the pages and located the word, reading aloud:

TEMPATION: 1. To entice to do wrong by promise of pleasure or gain: allure into evil: seduce 2. To make trial of: TEST: to try presumptuously: provoke: to risk the dangers of 3. To induce to do something: to incite, persuade, to lure.

Thoughtfully, Clay closed the dictionary.

At that instant, a black Lexus shot past; it was a dark blur clocking in at one hundred and six miles per hour. Clay disbelieved what he saw. He sat less than two hundred feet from the end-of-city-limit sign that stated, "fifty-five."

Throwing the dictionary back into the briefcase, he pulled the shift-lever into drive. Kicking up dirt and gravel, the Crown Victoria fishtailed onto the highway. For a big car, the Cruiser climbed quickly in speed...forty, sixty seventy-five, ninety and on past a hundred. The Lexus remained well ahead but Clay was confident he would gain.

They shot past the caravan of cars to include the Church Bus of singing children. The patrol car's siren yelped steadily, its loud warning cutting through the warm rays of the afternoon sun, but the speeding Lexus paid no attention, creating a highly dangerous situation.

Clay glanced at the speedometer now pegged at a hundred and twenty. The taillights of the Lexus came on; the driver was slowing. "About time." Clay said aloud.

Rapidly, the Crown Victoria closed the gap between them. When he was almost close enough to get a visual on the plate, the Lexus took off again. Clay hissed, "You son of a bitch."

Immediately he radioed county dispatch informing them of the chase, giving location, direction, and description of the vehicle. No help would be available for another fifteen or twenty minutes, so he acknowledged and remained in pursuit.

The Lexus maintained the lead, but because it had slowed momentarily, Clay had gained an edge. He was gaining much faster now. The two speeding cars shot through an intersection, causing a van to swerve and brake to a squealing stop; it careened sideways and slid several feet, luckily not overturning. They passed three more vehicles with the Lexus dangerously weaving in and out to maintain its lead.

Again, Clay glanced at his speedometer, this time wondering how far they had come. The odometer told him nearly eight miles, and he knew that to be true. They were approaching the old Brooke Grain Elevator ahead, a speck in the distant; it sat exactly eight miles from the sign by which he had been sitting. But that speck was growing larger quickly.

Because of their high speed, the old complex gave the allusion of literally rising up from the ground, growing and taking shape. Long abandoned, the old place sat two hundred yards off the highway, surrounded by empty fields. Rotting and rusted, the main building towered high above the others, housing five floors of elongated windows broken and weathered with years.

Strangely, Clay had a premonition the speeder would turn off and head straight for the place...but that did not happen. Instead, the vehicle's taillights came on again and it began slowing, pulling off to the side of the highway, stopping perfectly in line with the elevator.

Cautiously, Clay pulled in behind, positioning the Crown Victoria ten or twelve feet from its bumper. He adjusted the car's video camera to take in the entire vehicle, include plate. Sitting behind the wheel in close observation, he radioed dispatch with the number, and it came back reported stolen.

The black Lexus sat silent, no movement. Its windows were tinted and impossible to see into without practically putting your nose to the glass. Clay had always felt disgruntled with lawmakers for allowing such a dangerous thing.

Drawing the Glock from its holster, he slipped off the safety then pulled the slide. Slowly he stepped out of his vehicle remaining behind the door. Eyes locked on the Lexus, he reached in and switched his radio to outside speaker. Clicking the mike, he gave first warning. "In the vehicle, driver only, open your door slowly and step out with hands above your head." There was no response. He raised his tone. "Driver, step out of the vehicle, NOW!"

Several more seconds passed, and then the door opened. A white male, mid-twenties, climbed out. He was dressed in dirty jeans, scuffed motorcycle boots and wearing an army brown T-shirt in need of ironing. His hair was long, stringy, and filthy. On a face in need of a shave he was wearing a smile that told Clay he was used to the routine and not at all afraid. "Put your hands on the roof of the car."

He obeyed but didn't lose the smile.

"Is anyone else in the vehicle?"

Turning only his head to look at Clay, the driver told him, "Look for yourself, Pig Fuck."

Clay tossed the microphone on the seat and moved cautiously out from the security of the door, moving toward the Lexus. Gun pointed, he approached slowly, moving around behind the standing man for a clearer look inside. He continued to move until he stood against the driver side fender and behind the opened door, then said, "It's Mister

Pig Fuck to you. Now put your hands behind your head and get down on your knees." Again, the driver did as he was told. Clay saw no one else, but he could not see clearly behind the back of the seats.

The Lexus was a two-door, so he told the driver, "With your left hand hit the release and let the seat fall forward." When it did, it was clear no one else was in the vehicle. "OK, with your left hand again, reach in and pull the keys from the ignition, put your hands back behind your head and stand up, then move around to the back of the vehicle. Let's have a look in the trunk."

When it was done, they moved together to the rear of the car. The driver inserted the key but paused, saying to Clay without looking at him, "You know, Mister Town Marshall, Pig Fuck, you're robbing me of my constitutional rights. You have to ask my permission to look in the trunk."

Clay kept the 9-millimeter pointed. "I don't have to ask you anything. This is a stolen vehicle, that makes you a felon, now open the trunk."

The driver turned the key but stopped again, turning his head, this time to look at Clay. "No. Fuck you. You want to look in my trunk, you open it." He held open his arms and stepped back, adding defiantly, "And if you don't like it then shoot me right here in cold blood. But I'll tell you true, I don't think you've got the balls."

Clay made a face. "Don't tempt me."

The trunk lid moved just a fraction; he caught it with of the corner of his eye. The tip of a gun barrel poked out like the head of a turtle from its shell. Quickly Clay pulled the Glock around but was not fast enough.

From the trunk erupted two shots, both rounds striking him hard in the chest as though he'd been hit twice by a huge sledgehammer. He was knocked off his feet and slammed hard onto his back. Helpless, he lay at the edge of the road. Unconsciousness rushed in to take him to a world of blackness, but he fought it, instinct screaming at himself to stay awake!

His chest hurt over every inch, and he gasped for the air that had been knocked out of him. He wanted more than anything to hold onto his weapon, but he couldn't. It fell from his hand and onto the pavement. The bulletproof vest beneath his shirt had saved his life, but in vain; for now, he lay at the mercy of two cop killers.

His breath was beginning to return, but not yet sufficient to give him strength. He felt himself being pulled to his knees and dragged to the side of the road. As consciousness inched its way back, he could hear the two men talking, though they still sounded distant.

"Let's put a bullet in his head and get the hell out of here. You know more cops are coming."

"No, we were told to be creative and fuck with him a while." Clay recognized the voice as that of the driver. He thought of the man's remark-who had told them to stay?

"Fine," said the man who had been in the trunk, "I'm gonna cut out the bastard's Adam's apple and stuff it up his law-keeper ass. That's creative, right?"

Clay heard a click-a switchblade maybe? -then a hand gripped his forehead and pulled his head back exposing his throat, but instead of a blade the barrel of a pistol pressed tight to the top of his head. He closed his eyes. So, this was it, he thought. This was how it would end, a bullet not a knife.

He didn't wish to die, but strangely felt no fear. In his thoughts he told Nancy he loved her, and wondered which direction he'd take, Heaven or Hell. He hoped Heaven. His consciousness had returned, and his awareness was clear, but he was in no position to resist now. Fate would decide his destiny-and it did.

Two shots rang out almost simultaneously, one practically upon the other. They were the reports of a high-powered rifle echoing out over the open fields. Both men fell almost at the same instant, dead before they hit the ground. Dropping, Clay rolled swiftly to the far side of the black Lexus for cover. No other gunfire followed. He lay motionless for a minute taking in his first deep breath since being shot.

Except for the grain elevator he was surrounded by flat open land, the shots had to have come from somewhere within that complex. Slowly he raised his head, just enough to look over the trunk of the Lexus. He saw nothing. Aside from a constant throbbing in his chest he was now in full control of his senses.

The sun was hot on his back and face, and he felt himself sweating. But at least he was alive to feel it. Then four more shots rang out. He ducked. The right front and rear tires of both the Lexus and Crown Victoria burst and went flat.

From the elevator, echoing faintly across the openness between them, a voice shouted, "You see, Marshall, your destiny lies in my hands-and, as you will soon be made aware, mine in yours. You will be hearing from me."

There was a minute of silence, and he heard the distant sound of a car motor starting in the vicinity of the elevator. Cautiously he raised his head and looked, seeing a dark vehicle pulling away. He could not identify its make or model.

Clay remained behind the security of the Lexus for several more minutes. Then, climbing to his feet, he reasoned that whoever had done the shooting could have easily killed him too, had they so desired. Instead, it appeared they had saved his life…or set him up to be murdered, then saved his life. He shook his head. It made no sense.

After retrieving the 9-millimeter, he stuck it back in the holster and checked the dead men. Both had been shot in the head. The tires on both cars were shredded and he was going nowhere. He informed dispatch of what had happened and ordered an ambulance and two tow trucks.

In just under six minutes, a County Deputy arrived. Following a brief explanation, Clay sent him to the elevator for a look-see, but he was confident nothing would be found.

Walking to the Crown Victoria, he sat in the air-conditioned vehicle and waited for the ambulance. Sitting there, he replayed the video three times. The entire incident, from the moment the Lexus pulled over to arrival of the County Deputy, had taken twenty-one minutes, and not one vehicle had passed by, or backup officer had arrived. That added up to one hell of a coincidence.

CHAPTER NINE

FEEBLE, CHANEL MANAGED ENOUGH strength to lift her head when the door to her stone prison opened. It was Quinten.

Sauntering across the room, he walked to the front of her and smiled. Soft shadows created by the flickering torchlight danced on his face. Staring at him through eyes now dull and lusterless, she wondered why he was doing this. He was so handsome, so wealthy, a man who had everything.

Reaching out, he stroked her cheek gently. "And how is my beautiful Angel today?"

Chanel had no idea how long she had been hanging in the chains. It must have been a while; her lips were dry from dehydration, and she wet them before speaking. Her voice was frail and edged with pleading, although still hoarse and raspy. "Quinten, why are you doing this to me? For God's sake, let me go."

His smile slowly vanished, and he withdrew his hand. "I can't do that, Chanel, not yet. But soon you will know happiness like never before."

She cried, a single tear streaking her face. "Quinten, I'm happy now the way life is...was. Just let me go home. I won't bother you; I promise. And I won't tell anyone."

Quinten cupped her bare breasts in his hands and kneaded them with gentle fingers. Their incredible softness mystified him. Breasts had always been his favorite part of the female anatomy; they were so... fanciful.

"No, Chanel," he told her, his eyes studying them with boyish fascination, "I can't let you go. Besides, you have no idea the pleasures that await you. You're going to be a queen." His eyes lifted to hers. "Have you any idea what it is like to be royalty, crowds kneeling before you? Hundreds of thousands will be your slaves, male and female, existing only to do your bidding."

She stared at him blankly with no idea what he was talking about, knowing only that he was insane. She tried pulling away, but it was impossible, the heavy chains held her at bay, and she had no strength.

She grimaced as the iron cuffs cut into her flesh and caused her wrists to bleed. For the first time, she noticed blood dripping to the floor, coming out from beneath them. Panic rose within her. She had always been weakened at the sight of her own blood. Fighting the urge to pass out, she took a deep breath.

Quinten released her breasts. Reaching into his pocket, he removed a plastic syringe filled with a dark liquid. Chanel's eyes widened. "My God, what is that?"

Quinten pointed it upward and squirted a small arch toward the ceiling. Tears blurred Chanel's eyes once again, tears she thought had long dried up. "Quinten please, NO! Don't do this." She began to sob.

"Now now, Angel," he said soothingly, "the only thing that is going to hurt will be the initial prick of the needle. After that you will begin to relax. This is Curare, a muscle relaxant," he chuckled, "an ancient poison, actually."

He tied a narrow rubber tube just above the right antecubital fossa and watched as her brachial artery popped up. "There it is. What a beauty." He wrapped his arm beneath hers and held her arm steady. He was too powerful; there was no resisting. Chanel felt the pinch as the needle punctured through the skin and into the vein. With expertise he pulled back on the plunger to insure he was in the vein then slowly pushed the dark fluid into her body.

She wailed out loud, fear rushing wildly through her blood stream well ahead of the poison. When finished, he recapped the syringe then kissed Chanel on the cheek. "In just a few seconds you will begin to relax. Every muscle in your body will become useless." He placed the empty syringe back into his pocket and added, "However, your brain will continue to function normally...you will see and feel everything business as usual ...warmth, cold, pain; it's just that your musculoskeletal system will be unable to respond. You will become incapable of talking, humming, singing, screaming." Quinten shrugged. "Of course, none of that will matter anyway, since in just a few minutes your breathing will stop."

He turned then and walked away, saying over his shoulder, "I'll be back in a little while. See you in Utopia, Angel."

With effort, Chanel held up her head long enough to watch him disappear through the doorway. Already she could feel the poison relaxing her exhausted body. The muscles in her neck gave way and her head dropped. Weak, eyes red from all her crying, her voice barely a whisper, she called after the man who had everything.

"Wait, come back! I don't want to die; I haven't walked in the flower garden."

CHAPTER TEN

GENT LEMUS'S HEADQUARTERS IN the basement of the State Police post, just north of Lafayette, Indiana, was a twenty-eight-minute high-speed drive to Brooke. In addition to Doctor Spulder, there were five other agents on the Blue Eyes team, three in-house and two assigned to the job of tailing Clayton Cooper. The men had been personally selected by Lemus and were into the third day since tapping the phones in Clay's house and office. To date, nothing had turned up.

The makeshift H.Q. wasn't exactly home away from home. Crowded with three decades of stacked boxes and countless paraphernalia, the walls around them were white cement blocks, now turned yellow from years of neglect. The lighting was less then desirable too, but Lemus overcame that by bringing in lamps and placing them strategically about the room.

The post captain had cordially offered to clear an area upstairs, but Lemus had declined. Here, they had access to all the building wiring, plenty of wall outlets, total privacy, and a direct basement exit from which to come and go without a dozen eyes watching their every move.

On the east wall, they had set up a tag board where pictures of the latest victims hung along with maps of the city of Lafayette, West Lafayette, Purdue University, and surrounding counties.

Lemus would have preferred headquartering in Brooke, but by stationing a little further away he hoped Blue Eyes would not catch on as quickly. In the past, they had religiously followed FBI protocol, and he believed doing so had helped the killer maneuver safely around them.

Besides, his gut instinct told him, if this was the final stage four, Blue Eyes would be in need of a large audience. If his grand finale required young, blue-eyed victims, what better place to find them than a college community?

Also, the killer would want to make fools of as many law enforcement personnel as possible, so whatever was to happen, Lemus was confident it would take place somewhere in or around the city of Lafayette. From their basement location, they were five minutes away from the heart of both city and campus.

At precisely 1:32 pm, they got their first break when Cooper's home phone rang. Immediately, the youngest of the three assisting agents, Frank Lordds, turned on the recorder and switched to open speaker. Following four rings the answering machine picked up. There was a soft click, then Clayton Cooper's recorded voice. "We're unable to come to the phone right now but following the beep you have 60 seconds to leave a message. Give us a name and number and we'll get back to you as soon as possible. Thanks."

Beep.

The voice that followed was cheerful, confident, and upbeat. "Agent Lemus and friends, how are you?" Lemus turned red, not sure if it was anger or embarrassment. The voice continued, "I'll bet you're surprised to hear from me, aren't you; sort of bittersweet, wouldn't you say? And you thought hiding in that dingy old basement would throw me off the trail!"

There was a short pause, then Blue Eyes added, "Doctor Spulder, grab a pen. I've a riddle for you. Time is short, so get it quickly. How did Davy Crockett get his cap? What do gentlemen prefer? What color are the skies over Hawaii? And from the 'Wizard of Oz', complete this line: be it ever so humble, there's no place like____." Blue Eyes paused again briefly. Lemus glanced at his watch.

Blue Eyes chuckled over the speaker. It was as if he were standing in the room looking at the hope in the agent's eyes. "Forget it Bob, I still have eleven seconds before you trace me."

Lemus yelled it out loud, "FUCK!" They even heard him upstairs.

"Before I go," Blue Eyes said finally, "this is for Marshall Cooper. Please do not feel left out. You'll be hearing from me soon. I just want you to know that until my business, our business, here is finished, wherever you are, there I am also."

There was a click followed by a dial tone. Lemus slapped the top of the table holding the recorder and shouted again. "Fuck, Fuck, Fuck!"

He turned quickly to Spulder. "Talk to me about that riddle."

While two of the agents filled their coffee cups, Spulder wrote the four Iines of the riddle on the large chalk board set up for just such a purpose. As soon as everyone was seated and facing the board, Spulder underlined the first line with his chalk. "How did Davy Crockett get his cap?"

Immediately the team began dissecting the line by throwing out thoughts. "From a raccoon."

"He killed the raccoon."

"He hunted it down, then killed it."

"No, he trapped it, then killed it."

"He gutted it, cleaned it, and sewed the hat." Lemus took a sip of coffee. "Ok, simple. Blue Eyes is planning to kill again."

Beside the underlined sentence, Spulder wrote the words, "kill again." Then, he underlined the next verse.

"What do gentlemen prefer?"

"That's easy," Lordds yelled out. "Blondes." Everyone nodded in agreement and Spulder wrote, "Blond," beside the sentence.

Then he pulled his piece of chalk beneath the third line.

"What color are the skies over Hawaii?"

Almost in harmony every man shouted, "Blue."

With the word "blue" written, Spulder underlined the last sentence.

"Be if ever so humble, there's no place like______."

Everyone knew that one, too, and yelled out the word.

"Home."

With the last word written, Spulder read them collectively aloud. "Kill again, Blond, Blue and Home."

Lemus rose from his chair and shook his head. "Too, easy. He's making it too damn easy. It's a given he's going to kill again, the victim will be blond, have blue eyes...so what's new? If he's telling us something, it has to be buried in that last line." Reaching behind his head, Lemus smoothed his hair and repeated aloud the last word "Home." He looked at Spulder, then at the seated men. "Is he telling us the next victim will die in his or her own home, or Blue Eye's home? Is he wanting us to guess where he lives, or at least once lived?"

Lemus began to pace the floor, as was his habit when thinking under pressure. He continued, "Is that why he chooses this area? Is he from here originally and wants the final stage to take place on his own home turf?"

Spulder spoke out, "Could it be his childhood home is here somewhere?"

Lemus nodded, looking at his comrades. "That's got to be it." Pulling a cigarette from his pocket, he began barking orders. "Lordds, get on the computer. Check with the Bureau of Motor Vehicles, this county and the three surrounding as well, and get a list of all male subjects issued a driver's license over the past fifteen years who have blue eyes and are now between the ages of twenty-five and thirty-five."

Lords looked dumbfounded. "Sir, do you realize how many names that will be?"

Lemus frowned. "Of course, I realize how many names that will be. I also want their addresses, so you better be getting your ass in gear."

Lords rose to go to the computer and Lemus said after him, "Then when you get that done, I want the names of all males on the same list worth five hundred thou or more. I want matches…those with blue eyes and money."

He then turned to the two older agents, Ted Tornington and James Building, both seasoned and as close to being friends as Lemus would allow. "You guys get your suited asses over to the campus. Take your briefcases; I want you looking like professors. Contact the University Police and let them know what's going on. We want their officers on the lookout too. Stay on campus and watch for someone between the ages of twenty and thirty-five-ish, with blue eyes, who you think may be stalking and not just hoping for a piece of tail."

Lemus lit his cigarette. "And if you make a grab for someone and want to see retirement, and I mean this with all the weight in my FBI ass, don't miss!"

CHAPTER ELEVEN

AGENT CLENDES LOOKED AT his watch: 3:02 am. Turning to his partner sitting vigilantly behind the wheel, he yawned and then spoke into the near total darkness of the car's interior. "God, I hate surveillance."

Glancing back at Clendes, more peripherally than directly, agent Jones grinned. "Then take a nap, you weenie. I'm awake, no problem."

Clendes yawned again, "OK, but don't tell Lemus. He'd have my gonads cut out and used for golf balls."

Having been chewed out more than once by Lemus, the agent sitting behind the wheel nodded in agreement.

The Cooper residence sat dark and quiet. The couple had gone to bed a few minutes after ten. They had shut off all lights except two: one in the garage, which in the darkness shined out as a wispy-thin strip beneath the closed overhead door, and an outside porch light.

Clendes laid his head against the back of the seat and closed his eyes; his sockets felt as if they were full of sand due to lack of sleep.

Except for a scant scattering of other porch lights, the little town of Brooke lay in a chilling black lair of darkness. Things once recognizable had long ago turned into strange, obscure shapes. Crickets chirped so loudly it was unforgivingly irritating, and everywhere tree branches swayed to the restless push of a pre-dawn wind. All signs of human life had vanished, fallen prey to the world of dreams. And apart from the occasional bark of a dog, the small community lay seemingly isolated from the world.

Agent Jones glanced over at his resting partner and smiled. The man was right, surveillance sucked. After filling his coffee cup from the large silver thermos lying between them, he tossed the thermos into the back seat and took a sip from his cup. Truth be known, he was just as bored and tired as Clendes, and if that weren't bad enough, now they were out of coffee. Jones shook his head and took another sip. "Come on, daylight."

At 3:46 am, Nancy opened her eyes. Clay was not in bed beside her. Then she remembered he had chosen to sleep in the chair beside the bedroom window. Earlier in the evening, after listening to the disturbing message on their answering machine, he had elected to sleep in his clothes, in the chair, with his side arm clutched in his hands.

Nancy threw back her covers and quietly walked across the darkened room to his side. The gold and black afghan he had used had fallen to the floor, so she picked it up and covered him again. Clay moaned softly but never opened his eyes. He had planned not to sleep, to stay awake through the night.

Nancy smiled affectionately at his sleeping form, then went into the bathroom to pee. There were two trained and experienced FBI agents standing watch outside; he could have slept comfortably in his own bed without worry. But at least now his body was taking the sleep it needed, and for that she was glad.

The small wall clock above the bathroom sink ticked methodically away... tick, tick, tick.

When finished, Nancy stood and let her nightgown fall down around her. She never wore panties while sleeping. Being thoughtful, she elected not to flush for fear of the noise waking her slumbering love. The room was pitch-black, but she needed no light to find her way back to the bed.

Three more hours of sleep and she'd get up to make a hearty breakfast for Clay and the two agents. Like her husband, their attitude was one of just doing their job, but she appreciated it. It was for her and Clay they were out there.

Like a striking snake, the arm came suddenly out of the darkness. He was strong, pulling her painfully against him, almost as if he might crush her face. His large handheld a cloth saturated with odd smelling something or other, which he pressed tightly over her mouth and nose.

The other arm, like a thick run of cable stretched across her chest, pinned her upper body. There was little moving, no success in fighting; and whatever was on the cloth, it quickly took her will away. The thought of chloroform flashed through her mind just before she slumped unconscious in his arms.

The dark form dressed in black coveralls, combat boots, ski mask, and gloves tossed her easily over his shoulder and entered into the dusky bedroom, moving to where Clay sat sleeping. He paused there momentarily, two stark blue eyes staring out through the holes of the dark mask, as if daring him to awaken, but he did not.

Leaving the bedroom, Nancy's captor entered into the hallway and descended the stairs. On the way down he slid his hand beneath Nancy's gown and messaged her naked buttocks.

"Nice," he said softly to himself, "firm, round, and honed to near perfection. I like that." Unconscious, oblivious to even being alive, Nancy's lucid body bounced like a rag doll with each silent step he took.

CHAPTER TWELVE

THE RINGING OF THE phone startled Clay awake. Darkness still possessed the town, but soft crimson light lay stretched across the eastern horizon. Inside the house, a thick murkiness filled the upstairs.

The phone rang again. Clay rose from his chair, alarmed at first, but a glance out the window and the sight of the surveillance vehicle put him at ease. Sleepily, he crossed the room to the bedside phone, noticing immediately that Nancy was not there. The bathroom was dark, so he guessed she was downstairs making coffee. On the third ring, he picked up the receiver, his mind barely free from the cobwebs of sleep.

"Yeah, hello."

"Good morning, Marshall Cooper." He did not recognize the voice. "I trust your sleep was sound, although not altogether comfortable, I'm sure. Do you know who this is?"

"No."

"Well, don't worry, Bob will vouch for me. Won't you, Bob?" Back at the police post in Lafayette, Bob Lemus stood listening with hopeful expectation. He held a cigarette in one hand and a cup of coffee in the other. Taking a long draw, he exhaled forcefully, speaking into the air. "Don't blow this, Cooper."

At the same instant, Clay figured out who the caller was and spoke his name into the receiver. "Blue Eyes?"

"Yes, it is, thank you."

Cooper looked at his watch, but it was still too dark to see the hands. Knowing the importance of holding the killer on the line, he began what he hoped to be a successful stretch of conversation.

And what is it I can do for you, *mister Blue Eyes?*"

The voice on the other end laughed lightly. "Did you hear that, Bob? Respect. This fellow has manners." There was a lull, then Blue Eyes added, I have a favor to ask of you, Marshall Cooper. A rather simple favor, actually. One that will put an end to this cat and mouse venture."

Cat and Rat, you mean?" Clay taunted.

Blue Eyes made a clicking noise with his tongue. "I'm sorry you see it that way, Marshall. I take it you do not approve of me...of my work. Personally, like to think of what I do as art."

"Art!" Cooper snapped. "You kill innocent people! How in the hell do you call that art? You're not an artist, you're a fucking lunatic."

"Now now, Marshall, let us maintain our temper. You're not visualizing the entire picture. You need to take time and understand the artist behind the picture."

"The picture! The picture is simple. You butcher and sodomize human beings. As for the artist, what is there to understand? You're a deep-end schitzo freak who ought to be hung by his balls with piano wire, then left hanging for everyone to see."

"Ouch. That certainly would hurt, now wouldn't it, Clay? May I call you Clay?" He gave no time for reply.

"Let us get back to my original purpose for calling. I request but one simple favor."

Cooper took in a deep breath. "Favor? Now why in the hell would I want to do you a favor?"

"Because what I ask will benefit everyone. You see, I want you to kill me! Just you and I alone, a small simple ceremony, using a special knife I have in my possession. Just one well-placed stab, and it's all over. No more innocent people will die. Now what do you say? Will you be a good sport?"

To give Cooper time for thought, Blue Eyes redirected his conversation to agent Lemus, listening at H.Q. "Bob, I suspect you have traced me by now, but don't get your hopes up. By the time a Black and White arrives, I'll be gone."

He returned to Cooper, "Well, what will it be, Marshall? Yes, or no?"

Cooper shook his head even though the killer could not see him. "I'm afraid my answer has got to be no, Blue. May I call you Blue? You see, I'm not a sick twisted weirdo like you. I believe in the value of human life, and because of that it would be against my principles even to kill a dumb fuck amoeba like you. But I will tell you what I can do, Blue. I can ring your psycho neck; kick your schizophrenic ass, put you in a nice tight pair of cuffs and come visit the day they fry you. How does that sound?"

Blue Eyes sighed. "I was afraid you would take this approach, so here goes. I have prepared a surprise for you. Something to, how shall I put it, empower you with motivation. It is simple, actually, but does require you to jump through two hoops, so listen closely. For hoop number one, hurry downstairs like a good little husband to your refrigerator." Blue Eyes gave him just enough time to form a mental picture of the refrigerator in his mind. "As for hoop number two, well, that will be self-explanatory via hoop number one. Got to run-and so have you."

The phone clicked and the dial tone played in his ear. Immediately Clay shouted Nancy's name. Panic stricken, he dropped the phone and, clutching the Glock, ran through the door and out into the hall. Turning, he bolted to the top of the stairs and bounded down.

The area below was dusky, filtered with but a wisp of dawning light. He tripped over his feet and tumbled head over heels down the stairs. His gun flew from his hand and slid noisily across the hardwood floor below, coming to a stop somewhere unknown.

Even as he rolled, end over end, his mind remembered the strange dream he had had two days ago. Then he came to an abrupt stop at the bottom of the stairs. Just as it had happened in the dream, he had injured his ribs in the fall and now held them with his hand, finding it painful when he breathed. Quickly, he climbed to his feet and dashed for the kitchen.

Outside, rays of light were rushing the earth like a welcomed army, but inside, the house remained a den of sabled shadows. Despite the hazard, he could see well enough to bolt past the couch and through the archway leading into the kitchen. Taped to the refrigerator door was a note. Ripping the note free, Clay held it beneath the window and read by the bit of light filtering in. The words were actually a rhyme.

A look inside will make you cry.

But I'll bet now you change your mind!

Crumbling the note in his trembling hand, Clay threw it angrily to the floor; his heart was pounding. Fear gripped his senses. Teeth gritted, he pulled open the door and bright light exploded into the room; instantly his dark pupils constricted, but despite the infarcted vision, he saw it immediately. There was no stopping his scream-it was the cry of a mortally wounded animal. *"Oh God!"* The words echoed with horror through the two-story house.

Sitting by itself on a cleared shelf, a fresh, bloodstained blond scalp sat draped over the milk carton, the hair neatly brushed and decorated with two of Nancy's hair barrettes. Below it hung another note, one whose words jerked the strength from his legs and brought him to his knees.

Remember the song Bits and Pieces, Bits and Pieces?

Better check the Garage.

Stunned, he could not move. There on his knees he glared frozen at the horror before his eyes. Holding open the refrigerator door he looked on in cold, disbelieving shock. He began to sob. The world around him became a soundless void and he was but a tiny speck in the middle of its vast expanse, numbed and incapable of moving. The door leading out to the attached garage was just to the right of the refrigerator, but it was a hundred miles from his reach. He could feel his strength draining, taking with it his will to live.

With a shaking hand, he reached up and touched the hair, stroked it gently, his sobs becoming a hard, painful cry. Nancy, his lifesaver, was no more. Pictures of her, of them, flashed in his mind. He could hear her laughter, feel her arms around him and the touch of her soft kiss. In seconds, his numbed mind relived every memory of their short time together. Time passed immeasurably.

He had no inkling of how long he knelt there, staring and crying; he knew only that he came to the stark realization that at some point his tears had finally dried up. Closing the refrigerator and using the counter, he pulled himself to his feet. Weakly, he began to move, inching his way past the refrigerator toward the garage door. To the entranceway leading to the horror awaiting him on the other side.

Clendes and Jones had left the car and were making their way to the house using tactical caution, guns raised. They had heard the scream and wanted very much to bust open the door and rush in, but experience and temperance took over. Clendes glanced quickly through the window beside the front door. The living room was clear. Morning light was incessantly chasing away the remaining darkness now, so seeing was no problem. Ducking to stay below the front windows, Clendes ran quickly across the front of the house and stopped at the corner, looking quickly around it; he saw no one. Calling to Jones, he motioned for him to enter the front; he was going around the back. Jones nodded, then slipped the key they had been given into the slot and slowly opened the door. As it had been with his partners glance through the window, the living room was empty. Quickly he darted inside, placing his back against the wall. Remaining motionless, he listened intently. The house was silent. Glancing through the archway leading into the kitchen, he noticed that the garage door was standing open; he guessed, under normal circumstances, that it should have been closed.

Carefully he crossed the room, placing his back to the wall dividing the living room and kitchen. From somewhere inside the garage, he thought he heard the faint sound of someone crying.

With extreme caution, he moved into the kitchen beside the opened door. Following a deep breath, he whirled around with gun poised, centering himself in the doorway ready for the worst, but nothing happened.

The garage was well-lit, so it took only a second to realize where the crying he had heard was coming from. Clayton Cooper sat on the floor, his back to the wall and sobbing. Jones shifted his eyes from Cooper to the center of the garage. What he saw startled him nearly speechless. But he did manage four words: "Jesus, Son of God."

He had seen the worst in his career working with Lemus, chasing killers, but this was it, the number one horror. Slowly he lowered his weapon and held it at his side. The body hung by its feet from the center rafter. Heaped below it on the cold cement floor lay the pile of flesh that had been skinned from its body. Like a perfectly sculpted cadaver used to portray the muscular structure of the human body for medical students, the blood-soaked figure hung motionless, fingertips dangling only inches from the floor.

Suddenly Clendes appeared beside Jones and looked into the garage. Despite his being far more seasoned than his partner, his own reaction was not surprising: "What the fuck?"

CHAPTER THIRTEEN

NAKED, BLUE EYES WALKED to the middle of his motel room and sat cross-legged on the floor. He had drawn the curtains to darken the room so that the forty-one candles, one for each of his victims, burned with twinkling warmth. He had already disarmed the smoke detector.

As was always his practice, he had streaked his face with three single lines using the blood of his latest sacrifice. To him this ritual was symbolic of the union created with each of his kills. The streak running down the left side represented himself, the one on the right his most recent victim, while the middle one, both wider and longer, represented his beloved master.

Closing his eyes, he took in a deep breath, held it a few seconds, then let it out slowly, making a hissing sound. Then, cupping his genitals in one hand and holding his penis in the other, he began to pray aloud.

"Belial, master demon of lust, hearest thou, my prayer. I have done all that thou hast asked of me and now await the death of this body, that I may come to you, your humble servant. I beseech thee, bestow upon me thy power, maketh me your Incubus that I may return to this plane again and create wickedness, guilt and perversion among man and woman as they have never known."

From the bed just behind him came a soft moan. The naked body tied face down, blind folded and gagged with duct tape, pulled against the half-inch yellow nylon rope restraining their arms and legs. Blue Eyes ignored the struggle, knowing there was no threat of escape; knots were one of his specialties.

Refocusing his concentration, he continued his supplication. "I have distressed Marshall Cooper as thou hast commanded. Now I beg of thee, fill his soul with hatred and despair, inflame his anger that he will do as I have asked, kill this worldly body, and send me home to you. This do I pray in your most adored name, may evil forever prevail. Amen."

Blue Eyes sat several more minutes in silent meditation before opening his eyes. Initially they were black, but they quickly returned to blue. Leisurely he rose to his feet and walked slowly toward the bed, a small sensual smile on his face.

Feeling himself grow aroused, he approached the bed and lay down beside his helpless captive, letting his now deep blue eyes sweep the naked body. Candlelight accentuated a sculptured figure.

Lightly Blue Eyes traced his fingers down the victim's spine, pausing to roughly knead the nicely rounded butt-cheeks when he arrived. How perfectly built, so young and perfect, and so willing to come to his room for a drink; the drink that had drugged this beautiful creature.

Now the bound victim was awake and no doubt in fear. Blue Eyes closed his eyes and smiled into the shadows of the candlelit room. Oh, how he loved that fear. It caused his head to swim, and he grew drunk with its intoxication.

Slowly, he slipped his hand between the victim's legs, caressing the victim's testicles; then slid his hand forward and grasped the soft, fleshy manhood.

Opening his eyes, he exhaled with exuberant pleasure. Even in fear, he could feel the naked man beside him began to respond to his touch.

CHAPTER FOURTEEN

TWO FULL DAYS HAD passed since on-scene paramedics had injected Clayton Cooper with 15 total milligrams of Valium to sedate him. His refusal to leave the remains of his wife had been distressing for all. Ongoing sedation had kept him in a sleep-induced, incomprehensible world, but over time the doses were reduced to allow a gradual return to reality. Now, on the morning of the third day, he opened his eyes and gazed around the hospital room in which he lay.

A heart monitor showing normal sinus rhythm darted its pattern across a small blue screen, and an IV of normal saline flowed slowly into the angio fastened to his right hand. With blurry eyes, Clay studied the tubing's small loop taped there, then slowly moved his fingers. He was pleased they still worked. It was his shooting hand, the hand that would pull the trigger when he emptied his clip into Blue Eyes' heart.

Still groggy from the persistent sedation, he wet his lips, then closed his eyes and opened them again. His lids felt weighted down and he was in need of a shave, but most of all he wanted his toothbrush and the removal of the catheter running up his penis.

He stared into the ceiling for an unknown period of time, moving in and out of conscious awareness. At 12:13 a stocky nurse with short, graying hair, flowered scrubs, and a face like Adolph Hitler minus the mustache, entered his room.

Moving to his side with syringe in hand, she prepared to give him his scheduled sedation. He refused it. Irritated, she wrote on the chart at the foot of his bed then stormed out, mumbling. Clay knew just what she'd do: march straight to the nurse's station and call the doctor. Actually, that was just what he wanted, and he was not surprised when the doctor showed up in less than five minutes.

When he walked in, the old nurse was right on his heels, wearing an expression that said, "I brought the big gun this time, and you won't tell him no!" Just like in every movie he had ever seen, the doctor went immediately to the foot of the bed, picked up the chart, read its contents then came around to his side. Nurse Adolph remained at the foot of the bed with smugly folded arms.

When he spoke, the doctor's tone was soft, therapeutic in its own way. "I'm Doctor Pecard. Pecard with an 'e', not an 'i'. No relation to the Enterprise Captain. The nurse tells me you refused your scheduled sedation. Based on that fact, how do we feel this morning, Mr. Cooper?"

A tall elderly man in his mid-sixties, Doctor Pecard sported a gray bushy mustache that brought Sam Elliot to Clay's mind. Because he was armed with a warm smile and boyish mannerisms just like the actor, Clay liked him almost immediately.

"I can't speak for you, Doc, but I'm doing ok."

"Good." The doctor smiled briefly, then removed his stethoscope from around his neck. First, he listened to Clay's heart and lungs, then checked his pupils with a penlight. He nodded approval at his findings. Throwing a quick glance at the stone-faced nurse, he turned back to Clay, leaned down to his ear and whispered. "Do you know what most blond nurses get on their SATs?"

Clay shook his head weakly, "No."

"Nail polish," Pecard whispered.

Clay laughed lightly.

"That's what I needed to hear," the doctor told him, standing up straight. "If you can laugh, you're eligible for parole. I'll make arrangements and have you sprung within the hour. But on the way home, it's an order that you stop and get a good meal; you haven't eaten in over forty-eight hours. You can order hospital food if you wish...but

I'll trust your better judgment." He turned to leave, then stopped after a couple of steps. Looking back, he added, "And one more thing, Mr. Cooper. You cannot have the gown, so please don't ask." At that, he turned and walked past the nurse, speaking over his shoulder. "Come along Nurse Fraulein." She threw Clay an unpleasant look, then turned on her heels and followed the doctor out the door.

Alone again, Clay lay motionless on his back staring at the ceiling, his mind drifting back to the garage. His eyes filled with tears, and he wiped them, blinking several times. It was paramount he remain strong; if he did not, they would keep him in the hospital and sedate him once again. And if that were to happen, Blue Eyes might lose interest and disappear into the big, crowded world and never be found.

Picking up the phone, he dialed Ron. "Hey, it's me."

It was obvious his best friend was pleased to hear from him. "Clay, how you doing, buddy? I'm coming up to see you in a little bit."

"You bet you are. They're setting me free. Can you meet me here within the hour?"

Ron glanced at his watch. "You bet."

Clay hesitated a second, "If you don't mind, I'd like to stay at your place a couple of days."

"Sure. Stay as long as you need."

"Great. Bring me a change of clothes, will you?"

"You got it, buddy."

When the phone went silent, Clay laid it back in the cradle. He fell back against his pillow, tears welling in his eyes once again.

"*Stop it,*" he admonished himself. He was going to have to find a way to get the sight of Nancy's hanging body out of his mind. And although he was in control enough to know that time had a way of easing pain, right now it seemed impossible. He wiped his eyes again, then hit the call button clipped to his bed.

In just a few seconds, Adolf the nurse was back, and upon his request, discontinued the IV, monitor and catheter, but not before letting him know it was only because the doctor had ordered it to be done. She had also retrieved a toothbrush and paste, a razor, and small container of shaving cream. With those in hand, he made his way to the bathroom, shaved, and showered.

Ron arrived at ten minutes after one. By 1:30 they were sitting in a restaurant, where Clay picked at his food in silence. Finally, taking a sip of coffee, he worked up enough courage to ask.

Ron what he been avoiding. "What have they done with her?"

Ron put down his fork and looked at him from across the booth. "She's at Hyperstole Funeral Home. They're waiting to hear from you. I didn't want to bring it up until you were ready."

Clay nodded his appreciation. With wet eyes he told him, "I'll give them a call from your place."

"Whatever you say, buddy."

Ron's house did not turn out to be the quiet haven Clay had expected. Throughout the evening he was visited by an endless trail of concerned family and friends. Both Nancy's Parents and his had been waiting, and together they spent nearly an hour crying and reminiscing.

It was hard on all of them, but worst on Clay. He had a sense of guilt, feeling he was the reason Nancy was dead. Understanding and compassionate, both sets of parents assured him he was not to blame.

It was just past midnight when the last guest left, so Ron and Clay grabbed two Bud Lights and went out on the porch to sit. The sky was alive with a million glowing stars. Clay stared at them a long while before speaking. "I'm going to miss her, Ron. God, I'm going to miss her."

Ron squeezed his shoulder, not sure what to say. "I know." They were the only words he could think of.

"She was everything to me, Ron, my whole life. Hey, remember the wedding? When we kneeled at the altar, and on the bottom of my shoes you had stuck two wide strips of masking tape with the words 'help me' written on them? Half of the congregation lost it." Ron chuckled. "Yeah, man, that preacher sure was pissed."

For a moment, Clay grinned. "Yeah, it was a good thing we were in the middle of the ceremony, or he'd have thrown us all out. Of course, Nancy was just as mad, swore she'd never talk to you again." Pausing, Clay looked at his best friend. "And now she never will, will she?" Clay began to sob. Ron put his arm around him and held him, wiping at his own eyes. And there, beneath the stars, the two cried together.

CHAPTER FIFTEEN

ONE HUNDRED AND SIXTY-THREE guests attended the visitation. On Thursday, that many and more turned out for the funeral; because of heavy drizzle, a sea of umbrellas festooned an immense area surrounding the tent shelter. Standing chilled on soggy grass, some prayed, some dabbed at their eyes with handkerchiefs, and others wished it would end so they could go home where it was dry.

Less than half could see or hear what was going on inside the tent. They had come out just to show respect. Although Clay appreciated their presence, he would have dismissed them long ago had it been proper etiquette. But he had attended enough funerals himself to appreciate their sacrifice.

Attending the services also, working their way inconspicuous amid the crowd, Lemus and his men searched for Blue Eyes, confident he would show. Of nearly seventy men, at least forty had blue eyes and looked between the ages of twenty and thirty-five. It was the proverbial needle in a haystack, but worth the possibility.

Without realizing it, however, they were only partially correct about Blue Eyes attending. The killer, a quarter mile away, watched through a Swarovski Spotting Scope. And from his position on a high bluff, he could see into the open tent, even the expression on Clayton Cooper's face, down to the tears in his eyes.

Strangely, Blue Eyes shared his pain and cried himself, yet at the same time felt elation. He was confident the town Marshall would now do as he had requested and kill him; but if not, then tomorrow's surprise would push him over the line for sure.

Following the services, Clay returned home for the first time since leaving the hospital. He wanted to be alone, and felt it was time to face the last hurdle. Three newspapers lay on the porch, so he gathered them up and tossed them onto the couch once inside. The house looked exactly the way it always had, just quieter, empty...lifeless.

Ron and Michelle had hired a crew to clean up. The cleaners even scrubbed the garage floor, although a small dark stain remained.

Clay showered and changed into blue jeans and a T-shirt, then went downstairs to make a pot of coffee. At the kitchen door he paused momentarily, glaring at the refrigerator. His stare lasted only a few seconds, and then he went into the kitchen. The coffee was in the cabinet above it and although it was silly, he was thankful to have reached it without touching the refrigerator itself.

While the coffee brewed, he went into the living room and sat on the couch to read the papers and catch up on news. Wednesday's headline caught his attention... *Bizarre Killing at Local Motel.*

A 23-year-old male, identification withheld, had been found gruesomely murdered in one of the motel rooms. Details were sketchy, so he did the logical thing: he called Ron for the whole story. Michelle answered.

"Hi, it's Clay."

"Clay. How are you doing? Are you OK?"

"I'm fine, Michelle. Hey, thanks for all your support. Is your hubby around?"

"You're certainly welcome, and yes he is. Hang on."

He heard her yell Ron's name as a soft thud clattered through the receiver. A few seconds passed, then Ron came on. "Hey, buddy, how are you doing?"

"Fine. Ron, I'm calling to get the skinny on the motel murder."

Ron paused. "It was homosexual in nature. So how are you doing over there by yourself?"

"Doing fine. How did the guy die? The papers mentioned it was gruesome, so give me the details."

"Buddy, you don't need them right now."

Clay shook his head. "It was him, wasn't it? Blue Eyes!"

Ron conceded. "It was him...the sick freak."

"How?"

"'Are you sure you're up to hearing about it?"

"Yes, Ron, I'm up to hearing about it. This guy killed my wife, remember?"

"Ok. Like I said, the victim was a known gay, worked the bars, especially campus. Blue Eyes charmed him to his room and tied him up with nylon rope, naked, face down. He'd been drugged."

"Sodomized?"

"Oh, yeah. Had semen running out his ass."

"Damn. How did he kill him?"

"It's sick, buddy. First, the son of a bitch cut a plastic one-gallon milk jug in half, and securely duct-taped it airtight to the poor guy's face. After punching two small air holes through the plastic, he ran an IV line just inside the snout and taped it so it wouldn't leak. Then he started an IV in the guy's left arm and attached the IV line running from the snout, directly to it. The poor bastard's own blood began filling up the milk jug. He had to literally drink his own blood to keep space enough for air inside the container to breathe. Doc says he doesn't know which happened first, bleeding to death or drowning. It was a freaking bloody mess; I'll tell you that."

Clay sighed and shook his head. "What was the name on the register?"

"Doctor Michael Forthy, surgeon from Chicago, in town for a Medical Convention. Blue Eyes used his credit card to secure the room."

"Any notes on the victim?"

"Yep. Another parchment, wrapped around the poor Bastard's Penis with a neat little bow."

"Was I mentioned?"

"Oh, yeah." Ron paused briefly before he told him. "Said the victim was dedicated to the late Nancy Cooper."

Clay closed his eyes and took in a deep breath. There were several seconds of silence before he spoke again. "He's going to call me again, Ron, you know that."

"I'd count on it, buddy."

Clay's face grew cold. "Oh, I am counting on it, Ron. And when he does, you can bet your ass I'm going to grant him his wish."

CHAPTER SIXTEEN

THAT NIGHT, CLAY TOSSED and turned restlessly. More than once he awoke reaching out for Nancy, only to realize she was not there. He slept and he awoke, and he dreamed in between. And in each of his dreams he and Nancy were together, laughing and sharing, or making love.

Although restive, it was a good night for him. He had been with her, even if only for small, subconscious fragments of time. Repeatedly, throughout his awake-asleep state, Clay had prayed the night would not end; but as all things do, it did, and he opened his eyes to the light of morning.

By seven, he was dressed in jeans and a T-shirt again. With Nancy still on his mind he descended the stairs, thinking about a cup of coffee. Every morning she greeted him at the kitchen door with a kiss and a cup. It had been an assiduous ritual he had taken for granted. Guilt and remorse weighed heavily on his heart, and he admitted the old adage was true: you don't miss something until it's gone.

Halfway down the stairs, Clay realized the aroma of brewing coffee was drifting his way. Descending the remaining steps, he approached the kitchen with apprehension but found no one there.

Within seconds, his eyes spotted his old coffee cup from the office sitting on the counter. Beneath it laid a neatly folded piece of paper. Pulling it free, he opened it. It was a short, hand-written note:

Clay,

I brewed your coffee since Nancy couldn't be here to make it for you. Also, as you can see, I brought by your favorite cup. I'd have given you your morning kiss, too, but what would people think? Anyway, about my wish. I suspect by now you've warmed up to the idea of granting it to me. Here's the game. Eight o'clock-be at the pay phone in front of the IGA store up town and wait for me to call you. Make sure you're there, or I promise you will truly regret it. Trust me when I say things could get worse...or maybe even better! Cooperation is everything! **Tell NO ONE!**

Blue Eyes

Clay held the note, staring blankly for some time. Hatred pounded in his temples. He knew he could tell no one; it was impossible to guess what this maniac would do next, and to whom he would do it. Going alone was the only way. Soberly, he glanced at his watch: 7:10.

After pouring a cup of coffee, he went back upstairs and removed his sneakers, replacing them with Magnum Hi-Tech Trooper Boots. He then strapped his ankle holster with his .380 to his right calf and slipped a knife into his left boot. Finally, after clipping the Glock to his belt, he went back downstairs to wait out the remaining time.

He paced restlessly. It was imperative he maintain composure and think everything out with precision, for this could be the only chance he would ever have to get close to Blue Eyes. Twice he picked up the phone and began dialing Ron's number, but both times hung up the phone before Ron answered.

On one hand, calling Ron seemed like the smart thing to do; it was always a comfort knowing back up was there in the shadows, especially if it were Ron. But this time was different; this killer was far too smart to be fooled. Besides, he thought, when they met it would be far better if there were no witnesses. The time passed idly by. Anxiously he paced and twice checked the rounds in both the Glock and ankle weapon. Finally, after four cups of coffee, the moment of truth arrived. After shutting off the coffeepot, he walked vigorously to his truck and drove to the IGA.

He waited by the phone nearly sixteen minutes, twice having to turn away others in need of its use. He had begun to fear Blue Eyes would not call, but at exactly 8:17 it rang. When it did, he snapped it free of the hook. "Hello."

"Sorry for the wait, Marshall Cooper. I had to take care of a last-minute detail."

Clay wondered for a second what that detail might have been, then replied, "Well, I'm here, so what now?"

Blue Eyes was beside himself; confident Cooper was anxious to do as he had asked. "Now I want you to get in your truck and drive out to the abandoned grain elevator. Once you arrive, park on the north side, out of sight. Get out of the truck and look all the way up to the top of the building to the highest window-what would you say it is, a hundred and fifty, two hundred feet? After you've looked up and spotted my ... *assurance,* walk straight into the building using the large doorway in front of you and stop just inside the shadows. Remember, walk just inside, and stop. Do not let what you see at the window spur you on. Self-discipline will be the key here."

"Is that it?" Clay asked.

"Pretty much. You did not invite any friends, did you?"

"No."

"Promise? After all, we wouldn't want to spoil the festivities, now, would we?"

"Cut the shit! I'll be there in five minutes, alone."

"Wonderful, see you in five." Blue Eyes hung up.

Clay hurried to his truck and, tires squealing, pulled out of the IGA parking lot. His face showed no expression, except for his cold, calculating eyes. Never had he wanted to kill anyone like he did right now. He wondered what assurance this maniac would have at the elevator window. In all honesty, it scared the hell out of him. The twisted bastard was capable of anything.

Clay wished he had called Ron for backup, or even Lemus, but he could not have taken the chance. Besides, if...NO. When, he killed Blue Eyes, both would give him a hero's hurrah anyway, with no questions asked.

Just as he had been told, he pulled around to the north side of the elevator, out of sight. Then he stepped out of the truck and ran his eyes up the full length of the tall, abandoned structure. There were five windows, each representing their own floor, each without glass and looking like darkened eyes of evil staring out over the open fields. Many of the old shingles that had once dressed the building were missing, and anything iron was rusted. The entire complex should have been torn down long ago, but no one had wanted to front the cost. Now, in its hundredth year, the old grain elevator remained a long-deserted testimony to the days of sweat and hard work.

Clay's eyes finally rested on the highest window, guessing the height to be nearly two hundred feet. He saw nothing but the dark rectangular hole: no movement, no sign of life. But Blue Eyes was here, of that he was certain, no doubt watching his every move. He could hear cars passing by on the highway south of the building and the morning sun was already feeling warm on his face.

Lowering his eyes, Clay studied his surroundings. Straight ahead was the entrance he was told to walk through. At one time, it had been a wide, sliding door, but it had long ago rotted and fallen, and now lay in a heap of decaying lumber and rusted framework. Five other outreach buildings spotted the complex, along with seven towering silos connected by an intricate network of piping. A noise from the high window caught his attention, and he looked up again.

A man in a ski mask was forcing another person, dressed in coveralls, out of the long window and lowering them by a rope tied to their wrists. The victim was lowered until they hung helpless two feet below the sill. Arms stretched above their head, the victim struggled only briefly before realizing the predicament, and at that point remained absolutely still.

A hood had been placed over the victim's head, so they were unable to see anything but the drop beneath them. There had been no pleading or yelling on the victim's part, so Clay guessed the victim had been gagged.

The man in the ski mask paused momentarily, staring down at him, then turned and disappeared into the darkness beyond the window. Seconds of silence passed before the voice of Blue Eyes came out of the dark somewhere beyond the doorway in front of Clay.

"Welcome, Marshall Cooper. In less than twenty minutes, it will all be over. I have prepared a place here inside for this most monumental of moments. I have been waiting a very long time for this. And now, thanks to you, Master Belial is going to make it happen. But before we get on with the business at hand, allow me the pleasure of giving you something in return." Blue Eyes paused briefly before adding, "In regard to what is about to happen next, you must under all circumstance remain in control…no matter what you see or hear. So please, if you will, look up at the window once again?"

With apprehension, Clay's eyes traveled back up the lofty wall. Whoever the hanging person was, they chose to remain still, knowing full well the peril of their predicament. The person in the ski mask reappeared immediately and Cooper whispered under his breath, "You couldn't have climbed those stairs that fast; you have a partner, you son of a bitch."

The hangman knelt, and fumbled beneath the hood, untying the victim's gag. Then, in one quick motion, he pulled the hood from their head.

Clayton Cooper stood in awe, disbelieving what he saw. He yelled her name. *"Nancy."*

In the same instant she yelled his. *"Clay!"*

CHAPTER SEVENTEEN

BLUE EYES WAS QUICK to remind Cooper of the rules. "Remember Marshall ...control! Stay where you are until told to move."

Clay used restraint. He wanted to charge the open door but knew doing so could place Nancy in greater danger, or worse, become the cause of her death, and that of their new developing baby. So, standing steadfast, he did the only thing he could-grit his teeth and curse under his breath.

"Now if you will, Marshall. Drop the handgun onto the ground in front of you."

Without removing his eyes from his wife, Clay withdrew the Glock from its holster and laid it at his feet.

"Also, the ankle weapon, please."

That shifted Clay's thoughts. How did the killer know he was wearing an ankle piece? Had he just assumed it? For the first time since setting eyes on Nancy, Clay broke his stare, slowly pulling away to glare into the open darkness of the doorway. Kneeling, he removed the .380, placing it beside the 9- millimeter, then stood. His eyes narrowed, straining to penetrate the black confines, but it was no use.

"Wonderful," the hidden voice told him. "Now, understand that if you do not do exactly as told, my colleague will sever the rope holding your wife, and sadly, she will drop to her death right there in front of you. And we do not want that to happen, now, do we? After all, you've lost her once, and this time it would be...so final."

Clay grimaced, glancing quickly back to the high window. The figure in the mask had brandished a knife, its silver blade glistening against the sunlight. A mixed array of feelings whirled in his thoughts; his sweet Lifesaver was alive and that brought unimaginable elation, but now there were two madmen holding her new life in fragile balance. While he wanted to help her, his not helping was the best help. Frustration and anger lay pitted in his stomach.

Again, he brought his eyes back to the dark doorway. Above him the sun was rising, slowly reducing the dark opening to an assemblage of striped shadows. Visibility was slowly improving, but time was quickly running out.

Moving only his eyes, he glanced down at the Glock. Could he get to it and fire true before the man in the mask could cut the rope? Then, could he run fast enough through the door into a darkened area, let his eyes adjust, and beat Blue Eyes to the top floor where Nancy was tied?

Clay knew the layout of the building; he had played there countless times growing up. Once through the door, he would enter into a foyer, turn right onto a huge open floor, then turn left and make a mad dash across fifty or sixty feet of open bay to the foot of an old stairway leading to the top.

The foyer was an enclosed recess, so Blue Eyes had to be standing within its shadows, thus giving the killer a slight lead, but Clay was a fast runner. In the sky above, an aircraft too distant to see raced across the sky, leaving a stream of white exhaust in its wake. The highway hummed with passing traffic and the sun's warm rays caused a bead of sweat to run down the side of Clay's face.

Blue Eyes spoke again from his concealed position. "Now if you will, Marshall, enter through the door and stop just inside."

Clay glanced quickly at his hanging wife, then back into the shadowy entranceway. He also looked once more at the Glock, rapidly contemplating the odds, but Blue Eyes interrupted before any decision was reached.

"I would not if I were you, Marshall. The knife my friend is holding is very sharp and would cut the rope long before you took safe aim. The range would be what, six hundred yards? I would think the possibility of shooting your own wife would not be worth the gamble, wouldn't you agree?"

Reluctantly, Clay did agree; the probability of success was dangerously low. Left with no other choice, he walked grudgingly to the door and stepped into the shadows. Just as he was told, he entered into the foyer. Three steps in, he stopped.

His pupils adjusted quickly, and he looked to the right, staring out over the old plank flooring. Steeped in diffuse shadows, the well-worn floor swept away into dim obscurity. Rays of sunlight filled with floating particles shot brightly through the open windows.

As though he'd materialized out of nowhere, Blue Eyes stepped suddenly into the nearest beam of light. For the first time, Clay viewed the elusive madman. Just as Spulder had suspected, the killer was handsome. And, at least for this day, he believed in dressing for the occasion. A white swallowtail tux highlighted his perfect golden tan. Blond, shoulder length hair fell just within reach of unmistakably broad shoulders, and a close-shaved, dimple-chinned face held a warm, amiable smile.

Although possibly older, he looked to be in his late twenties. He radiated culture, education, and innocent boyish charm. Yet none of those perfect features captured the true pulse of his charisma. That privilege belonged to a pair of the most intense, bright blue eyes Clay had ever seen. In fact, he wondered if perhaps the man was wearing contacts. Even so, he thought, Lemus had appropriately nicknamed the killer.

It was no challenge understanding how he had been able to deceive his victims and gain their trust. Doctor Spulder had called it correctly. This was a man who had everything—everything, that is, but a sane mind.

Then Clay frowned in puzzlement. Despite the lunatic's careful effort to look perfect, he had forgotten to dress his feet; his shoes and socks were missing. Blue Eyes spotted Clay's curious expression and wiggled his toes.

"You must think me senile, Marshall, but I assure you that is not the case. Remaining barefoot is simply part of the ceremony you and I will soon be undertaking. Actually, I will be asking you as well to remove your shoes and socks when we begin."

Blue Eyes stuck his hands in his pockets, adding, "Really, it is nice to finally meet with you. When both of us are awake, I mean. I must tell you, I consider you a most fortunate man, as worldly men go. You have a beautiful wife, a comfortable home, close friends, and to say the least, an interesting job. After all, who else other than those chosen for Belial get to meet such a colorful personality such as myself? And, as agent Lemus would attest, there is a long list of those who would like very much to meet me."

Blue Eyes smiled at his self-portrayal. Pulling his hands from the pockets of the tux, he held a small, flat gold case. Clay's eyes darted to the object, watching the killer open it and remove a cigarette. He snapped it shut, then gently tapped the end of his cigarette against it. Clay stared at it tentatively. Placing the cigarette between his lips, Blue Eyes lit it using a matching gold lighter, then inhaled deeply.

Except for the tiny dust particles floating within the rays of light, the two men remained encased in a silent, motionless world. Clay wanted to charge the killer, take him out, then make his way to the top floor to the man in the ski mask. The knife was still in Clay's boot.

Clay studied the man standing before him. His shoulders were broad, and he would be fast and strong. He was a killer and would not surrender. If tackled, he would make it a fight to the death...but Clay was confident he could take him, so he made up his mind. On the count of three he would charge and tackle him. He began his count... *one.* Blue Eyes closed his eyes. Clay would do his best to take him alive, but if killing him meant saving Nancy, then that's the way it would be.

Two. Suddenly the killer opened his eyes...and Clay caught his breath, lost his concentration. Shock tingled his spine and the hair on the back of his neck prickled.

The magnificent blue of the killer's eyes had vanished, replaced by a cold blackness as dark as the interior of a sealed casket. Two eyes of tarmac, lifeless yet alive, stared sternly. It was as if the killer had read his thoughts, and the very idea of an attack had enraged him, releasing some form of internal evil.

Cooper stared, speechless and stunned, not sure what to do. Never had he seen anything like it, and never before had he considered turning to run. Seconds of eerie silence prevailed as the demented killer gazed into Clay's eyes. They stood staring. This was evil incarnate; no human eyes could change color like that. His mind processed but one single thought: this man, or whatever the hell he was, would not be that easy to kill.

Without breaking his stare, Blue Eyes exhaled the draw he had taken seconds ago from his cigarette. Smoke floated from his mouth, rising upward to encircle his head in a perfect halo. The bizarre ring lingered a few seconds, then dissipated.

A slow smile began to appear on the killer's face. Clay watched, speechless, as the dark of his eyes began to change slowly back to blue. Shaking his head, Clayton Cooper whispered, "What in God's name are you?"

In a soft, gentle voice, Blue Eyes apologized. "Please forgive me, Marshall Cooper, for that inexcusable spurt of anger. I do not wish to alarm you. It is just that any effort on your part to apprehend me will not only be futile, but very unfavorable to both your wife and my goal. Truth be known, I have been waiting a very long time for what is about to happen, longer than you can imagine. And whether you like it or not, Marshall, you are my aide-de-camp-the chosen one if I may. You simply have no choice. And if it means anything. I do have a strong appreciation for your boundless tenacity."

Barely noticeable, Clay shook his head. "Blue Eyes, trust me when I say that what I just witnessed-that thing with your eyes-well, it scared the shit out of me. But let's get something straight; I am not your aide-de-camp, your bud, your helper, your friend, or anything else. Originally, yes, I came here with every intention of killing you. But now the only thing I want is to get my wife and go home." He paused briefly. "And let's not forget about arresting your sick evil ass, too."

Blue Eyes smiled. "Sorry, Marshall, but arresting is me is not an option today. You have only two choices: kill me or kill your wife." Unbuttoning his tux jacket, he lifted the right side to expose the inner lining. Clay saw the small microphone with attached wiring immediately. Blue Eyes pressed his lips together and breathed deeply through his nose, then exhaled slowly out his mouth.

"You see, Marshall Cooper, my helper upstairs is listening to our every word, knows our every move. Should you not do exactly as told… well, your Little Life Saver won't feel the sting of a skinning knife, but she will experience the few seconds of terror as she falls to her death."

Clay cursed silently, fighting the rage that boiled inside him. He was unsure which was stronger, his anger or the despair that tried to overpower what little bit of hope remained. The situation seemed impossible, yet despite his feelings he held a poker face.

Blue Eyes dropped what was left of his cigarette and crushed it out with his bare foot, showing no expression. "It is time, Marshall. So, if you will, please follow me."

Turning, the killer stepped out of the light and into the shadows of the huge open floor. Frustrated, Clay followed. They moved south, toward a distant stairway that would take them not in the direction he wanted to go, which was up, but rather would lead them down, deep into the dank bowels of the old building. Down there, the only light would be that which a man took with him.

CHAPTER EIGHTEEN

AT THE DOORWAY BLUE Eyes paused, pulling two short, white candles from his tux pocket. After lighting them with the gold lighter, he handed one to Clay, then turned and descended into the darkness. Reluctantly, Clay followed.

Although mindful that Blue Eyes may possess the ability to read his thoughts, Clay considered their descent yet another opportunity to take the killer out. His back was to him, and a simple shove was all he needed. The steps were traitorously steep and would themselves do all the work, but the wire beneath the killer's coat created a dilemma. His direct communication to the other psychopath above greatly complicated matters.

Clay had to admit, Blue Eyes was no bungler. In terms of criminal demeanor, he possessed the I.Q. of a genius, remaining always at the top of the FBI's Most Wanted list. He never made mistakes. Certainly, many past serial killers had made that infamous list, but not one had ever made it *personal*.

The old, wooden steps strained beneath their combined weight, moaning into the profound darkness. Below them lay a lightless world which Clay had no desire to enter. Because of the killer's demented mind and deviant eyes, Cooper thought of their descent as entering the gateway to hell.

Their candles cast prolonged shadows on dank, wooden walls. The tight confines made Clay uncomfortable, but it was what lay at the end of the stairs that bothered him most.

Like a long-lost mausoleum, three dark, cold rooms of dirt walls and decaying plank flooring lay in wait. The first would be an empty ten-by-ten space with a low six-foot ceiling. Both, Clay, and the killer would have to stoop going through the doorway. The second, slightly larger, was once a storage area separated from the third room by a wide split iron door. Clay was confident that the third room was their destination.

Since the elevator's inception, the space had served as the lunchroom. Clay had known this since it had contained a long-rusted iron table surrounded by rotten wood benches; also, there were sagging plank shelves that still held old glass bottles and rusted cans. The entire space would host an immense embroilment of spider webs and emit the disquieting smell of a freshly dug grave. Although now a grown man, Clay was confident the place would still give him the willies, just as he felt when he was a small boy.

A second before stepping onto the floor at the foot of the dark stairs, Clay paused long enough to slip the boot knife from its sheath. If for no other reason than desperation, he had formed a plan. In one swift sweep he would clamp a hand over Blue Eye's mouth and slash the wire beneath his jacket, thus severing communication with the man at the top. Then he would take the killer to the floor and place him in cuffs, or if he had no choice, kill him.

Clay's pulse was pounding. He would have but one shot at it; if he failed, Nancy would be dropped to her death. Clutching the knife tightly he drew in a deep breath and lunged.

Blue Eyes moved promptly to the right a second before Clay's hand shot out. The momentum of his weight sent Clay off balance, and he stumbled past the killer. Blue Eyes laughed into the semi-darkness. "Really, Marshall, did you actually think I would not anticipate a play on your part?" He spoke into the tiny microphone attached to the collar of his shirt. "Everything is fine, stand fast."

Clay recovered quickly, angry with himself but thankful that the killer had ordered the man with the knife to stand down.

Blue Eyes spoke softly over the flame of his candle. "Now please, Marshall Cooper, drop the knife to the floor, and let's have no more antics." Following an angry squeeze of the handle, Clay let the weapon fall. It struck the planking with a soft thud of finality.

Blue Eyes moved on, and just as Clay had suspected, their journey ended in the last of the three rooms. Upon entering, Blue Eyes began lighting candles that had been set about in a circular fashion. When they were all lit, the area glowed with a bright but gentle luminescence.

A rusted table lay draped with a white sheet and sat in the center of a giant pentagram painted on the floor around it. Clay's eyes scanned the room. He estimated a collection of at least thirty burning candles, their flames glowing motionless within the stale, cold void.

Blue Eyes removed both his tux jacket and wire set, laying them carefully on one of the shelves. He pulled the earphone from the unit and automatically the device transferred to audible speaker. While staring into Clay's eyes, he began speaking into the open air. "Upstairs, how do you copy?"

"Clear," came a raspy, single word.

Blue Eyes continued speaking to the man above. "Beginning now, we have twenty minutes. Unless Marshall Cooper reaches you in that time frame, with proof that the ceremony has been completed, cut the rope."

Blue Eyes then smiled for Clay. "My colleague and I have it worked out. A game plan if you will. Unless you kill me with the knife, I will give you and reach him within twenty minutes from now, he will cut the rope and allow your lovely wife to drop to her death." He paused, then added, "I have already given you the painful taste of losing her, so please cooperate. As proof you've completed your assignment," he held up his right hand flashing a large gold ring sitting snugly on his little pinky "you must take this ring to him...along with a certain number which I have written with a fine point permanent marker on the front of my testicles."

Clay made a face.

Blue Eyes smiled. "I know what you are thinking Marshall-that I am crazy. Well, perhaps, but I see the *burden of proof* as a form of dark humor. In any event, I also imagine you are wondering why I did not set up a video camera so my colleague could simply watch the event and save us all this trouble. Well, the ceremony you are about to participate in is not allowed an eyewitness; only Belial's chosen one, me, and *my* chosen one, you, are allowed." Now, since we only have twenty minutes-actually eighteen now-I suggest we not waste another second."

Beside his jacket, Blue Eyes retrieved an item wrapped in burlap. He unfolded the material while walking to where Clay stood. Once at Clay's side, he presented it on raised hands. "This is it Marshal Cooper, the ceremonial knife you will use to save your wife and send me to Utopia."

"You mean Hell, don't you?" Clay told him, stone-faced.

Blue Eyes nodded curtly. "Actually, yes."

The blade was short and exceptionally wide, with a handle of ivory shaped in the form of a demon with long, fanged teeth. Blue Eyes nudged his hands closer.

"Go on, Marshall, pick it up. Take it. It's our salvation."

Reluctantly, Clay's hand reached out. Repulsed, he gripped the handle and let his arm fall to his side. Blue Eyes turned and walked to the edge of the pentagram where he glanced back toward Clay.

"Please, if you will, Marshall, remove your boots and socks. You are about to step onto sacred ground."

Clay's eyes narrowed. "Sacred to you, you sick-0, but not to me."

Ignoring his remark, Blue Eyes walked to the sheet-covered table and sat on the edge, staring thoughtfully at Clay. "You see, Marshall, that is exactly the thing I was talking about: tenacity. Trust me when I say, there could be no other."

Cooper fought with himself to remain where he was. He wanted desperately to rush the killer and begin beating the mental sickness out of him. But he envisioned his wife hanging at the mercy of the other madman ready to end her life. Given no other choice, he did as ordered and removed his boots and socks.

The floor was cold and sent a shiver through his body. Anxious, Clay glanced at his watch.

Observing him, Blue Eyes spoke out. "We have fifteen minutes and thirty-two seconds remaining, Marshall Cooper; time is quickly running out for your little Life Saver."

Clay shook his head. This maniac hadn't even looked at his watch. How could he possibly know the time left? Yet he was right!

At the head of the white sheet, just beyond a small black pillow, sat a dark ceramic bowl filled with red liquid. Following a glance at Clay the killer picked it up, kissed the side of the bowl, then dipped a finger into its dark contents. Slowly he ran a long streak down the left side of his face. He dipped again and painted one down the right side. Lastly, he inserted two fingers, and this time made a much wider strip down the middle of his face, pausing just long enough on the way down to taste the liquid. Clay shook his head.

"You're infected with a discusting sick kind of insanity.

Again, ignoring him, Blue Eyes set the bowl down and stretched out on his back. "Come, Marshall, stand by my side. I have something I must tell you." The words were soft and pleasant.

Clay remained where he stood. Blue Eyes stared into the ceiling a few moments, then turned his head to look at Clay. "Please. I will not bite you; I promise.

Still, Clay did not move. Seconds of awkward silence passed as the two stared. The room remained silent, void of movement and sound yet alive with the pungent odor of dirt and earth and damp, rotting wood. Clay thought of the room as a giant grave, and the man on the table as the angel of death stripped of traditional robes. Then Blue Eyes broke the stalemate by saying, with irritation in his voice, "Obviously, Marshall, we have come to an impasse. Tell you what. We have a few minutes, so allow me the pleasure of granting you a glimpse of what I stand to lose by your not cooperating. We already know what your loss will be. So, bear with me." Pulling himself into a sitting position facing Clay, Blue Eyes told him, "Observe."

Slowly, he raised the hand donning the gold ring, and instantly, it began glistening brightly in the light of the twinkling candles. Clay's eyes followed its slow assent upward. Throughout the room candle flames began to flicker, and out of the still nothingness was born a chilled presence. It was not a breeze, yet cold; nothing was there, yet something was present. Clay felt goosebumps rise from his skin. An invisible entity moaned and howled, not like the wind, but with sounds eerily human yet not quite audible. As if alive, possessing the ability to reason and think with purpose, a sudden bolt of polar ice shot out of nothingness, streaking its way to where Clay stood, halting abruptly only inches from his face. There, as if raising like a snake, it coiled, studying him; then it slowly stretched outward and began encircling his body from head to toe, a serpent of ice binding him beneath its frigid power.

Despite the unforgiving temperature, Clay found himself unable to pull his eyes from the ring, now gleaming with implausible brilliance. Without any warning, thoughts exploded inside his head, violent flashes of forgotten scenes buried deep within his subconscious: haunting pictures of murder victims, suicides, and terrible highway crashes that had left bodies bloodied, life-less, or mutilated.

One after another they ignited; short, second long bursts of horrible images in a mad endless chain. Clay cursed their frenzied onslaught, but there was no stopping it. He struggled to make sense of what was happening to him, and feared he was going mad.

Throughout the room, spider webs danced against the mysterious tempest so cold that his breaths were now clouds of moisture. Wildly, his heartbeat raced, pounding at a dangerous rate. And somewhere, somehow, out of his icy encasement arose an eerie lamentation, this time clear and very human.

What he heard was the wailing of people, flesh and blood people, men and women screaming out of pain and agony and fear. The sound at first was loud and startling, but waned gradually, as if its source were being pulled away, down into an empty void.

Blue Eyes slowly lowered his hand and stood, approaching Clay whispering in his ear. "Sleep, Marshall; enjoy your visit."

Deeply entranced now, Clay's eyes were fixed and dilated, his stare vacant, as if his body were empty of life. He was unaware of two things: that the killer's eyes had faded to black and that his own heartbeat had stopped. Clay's eyes fluttered and closed.

Then they reopened, and he was standing alone in a dark world poised upon a high ledge. Below him burned an endless sea of fire. Millions of bodies, male and female, roamed naked within its flames, screaming for help...help he knew would never come to them. Amid their cries, there drifted up the repulsive stench of sulfur and burning flesh.

Lessons learned in Sunday school jolted though his mind like a speeding train of religious knowledge. These were the lost souls, the non-believers, the lukewarm, those who had been spewed from the mouth of God and cast into the lake of fire. Their screams of pain and fear rose from the giant pit like the intense heat and flames that lapped high above their heads. Tears of remorse filled Clay's eyes.

Then, from behind, something cast a great shadow over him. He turned to look and was snapped up by a bird-like creature with a head resembling the one on the knife Blue Eyes had handed him. Long black claws dug painfully into his shoulders as the beast set its grip, sweeping him from the ledge. With a wingspan of fifty feet, he could hear the fluttering and feel the breeze.

Clay hung helpless, his fear reaching new heights. For an endless time, they sailed over the sea of fire and burning people, always the flames lapping but inches from his bare, dangling feet. Those below, in the lake of Hell, appeared blind, adrift, lost and groping, reaching out for someone or something familiar, every face expressing fear and terror, and all were crying incessantly. Clay's own eyes stung with wetness, recalling the Bible's description of Hell.

Christ himself had said there would be darkness and gnashing of teeth. Until now he had never understood, or even given it thought. Fear gripped his heart like the powerful claws holding him only inches above the searing flames. Even now, his feet burned to near blistering from the closeness of the fire.

Then the beast with the giant wings sailed over a ledge and descended downward to a massive, marbled floor where Clay was dropped. It was a short, easy plummet, enabling him to land on his feet. Before him towered double doors of crimson, sealed tightly in a wall of black onyx stone. With the back of his hand, Clay wiped wetness from his eyes and looked about. On three sides, black lava cliffs, sheer and glossy, towered high above his head, imprisoning him within their walls.

The floor on which he stood was a vast open area consisting of white marble squares, each etched with a black pentagram. Easily the size of a football field, he had been dropped squarely in the middle of its enormity.

Then, suddenly, the massive doors began to open. Fear carried his mind to a level he had never before reached. Swallowing hard, he stood mesmerized, his eyes widening. This had to be a dream, he told himself, then shook his head. "No," he said aloud, "This is a NIGHTMARE!" NIGHTMARE!" None of it could be real. Blue Eyes must have hypnotized him, placed him in some sort of trace.

Three stories high, the gigantic doors pressed unhurriedly open, inching wider, creaking, and groaning. Frozen in place, Clay looked on, wondering what lay beyond them. He was already in Hell, so what could possibly be on the other side? Could Hell actually be worse than the horror he had already seen, or consist of more than what was told in the Bible?

He was about to find out.

CHAPTER NINETEEN

NANCY COOPER HAD BEEN hanging below the window for nearly half an hour. The rope binding her wrists had worn away a layer of flesh, and now blood seeped through the raw skin. It burned, and she likened it to the consistent rubbing of a shoe against an open blister. Nancy fought tears because of the pain's intensity.

Below her, the ground appeared a long way down. It took no effort to know that if she fell, death was most assured. Even if she were fortunate enough to survive, the resulting injuries would be debilitating and permanent.

Her predicament was not good, but it was her husband she thought most about. Silently she prayed for his safety, and although she understood her greatest hope of surviving rested with him, it was his personal welfare that preoccupied her mind. She loved him and, although it was not something she wanted to do, she would die for him if need be.

The sun was warm on her skin. Actually, aside from the circumstances, it was a beautiful day. High above her head, birds sat perched on the building rooftop, chirping at the world. The highway on the other side was busy with motorists going about life.

On this side, only one car had passed so far; at least she assumed it to be a car, since she had been blindfolded at the time. In the beginning, she had hoped to be spotted and reported to authorities, but no one had come. Now she was conceding to the possibility of being dead long before help arrived.

Nancy Cooper had no way of knowing what was taking place far below her in the dark interior of the elevator. She had not even a hint that if her husband refused to cooperate in the ceremonial slaying of the Blue Eyes killer, she would be dead in less than twelve minutes.

Above, her captor in the mask moved continually back and forth, checking both the north and south side of the elevator, ensuring no one crept up on them.

The intensity of pain around Nancy's wrists increased as she hung. Yet despite her agony, enduring the pain was far better than the alternative.

Despondent, she stared out across the open expanse. The fields before her stretched to the far horizon acre upon acre, just miles of open farmland. She personally preferred the mountains or ocean beach but understood this was what it took to feed a big world.

A tiny movement caught her eye in a distant field to the right. Her heart leaped. Although far away and barely distinguishable, she made the object out as a farm tractor with giant rear tires and a closed-in cab. It was too far to see the driver, but she didn't care. Her hopeful eyes watched it amble slowly forward, rolling deeper into the field before coming to a stop, almost in line with her hanging form.

The man in the ski mask raised binoculars to his eyes and at the same time warned her, "Keep your mouth shut, bitch. Open it and I cut the rope." Believing he would, Nancy remained silent, calling out the only way she could: telepathically, praying their minds would somehow connect. Her thought waves screamed across the great distance edged in hope and desperation, "Up here! Look up here!"

After a few minutes, a tiny figure climbed down from the cab, walked to the front of the tractor and kneeled. Nancy guessed he was checking soil. She continued with her silent, desperate cries. "LOOK UP! I'M HERE. FOR GOD'S SAKE LOOK THIS WAY!" Whoever he was, he rose, walked a little farther, and kneeled again.

Above her, the man in the ski mask squatted at the edge of the window and placed his binoculars on the floor. In exchange, he picked up a Remington Model 700 BDL chambered in .308 with 3-12x Kahles scope and laid it to rest on the windowsill for stability. Pointing it toward the man kneeling by the tractor, he carefully adjusted the Kahles, bringing the figure into close, crisp view.

The farmer was dressed in pin-striped, gray bibs, a light blue long sleeve shirt and a Carhart ball cap. He was middle-aged, thirty-five or forty. Through the scope, the masked observer watched him pick up a fistful of soil, sniff it, crumble it with his fingers then let it funnel out of his hand. This activity was not all together unusual, but the man in the mask questioned two things. First, the blue shirt looked new and well-pressed, with partial creases near the cuffs. Secondly, why would a farmer going to the field be wearing black, high gloss Oxfords for shoes? He shook his head, mumbling to himself. "Idiot."

Speaking softly into the microphone clipped to his black turtleneck shirt, he said, "Below. We have a visitor up here, possibly more than one." There was no reply, but he knew to be silent a while before trying again. Rising, he crossed to the south side of the elevator and stood watching below. There was nothing out of the ordinary, only traffic passing up and down the highway. The grounds appeared clear, so he returned to the other side and refocused the Kahles on the man in the field.

The figure rose and returned to the tractor. Climbing back up into the cab, he put it into gear and drove on. Nancy shook her head in desperation. "NO! FOR GOD'S SAKE, LOOK!" She began to cry as she watched it putter away, taking with it her hope.

However, if she knew Agents Lemus and Clendes were now standing stone-still just inside the elevator below, she would have felt better. Backs against the south wall, the two agents listened intently. Light shadows played across the huge open floor before them, but visibility remained good.

Although well aware of the man above and the crucial predicament facing Mrs. Cooper, it was the unknown whereabouts of Clay and Blue Eyes that worried them most. Somewhere off the main floor had to be a stairway leading up to the killer holding Mrs. Cooper. When found,

Clendes would climb it and attempt her rescue. Hopefully Agent Jones's diversion with the tractor would hold the masked man's attention long enough for him to get safely to the top and get off one well-placed round. Turning back-to-back, Lemus and Clendes moved off in opposite directions.

Slowly, maintaining a shoulder to the wall, each man circled the outside perimeter of the large, open floor, searching for entrances or exits. Lemus was the first to come upon the stairway leading to the top floors. Cocking his head, he stood at the foot of the open entranceway and strained to listen but heard nothing. Moving on, he passed two windows and a boarded outside exit before reconnecting with Clendes.

Pausing and speaking in whispers, they exchanged information. Clendes had located a stairwell leading down on the west wall and informed his senior officer that it looked darker than the inside of an Australian dock rat's ass. Lemus acknowledged and noted that he would check it out.

Wishing one another well, they moved on: Clendes to the stairway leading to the hopeful salvation of Mrs. Cooper, and Lemus below, deep into the building's black entrails.

CHAPTER TWENTY

CLAYTON COOPER STOOD IN awe, staring at the mammoth doors. They had opened fully, and he thought of their gaping hole as an unholy mouth of venom. While he could not see into its depth due to the presence of dark, churning fog, he did sense *something* on the other side. It called to him, a silent voice weaving its way into his mind, slithering like serpents into his thoughts.

Whatever it was that lay beyond the doorway's haze, he didn't want to see it. He just wanted to return to reality, to reunite with his sweet Lifesaver and go home, to be happy again and live a normal life of weekend barbeques and Saturday football.

Then, rising no higher than a foot from the surface of the floor, fog began to creep out of the dark aperture and into the open area. He watched it spread unhurriedly across the white marble tile in his direction, and in his mind, Clayton Cooper somehow knew it was coming for him.

His initial reaction was fear, near panic, but it lasted only a few scant seconds, for out of the emerging murk he also experienced a strange beckoning, the want to dash through the encroaching mist and into the presence of whatever was waiting for him on the other side. Though his mind was fragmented, minute vestiges remained clear and sensed the terrible unholiness. Weakly, in little more than a whisper, perhaps closer to mere movement of his lips, he spoke the words, "Jesus, help me."

Whatever evil thing called him to its darkness, its power was resolute. And he knew it was eternally destructive, yet he found himself helplessly drawn to it. His mind sought to meld with it and his flesh tingled for the touch of it. The fragmented waves of thought told him to run, to flee from this place-but where? The power of this thing was already attaching itself to the cells of his brain like millions of tiny demonic leeches sucking from him both life and will.

At first his heart had been a fierce battlefield over right and wrong, evil, and good. There had existed an acute awareness that what existed around him here, and especially in the darkness beyond, was nothing more than hidden traps, purposed wholly to capture his soul. Rapidly, its wickedness was overpowering him, consuming his resistance, and he was losing sight between right or wrong.

The dark fog was nearly upon him now. Little more than a foot away, there arose out of its unlit mist, strange sounds: human cries, but this time they were unlike those coming from the burning Hell beyond the high walls. These were alluring and familiar, inviting sounds that reached deep into the primordial need of man-moans of soft, sensuous ecstasy, a symphony of fleshly pleasures, the unmistakable sound of men and women copulating, giving, and taking, invisible bodies lustfully engaged in the desires of the flesh, sliding, pounding, wet and sweat laden, sending one another to the highest peaks and over the edge of explicit erotic pleasures. Clay knew he should not listen, and he didn't want to listen, but he could not help himself. The sounds had struck the cord of that secret place every man keeps hidden, locked securely away for the sake of sanity-then Hell consumed him.

Weakened to the point of no return, morally malignant, unable to resist any longer, he closed his eyes and embraced the sounds as succulent melody. He moaned softly.

From within his loins, pleasurable sensations began to radiate. His heart pounded and his manhood stirred. He clearly understood that beyond the doors the most splendid sensations awaited him, an orgy like nothing his world could ever know.

The creeping haze had reached him and was now wrapping itself around his feet, drifting up inside his trouser legs and against his flesh. As if they'd risen out of the black mist, the sensation of a dozen sexually hungry hands began moving up his inner thighs toward his swelling manhood. He felt his breath quicken; he grew dizzy with desire and yearned for their touch. His senes lay crippled, he wanted to call out for Jesus to help him, BUT, the pleasures were so Powerful.

In his head the voice beyond the doorway called to him and, although clearly evil, he could not resist its affluent coaxing. It invited him to come and share, to experience the very height of ecstasy, to push his senses over the edge. Waiting for him was a world of sensations far beyond what he had ever known, and it was his for the taking.

Then the dark mist began lifting him from the floor, slowly at first, into a sitting position, then gently onto his back. As though he were floating on a cloud, his eyes remained closed; he savored the added sensation of hot, sensuous kisses being planted over his body. Testosterone poured into his bloodstream and pure, unadulterated desire clouded his mind. Endorphins rushed to his brain and exploded. Lust burned within him, driving him to the edge.

Affected by something more potent than Demerol or morphine, he sailed toward a world of dark debauchery, one of want and need, *a terra incognita* that lay far beyond the realm of reason...and he hungered for it.

The hands that glided over his skin were soft, gentle hands, and hot. He burned at their touch, his flesh afire. Out of the mist, the orgy of lovers continued their cries of desire, adding fuel to the inferno of need raging within him. Although a faraway sensation, he felt the mist begin to shift around him, maneuvering his body into an upright position so that he faced the open doorway. His eyes opened. Out of its evil gap stepped a woman of unblemished beauty. Walking atop the black mist, she slowly closed the distance between them. Raven-haired and naked, she sauntered sensuously toward him, her perfect breasts trembling with each provocative step. She possessed eyes of coal and skin of alabaster, and her gaze told of the exquisite pleasures her body was going to bring him.

Clay was fully hard now, his erection enormous and ready to be set free of its imprisonment. Like the stunning beauty approaching, he too wanted to be naked, to tear off his own clothing and revel in erotic freedom...and he wanted the approaching female, needed her, and would run her down and take her by force if she did not consent... but he knew she would. His face felt flushed, hot, his skin searing like the flames behind the high walls surrounding him.

In seconds she was there, inches from him. He breathed in the scent of her; it was exhilarating. Bending his head, he ran his tongue slowly up her cheek to taste her. She smiled for him, knowing he liked it. But what most intoxicated him was the sense of her vulnerability, the feel of dominion over her. He was the master, and she was his to do with as he pleased.

Her hands rose to his chest, caressing his muscular pecks, almost to the point of causing him pain, kneading them with notable force. Clay sighed; his eyes closed. Slowly, sliding her hands down his body, she lowered herself to her knees and traced the hard form of his penis now bulging from beneath his trousers. She moaned her desire for him. Slender, long nailed fingers gripped the tab of his zipper and at that instant the sudden explosion of bright light nearly blinded them. It filled the giant open floor with indescribable radiance.

Instantly drained of all strength, Clay collapsed, falling through the dark fog and slamming hard onto the tiled floor beneath. Stunned and suddenly confused he tried to rise but could not find the strength. Lying on his side he curled into a fetal position and lay half-in and half-out of consciousness.

The naked female faded mysteriously into the black mist, now retreating back into its decedent world beyond the giant doors. Standing silent, the tall, noble figure watched it vanish, well aware of its sin and decaying death.

He was tall and stately, with flowing, beautiful blond hair reaching to his shoulders. His skin was perfect and smooth. Broad shoulders, straight nose and high cheekbones gave him, in worldly standards, the look of the perfectly chiseled model. But it was his eyes that told the most about him. They were eyes of kindness, filled with a gentle trust and love that radiated like the warming rays of sunshine. The white toga draping his shoulder and the sandals on his feet gave reverent tribute to the knowledge and wisdom given him by his Creator.

Kneeling beside Clay's coiled body; the figure's gentle hand touched his forehead. Clay felt a rush of cool tingling serge through him. He moaned, his head spinning dizzily for a second.

But the uncomfortable feeling passed quickly, and he rolled onto his back. Blurry at first, his eyes stared up at a fuzzy, indistinguishable form kneeling beside him; at the same time, he tried recalling what had happened, where he was and why he lay weak and trembling.

Clay looked about, blinking vigorously to clear his vision. Time seemed to pass slowly, but little by little his sight returned and for the first time his eyes made out the blond man kneeling there beside him.

Whoever he was, and despite his yet lingering confusion, Clay knew this man had saved his life...his soul. Staring into the stranger's eyes, as though some miraculous healings were taking place, Clay's mind began to clear at great speed and all was coming back in lucid images- his flight over the burning pit of lost souls, the opening of the crimson doors, the sensations and sounds of the evil fog, and the naked female with dark eyes and alabaster skin. He recalled his immoral hunger for it all.

Then instantly, like the demon beast that had carried him over the sea of lost souls, the vision took flight and was replaced with the image of his wife, standing before him. His sweet Lifesaver, smiling radiantly. His heart leaped and he closed his eyes to savor the feel of her touch and breathe in the very fragrance of her presence. He ached to embrace her, and there radiated a love for her like he had never known.

But joy was elusive, for a sudden shaft of rainbow-colored light exploded out of nowhere and pierced his heart like a lance. He screamed from the instant pain of realizing his disgrace and shame. He cried out with the knowledge that he had done wrong, sinning against God nearly to the point of blasphemy, and within him there arose an unbearable weight. Sadness crushed his heart like a sudden implosion, and he began to wail aloud.

The gentle stranger smiled tenderly and touched his shoulder, speaking for the first time, his voice kind and forgiving. "Let not your tears fall and your heart be saddened, for He is merciful. That which has happened to you was with purpose. All fall short of his Glory, and you are no different. The Evil One is a strong enemy, and now you are aware. And because of what has happened here, you are stronger and wiser. It is not your time. I am here to send you back."

"Back home?" Clay asked.

"Yes. More specifically, to your body. We must hurry. Many minutes have passed."

"Minutes? Passed?"

"Yes, and your friend will find you soon."

Clay moved into a sitting position. "Wait! I have so many questions!"

"We cannot wait."

"At least tell me who you are!"

The stranger with blond hair and a perfectly chiseled face smiled. "Sleep now, and return."

Clay's eyes fluttered wildly and the closed, but unconsciousness lingered just long enough for him to receive his answer.

"Michael is the name He has given me. Now go and be strong."

CHAPTER TWENTY-ONE

AGENT CLENDES CLIMBED THE stairs with slow, deliberate steps, moving at a nearly noiseless pace. There was no avoiding the occasional squeaky board, however, and each caused an internal cringe.

Above his head were the five floors he needed to bridge before reaching Mrs. Cooper. He hoped Jones's diversion with the farm tractor kept the man in the mask occupied long enough for him to reach the top and maintain the element of surprise; it took but a fraction of gray matter to realize he was a sitting duck while advancing. Far too much of his task depended on luck. He tried thinking of the adrenaline rush as a trade-off.

Time was quickly running out, and so much depended on finding Blue Eyes. It had been their analysis that the man in the mask was not him, but that the killer was in fact somewhere in the elevator with Cooper, and somehow pulling the strings regarding the fate of Cooper's wife.

This increased the pressure Clendes was feeling. Not only was his stairway climb leaving him dangerously vulnerable, but his experience told him that if he failed in his mission, Mrs. Cooper would surely die. And while he received great joy in helping others, he loathed having someone's life resting solely upon his shoulders.

Atop his well-pressed button-down collar shirt, the black departmental issue bulletproof vest rested snugly about his upper body. With the exception of high velocity rounds, it would afford him sufficient protection against nearly all handguns. However, because the Blue Eyes killer had proven himself a most formidable foe, Clendes feared the worst: that a shot from the masked man's weapon would most likely be directed toward his head.

It was his calculation and hope that the first three floors, and possibly the fourth, would be safe climbing, primarily because the few noisy steps he struck could not be heard by someone way up on the fifth. Also, he guessed that the masked man would not leave his post to intercept him; any protégé of serial killer as successful as Blue Eyes would adhere strictly to orders. And it took little thought to realize that Blue Eyes had placed him by the rope for a definite purpose.

The elevator was stilling. The higher Clendes climbed, the hotter it became. Sweat trickled down between his shoulder blades, tickling the middle of his back. Because of the vest, he was unable to scratch, and it was undeniably irritating. Salty beads were also forming on his forehead and beneath his nose; at least he was able to wipe them away.

Each stairway emptied onto the appropriate floor. Then began the next flight, forcing him into the open for several seconds at a time. When he finally reached the start of the fifth floor, Clendes paused briefly and took in a deep breath. While he was not necessarily a religious man, he considered himself a good Catholic and spoke a short prayer, then crossed himself. Weapon raised; he began his climb up. To his right would be the window from which Mrs. Cooper hung, and hopefully the masked killer would be there, too, with his back to him and staring out into the open field.

To his surprise, none of the steps had squeaked. He couldn't believe his luck and was thankful. Finally at the top, hugging the wall, Clendes slowly raised his head just enough to see.

The rope that held Mrs. Cooper was tied to a large, upright wooden beam and stretched downward at an angle, its leading end disappearing out the window. The masked man was kneeling at the window's edge with his back to him. Clendes shook his head in disbelief. Things were going too well, and it worried him.

With his gun pointed toward the killer's back he slowly advanced the last remaining steps, moving quietly onto the open floor. Slowly, gingerly, he placed one foot in front of the other, stepping lightly while edging closer. He much preferred taking the masked man alive, but if killing him became necessary, it would cause him no heartache.

Clendes used his peripheral vision as well as concentrated on the kneeling man; his training, as well as his experience, had instilled in him the importance of leaving zero to chance. When they had driven past earlier that morning, posing as typical passers-by, they had glimpsed only two people-the masked man and presumably Mrs. Cooper. However, it was possible a second perp was present-and if so, Clendes at least wanted a fighting chance.

Not turning, the figure in the mask spoke suddenly to Clendes. It took the agent by surprise, and he froze in place. But he did not lower his weapon.

"Well, Fed. It would seem you have me by the short hairs, now, wouldn't it?"

Clendes remained silent.

"I am going to turn Fed, so hold your fire."

Slowly the masked figure turned but remained in a kneeling position. Immediately Clendes saw the knife in his hand, with its blade resting on the rope holding Mrs. Cooper. He had already cut through nearly all the fiber, and it now held her by only a few strands. Clendes swore under his breath. The man in the mask chuckled.

"Drop your pistol on the floor, kick it to the side then lay down on your stomach with arms stretched out in front of you."

Clendes hesitated, figuring his options. Seconds went by.

The man in the mask spoke sternly. "Fucking do it or I will cut the rope and let the bitch drop. You will shoot me, and I will be dead...that will not piss off your boss. But if the woman dies because of you, he will really be unhappy. *Now drop the fucking gun.*"

Agent Clendes hated the situation, hated the son of a bitch with the knife and hated himself for considering doing what he was being told. His mind raced as he calculated the options. If he shot the perp there was a chance the impact of the bullet would simply throw him out through the window. The knife would drop from his hand and the rope would hold long enough for him to grab hold before the remaining strands gave way.

On the other hand, there was equal chance the bullet would cause him to jerk, and even the slightest cut of the blade could cause the rope to snap and send Mrs. Cooper to her death. Hell, just stalling alone, with the rope cut so closely, could cause it to snap any moment.

Damned if you do and damned if you don't, Clendes, he told himself.

The agent shook his head, speaking to the masked figure. "Ok, I am going to put the gun down." Beneath his mask, the killer grinned. Then Clendes added quickly, "Right after I shoot your fucking ass."

Clendes fired one shot. The nine-millimeter recoiled, and the bullet tore through the black ski mask, searing into the killer's brain. He flew backward through the window and the knife flipped up into the air and outside; it followed the body to the ground below.

Clendes dropped his weapon and dove for the rope. it snapped as he grabbed it, and for a short distance the weight of Mrs. Cooper's descending body pulled him along the floor toward the opening. But he far outweighed her and quickly regained his balance. Climbing to his feet, he slowly pulled her up and inside to safety.

Untying her hands, he asked if she was alright. Following a glance at the body below, she nodded. "I am now thanks to you. But I'm worried about my husband. Do you know where he is?"

Agent Clendes walked over and retrieved his weapon. After holstering it he returned to her side and told her grimly, "No, Mrs. Cooper, I'm afraid I don't."

CHAPTER TWENTY-TWO

AGENT LEMUS HAD DESCENDED the full length of the dark stairwell, using a small mini-mag flashlight. Now at the foot, he stopped and shut it off, hoping the total darkness might better aid him in hearing sounds.

While he'd been descending, the small light had prevented him from noticing the soft illumination emitting from another room somewhere beyond. It was dull, and wherever it was coming from, it did not provide sufficient light by which to navigate. Clicking back on the mini-mag, he began moving in its direction.

He had crossed his wrists, and his right hand held ready his sidearm, an Ultra CDP .45 ACP. His left gripped the light with the beam shining along the gun's slide and off into the distance.

Lemus would have preferred advancing while shrouded in the cover of darkness, but because he did not know the layout ahead, that was not an option. Besides, it would be far easier for someone familiar with the layout to overpower him in total darkness-especially if he or she lay in wait with donned night vision headgear. In defense of using his light, the beam could render their equipment useless.

Lemus wanted the Blue Eyes Killer so badly that the cat and mouse chase had ultimately given him a painful ulcer, one he kept secret and was quietly seeing a doctor about. Standing alone, he much preferred taking the madman alive, but if Blue Eyes were killed during capture, so be it; at least he would be off the street and out of his life. His thoughts also focused on Clendes, wondering if he had been successful in rescuing Mrs. Cooper. The distance between them was great. If there had been screams or gunplay, Lemus would not have been able to hear them.

Privately, Lemus cared for the men who worked for him. Although often came across as harsh and calloused, in his heart there existed a much different man. After years with the Bureau, agents could grow bitter and cold, building a wall around themselves and becoming desensitized. He had always kept himself consciously aware of that possibility and had admonished himself whenever those ugly signs appeared. His hard approach to management was first and foremost a means of keeping his agents alert and alive, but it also was a way of covering his soft spot and thus safeguarding his reputation.

Lemus entered through a small doorway and into what appeared to be a somewhat larger but empty room. So far, the path he moved through was clear, with no obstructions or apparent booby traps. It became evident that the light source he hunted was coming from the next room. It was now just barely bright enough to see by, so he shut off his mag and placed it in his pocket. He then allowed his eyes to adjust a few seconds and continued on with weapon ready.

There had been, so far, no sound, no movement, and not one trace of opposition. It worried him; someone had placed lights down here. The question was, why? And where were the people who'd placed them?

He moved through a second door into the third room since his stepping free of the stairs. Dozens of candles twinkled softly, and a white sheet lay draped over what seemed to be a long stand or table. The room appeared unoccupied. Strangely, it felt abnormally cold, so cold in fact it caused his body to shiver. The covered table sat directly centered in the room, and he made note of the satanic pentagram painted on the floor around it.

Remaining still, his eyes vigilantly scanned the area, section-by-section, inch-by-inch; nothing appeared life-threatening. Satisfied that he was alone and that the room was safe, he holstered his weapon. Then, in a systematic, clockwise pattern, using the head of the sheet nearest him as 12 o'clock, he began a search for clues as to why the room was now vacated. Lemus recalled the recorded phone conversation Blue Eyes had with Cooper, and Blue Eyes' desire that the Marshall kill him in a ceremonial execution. The surroundings here evinced that request.

Dust covered nearly everything. Tin cans, bottles, and rusted objects lay scattered on old shelving, but nothing gave a hint that anything had already happened. His fingers were growing cold, so he stuck his hands in his pockets for warmth. It remained cold enough that he could see his breath. The anomalous temperature made no sense and created an uneasiness that increased his awareness.

According to the search-clock system, he was just about seven o'clock when he spotted Clayton Cooper lying face down on the floor unconscious. Hurrying to his side, Lemus kneeled, recalling his long-ago CPR training.

Lemus grabbed Clay's shoulders and shouted, "Cooper! Cooper, can you hear me?'

Cooper did not respond.

Lemus rolled him onto his back and opened his airway, placing an ear over his mouth to check for breathing. Clay's chest was not rising and falling.

Immediately agent Lemus pinched Cooper's nose and gave him two breaths of air, then moved to the side of Cooper's neck and felt for a carotid pulse. There was none. "Fuck!" Lemus yelled out loud. Hastily, he located the landmark on the chest, positioned his hands and began chest compression, counting aloud. "One and two and three and four and five and six and seven and eight and nine and ten and eleven and twelve and thirteen and fourteen and FIFTEEN."

Again, he opened Cooper's airway and gave two breaths, then returned to the chest for fifteen more compressions. He remembered it was four cycles of fifteen and two before stopping to check progress, but he hoped Cooper would come back long before that. Although his CPR training had not included it, he began giving Cooper some adrenaline induced Bob Lemus motivation. "Come on, you son-of-a-bitch. You can do it. BREATHE! Ten and eleven and twelve and thirteen and fourteen and FIFTEEN." Again, he gave him two breaths, then went back to the chest. "I'm telling you Cooper, BREATH!" Clayton Cooper's color was not good. Even in the candlelight Lemus could tell he was turning blue from lack of oxygen. Frustrated, still doing chest compression, he raised his eyes and looked up. "God, you know I'm doing what the hell I can do. I could use a little help here!"

Lemus moved to the head and gave Cooper two more breaths. Back at the Chest, he had completed eight of the compressions when Cooper spontaneously gasped. Instantaneously, Lemus stopped and shouted into the dark ceiling, "Hell yes! Me and you, Lord!"

Clouded with bewilderment, Clayton Cooper opened his eyes and looked at Lemus. He blinked several times, then took a deep breath. His color was rapidly returning, and Lemus sighed, moving off his knees and into a sitting position. Cooper raised himself up on an elbow, his mind now clearing. Looking at Lemus, he asked, "Were you just doing…did you just give me…was your mouth just on top of mine?"

Lemus nodded. "Yes, I was, yes I did, and yes it was, and if you tell one single soul, I will personally kick your ass right back into Cardiac Arrest and shoot anyone who tries to revive you."

Realizing Lemus had just saved his life, Cooper pulled himself into a sitting position beside him and offered his hand. "No need for that. Thanks."

Lemus took his hand and smiled ever so slightly. "You're welcome. Now let's get the hell out of this makeshift morgue. I need a damn cigarette."

CHAPTER TWENTY-THREE

HE REUNION BETWEEN CLAY and Nancy Cooper was heart-warming. Both hugged the other and it was obvious neither wanted to let go. Both cried and shared the joy of being alive. Clay especially, having felt the pangs of loss-although cruelly misleading-saw the moment as a new beginning.

The world seemed bright and alive, its colors vivid and beautifully blended. Noon sunshine felt exhilarating on their faces and birds on the roof of the elevator sang with a joy auspicious to the occasion.

Agents Lemus and Clendes stood by Clayton Cooper's truck, Lemus smoking a cigarette, watching. He was happy for them, pleased they were both alive and together again, and he was delighted Clendes had been successful and was himself unharmed.

But there was disappointment, also. Blue Eyes had escaped, vanished once again into nowhere and everywhere, free to kill again. This event had been the closest they had come yet to his capture. Sick in his heart, Lemus knew the final stage four they had hoped for was not to be.

So many questions remained. He wondered if Blue Eyes would move on now in search of new victims, or stay, feeling his work here was not yet finished. Although thankful that he hadn't, Lemus wondered why he had not killed Mrs. Cooper, and wondered about the hoax mocking her death. Perhaps his reasoning was that by keeping her around, there would remain a frightening burden in Cooper's heart. In retrospect, who was the poor soul that had been skinned in Cooper's garage? As of yet he had not received the autopsy report, kept hidden from Cooper, and now he would order it priority. Above all, he wondered the proverbial million-dollar question: Who would be the killer's next victim?

Lemus finished his cigarette and tossed it at his feet, crushing it with the toe of his shoe. He sighed, wondering if maybe it was time to retire. Of all the cases in his thirty-one-year career, no one had caused him the agony and frustration Blue Eyes had. For that matter, no one had caused him more embarrassment. Several at the Bureau had begun to wonder if maybe the almighty Expert was losing his touch. He detested that nickname-Expert-but whether he liked it or not, he was in fact damn good at what he did. Until Blue Eyes had come along, no one had escaped his persistence.

He personally disliked boasting, but to date he was the best, recognized throughout the business as a world-class hunter. Over the years, numerous countries had called him, seeking advice and personal assistance. Yet, when the truth is picked from the bullshit, it is a given that sooner or later everyone meets their match, and it seemed Blue Eyes was his.

He lit another cigarette and inhaled deeply. Fact of the matter was that this thing was far from over and retirement was out of the question. He knew it, and Blue Eyes knew it. And one day, sooner or later, one of them would taste his own blood at the hands of the other.

While Clay appeared to be in great health after having a full cardiac arrest, there was still risk. Because much of Nancy's wrists were raw exposed skin, Lemus had ordered an ambulance. Actually, he had requested two-a second to transport the dead perp to the morgue.

In addition, he had cell-phoned the New York Bureau and ordered his personal crime scene team to be dispatched. The State Police would have gladly sent in their own, but although he was sure their skills were commendable, the FBI were better trained and experienced. This was true in part because of frequent activation, but also because of funding availability for training; money was always better at the federal level.

By the time the ambulances had arrived, the body of Nancy's would-be killer had been de-masked and searched; they found no ID, nor did anyone recognize the face. And Lemus was grimly certain prints would turn up a dead end as well.

Medics sat Nancy on the squad bench and dressed her wrists with soft Surgi-pads and gauze compress rolls. But it was Clay who became their primary patient. Upon being informed he had been in cardiac arrest and CPR had been administered, they immediately placed him on the cot and loaded him into the back.

While he respected protocol, he felt embarrassed over the fuss and grew concerned that it was scaring Nancy. Except for his chest being a little sore from compressions, he was experiencing no problems, no traditional signs or symptoms related to heart attack: no chest pain, no nausea, no profuse sweating, no shortness of breath, nothing. He felt fine.

Still, they placed him on high-flow oxygen via a non-rebreather mask, started an IV of normal saline at KVO rate, and hooked him to a twelve-lead monitor. Once connected, they ran a strip and studied it: there were no abnormalities. In fact, it was a picture-perfect normal sinus rhythm.

At the hospital, it turned out the same. The ER physician could find nothing out of the ordinary and could give no explanation of what had caused the arrest. Following a brief consultation with the on-call cardiologist, who was also at a loss, Clay and Nancy were released.

Lemus had waited by their side through the entire process. Upon their signing of the release forms, he drove them home. Jones had returned Clay's truck and had parked it in front of the garage door. After pulling onto the driveway and placing the car in park, Lemus turned to face Clay and Nancy in the backseat. "Look," he told them soberly, "I don't want to frighten anyone, but you both know what this killer is capable of. Get some rest. If anything, out of the ordinary catches your eye, makes a sound in your ear or puts a feeling in your gut, give us the signal. Clendes and Jones will be outside for the remainder of the day and night, and this time much the wiser."

Clay and Nancy nodded, then got out of the car and walked to the house holding hands. Lemus followed them with his eyes. They were lucky people, he thought. Very lucky people.

CHAPTER TWENTY-FOUR

THE ENTIRE ORDEAL WITH Clay and Nancy had taken its toll, especially on Clay. He refused to go to work for the next week, remaining at home and spending every moment by his wife's side, almost to the point of smothering her.

She had tried calm reassurance and rationality in encouraging him to return, explaining she had learned from their experience and would remain at peak alert with her Lady Laser .25 always at her side. However, he refused to believe that would be enough and stayed home anyway.

She was secretly thankful, but she also understood that there was a downside. Regardless of how safe her husband's presence made her feel, Blue Eyes had effortlessly entered their secured home not only with Clay present, but beneath the watchful eye of an FBI surveillance vehicle as well. In her heart, she harbored the fear of knowing that if Blue Eyes so desired, even though he had not laid a hand on her during her captivity, he would have little difficulty in kidnapping her again. If he did, this time Clay might be harmed or possibly killed in the process.

Nancy also understood, or at least felt she understood, the sense of guilt and anguish her husband had endured since he had found the skinned woman hanging in their garage and assumed it had been her. Because of that, his remaining at home and following her around like a lovesick puppy stood as a mixed blessing.

In her heart, she prayed the killer was gone. This bastard had caused enough torment and anguish in their lives. She disliked cursing even in her thoughts, but it felt good, and appropriate.

Why would he hang around, anyway? She tried reasoning. Clay had clearly refused to be part of his sick death wish, so there remained no justification in lingering. Surely, he was gone and now someone else could risk all in arresting him.

On Thursday night that same week at exactly 7:00 p.m., Clay and Nancy arrived at Ron and Michelle's house for pizza and a few hands of Euchre. After devouring one large pepperoni with mushrooms and three-quarters of an Italian Sausage with anchovies, they broke out the Euchre deck and a bottle of chilled red wine.

Pitting themselves against the women, Ron and Clay took their seats at the card table with boyish male egos. Both Nancy and Michelle smiled at them.

While shuffling, Ron grinned. "You girls realize, of course, you're goin' down. You gonna be begging, Please guys, let us win at least one game tonight! You're just such better players then we are."

Satisfied the deck was sufficiently shuffled, he began passing out cards, adding, "And girls, you'll be begging before the clock strikes nine."

"Before nine, you say?" Michelle said, smiling at Nancy.

"Yep," Ron told her, "It's gonna' be a pitiful sight, I admit, but nonetheless it'll happen by nine, and it's a sure thing."

Michelle winked at her partner, then looked back at Ron.

"Well, let me just say-and I speak for both of us, Mr. Superior Card Player-if we haven't won at least two games before that clock strikes nine, it won't be the girls begging tonight, and you can bet it won't be the girls going down, and *that's* a sure thing."

Setting the remainder of the deck on the table, Ron turned up trump and glanced at Clay, grinning. "Listen to that, will you, partner? We haven't even bid, and they're already playing dirty."

"Not dirty," Nancy chimed., "Strategy."

Clay fanned out the cards in his hand, then glanced at the deck. Ron had turned up the Jack of clubs.

Michelle, sitting to her husband's left, passed. Everyone turned to Clay, next in line to bid. He pressed his lips together as though unsure of what to do, but in his hand, he held the left bower, ace, king, and ten of clubs. His fifth card was the ten of hearts. Looking at Ron, he said, "Better give me your best, partner. We can't let idle threats tarnish our love for the game." Grinning, Ron picked up the right bower and slid it across the table. Immediately Clay laid down his hand. "Read 'em and weep, girls. Give us two, partner."

Michelle and Nancy looked at one another, and in almost perfect harmony asked, "What time is it?"

At 10:03 pm, the untenanted Cooper house lay draped in a mottled patchwork of evening shadows. Despite the silvery shine of a near-full moon, a myriad of twilight, and the dwarfed glare of the porch light, more than sufficient darkness existed in which to maneuver unseen.

The indistinguishable form crawling close to the deep, shadowed hedge wall was well aware of Lemus's newest strategy. The lead agent had abandoned the traditional surveillance vehicle and placed Clendes and Jones farther off in the distance, each set up with the best scope equipment the FBI owned.

The families of the two neighboring houses, one across the street in front and one just beyond the back yard, were thrilled, he suspected, to have been asked to assist the FBI. But strategically, even with their help, the plan offered only a limited challenge.

Clendes and Jones were totally unaware of the intruder flawlessly blended within the dark surroundings. Even pushing a small black gym bag ahead of him, the trespasser worried only modestly that they would spot him. But then, why should he worry? He was the Blue Eyes Killer, the FBI's perfect match. No, not match. He was their larger-than-life superior. Besides, the Coopers were away, so the agents would be lost in their own little bored-to-the-gills world, thus paying imperfect attention.

Meticulously, he inched his way to within an arms-reach of his destination, the basement window on the east side of the Cooper house. Once there, he lay soundless in the shadow of the hedgerow, motionless as the serenity of death.

The window was located forward of the center of the wall and totally out of sight from the surveillance house to the rear; as for the one in front across the street, there was only partial visibility since it sat more to the right than to the left.

Lying quietly, waiting patiently for the perfect distraction, Blue Eyes wondered how Lemus could overlook such an obvious flaw. Was it any wonder he forever remained a step behind?

Crickets chirped in the hedgerow. The killer liked the sound, but he disliked insects in general, especially mosquitoes: they served no purpose but to irritate him. Spiders, on the other hand, held a worthwhile purpose. Their mere form terrified millions.

He heard the faint sound of voices and refocused his thinking. Strapped to his leg, holstered in a swat quick-retrieve frame, a silenced nine-millimeter lay ready. Slowly he reached for the gun, resting his hand on it. An old couple passed across the front of the house, talking softly. He could not make out their conversation entirely but could tell they were on a power walk and not a leisurely moonlight stroll.

He eased his hand away. He admired old folks out walking, working at beating death, or at least delaying it. In a short time, he himself would not have to worry about such a thing, just as soon as Clayton Cooper came to his senses.

It was a small, virtually unnoticeable event, but it caught his keen eye. A tiny cricket jumped to the top of his bag and sat soundless, inches from his face. Smiling, but careful not to show his teeth, Blue Eyes whispered to it ever so quietly.

"Now don't you hop away with that big bag, little bug, or you'll make me angry. I have a video camera in there just for Marshall Cooper-actually, for his wife, too. It's going in their bedroom. They don't know it, but they are going to make a video for me. One all of their friends and family will just *love* receiving a copy of. It will...."

Down the block a car turned onto the street and began moving toward the Cooper house. For a few seconds it caused him alarm as he thought it might be the Coopers themselves coming home, although he did not expect them back for at least a couple more hours. But a few seconds of listening told him it wasn't a car at all; it was a truck. Since the Coopers had driven Nancy's 2020 Chevy Impala to the Parks' house, he knew it would not be them. Easiness settled over him.

This was the moment he'd been waiting for. When the vehicle passed in front of where he lay, creating a blind spot, he would roll both quickly and tightly up against the house next to the window, then slip inside.

Once in, his task would take but a few minutes. Against the wall beyond the foot of the Cooper's bed stood a tall antique Armoire with beautifully hand -carved designs bordering the top; it was the perfect spot for his tiny micro camera. Blue Eves grinned into the darkness, again careful not to let the white of his teeth show. Damn, you're good, he told himself.

The headlights of the approaching truck brightly lit up the street in front, then rumbled past. Quickly grabbing his bag, he rolled, apologizing to the little cricket for disturbing him. Two rolls and he lay motionless, pressed to the house. He listened and heard nothing out of the ordinary.

Opening the window required little effort; it was a typical half-moon latch with a Grand Canyon gap between the window top and frame. Within twelve seconds he had it unlocked, opened, the bag dropped through it, and he himself standing just inside it in the dark basement.

For the most part he stood in extreme darkness, except for the fraction of moonlight filtering in through the glass. Moving away from the window, he pulled a small hand-held red-lens flashlight from his pocket, turned it on, then bent and picked up his bag.

That's when the red laser beam appeared suddenly on Blue Eyes forehead, shooting out of the darkness from somewhere directly in front of him. Blue Eyes froze. He dropped his bag and at the same time smiled with a resigned grin, greeting the man who he knew held the weapon that could takeoff half his head. "Hello, agent Lemus."

"How are you, Blue?"

"Obviously not doing so well, but how about you? How's that ulcer?"

"I feel it healing as we speak."

"That pleases me, Bob."

Lemus hit the wall switch and the basement filled with light. For the first time in over a three-year hunt, Agent Lemus looked into the eyes of the killer he both hated and respected. And just as he had profiled, the man was tall, handsome, and possessed beautiful blue eyes. "Put your hands behind your head and get on your knees, Blue." Lemus said.

With no hesitation, Blue Eyes did as he was told.

Moving around behind him, positioning himself to place Blue Eyes in cuffs, Bob Lemus radioed for Clendes and Jones. And he did it smiling all the while.

CHAPTER TWENTY-FIVE

BLUE EYES WAS TAKEN to the Tippecanoe County Jail and held under double guard. In addition to the assigned uniformed officer, Lemus had ordered his own staff to rotate watch outside the cell holding area; he was taking no chances.

Just under two hours from the time Blue Eyes was fingerprinted, stripped, and dressed in a pair of bright orange coveralls, James Johnson Montgomery arrived in his 600 Silver Arrow Mercedes Convertible. He was dressed in a dark, pinstriped, double-breasted suit. His arrival was the result of the killer's allotted phone call.

Lemus knew Montgomery and disliked him to a revolting degree. Montgomery was aware of it and found it amusing, and this infuriated Lemus. The lawyer was a middle-aged, wealthy, flamboyant criminal defender with a main office out of Chicago, although his assignments often took him throughout the world. He had made millions defending the biggest names in crime, and always winning-one way or another.

When Montgomery approached the cell holding Blue Eyes, he smiled for the FBI's most noted criminal hunter. And since he was a southpaw and carried his briefcase in the left hand, he extended his right to Lemus, widening his smile. "Good to see you, Bob."

Lemus did not return the smile. "Can't say the same, J.J." When Lemus took his hand, he squeezed it painfully. J.J. was the nickname Montgomery allowed only certain people to call him-those rich and/or famous.

Although three inches taller and ten years younger than Lemus, Montgomery wasn't nearly as powerful. He felt the pain of Lemus's grip and let his smile dwindle to a grin. "Gee, Bob, better lighten up on the caffeine."

Spulder was standing next to Lemus, but Montgomery offered only a curt nod to him. Following a glance toward Blue Eyes, then back to Lemus, Montgomery said, "Now, if you don't mind, I'd like some private time with my client."

Lemus wanted to forbid it but knew he could not. Resigned, he left the cell block with Blue Eyes still behind bars and Montgomery remaining on the outer side. He and Spulder ambled out and stood just on the other side of the cellblock door.

Montgomery's session with his client lasted only a few minutes, and Lemus observed nearly every minute through the door's reinforced glass window. Several times the counselor turned and smiled for him, and each time Lemus remained stone-faced.

While undergoing the administrative process, Blue Eyes had given his name as Charles Farmsman, a self-employed handyman from Evansville, Indiana. In his wallet they had found a driver's license, two credit cards, membership card to a health spa and an Indiana license to carry a handgun. It all matched up, but Lemus didn't buy it. Even though the driver's license appeared legitimate, and the fingerprints came back clear, it stunk; this killer was too sharp, smarter than the whole lot of them put together.

Montgomery finished his conversation and walked casually to the door, rapping on the window. The uniformed officer standing watch pushed the automatic release button and a loud buzz reverberated through the hallway in which they stood. The door jarred open, and Montgomery exited. He spoke directly to Lemus.

"Let's get this over with, Bob. I want my client taken before the magistrate immediately to determine bail."

Lemus became livid. "Bullshit Bail, He's staying right where he is. He's a serial killer that has murdered 34 people, and it has taken the Bureau over three years to catch him. The man is going nowhere."

Montgomery remained calm, knowing he possessed the legal advantage.

"You can't deny him his rights, Bob. The magistrate may refuse bail upon hearing the case, yes, but even the FBI cannot change the fact that he has the right to be heard."

Lemus stared coldly at Montgomery, wanting more than anything to punch him in the jaw.

"Look, Bob," Montgomery went on, "I'm not the bad guy here. Do whatever you wish. Bring him before a judge here in Tippecanoe or transport him back to Newburn County where you arrested him. It's your choice. But I want him standing in front of a judge tonight."

Wholly pissed and restraining his punch, Lemus reluctantly agreed to transport him back to Newburn County, since that was where the Cooper house was and the murders at Fisher's Point had taken place. A judge there would be more apt to deny bail since the horrendous crime had taken place within his own jurisdiction. Like it or not, Lemus clearly understood the importance of following the letter of the law; otherwise, he would have to watch Blue Eyes walk due to some frivolous and ridiculous technicality.

As finalization for the transfer neared completion, Lemus seized the opportunity and walked outside for a badly needed cigarette. After he lit it, he inhaled deeply, relishing the feel of the warm smoke in his lungs. Almost instantly it helped to calm him. With the first draw out of the way, he pulled out his cell phone and dialed the Cooper residence. The ring brought Clays sleeping form to an abrupt sitting position. The room was dark, and he shook his head to clear the cobwebs. He had been locked in deep sleep, a blackness where no thought existed. While reaching for the receiver, he glanced at the bright red numbers on the nightstand clock: 2:42 am. "Hello."

"It's Lemus."

"Hey." Clay wasn't sure how to react to the call, since it could easily be good or bad news. Either Blue Eyes had been caught or he had killed again. He chose to hope for the best. "Tell me you caught him?"

"We did. He's here in the Tippecanoe County Jail."

Clayton Cooper sighed. "Thank God. It's over."

"Not so fast."

Cooper frowned into the darkness. "What? What do you mean, not so fast?"

"We've run up against a technicality. His lawyer is here and demanding he stand before a magistrate for bail."

"Bail? The guy's a fucking killer, a damn lunatic."

"A lunatic with rights. Like it or not, we can't afford any mistakes. We have to do everything by the book: dot every 'I', cross every 't', and walk on eggshells."

Clay sighed, while nodding at the same time. "You're right. I've been there."

"We're taking him back to Newburn County where I arrested him for breaking into a house. I'm hoping the judge there will be less lenient. You need to meet us at the courthouse ASAP. At this point, his lawyer is standing on the premise that *breaking and entering* is all we have on him. And without you, he's right."

Clay nodded again. Nancy had awakened and sat up. "Who is it, Clay?"

Holding his hand over the receiver, he whispered, "It's Lemus."

"Are you there, Cooper?"

"Yeah. Look, I'm a lot closer than you are. I'll meet you there, no problem."

"Good."

Lemus shut off the cell phone and Clay cradled the receiver. Turning to Nancy, he told her, "Got to go, babe. They caught Blue Eyes and are taking him to the courthouse here in Newburn. I have to meet them there. The judge on call will be coming in to hear bail."

Nancy's voice echoed loudly through the dark bedroom. "*Bail.* How in the world could they even consider it?"

"It's like Lemus said. The man has rights, like it or not."

At 3:02 am, with Blue Eyes in shackles and sitting in the back seat of the Bureau Mobile between Clendes and Jones, the vehicle pulled out of the Tippecanoe County Jail parking lot and headed for the Newburn County Courthouse. For the second time in a week, Lemus prayed— the first had been during Cooper's CPR rescue. Silently, he now asked to be given a good judge, a hard and honest judge. One who understood the grave consequence of turning a criminal of Blue Eye's caliber loose on bail.

Lemus drove while Spulder rode in the passenger seat, staring out the window into the chilled, murky darkness beyond. Montgomery followed behind in his Mercedes, his headlights a dim glow in the distance.

The night was cold, and the mellowed light from a flawless, round moon did nothing to warm it. In every direction vacant field vanished into dark, open nothingness, and because of the possible decision that could be waiting, a sense of gloom lingered. Conversation was void and even unwanted. Within the car, dismal silence hosted an assortment of concealed thoughts and feelings.

Because the shackles binding his feet and hands were linked together by a wide leather waist belt with a short run of chain, Blue Eyes lowered his head closer to his knees so he could scratch the tip of his nose. The shackles rattled and he closed his eyes, liking the sound. While his head was bowed, he remained in that position and prayed silently. Both Clendes and Jones watched him with suspicion, anticipating some outlandish attempt to escape. The killer remained in supplication for nearly three minutes before finally raising his head, smiling for the two agents. He then surreptitiously diverted his attention to the shadowy figure driving the car. Both Clendes and Jones relaxed.

The fact that the FBI's most famous tracker had outsmarted him had left a great impression on Blu Eyes-actually, he found it refreshing. No one else had even come close. Over the past three years, he had grown fond of Bob Lemus, and openly admitted the man was very good at what he did. In fact, on three separate occasions, he had come closer than he knew in nearly capturing him; in each of the cases, nothing but sheer luck had been the avenue by which he had escaped.

While it was clear his beloved Master had no designs on Lemus, Blue Eyes personally found him attractive and felt that making love to him would prove quite exciting. He suspected Bob Lemus had never felt the swollen maleness of another man, and given the opportunity, would very possibly find the experience quite exhilarating. However, had Bob Lemus known Blue Eyes harbored such a thought; he would have stopped the car, turned in his seat and shot him right then and there.

CHAPTER
TWENTY-SIX

OTH CLAY AND NANCY Cooper were beside themselves
with jubilation that the Blue Eyes killer had been caught.
As Clay readied himself for the drive to the courthouse, a feeling of
rebirth surged through his veins. He could not believe the madman was
finally captured, decommissioned, stripped of his evil rank as Satanic
Mercenary, no longer able to murder innocent people.

Pleased though he was, he imagined Lemus was more so. After
having spent over three years hunting him, always coming close yet
missing by as much as the expanse of a state or the distance of a country,
he was finally reaping the rewards of his hard work.

Clay was happy, yes, but on the other hand, he shared that sick-
with-worry feeling Lemus had been experiencing. All of his hard work
cleansing the world of the sick bastard's atrocities could very well be
overturned by one single, unknown, small-town judge, literally sending
the FBI back to square one and in so doing allow the senseless killing of
more innocent victims. Like Lemus, Cooper prayed the judge they drew
would be a good one. At one time or another he had stood before most
of them, and as far as he knew they were all good men.

But of it all, what made Clayton Cooper the happiest, at least for
now, was that the threat of his sweet Lifesaver being hurt was over, and
they could now get on with their lives. He vowed that, the day they
incarcerated Blue Eyes, he would take a week off so that he and Nancy
could fly to Vegas. They would drink to the perfect buzz, dine at the
best restaurants, gamble away the nights, and make wild passionate love

every spare moment in between. The "do not disturb" sign on their hotel door would become their maxim. By the time vacation would end, both of them would have to limp out of the brightly-lit city. He smiled at the thought and decided that there was no better place in the world in which to celebrate their new *freedom* than Las Vegas.

Dressed in jeans, sneakers, and a white T-shirt, Clay clipped the Beretta to his belt and headed downstairs. Nancy followed, dourly. She had no desire to go with him and look into the face of her former captor again, to feel his impious stare on her and recall the terrible ordeal of her captivity. That was something she had secretly been fighting hard to be rid of.

Unaware of his wife's inner feelings, Clay agreed to let her remain home alone. Blue Eyes was in custody, even though he could not entirely shake free a feeling of uneasiness.

At the door, he placed his ball cap on his head and slipped into his Carhart jacket. Taking Nancy into his arms, he held her a moment, then released her, saying, "You stay inside and keep the doors locked. And keep the .25 under your pillow."

She smiled, trying to hide the apprehension gnawing away at her nerves. The feeling bordered on fear, ever near panic at the idea of being left alone. But she did not wish to worry her husband or appear childish. Despite having been abducted from the house, she still felt safest within its confines. Widening her smile, she told him, "The man is behind bars; I'll be fine."

He kissed her softly on the forehead and went out the door, closing it softly behind him.

Moving to the window, she watched him walk through the muddy shadows to the truck and climb in. The engine started and headlights came on. It was cold, and she was glad to be inside the warm house glancing out through the glass. The truck backed out of the drive and onto the street, then pulled away. Gradually the red taillights faded into the distance.

The instant they disappeared; an immediate sense of foreboding racked her body. Panic filled her brain, and she felt an overwhelming desire to throw open the door and run after the truck, to shout for him to stop and come back, but it was too late. He was gone, and she was alone. Worry lines showed around her eyes.

She tried talking herself down to a calm, controllable level. "Stop it, Nancy Cooper. You're fine. You're being ridiculous." But her thoughts haunted her, planting terrible, unwanted feelings, and she found herself arguing with a dark subconscious. *You're alone in the house! What if he gets bail and beats Clay back to the house? Gets to you first?* No, Clay will be gone only long enough to ensure the maniac stays behind bars. Then he will come straight home as fast as he can and be with me. *Yes, maybe. But what if Blue Eyes; has another partner, waiting in the darkness outside-or already in the house?* She spoke the words loud..."Then I'll shoot the son of a bitch dead."

Raising her hands to the sides of her head, she closed her eyes. "Stop it!" A few seconds passed. She opened her eyes slowly. It was then she realized was it was not for her safety she worried. It was for someone else's. Someone was in grave danger; she could sense it. She felt knots in her stomach, almost to the point of nausea. "My God," she said with a shudder, "someone is going to die tonight."

She told herself it was not going to be Clay. It couldn't be Clay. But it could be someone she knew. Yes, someone she knew, someone close to her. Nancy went pale for a second, but the color returned quickly. She felt sick to the point of nearly throwing up. Where were these thoughts coming from?

She shook her head, once again speaking aloud, this time through angry gritted teeth. "Damn it, stop it right now!" taking a deep breath she closed her eyes, then opened them again. "This is ridiculous," she told herself, "No more. No one is going to die. It's all in your imagination."

As a means of gaining control, she filled her head with memories warm and sweet, recalling last Christmas, envisioning the nine-foot Douglas Fir so beautifully decorated in front of the big picture window and all the neatly wrapped, differently shaped presents beneath. This Christmas would be even more extravagant, she promised herself. It would be fun, the best Christmas ever.

She walked to the door and checked to ensure it was locked. It was, and she breathed a sigh of relief. The lamp near the couch was glowing softly. Leaving it lit, she went into the kitchen and turned that light on as well. She then started up the stairs. Above her an unyielding blackness engulfed the top half of the house, but that was okay. She would turn on every light up there, too. Then she would climb into bed, place the .25 under her pillow just as Clay had suggested, and read a book until he came home.

She ascended three steps, then stopped abruptly, her eyes widening. Somewhere in the dark, something had made a noise.

CHAPTER TWENTY-SEVEN

CLAY'S DRIVE TO THE courthouse was less than twenty minutes. Anxious but with no need to hurry, he edged along at a leisurely fifty miles per hour. This would allow time for Lemus to make up the difference in distance.

Inside, he was feeling distraught over having to leave Nancy alone. As a means of appeasing his guilt, he told himself it was alright, that Blue Eyes was in custody, and it was this trip that would insure he stayed there.

Glancing out his window, he stared up at a full, radiant moon. He could see the eyes, the nose, and the dark shadowy mouth; the old man appeared to be smiling, and Clay took that as a good sign. Thoughts bounced in his mind like rubber balls in a spinning dryer; they tumbled and clashed to the point of making no sense. What had happened to him at the elevator was not possible. Certainly, Heaven and Hell existed-he had believed that since earliest childhood. But people did not go there until they were dead, permanently dead.

Even the stories of those who had died and experienced seeing a bright light at the end of a long tunnel seemed believable. But never had he heard of anyone being taken to Heaven or Hell for a personal tour and then being sent back to live a normal life. Not without some lingering injury or disability.

Yet still, believable, or not, he had been dead, at least clinically dead. Lemus's CPR had proven that. And he had been in Hell. The movie *Flatliners* popped into Clay's head for a second, but he quickly dismissed it and returned to his futile efforts at making sense out of what had happened.

Maybe the devil did have the power to allow certain individuals a sneak preview of that unspeakable place, just as God possessed the power to allow a clandestine trip down the dark tunnel with a privileged look at the light.

Suddenly something darted across the road, just within range of his headlight beams. It was a small black form he couldn't positively identify. Probably a possum or raccoon, he reasoned, although it seemed to move at a controlled pace, as if it wanted to be seen but not recognized. Clay frowned. 'Don't be ridiculous" he told himself.

He shifted his thinking to Nancy. How he loved her! Blue Eyes had cut to the quick when he'd taken her away, leading him to believe she was gone forever. The sight of the scalp and the skinned body hanging in his garage would forever linger within his subconscious, along with the remembrance of a pain far worse than anything he had ever experienced. But that day he had seen her again, alive, dangling from the elevator window, and had heard her call his name-that feeling of joy, of pure jubilation-far outweighed the agonizing pain of loss.

Wrapped warmly within that memory, Clay felt the sudden thud of the truck running over something, something of notable size. The huge vehicle bounced, and the jolt nearly pulled the steering wheel from of his hands.

Slamming on his brakes, he came to an abrupt stop, turned the truck around in the middle of the road and slowly drove back. The headlights gave light only the width of the road, but he saw nothing.

Stopping the vehicle, he placed it in park and got out. The interior light came on but went out again when he closed the door. Clay stood in the dark his pupils dilated, adjusting quickly to the moonlight. Headlights lit several feet into the fields before fading, leaving the area beyond sheathed in dark obscurity.

Above, stars twinkled in a heaven of velvet. There was no sound, no one crying or moaning, no animal howling in pain. The only noise was that of the truck's idling engine. He could find no trace of blood to indicate that whatever he had hit was wounded. There simply was nothing. It was as if it had all been his imagination.

Then, in the field to the left of the truck, somewhere beyond the shine of the silvery lights, he heard it. It was faint at first, so soft he nearly missed it. Straining his ears, he listened more intently.

It was a sound he recognized yet didn't. He heard it again. Certainly, it was not the noise of a dying animal. And it was not the cry of a man bearing the agony of pain. Quite the contrary...this was a soft, self-possessed laughter, perhaps more of a snickering. Strangely, although he thought it ridiculous and difficult to explain, it did not sound human... but yet it did.

For the second time, something dashed quickly across the road within the beam of the truck's headlights. He turned quickly to look, but it was gone. Whatever he had glimpsed, it was not the person or thing laughing from the darkness beyond the moonlight, for that thing was still there, continuing to snicker and sounding as if it might be moving closer.

Slowly Clay's hand inched its way to the Beretta, and he eased it out of its holster. Even slower, although he sensed the urgency to turn and move as fast as possible, he backed to the door of the truck and reached for the handle. Whatever was there ceased to snicker, paused briefly, and spoke for the first time, causing the blood in Cooper's veins to turn to ice. The hair on the back of his neck prickled. He had heard the words before, in a vision. Only now this was real, and he was in the middle of nowhere. The voice was guttural, not animal and not human, and its words ended with the hiss of a snake. The sound sliced through the darkness and fear blazed through his mind like a consuming flame, turning any remnant of confidence into weightless ash. He fought panic.

"Kill him, Cooooooper. Sssssssssssssss."

Clay's fingers touched the truck's door handle; his hand was shaking. The creature, or whatever the hell it was, was now just bordering the edge of the moonlight, ready to step into his range of vision. He had no desire to see it. Two more dark forms dashed through the headlight beams, this time speaking while scurrying out of sight, "Kill him. Kill him." Their little voices were a piercing shrill.

Quickly Clay lifted the truck's handle, but it didn't give. He tried again. Nothing. Under his breath he cursed, a feeling of terror stabbing into his senses. The door would not open. He was locked out.

Then the thing in front of him stepped out of the dark and into the dim light; it resembled the form of a man but with wings pointed and folded against its sides like those of a bat. In place of hair, it was covered with dark scales. Hunched on thick, powerful limbs, it gave the appearance of being curled within itself.

Even in the moonlight the anomaly remained obscure, but he could easily see that it was huge. It began to uncurl slowly, methodically straightening, angling up on its hind-quarters and turning into something neither human nor animal. With its unfolding came the repulsive stench of something dead. Clay placed a hand over his nose and mouth to help ward off the odor. The creature grinned at him, with a mouth the size of a football, exposing sharp, elongated teeth that glistened beneath the moon's gray, muted light.

Two bright yellow, elliptical eyes with black, triangular pupils pierced Clay's mind shattering what tiny bit of confidence he possessed into shreds of cold-blooded fear. Thick snake-like arms with near human hands twisted and curled restlessly. Clay noted their huge size with scaly fingers and knife-like nails nearly a foot in length.

Then suddenly, its arms stopped moving. It intentionally pulled its hands together, just enough to work its fingers so that the long razor claws clattered and clicked against one another. It stood staring at him, as though contemplating something. The sound was eerie, and its gaze was terrifying.

In silence, eyes big, Clay mouthed the words, "son-of-a-bitch." The clicking noise increased, becoming alarmingly amplified in the still, soundless night.

Its grin widened, and with it the long, pointed teeth seemed to grow before Clay's very eyes, as if adjusting to the size of its mouth. Slowly it raised its head to the stars, then screamed, a sharp penetrating shriek that sliced through the open fields in every direction.

Clayton Cooper stood frozen in disbelief; eyes fixed on the creature's monstrous size. Then its head lowered, the grin disappeared, and it slowly began moving toward him. Clay's knees grew weak.

In his head, beginning in the dark recess of his mind, a voice began to shout while clawing its way through his subconscious, moving rapidly toward what was left of his intuitive awareness. Its frantic tone grew louder while pulling and pushing its way, knowing time was short. Finally, it reached him, and a piercing scream exploded violently in his brain: RUN YOU FUCKING IDIOT!

As if suddenly awakened from a trance, Cooper yelled, Oh my God!" into the night. He raised the 9-millimeter and fired three shots into the approaching thing, then turned and fired point-blank into the window of his truck, the glass shattering. Frantically, he pulled up the door lock and scrambled in behind the wheel. The thing was closing quickly, now just a few feet away.

He pulled the transmission into gear, and the tires squealed on the pavement as he rocketed forward. The engine raced as he gathered speed, reaching seventy in just several seconds. His eyes rose to the rear-view mirror. Again, he yelled, "Oh God!" The creature was at his tailgate, easily matching the truck's speed. Then it leaped and Clay felt the truck bounce: it was in the bed.

Turning, he fired through the rear window, shattering glass once again. He emptied the clip of the Beretta into it. When he spun back around his eyes widened and he shouted, "OH SHIT!" The truck was leaving the road and tearing into the soft ground of a freshly plowed field.

The front tires dug deep into the dirt. The truck flipped end over end-a giant mass of steel and plastic somersaulting time and time again.

Among the shriek of tearing metal, the cab crumbled and twisted. The windshield shattered noisily, sending hundreds of glass fragments flying. In his head Clay likened it to a wild carnival ride without built-in safety features.

He had not fastened his seatbelt and he tossed and tumbled harshly. But even as he toppled, he considered himself lucky and prayed that his luck held out. In most highway fatalities, the cause of death was often being thrown from a rolling vehicle.

The truck made one last flip and then landed upside down on its roof, pinning like a top and finally coming to a slow, gradual standstill. The cab was horribly crushed, and Clay lay pinned within its twisted confines.

Half in and out of consciousness, he tried collecting his thoughts. He could hear the incessant spinning of a tire and the hissing of steam. He felt wetness covering his face and soaking into his T-shirt somewhere in his lower abdomen. His right leg ached with pain and his head throbbed.

He moaned and tried to move, but there was no way. Out through a small gap where the windshield once was, he could see into the field a short distance thanks to the gleaming moonlight.

With the back of his hand, he wiped at the wetness that would not stop running into his eyes. He was hurt badly, and Clay knew it. But it was not the bleeding from his face and scalp that worried him; they were extremely vascular and almost always appeared worse than what they really were. No, that bleeding would stop soon enough. It was the wound on his abdomen that concerned him.

Reaching down, he felt a laceration that was six or seven inches long and was bleeding profusely. Immediately he placed his hand over it and applied gentle pressure. At the same time, he tried freeing his right foot. It had become pinned within the wreckage of the dashboard, and the effort was useless. The movement only increased his pain, so he stopped. Realization set in. He was there until someone found him or he died of his injuries, whichever came first. Besides, even if he were to pry his foot loose, there was no climbing out. He Was trapped within the twisted cab.

Clearing blood from his eyes, he once again stared out through the narrow gap. Dozens of small black creatures like the ones that had crossed the headlight beams and he had seen in his vision days ago were now scurrying about everywhere. Clay could hear them climbing over the ruins of the truck. Softly, in voices barely audible, they were chanting the same message: "Kill him, Kill him, Kill him, Kill him"

Clay knew who they were, what they were, and who had brought them here, but he no longer cared. There was nothing he could do about it now. Besides, he had far more serious problems. If the hemorrhaging from the laceration on his abdomen did not stop soon, he would die of blood loss anyway. Even since he'd first applied direct pressure, blood had been steadily seeping out of the wound and through his fingers.

It was clear now he didn't have a snowball's chance in July of getting to the courthouse in time. Blue Eyes now stand a greater than average chance of walking.

Clay shook his head. "And to top all that, Cooper, Demon Big Mouth is probably right outside just waiting to tear open the wreckage and jerk you out, then bite your head right off your torso."

He laughed at his predicament. It was a cynical laugh that lasted only a second since it hurt too much to move.

He was beginning to feel lightheaded and felt the steady encroachment of unconsciousness. It would overpower him within minutes, and he knew it. he had simply lost too much blood.

As he lay there feeling himself drift slowly into that sleep-craving state, one thought raced through his mind in an endless loop, and the thought terrified him. If he did die here, alone in this twisted mass of metal, would he go to Hell? He certainly hoped not.

CHAPTER TWENTY-EIGHT

WHILE THE TOWN OF Brooke was located in the southwest corner of Newburn County, the courthouse sat dead center in the city of Kenter, nearly fifteen miles north. It was exactly 4:05 am when both the Bureau Mobile and JJ Montgomery's $130,000 Mercedes Benz pulled around to the west side of the courthouse and stopped, both shutting off their headlights in almost the same instant. Much to his disappointment, Agent Lemus saw no sign of Clayton Cooper.

Hidden within the thick shadows of a giant sycamore, the Honorable Judge Roy Burshine sat watching from inside his deep blue Cadillac Seville. The judge observed Clendes exit the right-rear door of their vehicle and walk around to the opened door on the left-rear side. Once there, he assisted agent Jones in removing Blue Eyes who was bound in chains.

Attorney Montgomery came up beside them and spoke at a level barely audible to Burshine. "Easy, gentlemen. I do not want my client injured." Both Clendes and Jones ignored him.

The shackles around Blue Eye's feet allowed only a fifteen-inch step, toe-to-heel. Actually, it looked more like a Chinese shuffle when he walked, so Lemus, Spulder, Jones, Clendes and Montgomery all paced themselves to his speed. Their slow, awkward pace reminded Burshine of an assembly of first-time pallbearers, minus the casket. It wasn't until the five men had reached the locked west door of the courthouse that the judge stepped out of his vehicle.

When he did, his dome light lit up the car's interior and the key-reminder bell sounded, fanning out through the early morning tranquility. By the time Burshine leaned in and pulled his keys from the ignition, all five of the men had turned and stood staring in his direction. When the judge closed the car door it sounded like a slam. Lemus smiled. A pissed-off judge was less likely to say yes to bail.

Leaving nothing to chance, as Burshine approached, Lemus remained on the alert with hand resting on the butt of his weapon. He was trusting no one. Blue Eyes had a partner earlier, and since it appeared he belonged to some sort of satanic cult, there might be others around who would do anything to see him freed.

When close enough to be heard without having to shout, the Judge identified himself and proceeded to unlock the courthouse door. Upon entering, he held it open for the others, then closed it and gave it a quick pull to ensure that it relocked behind them.

Burshine was an older man, slightly stooped and pushing seventy. Since the early morning air was chilly, he was dressed in a dark cardigan sweater over a red and white flannel shirt. A navy Dixie Cup cap was pulled down over his ears, Gilligan style, and matched the color of his Docker trousers. Lemus read him as a man who marched to the beat of his own gavel, and that worried him somewhat. There was no way of telling which way a self-possessed man might lean.

The group followed Burshine down a short narrow hallway that exited into the huge, open center of the courthouse. Motion sensors were triggered, and bright lights clicked on everywhere. The place lit up as if someone were trying to break into Fort Knox. Burshine knew the sudden explosion of light would take them by surprise and grinned. In the past, it had shocked countless people who had come by for late-night hearings.

Raising a hand, he talked while continuing to walk ahead of the others. "Gentlemen, the sensors also send a signal to the local Sheriff's Department, but I have already called them. They know we are here."

The courthouse interior was impressively spacious. A glossy white marbled floor circled forty feet around them and the open area ran clear to the domed top of the building, four stories above. Each floor was bordered with a polished mahogany railing, and even from below they noted spacious murals and exquisite paintings covering the walls on all levels. A surprisingly narrow staircase with matching mahogany railing and notably worn wooden steps ran up both the north and south side of the room. At the top was a circled dome lined with a ring of small, round windows. However, the old stairway was not where Burshine went.

Instead, he led them to a small elevator, barely large enough for all of them to fit. Pressed tightly inside, they rode to the third floor. The car creaked and strained during its entire ascent. Seeming to take an eternity before coming to a stop. When it did, still another eternity seemed to pass before the doors opened. Lemus had begun to feel uneasy, and small beads of sweat formed on his brow, a small sign of yet one more of his well-kept secrets: he was claustrophobic.

Exiting, the party followed Burshine down the walkway to a locked office. Following a few seconds of fumbling with his keys, the old judge swung the door inward and entered, leaving it open behind him. The aged adjudicator marched straight to a brass coat rack to the right of his desk and removed his black judge's robe, slipping it over the cardigan sweater. The five men entered the room and stood patiently in front of his desk.

With his robe in place, Burshine pulled out the brown leather high back chair behind his desk and sat. There were three other chairs in the office, and he motioned for the others to sit with a sweep of his hand.

Sliding the three together in front of Burshine's desk, they placed Blue Eyes in the center while Lemus and Montgomery flanked him in the other two. Spulding stood behind Lemus, arms folded. Clendes and Jones positioned themselves near the open door to watch and listen, for Clay and what the judge had to say. When he spoke, Burshine's old voice crackled like a cross between laryngitis and emphysema. "Now, what is the situation here?"

Montgomery spoke first. "Your honor, my client is here to request bail."

"What's the crime, counselor?"

"Breaking and entering with no property damage and nothing stolen. In fact, his prints were run and came back clean. As far as we know, this is his first offense."

"Who arrested him?"

"I did, your honor." Lemus spoke quickly. "I personally apprehended him while the crime was in progress. But B&E is not the reason I wish you to withhold bail."

Burshine raised his eyebrows. "Oh?"

Lemus pulled his bureau ID. "My name is Bob Lemus, Your Honor, and my specialty with the Agency is tracking serial killers. I have been hunting this man, otherwise known as The Blue Eyes Killer, for over three years. He murdered 34 people, the latest of which were here in your county at Fisher's Point, less than a week ago."

Burshine nodded. "Yes, I read about it. A young man and woman were hung."

"And then some, Your Honor," Lemus added. "I believe if you release this man, he will definitely disappear and kill again. I assure you, Your Honor, he will in no way show for his assigned court date if bail is granted."

Lemus slid forward in his chair. "Sir, he is an insane, sadistic killer, and to release him would be an atrocity after having chased him for three years. He has been the Bureau's most difficult and trying case to date."

Montgomery chimed in. "Your honor, my client is accused of B&E, and that is his only crime. Agent Lemus has absolutely no proof he is in fact this Blue Eyes Killer."

Lemus threw Montgomery a sour look and continued.

"Sir," Lemus went on, "if it would not be too much to ask, I have another person arriving any minute who will verify my facts. He is an individual whom this man has tried to kill."

Burshine glanced at his watch. "Well, I will tell you what. Your witness has exactly twenty minutes, no more. If he's not here, then I will pass on to you, my decision."

Burshine rose from his chair and the other three followed. The old judge told them, "In the basement, there is a small cantina with vending machine coffee. It's actually not bad. You all go have a cup, and when you return, I'll make one of you very happy. Now go and allow me time to think."

Lemus and Montgomery felt enough had not been said, yet both knew nothing more was left to say short of weightless rambling. Reluctantly, the group left the office and walked to the elevator. After crowding in, Lemus pushed the button and they descended to the basement.

The old car creaked and wobbled as before, and Lemus experienced the same discomfort he had earlier. However, this time the claustrophobic anxiety was overshadowed with the fear that something had happened to Cooper.

CHAPTER TWENTY-NINE

NANCY COOPER SLOWLY BACKED down the stairs, stepping soundlessly onto the living room floor. Fear gripped her with an almost crushing sensation. She was finding it difficult to breathe.

Teetering between two choices, she ran both hastily through her mind. One was to rush to the kitchen and retrieve a large knife, one big enough to do serious damage. The second was to charge the front door, unlock it and run as fast as possible to a neighboring house, praying they were home and would be willing to help. But how many times had she read or heard the stories of someone begging and pleading for help, only to be turned away or locked out? Then, right there before them, the victim was brutally raped or murdered.

Eyes locked upon the darkness, frantically debating her decision, Nancy remained motionless, ears straining for the sound she had heard only seconds ago. Above her the blackness lay like a night sky without stars. The dark, foreboding threshold fiercely warned her not to come up.

Was she being silly and simply overreacting? The house was old and had been making unexplained noises since they'd moved in, over five years ago. Never once had they given it a thought.

It was time to put her ridiculous jitters to rest. She had to make a decision-and she made it. Taking a deep breath, she stepped back onto the stairs and began a slow climb to the top, one hand on the rail and the other holding a stomach on the verge of giving up its contents.

The house around her remained silent. "There is no one in here, you are safe," she whispered to herself. The steps made the slightest sound beneath her weight, but she grew more confident with each one. The darkness that lay waiting wasn't so bad. It was simply a room without light, and soon it would have that.

Below her, near the couch, out of the corner of her eye-did something move, something small and dark? She glanced over quickly, but nothing was there. She continued on. The darkness was close now, and the once foreboding feeling was, waning, though only slightly. This was *her* house, and she would not be chased from it by an overactive imagination.

Outside, a car drove past. For a second, its headlight beams streaked in through the window, casting the living room in gray, ghostly light. God, how she wished Clay were with her. Her ears now sensitive to the deathly silence, she picked up an ever so soft sound, a clicking; it lasted five, maybe ten seconds, then stopped. She was at a loss. Frozen in place, Nancy listened intently. Nothing! She took six more steps and heard it again. Once more she halted, now nearly at the top of the stairs.

She could see slightly into the uninviting blackness. Nothing seemed out of the ordinary. Directly in front of her was the door to their bedroom; it was open just as she had left it. To the right, the bathroom door was open as well, again as she had left it. And to the left, fifteen feet give or take, down the shadowy hallway, was the closed door to the guest room. It too was just as it should have been.

Stepping onto the floor, she crossed into her bedroom and quickly struck the switch. The room burst into a bright world of light, and she sighed. Quickly, she walked to the nightstand beside her bed and retrieved her pistol. Pulling the slide, she slid a round into the chamber and closed her eyes with relief. A wonderful sense of security washed over her.

Smiling, feeling triumphant over her fears, she went to the closet to get her nightgown. At the door she hesitated, her nervous hand reached for the knob. Quickly, she jerked it open. There was nothing. Grabbing the gown, she turned, and screamed-a mouse was scurrying across the floor, disappearing through the door, its tiny feet clicking frantically against the hardwood floor. Placing a hand over her pounding heart she sighed, at the little rodent for scaring the daylights out of her. It must have been his tiny little claws that had created the clicking sound she'd heard.

After slipping into her nightgown, she opened the door that connected the bathroom to the bedroom, entered, splashed water on her face, brushed her teeth, peed, and then went back into their bedroom, leaving the bathroom light burning.

After placing the .25 caliber automatic beneath her pillow, Nancy picked up the novel she was reading and turned to the page she had marked. Settling comfortably into the pillows, she began to read.

The house was quiet, and the lighted rooms gave her a feeling of relief and liberation. She would read now until her husband came home, at which time they would share a good cup of coffee and make tender, fulfilling love...but not necessarily in that order.

CHAPTER THIRTY

MUCH TO HIS SURPRISE, the cantina coffee wasn't that bad. Agent Lemus drank two cups and smoked a cigarette with each, ignoring the "smoke free facility" sign posted above the vending machines. He restlessly paced the floor while the others sat huddled around a long break table in tired silence.

Blue Eyes sat between Jones and Clendes, sipping a Diet Coke through a straw, his only means by which to drink due to the restrictions of his chains. Montgomery sat facing Blue Eyes, with Spulder to his right. The room was actually small, maybe twenty feet by twenty feet, with a long stainless sink and a marbled counter with a microwave, a toaster, and a well-furnished condiment tray.

For Lemus, time passed slowly, partly due to his continuously checking his watch. He tried not to look so frequently; but couldn't help himself. Cooper should have been there long ago. Something had to be wrong but there was no time to find out what or to help him if the need existed.

While staring at the top of his Coke can, Blue Eyes broke the somber silence of those sitting around the long table. "Well, gentlemen, it's been twenty minutes. Shall we go upstairs?"

Lemus stopped pacing and glanced at his watch once again; the killer was right, it was time. He glanced around the room for a wall clock and saw none. He wondered how the killer knew, to the second, that it was time. He must have deceptively peeked at an agent's watch.

When it came time to return to the judge's chamber, Lemus felt both warm and cold. He didn't want to go, not yet. He wanted to stall just a little longer in the hope Cooper would show, even though in his gut he knew Clay wouldn't. Yet he understood the importance of hurrying back to Burshine, to not keep him waiting, as that would only piss him off. People with his kind of power in small communities could prove dangerous. Often, because of that power, they did more harm than good. He feared this was going to be just such a case.

On their way to the elevator, Blue Eyes shuffled his way to Lemus's side and taunted him with a smile. "Well, what will it be, Bob? Go free or go to jail?"

Lemus ignored him, but Blue Eyes persisted. "Come on, Bob, I know you're a wagering man. In your work, you have to be. I say I go free. I say the old codger tells you he doesn't have enough to not grant bail."

Lemus gave him a sidelong glance. "SHUT UP!"

Blue Eyes smiled widely. "Bob, is that any way to talk to a prisoner?" He paused, then added, "By the way, what do you think happened to Marshall Cooper? Do you suppose he took a sudden liking to me and decided not to show?" Lemus gave him another glance but said nothing. He picked up his pace in order to pull away, but Blue Eyes shuffled faster to stay at his side, adding, "Then again, maybe he's lying dead along the highway somewhere, the result of a terrible and most unfortunate accident. If he is, what a shock it will be to that beautiful wife of his. She is beautiful, you have to admit." Blue Eyes widened his grin. "Given he is dead, Bob, what do you think my chances will be of winning her heart? I sure would like to fuck her. Wouldn't you?"

Lemus swung around, grabbing Blue Eyes by the throat, and slamming him hard against the wall. His words were spoken between teeth gritted tightly. "Look, you sick bastard. I told you to...." Both Clendes and Jones moved in quickly and pulled their boss away while Montgomery stepped in front of him with a pointed finger.

"That is going to cost you."

Lemus pulled angrily away from Clendes and Jones, straightening his suit jacket. "No," he replied to Montgomery, "if that animal walks, it's going to cost you."

"Are you threatening me, Agent Lemus?"

Lemus's eyes were cold. "You can bet your legal ass on it."

When they entered the room, the honorable Judge Burshine was sitting behind his desk. The three took their seats. Leaning back in his chair Burshine folded his arms speaking directly to Lemus. "Well, I see your witness hasn't shown, so is there anything else you can say or do to convince me to withhold bail?"

"At this time, all I have is my word as an agent, Your Honor."

Burshine grimaced. "Well, I have to tell you, if I didn't require evidence and locked people up based only on someone's word, every citizen in Indiana would be pointing a finger at someone, and the entire state would have a high fence with concentina wire stretched around its borders. I am afraid I need more than that."

Montgomery grinned, speaking out loud. "Yes, Your Honor, that's right."

Burshine glanced at the counselor and made a face. Then, he looked back to Lemus. "Before tonight, had you even laid eyes on this man?"

"No, sir."

"Ever see a photo of him?"

"No, sir."

"And you have no connection in the way of prints?"

Lemus despondently shook his head, hating the sick feeling generating in the pit of his stomach, knowing full well the direction the conversation was taking. "No, sir."

"Then how in the hell do you know he is your killer?"

"At the Cooper house," Lemus told him anxiously, "when I engaged him, he spoke to me in the first person. Called me by my first name. Knew things, personal things, that unless he had intentional cause, he would not have known."

Burshine looked down at his desktop and back up. "Did he confess to you the crimes in question?"

"No, sir."

"There, you see, Your Honor?" Montgomery injected. "Agent Lanus has nothing against my client. Agent Lemus has done nothing here tonight but waste your valuable time."

Burshine looked at Montgomery. "Counselor, unless I ask for your opinion, shut your pie hole. Tell me, Agent Lemus. If I ordered this man held without bail for twenty-four hours, could you produce hard evidence, indisputable evidence, that this is your killer?"

Lemus thought a long while, running through his head all the things that had happened since arriving in Indiana. The possibilities were slim, and he considered them all...possibly a semen match with the male victim at the hotel, or maybe a print from the room at the bottom of the elevator where he had found Cooper. But even with those, without Cooper to verify, would amount to nothing. As much as he hated to admit it, Cooper alone was the trump card.

Lemus looked soulfully up at Burshine. "Nothing immediate, Your Honor. But I assure you, a case can be built. And the witness that was to be here could provide you with all you need. He is one of your Town Marshalls, Clayton Cooper."

Burshine raised his eyebrows. "Yes, I know Cooper. He's a fine young man. But unfortunately, here tonight, he is a no-show."

"That is true, your Honor. But given twenty-four hours, I can find him and have him standing before you, tall and honest."

Montgomery injected. "Your Honor, this is ridiculous. My client is-"

Burshine raised a finger in his direction without even looking, "Pie Hole, Counselor."

For some time, Burshine stared at Lemus, contemplating, considering all that had been said. Lemus knew he was looking for something to use, something to justify holding the man sitting before him in chains. He liked the old judge but feared what his answer would be-what his answer would have to be, by the fairness of the law.

Burshine sighed and settled back in his chair. "I am afraid, based on what I've heard here tonight, I must grant bail."

Montgomery smiled, speaking aloud. "Yes. Thank you, Your Honor."

Burshine looked at him. "Bail, Counselor, is set at two million dollars."

The smile disappeared, but Montgomery nodded his approval.

Looking at Lemus, Burshine shrugged. "It's the best I can do."

Under normal circumstances, the decision would have pleased Lemus, but to Blue Eyes, money was no problem, and now he was free.

Upon dismissal, when everyone rose to leave, Burshine called Montgomery to his desk. "Make sure your client stays close by. I am setting a hearing for one week from today." He wrote out a date on a piece of paper and handed it to him. "Make sure he's here, Counselor."

Montgomery nodded.

Back outside on their way to the vehicles, Blue Eyes leaned close to Lemus and whispered, "I'd like a private word with you, Bob. It will prove very beneficial, I promise."

Lemus looked at him, studying his face. Instinct told him listening would be the right thing to do, so he agreed and the two walked off in the distance.

"Bob, I know you've grown fond of the Coopers, so I want to share my...,"he looked up into the star-filled sky, then back. "...intuition with you."

Lemus stared at him, silent and waiting.

"I strongly believe that the Marshall has been in a very serious accident and, even as we speak, lies very close to death. If he doesn't get help in the next, oh, let's say, thirty minutes, he will surely die. And it just happens to be that my intuition can tell you exactly where he is."

Lemus shook his head. "And I'm supposed to believe that?"

"Believing is optional Bob. His dying is not. The clock is ticking. And trust me, your CPR will not save him this time. He is in need of much more than that. Now, here is my deal. You remove these chains and let me return with my lawyer, and I give you the location of your dying Marshall. You save his life a second time, you're a hero again, and everyone is happy. What do you say?"

Lemus turned and shouted for Clendes. Once at his side, he told him, "Unchain the son-of-a-bitch."

Clendes looked puzzled, and Lemus repeated it. "You heard me, unchain him. He's free to go with his lawyer."

Shrugging his shoulders, Clendes did as he was told. Lemus then told Clendes, "Go put the chains in the car."

Blue Eyes rubbed his wrists. "When you leave, take Highway 52 to 500 North. Marshall Cooper was taking the long way around to kill time. From the direction you're going, you will come upon a large farmhouse with two twin barns and a silo standing between them. One half mile past, look to your left. In the field will be the wreckage. Trapped in that wreckage will be Marshall Cooper. And, if I may, I suggest you call an ambulance now. Trust me, he will need it. If you do not take my advice, then you have wasted both my time and yours."

"How do I know you're not sending me in some phony direction?"

Blue Eyes' face went sober. "Because I'm giving you my word, Bob." He turned then and walked toward Montgomery's car. Strolling past Jones, Clendes, and Spulder, the killer grinned. "Good night, gentlemen." Their faces had a dumbfounded expression. Lemus approached at a near run. "Get your asses in the car. We're running out of time."

They looked at one another, each thinking the same thing: running out of time for what?

Lemus spun his wheels, pulling away from the old courthouse. Glancing at Spulder, he told him "Get on the radio, call dispatch, tell them there has been a terrible accident in Newburn County on 500 North, one half mile south of the farmhouse with two big barns and silo in the center."

Spulder stared at Lemus, trying to make sense of what he was being told to do.

Lemus sighed. "I'll explain later. Just do what I told you. Tell them it's a 10-50 P.I. with pin in. Tell them it's the Brooke Town Marshall."

CHAPTER THIRTY-ONE

T HE RIDE BACK TO the Tippecanoe County Jail for the retrieval of his clothes and personal belongings was enjoyable for Blue Eyes. The wind felt gratifying blowing through his hair. He loved convertibles, cherished their feeling of freedom and the uncontested success they symbolized.

The early morning air was chilly, but he didn't mind. At first his lawyer had protested that they leave the top up, but Blue Eyes had been more persuasive. Now he was enjoying it all: the stars, the wind, and moon. At the moment life was pleasing, but it was still certainly no match for the unholy paradise that awaited him. And because Lemus had listened, Marshall Cooper would live to finish what they had started.

It was all so wonderful, but what really excited Blue Eyes was his ingenious plan to dissolve the Marshall's intransigence. The plan was genius, with the additional promise of a rush. Hands down, it would push his need-be assassin over the edge and into an accommodating state of pure, uncontrollable fury.

After picking up his belongings and signing all appropriate paperwork, Montgomery and Blue Eyes climbed back into the convertible. Montgomery wanted to return to Chicago, but his client thought differently. "Take me to an all-night variety store, then to the town of Brooke. Just outside the limits, is an old grain elevator. I want to go there."

Montgomery frowned. "Why?"

"Because I want to. What is the problem? Don't I pay you enough money?"

Montgomery nodded his head. "You pay me well."

"Then do as I ask."

Shrugging, Montgomery agreed.

They found a gas station on State Road 43. Blue Eyes had Montgomery wait in the car while he went in alone. When he came out, he had two cups of coffee, one of course for his legal advisor and one for himself. He also carried a small white plastic bag, the contents of which he kept to himself. Montgomery thanked him for the coffee and pulled away. He was curious as to the contents of the bag but felt it inappropriate to ask.

When they arrived at the elevator, Blue Eyes had him pull around to the north side and park close to the entrance. The old complex sat wrapped in the last fading rays of moonlight. Morning was close, probably within the hour. They got out of the vehicle and Blue Eyes pulled a black flashlight from the white hag. He then tore open a package of batteries and placed them in the flashlight, pointed it in Montgomery's face, and clicked it on. Montgomery flinched away from the bright light and Blue Eyes laughed. "Just making sure it works, Counselor." After picking up the white bag, he spoke over his shoulder. "Follow me."

Across the doorway leading into the small foyer, police had placed yellow "Do Not Cross" barrier tape in the typical X fashion. Blue Eyes tore it down and they entered into the dark interior.

Montgomery followed Blue Eyes across a large open floor and down a steep set of old wooden stairs. At the bottom they crossed through two small rooms and into a third. The flashlight's beam gave the lawyer only quick, limited flashes of the room's interior.

Puzzled, he watched Blue Eyes begin to light candles stationed all around them. Soon the area was aglow with a soft light. In the middle of the floor was a table covered with a white linen sheet. It too puzzled Montgomery "What is all this?" He asked wonderingly.

Blue Eyes turned and smiled. "It's my den of iniquity"

"Your what?" Montgomery asked, again puzzled.

The Blue Eyes Killer leaned casually against the wall and folded his arms, his smile widening. "Rather than explain, allow me the pleasure of showing you. Take off your clothes, Counselor."

Montgomery frowned with shock and surprise. "What?"

"Please remove all your clothing and lie down on the table, on your stomach."

Montgomery shook his head in disbelief. "Are you fucking nuts?"

"I prefer the word psychopathic. And I will kill you, brutally, if you do not do as I have asked."

Montgomery stood frozen, fear beginning to burn hot inside him like a rising fever. His wide, incredulous eyes watched Blue Eyes remove an old opened can from the shelf and twist free its jagged top. After bending one side over to eliminate the shard edge, he placed it between his index and middle fingers, then crossed to where Montgomery stood. In one quick as-lightning slash, the counselor's right cheek opened. Blood spilled down his face and over his shirt and tie. Instantly his hand went to the wound, and he screamed. Fear turned to sheer panic and sudden helplessness, and then began to cry.

Blue Eyes calmly walked back to the wall, leaned comfortably against it, and again crossed his arms. In a nonchalant tone, he repeated himself. "As I said, remove your clothes and get up on the table, face down. Should I have to cross the room again, I will do a lot more damage to that pretty, million-dollar face. The bleeding you're experiencing will stop in just a minute or so, and you will be fine. Now stop that ridiculous crying and do as you're told. I am going to put the lid down. See?" He laid it on the shelf to his right and turned back to Montgomery. "Now this is the last time I will tell you: if you so much as hesitate one second after I've said the word, I will pick the lid back up and come over there, and then nothing from then on will matter for you, ever again. Now take off your clothes."

Hands shaking, Montgomery removed his tie, suit coat, and then shirt. He stood naked from the waist up. The deep dirt room was cold, and he shivered.

Blue Eyes found the counselor's physique mediocre: love handles were beginning to emerge above his hips, but they weren't too bad yet, and there was a lot of chest hair, Blue Eyes liked that. The counselor's stomach was flat, that was a plus; and, because of the cold room, his nipples had become tiny, raised pebbles. That excited him, too. The counselor wasn't exactly Hollywood quality, but he was acceptable.

"Keep going, you're doing wonderfully," Blue Eyes encouraged him.

Next, Montgomery removed his shoes, socks, and trousers. Clad only in his boxer shorts now, he pleaded, "Please, don't make me do this."

Blue Eyes raised a finger to his lips. "Shhhhhhhhh." He refolded his arms across his chest in a relaxed fashion.

"Now, Counselor, remove the shorts, and before you get up on the table I want to gaze upon your nakedness. To lust, if I may."

Montgomery bent slightly and removed his underwear, then straightened. Blue Eyes stared at his flaccid manhood with a soft smile, then told him, "Now turn around."

Montgomery obeyed, his eyes filled with tears of embarrassment and fear.

"I like it," the killer told him. "Have you ever been told by another man that you have a magnificent ass?"

Montgomery was too frightened to reply.

"Now get up on the table and lay face down."

The counselor hesitated; his fear now so dizzyingly overwhelming that he was close to fainting. He began to cry again. He now understood the horror a woman feels just before she's raped. Weakly, he climbed onto the table and laid down.

Blue Eyes reached into the white bag and removed a roll of gray duct tape, then approached the table. Montgomery lay frozen. Part of him wanted to jump up, say "fuck you," and fight for his life, but his years of law practice had honed the skill of sensing that which was winnable and that which was not... and this was not. He could only hope the killer let him live and if not, that death would come quickly.

Blue Eyes wrapped the tape tightly around Montgomery's right wrist, unraveled a long length from the roll, then pulled both arms beneath the table and taped his hands together, pinning him. Montgomery could not move. Rising to his feet, Blue Eyes gleamed at the man's naked form, now helplessly bound. With gentle fingers he swept down his spine and over his buttocks. Montgomery wanted to pull away, but where could he go?

"Now, counselor," Blue Eyes said softly, "If you will, please pull your knees up, thus moving yourself into a kneeling position."

Montgomery begged, "For God's sake, stop this." Tears were streaming. "You know I have done nothing to hurt you. I've only helped you."

Oblivious to his plea, Blue Eyes repeated, "Move into a kneeling position, please."

Realizing his appeal for mercy was useless, Montgomery reluctantly pulled his knees beneath him. Blue Eyes taped first one ankle to the side of the table and then the other. Montgomery's legs were now pulled slightly apart with his buttocks raised, his upper trunk lowered, and his chin resting on the sheet. With his hands pulled tightly beneath the table, he was barely able to raise his head.

"There," Blue Eyes said, stepping back and admiring his handiwork. "Very neatly done." He then moved to the front of the table to where

Montgomery could see him and began removing his own clothing; already he was erect. The moment he was naked, he walked behind the bound counselor and climbed upon the table between his legs.

Montgomery begged, tears staining the sheet beneath him. "Please. I am not gay. I have nothing against gays, but I don't go that way."

Running his hands over Montgomery's buttocks, Blue Eyes told him, "Yes, I know. That makes you a virgin. And I like virgins."

Montgomery's face was wet with tears as he whimpered helplessly into the sheet. Over the years since he'd graduated law school, he had helped countless underworld clients, many of which he was sure were guilty of murder and other hideous crimes, but all had paid him well and none had ever tried to hurt him. Because of them, he lived in a million-dollar estate, drove an expensive automobile, ate the best foods, and drank the most expensive wines. All of his clothes were tailored, and he dated only the most beautiful women. Was this his punishment for having lived so lavishly from tainted money? Blues Eyes interrupped his thoughts, " Did you know counselor, that your Jesus said it was easier for a Camel to go through the eye of a needle, than for a richman to het into Heaven?"

Then he screamed. Pained ripped into his anus as though he had been torn open. Torturously, his body began to rock, slowly at first but quickly gathering agonizing momentum. He screamed again and again, but no one could hear, no one but the spiders that dwelled in the cold, damp darkness, the same darkness that he feared would become his grave.

CHAPTER THIRTY-TWO

CLAYTON COOPER LAY UNCONSCIOUS within the tangled mass of metal that had once been his pickup truck. Deep within a dream state, he did not see or hear the four men running into the field toward the wreckage. Beneath him, cradled within the curvature of the inverted cab, a pool of blood lay like a small pond soaking, into his clothing.

All four men reached the scene at the same time, each searching frantically for a way in, but there was none. Cooper had been sealed in tightly.

Kneeling, Lemus peered in through the thin, long gap that had once been the windshield. It was dark, and he could just make out the outline of Cooper's body. It appeared Cooper was lying on his back, with his face only inches from what had been the floor of the truck. "Cooper. Cooper, can you hear me?"

There was no response. He tried reaching in through the narrow slit, but only his fingers would fit. Turning, Lemus ordered Jones back to the car for the flashlight stowed in the trunk. Frustrated, he glanced up at Spulder. "Where the hell is that ambulance?"

The moment Jones returned, Lemus took the light and shined it in through the narrow opening and onto Cooper's face, covered with blood. Not looking up, he shouted for the others to shake the truck. "But do it gently. Let's see if the movement arouses him."

The three men found suitable spots to grip and in unison began rocking the truck lightly back and forth. Cooper's head rolled flaccidly, side to side. Lemus didn't care for that. He clearly understood the probability of a spinal injury but felt it important to rouse him if at all possible.

Cooper groaned.

Lemus closed his eyes in thankfulness and said aloud, "Thank God. Okay, stop shaking." The men released their grip and the truck fell still. "Cooper. Hey, are you hearing me?"

Groaning once again, Clayton Cooper opened his eyes. He felt the crusty sensation of dried blood. There was only darkness, except for a bright beam of light shining from somewhere to his left. Several times he blinked but the light remained, enveloping him within its vortex. *"So, this is it,"* he thought. He was there, in the tunnel of light, on his way to Heaven. Thank God, for that meant Hell was the other way. Although thinking clearly remained a difficult task, his thoughts had become coherent enough to wonder why his body wasn't moving. He should be flying, traveling through the tunnel at the speed of light. Then, he heard God call to him.

"Cooper. Are you with me?"

He swallowed, tasting the stale, pungent tang of blood.

"Cooper, damn it, can you fucking hear me?"

Shock or not, his head had cleared enough to realize that that question had definitely not come from God. Grinning weakly, he turned his head slowly toward the beam of light and blinked into its brightness. "Is that you, Lemus?"

"Yeah. It's me."

"I thought you were God."

"That's OK, a lot of people think that."

With slow, calculated motion, Cooper stretched out his arm in the direction of the light and poked his bloody fingers through the narrow opening. Lemus placed his fingers on top of them. "It's alright. The ambulance will be here any minute."

Cooper took a deep breath, and it hurt. "I can't believe I'm still alive. What about Blue Eyes?"

Agent Lemus answered evasively. "Don't worry about that right now. You just stay awake for me."

"He got bail, didn't he?"

Lemus wanted to lie, to say Blue Eyes was behind bars, but he felt he owed Cooper the truth.

"Yes, but he won't be out for long. We have his prints now."

"What about Nance?"

Lemus looked up at the four men standing together. He mouthed the words in silence: *"Damn it to hell."*

One more time he had been set up and made the fool by his adversary. Pointing a finger, he motioned for Jones and Clendes to take the car and hightail it to Cooper's house as fast as possible. Acknowledging him with a nod, they turned and ran to the car. Turning back to Cooper, Lemus said, "We have help on the way even as we speak."

"Thank God," Cooper said, followed by a cough that brought blood to his mouth. "If he gets her again, there will be no getting her back this time."

The ambulance unit and rescue truck arrived only seconds apart. While the medics readied their immobilization equipment and tech supplies, Fire Department personnel began cutting Cooper out of the wreckage.

Because the field was soft, fire trucks and the ambulance remained parked along the road. As a result, long electrical lines connected to a fixed generator crisscrossed pneumatic air hoses needed to operate the jaws-of-life and other extrication tools. In addition, hose lays were stretched and charged in case of fire. Three halogen lights were set up on the ground surrounding the wreckage, and for the first time Cooper clearly saw the inside of his twisted prison.

The truck floor was less than two inches from the tip of his nose. His right foot was lodged within the tangled remains of the dashboard. Because he was able to wiggle his toes and feel it, he guessed his foot was probably not that badly injured. The bed had been crumpled up and pushed tightly against the back of the cab, with part of it actually poking through what had once been the rear window. The steering wheel had broken in half. One half was missing, the other now punctured through the metal roof only inches from his face.

Fire personnel had chosen to apply the jaws-of-life through the narrow opening where Lemus was shining his light. Slowly, in careful increments, the metal creaked and popped, bending readily to the powerful hydraulic jaws. But the process was tedious, since repeatedly they had to apply cribbing beneath the jaws for height. All told, it took nearly twenty minutes before access was achieved.

Then came the slow, careful removal of Cooper's foot. It had become necessary for a rescuer to wiggle in and intertwine himself with Cooper's legs to get to the twisted dashboard. The close quarters were uncomfortable for both, and work progressed at a crawl, but it was necessary for prevention of further injury.

The medics had wanted to go first and stabilize Cooper with oxygen and at least one large bore IV, but it was voted down due to the potential need of a cutting torch, the incredibly cramped quarters, and the high risk of pulling the IV loose during the extrication. Cooper could not risk the loss of any more blood. It took thirty-six minutes until Cooper was finally pulled free. Immediately he was log-rolled onto a long backboard with a neck brace and head immobilizers. Then the medics placed him on high flow oxygen with a non-rebreather mask and started three large bore IV's, two of normal saline and the other of Hespan. Blood covered nearly every inch of his face and the large laceration on his lower abdomen was still seeping blood as well. The wound was dressed, following a head-to-toe examination that revealed multiple abrasions and contusions, but nothing of great significance.

Once Cooper was packaged, they lifted the backboard onto the cot, strapped it down, and carried him hastily toward the ambulance. Lemus helped carry him through the soft dirt field.

The desire to float away to unconsciousness was washing over Cooper like a warm ocean wave. Still, forcing a smile, he looked up at Lemus and asked, "Do I look like death warmed over?"

Lemus looked down and grinned. "Yes, as a matter of fact you do."

"I'll live, won't I?"

"You can count on it," Lemus told him confidently.

"Good," Clay told him weakly. "I don't want you giving me CPR again."

Cooper's smile faded and he closed his eyes.

CHAPTER THIRTY-THREE

ALTHOUGH NANCY COOPER LAY cozily nestled into her pillows, she had chosen to lie on top of the covers. That gave her more freedom should the necessity to move hastily arise. Every now and then she would reach quickly beneath her pillow and wrap her hand around the grip of the .25, practicing a homemade reprisal of the quick draw.

Although the book she was reading, *Mindtalk*, had become one of her all-time favorites, she was absorbing very little this night. She knew she would have to reread, since a constant scattering of thoughts relentlessly interrupted her focus.

Rolling onto her side, she rested her head on her left hand and turned a page in her book. She blinked several times in an attempt to chase away the need for sleep now beginning to cause her eyes to burn. It had been nearly two hours since she had watched the taillights of Clay's truck disappear into the night. She knew it was a twenty-to-twenty-five-minute drive to the courthouse and the same back; at worst, it was just under an hour, round trip. After allowing another hour to argue the why and why not of bail, to the best of her calculation her husband should be pulling in any minute.

For the most part, the house had remained quiet since she'd retired to the bedroom to read. Every once in a while, her eyes closed and head dropped, but the sudden jerk always brought her around. The very thought of falling asleep sent slivers of terror slicing through her mind. Asleep, she would become completely vulnerable. It was of paramount importance she remains awake, at least until Clay came home.

Nancy was confident the Blue Eyes Killer would not be granted bail. After all, he was a serial killer! She had also been won over by the persuasive power of Agent Lemus, trusting he would insure the nut case went to prison and fried in the chair.

She closed her book and fell tiredly back against her pillows, staring up into the ceiling. "Yes, she said aloud while stretching and yawning, "definitely the chair."

Her eyes closed, and it was a feeling of warm comfort. In her mind, a tiny voice warned her to remain awake, but it was weak, quickly overridden by the need for sleep.

Outside, another car was passing. And were she awake enough to get out of bed and look, she would have admired its splendid beauty. Nancy Cooper loved convertibles.

CHAPTER THIRTY-FOUR

MAGNOLIA HEAVEN PLANTATION
BED AND BREAKFAST
ALEXANDRIA, LOUISIANA
SATURDAY EVENING, 9:10 PM

PRIVATE INVESTIGATOR JANIS BARR stood with her back pressed tightly against the trunk of a massive oak tree. She was not worried about being seen; her petite, five-foot four-inch frame, all one hundred and fifteen pounds, remained well concealed.

The man she hunted was somewhere inside the big house. Of that she was certain, despite the fact she had not yet made a visual. Sadly, it was probably too late for the unsuspecting occupants. Closing her eyes, she whispered a hurried prayer, then opened her eyes back up and made the sign of the cross. Glancing up into the star-filled heavens, as if asking for absolution, she mumbled, "It couldn't be helped. The call came too late."

As was the case prior to a potentially dangerous confrontation, her mind battled the one irritating thought always coming back to haunt her: that everyone she knew felt she was far too small to be a private investigator, especially in Louisiana. Cajuns could be so mulish.

Although that thinking did put a small dent in her armor of astonishing self-confidence, being small in stature was never an issue;

anyone, big or small, could be brought down one way or another. In physical combat, luck always figured in at twenty percent of winning the equation. The nine-millimeter clutched tightly in her hand amounted to another fifty percent. Then, adding in the Janis Barr human nature belief system that women are women and men are just little boys with bigger penises, the odds of outsmarting the opposite gender weighed well in her favor.

Evening darkness had long since covered the restored plantation house, leaving it visibly impenetrable. Except for the soft illumination of a burning lamp in the front parlor, the old structure stood steeped in ghostly obscurity. Since her arrival, Janis had seen no movement inside. Light from the parlor lamp radiated through one of the six porch windows and spread a long, rectangular patch across the decking. Aside from that, there was no other outside light, except for the sky of stars and three-quarter moon playing hide-and-seek with drifting clouds.

Motionless, Janis Barr planned her strategy. Rain had not fallen over Alexandria for some time, and a brown resurrection fern dangling from the limbs of the big oak tickled the back of her neck. Using the butt of the Beretta, she scratched the itch while biting thoughtfully at her bottom lip. She could work her way to the back of the house and enter there, forging her hunt through dark, unfamiliar hallways and rooms. Or she could cautiously make a frontal approach toward the lighted porch and go right in through the front door. She preferred the porch, but it had a potentially hazardous downside: *if she could see, so could he.* In the darkness, she smiled at her unintended poetic humor.

Running a hand through her short strawberry-blond hair, she began what she always did when stressful decisions needed to be made: she initiated a conversation with herself.

"Well, what do you think Barr, dark or light? You've got one choice, one chance. Mess up, and if you're lucky, he'll only kick the shit out of you. If you're not, he will break your back or snap your neck."

She understood full well the consequences of making a mistake. Lonzo Pardaux was a giant of a man, six-five if he was an inch. She knew him personally, knew what to expect: an occasional bather with long, stringy, greasy hair held in place by the same Red Socks cap he'd worn for twenty years. It had been a gift from his grandmother when he was fourteen. His chubby face would be in need of a shave and his trademark black T-shirt would come just short of covering the last quarter of his huge beer gut. And worse, a pair of loose-fitting rustler jeans would be riding low, revealing the upper most portion of his butt crack. Janis shuddered.

Almost everyone in Alexandria knew he was a little slow. Half out of kindness to his parents and half out of fear for their own safety, the citizens treated him kindly, knowing he was a potential killer if his medication, was not taken regularly. The mayor was constantly petitioned to have Lonzo put away, but there was never a strong enough case.

Tonight, however, he had gone over the edge, and his sister had called Janis, a friend of the family. Unfortunately for Janis, she lived close by. It wasn't a case of not wanting to help out a friend. Rather, Janis feared this confrontation could lead to the possibility of having to kill one, Lonzo. The Sheriff's Department had been called as well but were several minutes away.

Leaning against the tree, Janis recalled the phone conversation with Lonzo's sister. The giant man had not taken his Haldol for three days. Now he was on another spiritual mission for the little "Angel" who always flew down and sat perched on his right shoulder whenever he stopped taking his medicine.

Usually they were non-life-threatening missions, like super-gluing a set of insulated underwear to the family pit bull because it was snowing outside, and he wanted to take the pet for a walk or washing his crotch with bleach because he'd developed a rash. And once, he'd carefully cut out specific newspaper articles to wipe his butt with because he thought it would make him smarter. But on one mission, and shamefully it was Janis's favorite, he had been told to donate all of his underwear to Goodwill-even the pair he was wearing, which he nonchalantly removed while standing at the Goodwill cashier counter.

Lonzo had never been locked up or institutionalized, thanks to the tireless intervention of his loving parents. Because of that fact, Janis found herself mind-boggled by Lonzo's behavior this night. He had told his sister his new mission was to send the owners of Magnolia Heaven Plantation to Jesus. And he was to use the World War II machete her husband kept locked in their gun cabinet. When he'd broken the glass to take possession, she'd tried to stop him, but he had easily pushed her aside and disappeared into the night. Crying, she had scrambled to the phone and called the Sheriff's Department-and Janis.

Murder scenes were always unpleasant, but they were far from alien to Janis Barr. Blood and guts came with the territory. The thing peculiar about his psychosis-induced undertaking—and no doubt it would be Lonzo's last was that the owners of Magnolia Heaven Plantation were his parents.

Gripping the butt of the nine-millimeter, Janis closed her eyes and took a deep breath. "OK, Barr, we're through talking. If that's the way you want it, let's do it." she opened her eyes and rounded the tree, moving quickly toward the front of the house. Cautiously she watched the lighted interior of the parlor. The window was open but covered with a screen. She saw nothing, but just as she stepped onto the porch, a light came on in one of the rooms upstairs.

Following a brief pause at the front door to listen, she stood to the side and pushed it open slowly. It swung soundlessly inward, and she was thankful for the quiet. Weapon ready, she darted quickly inside and dropped down on one knee. Still nothing. No sound, no signs of life.

She knelt in a small, open foyer. Immediately to her right was the doorway to the lighted parlor. Straight ahead, affixed to the wall, a winding staircase led to the top floor where the light had come on. To her left was another room, it was dark. Beside the staircase the entrance to a hallway faded gradually into profound darkness.

Just when she was ready to move on, her eye caught a small puddle of blood pooled at the corner of the parlor door. Cautiously, she rose to her feet and placed her back to the right of the doorway. With a quick dart of her head, she looked into the room. It appeared normal, except for a wicker chair lying on its side below the windowsill. Believing the room safe, she entered. A shadowy body lay slumped against the wall in the corner, and it startled her. She recognized who it was right away. It was Charlie Pardaux, Lonzo's father.

She did not bother to check for a pulse. His head lay flush against his left shoulder, nearly severed; eyes still open, the corpse sat in a huge pool of its own blood. Janis choked back a tear and stepped out of the room to the foot of the stairs. Her hands were trembling. The sight of poor Charlie had shaken her, but equal to that, she was wholly pissed. Carefully, she began climbing the stairway, slowly, one step at a time. Once at the top, she could hear the faint sound of someone crying. It was coming from the first room on her left, the only upstairs room with a light on.

Except for the soft sobbing, the remainder of the big house was soundless. With extreme caution, Janis inched along. She wished strongly for the Sheriff's Deputy to arrive. She was nearly to the open doorway now and the light spilling out into the walkway had begun to engulf her, exposing her approaching figure. No longer were there shadows in which to conceal herself. This was it. if Lonzo was in there, the confrontation was about to happen.

At the corner of the door, she peered in. It was a small bathroom. Lonzo's mother lay tied in the bathtub, crying. Her sobbing stopped when she spotted Janis. Immediately Janis raised a finger to her lips for silence. Lonzo was not in the room.

Following one last glance down the hallway, Janis hurried to her side. Using her black-handled switchblade, a gag gift from her father when she'd begun dating at sixteen, she cut the rope binding her friend and helped her out of the tub. When they turned, Lonzo stepped into the doorway. He stooped so as not to strike his head, then stood staring. His huge frame blocked nearly all light behind him. His face was grim. "Ms. Barr, you ain't supposed to be here. I'm on a mission."

Janis kept the nine-millimeter hidden behind her back. Closing the knife, she placed it in her pocket.

"No, Lonzo, it's okay. Your angel friend has changed her mind. It's only your daddy that needed to go to Heaven tonight. It's alright for your mama to stay so she can help you here."

Lonzo looked confused. "No, ma'am. I've been told they both need to go to Heaven."

Janis forced a smile but kept her tone firm. "Lonzo, your angel friend just told me it was alright to let mama stay. Now put the machete down and go get your Mama a glass of tea from the kitchen."

He teetered, unsure of what to do. Cocking his head as if listening to the angel on his shoulder, he smiled suddenly "Ms. Barr, I got some great news. My friend says that you can go to Heaven, too, along with Mama."

Janis shook her head, knowing what was to come next, but she made one more attempt at solving the dilemma without any more killing. "Lonzo. We have been friends for years. I knew your grandmother back when she knitted your cap. I have known your mama and daddy for a very long time, too. They trust me. You can trust me. Your angel friend likes you but has made a big mistake. Your mama needs to stay here and not go to Heaven yet."

Mary Elizabeth spoke softly to her son, her voice pleading with as much love as fear. "Son, Ms. Barr is right. Your angel friend has made a mistake this time. Now, I'm your mama, and I'm telling you to do as Ms. Barr says. Put down the big knife and go get me a glass of tea."

"I can't, Mama. I got to do what I been told, or God will be mad at me. I was being nice, Mama. I done put you in the tub so I can wash you up when the blood stops running." Lonzo took a step.

Janis pulled the nine-millimeter from behind her and raised it toward Lonzo's chest. "No, Lonzo, stop where you are."

He froze, surprised, and confused. "You going to shoot me, Ms. Barr?

"I don't want to. But because your friend is lying to you, I may have to." Janis held the gun steady. "Tell you what, Lonzo. I will prove your friend is not telling the truth. Do you know where your medicine is?"

"Yes. But I don't need to take it anymore. My friend told me so."

"Well, I'll tell you what. You go get it take it, and we will all sit down right here. And when the sun comes up, if you still think your friend is right, I'll put the gun down and you can send both Mama and me to Heaven."

Lonzo stared at her thoughtfully a few seconds, then leaned again toward his right shoulder. After a few seconds, he said, "I can't do that, Ms. Barr. You can leave. But Mama has got to go to Heaven now."

He raised the machete and moved quickly toward them. Mary Elizabeth Pardaux screamed for her son to stop, and Janis Barr fired twice into his heart. He stumbled back, looked surprised, took two more steps, then dropped to his knees and fell forward. The mayor of Alexandria would receive no more petitions. Lonzo Pardaux was dead.

Mary Elizabeth cried fiercely as she kneeled by her son's side, bittersweet tears soaking the back of his dirty black T-shirt. Janis holstered the weapon and sat on the edge of the tub, her own eyes filling with tears.

Outside, in the far distance, a siren was wailing. Janis shook her head: better late than never. Following a short period of mourning, Janis grasped Mary Elizabeth by the shoulders and pulled her to her feet. "C'mon, let's wait outside for the Sheriff's car."

They walked out into the hallway and headed for the stairs. At the top, Mary Elizabeth turned to Janis. "Wait, I want his cap; I want to hold it."

Janis squeezed her hand. "Sure. Wait right here and I'll go get it for you."

She returned to the bathroom and removed the red sock cap from Lonzo's head. While she was walking out of the bathroom door, the strangest thing happened. A voice softly called her name; it was almost a whisper. Startled, she turned. There, sitting on the floor near Lonzo's shoulder, was a little black…thing. A creature, like nothing she had ever seen before. It was small, not much bigger than a football-not a monkey, yet similar.

Janis Barr stared at it with disbelieving eyes. It frightened her, and not knowing what else to do, she pulled her weapon. For the second time that night, her hands trembled. The barrel of the gun would not stand still.

The little creature laughed and said to her, "You are warned. Do not help him."

Then it walked out of the room, disappearing into the darkness of the hallway. Janis watched until it was out of sight. Placing the weapon back in its holster, she asked herself, "Help who?"

CHAPTER
THIRTY-FIVE

FOR THE SECOND TIME in just over a week, Clayton Cooper awoke lying in a hospital bed. And just as before, he found himself connected to an IV and heart monitor. His first waking thought was, *Here we go again*.

This time, however, he was not drugged and could think clearly. There were several familiar faces milling around the room: Lemus, Jones, Clendes, Spulder and even Ron. But there was no Nancy. Where was his Lifesaver?

Looking directly at Lemus, he fearfully asked. "Where is she?"

They exchanged glances, then every eye turned to Clay. Lemus moved immediately to his side. "She's not here right now, but she's fine."

Clay grasped his wrist with a strong grip. "You're lying, aren't you."

While prying Clay's hand free, Lemus glanced worriedly at Ron, then back to Clay "No. She will be here in a little bit. She's on an errand."

Lemus turned and ordered Clendes to get the nurse. Lemus turned back to Clay. "Look. You're upset. Try and relax. When the nurse comes, we'll have her give you something."

Clay gritted his teeth. "I don't need anything to relax me, and they are not putting anymore drugs in my body. Now tell me the damn truth. He has her again, doesn't he?" Tears were filling his eyes as despair mounted.

Lemus smoothed out the back of his horseshoe hair, wishing he had a cigarette. "No, it's okay. Everything is under control, I promise."

Ron moved to the opposite side of the bed and placed a hand on Clay's shoulder. "Hey, buddy. Take it easy. She's gone right now, but she will be back. I promise."

Clay turned his head to look at his closest friend. "Not you, too?"

The nurse came through the door and both men stepped away from the bed, not sure to which side she would go. Marching straight to Clay's left, she immediately wrapped fingers around his wrist to check his pulse.

"What's going on here?" She asked the question while looking into each face, in turn, not caring which man answered, just so long one of them gave an explanation.

Before anyone got a word out, Nancy walked in with a cardboard tray holding six coffees, a plastic bowl of creamer, and sugar packets. When she saw Clay awake, she smiled exuberantly. "You're awake, sweetheart." Passing the coffee off to Ron, she went straight to the bed, taking his hand and kissing him lightly. "I was beginning to think you were never going to wake up. You had me worried." Smile remaining, she glanced around the room and teasingly asked, "Did you guys get all the man-talk out of the way before I got back?"

Realizing there was really no problem, the nurse quietly slipped out the door. Ron, looking into the face of his best friend, grinned. "No man-talk, Nancy. Didn't have a chance. Mr. 'I love coming to the hospital' wouldn't shut up about you long enough to talk about anything else."

She looked back to her husband and kissed him once again. "How sweet."

Looking around Nancy's shoulder at Ron and Lemus, Clay mouthed the word in exaggerated silence: "S-O-R-R-Y."

Clay felt like an ass – but he was a happy ass.

CHAPTER THIRTY-SIX

CLAY REMAINED IN THE hospital a day and a half. Late afternoon on the second day a nurse wheelchaired him out to Nancy's car. He was happy to be going home.

The house was heaven. The seventeen sutures in his abdomen pinched as he gingerly lowered himself down on the couch. Nancy covered him with a light throw, propped him up with pillows, kissed his forehead, then handed him the remote.

On the way home, he had pleaded for a good, home-cooked meal of meatloaf, mashed potatoes with gravy, creamed corn, and homemade lemon-meringue pie. The moment he had the TV going, Nancy went into the kitchen to begin the king's feast.

The sound of pots and pans rattling and the smells of cooking warmed Clay's heart. He was sure that feeling, which he classified as near utopia, was heightened by really great pain medication.

Sleep drifted easily into his worry-free awareness. It was a peaceful settling that came slow and ever so softly. Because of the medication, blue-eyed killers, demons, and nighttime monsters from Hell were far removed from his happy, contented mind. He welcomed the sensation of sleep with a gentle smile. The last thing Clay remembered was thanking God for a wife with a smothering maternal instinct.

While cooking, Nancy checked in on her husband three times, and each check found him sleeping like a contented newborn. She was pleased, considering that during the last two weeks he had been through hell--although she was sure she didn't know the half of it. Now he was getting the sleep he so desperately needed, even if he didn't realize it.

Dinner preparation took a total of ninety-eight minutes, including the baking of the lemon-meringue pie. Although noticeably warm from the heat of the oven, the kitchen smelled sinfully delicious. At first Nancy had not been hungry, but now the smells had stimulated her taste buds and she was looking forward to a relaxing dinner in front of the television with her husband.

Checking on him one last time, she debated letting him sleep or walking him to eat. Sleep, she felt, could be had anytime, but a warm, home-cooked meal could not. Therefore, because nourishment was as vital as sleep, she chose to wake him. Kneeling beside his slumbering form, she shook him gently. The medication coupled with near exhaustion had put him into a deep sleep and he was slow to rouse.

Eventually he opened his eyes, and upon realizing what was going on, smiled.

"Hi."

"Hi," Nancy smiled back. "Ready to eat?"

"Yeah."

Nancy set up two TV trays, then helped Clay into a sitting position. "You stay where you are. I'll fix your plate."

While eating, they watched an old rerun of Saturday Night Live. However, Clay laughed very little and only picked at his food. The utopian state was rapidly falling away. Although the medication kept the pain down to a barely noticeable level, his thoughts inevitably drifted to the same thing. Little dark demons and hellish monsters that walked out of open fields.

Perhaps it was the medication that lowered his threshold of mental resistance, but he was feeling more anxious and nervous than peaceful. When Nancy asked what was wrong, he opened up. He set his tray to the side and carefully lay back down.

Nancy rose and helped him, covering him again with the throw. When she returned to her chair, Clay took a deep breath and began. "I'm scared, Baby. I'm scared for you, for me, for the world."

She flashed a reassuring smile, although behind it was confusion. "I understand being scared for me, and you. But the world?"

Clay shook his head and swallowed, searching for words. "Less than a week ago, Nance, I took a trip into Hell. I saw it. I felt it. I cried because of its horror and insanity. I saw a multitude of millions burning as they roamed through flames of fire. They all cried out for help, for mercy, but could find none. A demon with giant wings flew me over them." Clay paused. "I know it all sounds crazy, but I was there."

"You were hypnotized, sweetheart."

He shook his head emphatically. "No! I realize you think I would not be able to know the difference, but I was there. And there is something else."

Nancy was beginning to feel uneasy with the direction of conversation. "Something else?" She wasn't sure she wanted to hear it but asked anyway. "Something else what?"

"There's another side to Hell."

Her brow wrinkled. "Another side?"

"Yes, another part, section, addition. Whatever you want to call it. My guess is it's the place where Satan himself lives, a private residence or whatever."

Nancy frowned. "You have me confused. Hell is Hell. In all my Sunday School days and listening to sermons, I have never heard of a private residence for the Devil."

"I know, me neither."

She settled back in the chair, crossing her legs and interlacing her hands. "So, what was it like?"

A small grin showed at the corners of Clay's mouth. "Do you have to sit like that? I feel like I'm talking to a psychiatrist."

Pulling her hands apart and resting them on the arms of the chair, she grinned back. "Better?"

Clay nodded. He went on to tell of the giant doors and drifting fog. And although it was difficult, he confessed his desire for the woman with dark eyes and alabaster skin, explaining how he burned for her while consumed with lust and greed and power. And finally, he told of the brilliant light, his falling through the mist and the piercing rainbow that had bolted through his heart and brought him to his senses. He explained how she herself had appeared before him and that it had been the Archangel Michael that had come to send him back to her.

He knew it all sounded crazy, yet he trusted his Lifesaver to believe what he was saying. She would not think him crazy. Admittedly, it sounded more "witches and goblins" than truth, like some fabricated story written in the spirit of Halloween, but that had been only half of it. It would be the events that took place the night of the wreck that would require his beloved wife to believe by faith.

As he told of the countless small dark demons clambering over the wreckage, he described the frightening beast that had chased him into the field. He could see her face growing sober, uneasiness and fear spreading across her face.

He had not wanted to tell her everything because he knew it would frighten her, but now there was no choice. It had become a fight they must face together. Both were now enemies of the netherworld, hunted prey to the hideous things that crawled out of its darkness and haunted the world in which they lived.

Up to this point, Clay's adversaries had always been speeders, thieves, rapists, and drug pushers. But all, regardless of their records, were flesh and blood and bone, perpetrators he knew how to handle. Now, however, a new enemy had surfaced, one he knew little, if anything, about-one capable of stealing far more than gold and silver. These perpetrators were capable of stealing the soul.

Inside her head, Nancy agonized over the things Clay had told her, trying to make sense of it all. On the sixth day following their conversation, she invited Pastor Phillip Hart to supper. She did not consult Clay-something she'd never done before. While neither now attended church on a regular Sunday morning basis, Hart had been their Pastor while growing up.

Now retired, in his mid-sixties, Hart remained a well-loved and respected Clergyman, imbued with the belief that problems, worldly or spiritual, needed to be faced head on, that there was always a solution. Who better to talk with, she reasoned, than Pastor Phillip Hart? A no-nonsense, frontal attack was the approach she and Clay needed to take against this…unexplainable malevolence.

CHAPTER
THIRTY-SEVEN

QUINTEN EARLHUST CHRISTENSON, ALIAS Blue Eyes Killer, stepped out of the small three-room château and onto the attached wrought-iron balcony. Standing draped in the silvery essence of a magnificently full moon, he stared awestruck into the heavens.

An incalculable number of stars, gleaming sharply amid their abysmal backdrop, drew his spirit to them, and he pictured himself sailing like Superman around planets and stars and bright flaring suns, gliding from galaxy to galaxy and diving breathlessly into swirling black holes. He was convinced such a feat would be possible in the world to which he waited anxiously to go, but for now he was doing what he could to make the best of the one in which he was prisoner.

Behind him, inside his tiny, rented accommodations, naked upon the bed, lay the blond beauty that later, at least temporarily, would help lift his spirits. Breathing deeply, he took in the delicious smells drifting up to his wrought-iron perch. Few places could match the decadent beauty of a moonlit New Orleans night. He had been coming to the French Quarter for a very long time, and it still held a certain mystique.

Below, noisy crowds pushed their way down Bourbon Street with loud, boisterous anticipation, their minds filled with the desire to make memories, drinking themselves into oblivion and secretly harboring that dream of dreams, that want of wants, that hope of hopes: connecting with that perfect someone and experiencing the unforgettable, once-in-a-lifetime, mind-blowing, incredible, one-night stand.

Quinten smiled as he watched them. The human race was so spurious. No matter what their faces and actions said, only four things really meant anything to them: God, money, power, and sex.

No, actually only three, he thought; money was power in itself. Either way, the crowd below had not come to New Orleans looking for money…or God.

Laughter and singing, mingled with the endless flow of Cajun music, drifted through the air freely. Below him, every walk of life, every nationality, people of every color, every creed, Christian and sinner alike, waded through the crowded street of pressed bodies, all adorned in colorful outfits fitting for an unforgettable night of free-spiriting.

The ice in the glass of straight Bacardi jingled as he raised it to his lips and sipped. Occasionally he would toast to the whistles and cheers of those below who happened to look up and spot his totally naked form watching them move through the jammed streets below.

He admitted to being a people-watcher. Humans had always fascinated him, their bodies and minds coming in an array of countless shapes, sizes and intellectual levels, tall and short, fat and thin, blue blood and trailer trash. The better lot of them were followers, flesh-and-blood human sheep, quick to join the crowds even when they didn't understand why. However, to him, the most fascinating human trait of all was their individualized reaction to fear.

The street below was a cacophony of sound. Frequent bursts of firecrackers exploded like machine gun fire. Blues music competed with country and hundreds of private conversations jumbled into one unrecognizable language, and parties of drunk singer's incapable of harmony obnoxiously tried to out sound them all.

Quinten Earlhurst Christenson, killer extraordinaire, smiled at it all. He then turned and entered back into the chateau. The blond on the bed, propped up with pillows, smiled as best she could. The cocaine surging through her body had put her in a world of perfection, a place of total compliance and surrender.

Moving to where she lay, he sat on the edge of the bed and lifted his wallet from the nightstand. He removed a small piece of paper from it, then picked up the phone and dialed the number scribbled across its face. While the phone was ringing, he half turned to the woman and ran his hand slowly up her thigh to her dark mound, inserting a finger into the warm-semi wetness. She stared at him with a blank expression. The narcotic high was peaking.

At the other end of the phone, someone picked up. "Hello."

Turning, Quinten refocused on his call.

"Yes, is this Michelle Parks?"

"Yes, it is."

"My name is Doctor Davidson. I am with Raven View Memorial Medical Center in New Orleans, Louisiana. I have some terrible news. Your husband's father, Sean Parks, has had a major myocardial infarction, a heart attack. I'm afraid it's gravely serious. His wife asked if I would call. She is quite upset and is by his side as we speak. She asked that you come right away. And, although awkward, when you get in, she would like for you to stop by the house and pick up the large brown envelope lying on the kitchen table before coming to the hospital. I am at a loss as to what it is. But in any event, I suggest you come as soon as possible."

Michelle nodded. "Of course. We will be there by tomorrow afternoon. Thank you, Doctor." She hung up, and Quinten followed suit.

Smiling, he rose from the bed and refreshed his Bacardi glass. After taking a sip, he returned to the bed and sat once again on the edge. Staring at the naked woman, he took another swallow, then removed an ice cube from the glass. Slowly, he ran it around her left nipple. It began to stiffen, so he dipped his finger in the glass and spread the golden liquid over the entire areola, then leaned in and began licking the fluid with his tongue. She smiled for him.

The cocaine high was diminishing but she still felt mellow. Stretching her arm, she took him into her hand and stroked while smiling into his eyes. Slowly he grew beneath her grip and delighted in the feel of her gentle tugging. He knew she would be pleased as well, the moment the surging blood had finished rushing into the huge, cavernous veins and he stood thick and long before her.

Moving his glass to the cleavage of her breasts, he pressed its coldness to her chest, and she gasped delightfully. Then he playfully poured the contents, ice, and all, down the front of her. She yelled at the sudden shock, then smiled as the liquid raced between her globes like a tiny stream amid two mountain peaks, spreading across her stomach and into the bikini-shaved patch of pubic hair.

Setting the empty glass on the bedside table, Quinten rose and moved to the foot of the bed. Gripping her ankles, he playfully pulled her free of the pillows and onto her back, throwing her legs over his shoulders. Hungrily, his face moved to her wet mound. Her eyes closed and she moaned, surrendering to the tingling wetness of his tongue. Wildly it danced, driving her to the edge, sending her closer and closer to that point of no return.

Wrapped warmly within a rocketing crescendo of overwhelming pleasure, she pushed his head forcefully against her sex, rhythmically rocking her hips. Her eyes were still closed when she cried out, as wave after wave of delicious sensation erupted in her brain. Face aglow, she smiled, lost to a God-given pleasure far greater than the poison of cocaine.

CHAPTER THIRTY-EIGHT

PASTOR HART ARRIVED EARLY. Time had been set for seven, but he actually arrived at 6:38. Clay answered the door, having just gotten over a short bit of irritation with Nancy. While he actually agreed with the idea of talking to a religious figure, he had been put out by the fact she had not consulted him prior to the invitation. Still, it was okay; truthfully; he felt something positive was going to come out of the visit.

At the door, Hart smiled warmly and stuck out his hand. "Evening, Clay. I apologize for being early."

Clay returned the smile, grasping his hand. "No problem, Pastor. Come in."

Nancy came out of the kitchen and greeted him just as Clay closed the door. "Hello," she said as she approached, offering her hand as well.

His smile widened. "Hi to you." Gently taking her hand, he asked, "Is that spaghetti sauce I smell?"

"Yes. I hope it's okay."

"Okay? Absolutely. I think I'm salivating already. The two things I love most in this world are Jesus and spaghetti; always in that order, I might add, although it sure smells like you could give the Savior a run for his money."

Nancy grinned warmly at his humor, relieved her culinary choice had met with his approval.

Glancing from her to Clay, Hart said, "I haven't seen you two in church in, oh, what has it been, ten years?"

Clay grimaced, feeling embarrassed. "A little over eleven, actually."

Hart made a face. "Wow! That long? I guess it's a good thing we're not Catholic-your confession would require an intermission."

Clay and Nancy looked at one another, unsure how to respond. Hart smiled.

"Just kidding." He paused a moment, then added, "So how have you two been?"

"Fine," Clay told him, motioning to the couch.

"Thanks," Hart told him appreciatively, while sitting down.

Nancy excused herself and returned to the kitchen.

Resting his arm on the couch end, the pastor said, "I read about your wreck, Clay. According to the paper, you're lucky to be alive."

Clay nodded. "It's true. I am."

"So how are you doing now?"

"Great. Sutures come out tomorrow. Or at least they are supposed to."

"Well, it appears you fared pretty well. I don't see any missing pieces."

"No, sir. Mostly cuts and bruises, and they healed up really quick."

"It appears God was looking after you."

Clay nodded. "Pastor Hart, you don't know the half of it."

Hart's expression became inquisitive. "Really?"

"Yes. In fact, after dinner, Nance and I would like to talk to you about a religious concern, if that's okay."

Hart gave him a nod. "Absolutely. Nancy had mentioned that when she called. And just in case you don't know, religion happens to be my favorite subject."

Suddenly, Clay realized he had forgotten to ask the pastor if he'd wanted anything. "I'm sorry, Pastor, would you like something to drink?"

"Yes, that would be nice." He smiled appreciatively. "What do you have?"

Clay counted on his fingers. "Coffee, Coke, Diet Coke, tea or red wine. And of course, good old-fashioned water."

"Coffee, please."

"Cream and sugar?"

"No, black is fine."

Clay excused himself and went to the kitchen. Nancy had just finished setting the table and was placing the food on the table. "We'll be eating in about five minutes, sweetheart."

"Great," he told her. "I'm starved."

"Imagine that" She quipped.

By the time he returned with the two cups of coffee, one for himself as well, he barely had time to sit down before Nancy called them to eat.

"Well, that conversation was quick," Clay apologized.

During dinner they ate and sipped red wine, discussing trivial things. Clay talked of his wreck and how he'd been pinned inside, and also about what had been appearing in the paper concerning his involvement as town Marshall.

Then, the subject came around to Pastor Hart's retirement. "Well, it's been nearly five years," he began. "I still preach occasionally as a guest speaker, but mostly I travel. Since my wife's passing, two years ago, I have been trying my hand at writing. I've nearly completed a book I'm calling *Know your Enemy and Live.*

"Sounds interesting," Clay told him, taking a sip of wine.

"Well, truthfully, it has been met with more opposition than encouragement."

"You're kidding. Why?" Nancy asked.

Hart looked at her.

"Well," he smiled briefly, "I like to think it's not because of writing ability, or perhaps I should say inability. The book actually focuses on understanding how the Devil works within the framework of our lives. Unfortunately, a large portion of the pastoral community feels it's an inappropriate subject for the masses. They like to think encouraging prayer alone is sufficient."

Nancy took a drink of wine, her interest piqued. "Why do you think prayer alone isn't sufficient?"

"Yeah, really," Clay added. "Prayer is the center of all religions, isn't it?"

"Well, yes, it is. It's our direct line to God, regardless of which faith you believe. But you have to know how to pray, when to pray, and what to pray for. And your prayers must be effective, more than just words. They have to be felt if you know what I mean."

He took a sip of wine, continuing. "Satan is the master of distraction and illusion, of knowing how to make the flesh weaker than the spirit is strong. And it works every time for him unless you're familiar with his tactics. Wars are won by knowing your enemy: how he thinks, what makes him tick. You have to be knowledgeable enough to anticipate his next move. Winning against the Devil is no different. In World War II, had we just sat home, closed our eyes, and prayed Hitler would go away, we would be a communist nation today. Fortunately, while he was dominating the world, there were staff officers over here studying him, his likes, his dislikes, his habits, and hangouts, his past-his personal demons, if you will. That, coupled with prayer, was why we won the war."

Clay refilled his wine glass, offering the same to Pastor Hart. Following the Pastor's appreciative nod, Clay refilled his glass as well. Nancy declined.

"I take it, Pastor Hart," Clay said, setting the bottle down, "that you believe in demons?"

"Yes, of course."

"If I may," Clay asked thoughtfully, "what exactly do they look like?"

Hart stared at Clay a moment, then told him. "They cover a broad spectrum, from horribly frightful to incredibly beautiful."

"Do they have horns and wings and tails and scales and all that?"

"Some do. Some do not. Some look just like us."

"Human, you mean?"

"Oh, yes. Hebrews 13:2 tells us, 'Do not forget to entertain strangers, for by so doing some people have entertained angels without knowing it.' Well, just as God's angels can take on human form, so can Satan's."

Clay nodded, drawn to the conversation. "You mean we can be talking to someone and all that time they can actually be an angel from Heaven or a demon from Hell, and we won't even know it?"

"Yes, but don't get paranoid. It's rare they transform into human form."

Clay's thoughts flashed to Blue Eyes and then he asked, "What about demon possession?"

"It does exist, yes," Hart replied.

"What's it like? I mean, are all crazy people possessed?"

Pastor Hart grinned, "No, of course not."

"Then how do you tell the difference?"

"Well, the demon-possessed are usually very violent, lewd, masochistic, and sacrilegious. To what extent depends on how many demons dwell within the possessed person. Some demons are more wicked than others."

"How many are usually in there?"

"It varies. Can be one, can be thousands."

"No shit!" Clay said it without thinking, then flushed slightly. "Sorry' Pastor."

Hart grinned again.

Clay took a deep breath, anxious. "Have you heard of a demon named Belial?"

Pastor Hart showed surprise. "Yes. How did you come to know of him? He is rarely spoken of."

Feeling a calming trust in Hart, Clay took a sip from his wine glass and began telling him everything, beginning with the night they had found the parchment with both his and Belial's name on it, continuing clear up to the creature that had chased his truck. He also retold the things Lemus had said concerning Belial.

Pastor Hart nodded in agreement. "All that agent Lemus told you is true. Belial is very powerful and, as mentioned, he supposedly serves as second-in-command, just under Lucifer himself. It's imperative you understand the capabilities of demons. Belial, and others like him, can masquerade as angels of light, perform what appear to be wonderful miracles, and quote scripture with the sweetest of tongues."

"Can they cause such things as statues to cry or bleed, or turn water the color of blood?"

"They can create these *stigmatas* and more. They can make you think they are a person of God, so you will follow them anywhere. But their hidden agenda is always to take souls. There have been several examples in the past, supposed pastors who lead their gathering in the name of God but in the end convince them, women, and children alike, to commit mass suicide. And suicide is a definite no-no in the Lord's eyes."

Clay took another sip. "Can a demon physically harm you? Can he rip out your heart or bite a big chunk out of your throat? Like you see in the movies?"

Nancy looked disgustingly at her husband. "Clay!"

Pastor Hart smiled, but it was short-lived. "They could if God allowed it. Demons are very frightened of our Lord Jesus Christ and God the Father. Bottom line, he holds the reins over them."

"If that's the case, then why does all the bad crap happen?"

Hart nodded, respectful of Clay's inquisitiveness. "You know, you really must read my book when it comes out. You see, a demon causing you harm and a demon-possessed person causing you harm are two separate things."

"How so?"

"Take the story of Job, for example. Satan was not allowed to do anything physical to Job without first going to God for permission. As you remember, Job was a man of God. A demon-possessed person is quite different. Most theologians agree that the Holy Spirit and a demon cannot dwell in the same place at the same time. Hence, if someone is demon-possessed, how can they be of God?"

"So," Clay injected, "so long as you believe in God, you're safe?"

"Absolutely not."

"No?" Clay exclaimed.

"No, I'm afraid not. In James 2:19 we're told, 'You believe that there is one God. Good! Even the demons believe that-and shudder.' Merely believing that God exists is not enough. Asking him into your life, into your heart, is the key. You remember from your Sunday School lessons? Once you ask Jesus for help, to come into your life, the Holy Spirit will come into you and find a place in your heart and dwell there. After that, Satan is locked out."

Pastor Hart paused, then went on. "Someone demon-possessed has allowed, that demon or demons to come into him or her and take possession. The demons, therefore, control them. And because of that, the demons can command the person they control to hurt you."

"So are atheists' demon-possessed?"

Hart's smile widened and he shook his head teasingly. "You know, it's because of people like you pastors preach a sermon on Sundays and don't offer question and answer periods afterward. Atheists can be possessed, yes. But because they do not believe in God, Satan pretty much leaves them alone, doesn't have to possess them. But bottom line is they can be demon possessed, yes."

"I know I'm driving you crazy, but..."

Hart shook his head, still smiling. "No, you're not. Please, keep asking. "

Only two more questions, and I promise I will quit. If Satan answers to God, then why does all the bad crap happen to innocent people? Why doesn't God stop it, prevent it?"

Pastor Hart looked down at his wine glass meditatively, stared at it a few seconds, then looked back up to Clay. "In a nutshell-and I want you to think on this one-*bad crap happens because God allows us to do it to ourselves.*"

Clay reflected on it for a short time, then nodded thoughtfully. Then he said, "One more question."

Pastor Hart took a sip of wine. "Shoot."

"How do I fight a demon?"

CHAPTER
THIRTY-NINE

MICHELLE PARKS CALLED HER husband the moment she hung up from her conversation with the person she believed to be Doctor Davidson. Ron had been at work, and upon receiving the news, immediately obtained emergency leave.

At home now, they packed hastily. The soonest flight out of Indianapolis was at mid-morning, and O'Hare had turned out to be no better in timing. It was decided to leave the children with Michelle's parents and drive. The agreement was that should the worst happen, her parents would come down then and bring both children.

Driving through the night, Ron estimated that with the hassle of baggage checks, lines, layovers, car rental and the other headaches a flight usually entailed, driving to New Orleans became the logical choice. In addition, he liked the idea of traveling with a weapon, something he could not do while flying.

Ron loved his dad dearly. Their relationship had always been closer than a lot of other fathers and sons he knew, so the news had devastated him. His father had been his original hero, a Lafayette police officer. It had been because of him that he had chosen to become an Indiana State Trooper.

Less than a year had passed since his parents had relocated to New Orleans, looking forward to the warmer climate. Saying goodbye had been traumatic enough; the thought of losing his father forever was almost too much to bear. As he packed, Ron's hands trembled slightly. Although he hid his emotion, in his heart he was crying.

Outside the sky was showing signs of nightfall, and Ron was glad. Being a policeman, he knew that late at night there would be fewer officers on the road as well as pedestrian traffic, and that would make for better time.

It was 7:00 when he finished placing the last suitcase in the van. After kissing the kids and bidding farewell to Michelle's parents, they began the long trip. Ron took the wheel. If he grew tired during the night, he would turn the driving over to Michelle, but he didn't anticipate that happening. The pain and dread of what lay ahead, of seeing his father dying, was enough to prevent any chance of sleep. And if that were not enough, his thoughts would be endlessly replaying memories.

CHAPTER FORTY

PASTOR HART, CLAY, AND Nancy finished eating, switched from wine to coffee, and sat in the living room with Clay on the sofa beside Nancy and Pastor Hart in a comfortable recliner. Of course, out of respect he did not recline, although he would have liked to. The conversation was a continuation of Clay's plaguing question about how to fight demons.

Pastor Hart took a sip from his cup, giving thought to the night's most important question. While he did not wish to *preach* to the young couple, reading from the Word was unavoidable. He realized the grave importance of explaining things precisely and clearly.

With permission, he excused himself, and walked out to his car to retrieve his Bible. While Clay and Nancy did not wish to be preached at, they agreed the subject had to be breached regardless of approach. Given its importance they would agree to whatever the situation warranted.

When he returned, Pastor Hart had two Bibles in his possession. Sitting back down in his chair, he placed a Bible on the chair beside him and held the other. Then he pulled a pair of reading glasses from his pocket and placed them low on his nose. Clay and Nancy watched as he thumbed through the Bible, located the spot for which he searched, then paused.

Glancing over the rim of his glasses, he noted their worried faces piqued with eagerness for information. Their expressions did not surprise him, though. After being told of Clay's skirmish in Hell and frightful encounter with demons the night of the wreck, he greatly respected their anxiety, and secretly feared for their safety.

Settling back in his chair, he closed his Bible for a moment but held his spot with a finger between the pages. Clay and Nancy waited, not knowing what to expect. Staring at them, Pastor Hart pressed his lips together tightly. "How old are you, Clay?"

"Thirty-two."

"And you, Nancy?"

She glanced at Clay, then back. "Twenty-eight."

"So, combining the years," Hart said, "as a couple, that makes you, sixty. Sixty years of combined wisdom, knowledge, and understanding how things work in life. And I would be willing to bet you both agree with the old adage 'two heads are better than one.' Not to mention your particular background, Clay. Through education, training, and experience, you have obtained superior insight into human behavior."

Clay nodded, and Hart went on. "Together, you have sixty years of total experience in your arsenal against the endless fight we face in life: against thieves, murderers, rapists, scam artists, politicians with hidden agendas, and on and on and on. It often takes everything we have to remain afloat and safe, and still sometimes we lose. You agree?"

Together they nodded. Hart smiled briefly and continued. "On a scale of one to ten, ten being perfect, how would you two rate yourselves in the ability to cope, to remain on top, paying bills, avoiding scams, possessing the things in life you want?"

Clay glanced at Nancy. Neither were quite sure where all this was leading. Facing Pastor Hart, Clay said, "Probably a six."

"Possibly a seven or eight," Nancy added, insuring she did not come across as arrogant.

Hart's smile widened. "And I'm proud of you two for it. As I look around, I would rate you the same. But let me tell you, even with your high rating and obvious proof of surviving in the game of life, you are no match against the Devil. Surviving in this world is only a small part of the whole picture-an almost insignificant part, actually. Let me read you something. Listen to this." He reopened his Bible and adjusted his head to position his lenses for focus.

"Ephesians six, verse twelve: For *we wrestle not*

against flesh and blood, but against principalities,

against powers, against the rulers of darkness of

this world, against spiritual wickedness in high places."

Hart looked up. Both Clay and Nancy were staring at him, pondering with uncertainty. From the pulpit he had seen the same expression many times on a sea of faces. Closing the Bible and picking up the other one, told them, "Allow me to re-read from another text, a paraphrased version."

Once again, he flipped the pages and found his spot. Glancing at them again he said, "This will clarify what I just read." He spoke without looking up.

"Same verse. 'For *we are not fighting against people*

made of flesh and blood, but against persons without bodies —

the evil rulers of the unseen world, those mighty satanic

beings and great evil princes of darkness who rule this world;

and against huge numbers of wicked spirits in the spirit world.'"

When he glanced up this time, Nancy was waiting. "I'm confused about a couple of things, Pastor Hart. A second ago you said our fight was against rapists and thieves and crooked politicians. Plus, I grew up believing it was God who made the world and owned it, not demons."

Hart nodded. "You're correct in both cases. It is those people we fight against, the rapists, murderers and so on. People of flesh and blood, human beings. And it is God who owns the world. He owns the universe, everything that exists. You both know the simple crux of life, good versus evil. In this life, this plane, not the spiritual world but the flesh and blood world in which we live, you have three-how shall I word it? -states, or conditions. First, you're a Christian, born again into the spirit. That is, you've asked Jesus to come into your life and your heart. And as we spoke earlier, the moment you do that, the Holy Spirit immediately dwells within us, locking out the possibility of demonic possession."

Hart paused a second to allow them time to visualize that, then went on. "The other two conditions are of a demon nature. One is demon possession, and the other is demon oppression. In demon possession, as you know, a person is literally possessed; their bodies actually host the evil monsters. In oppression, though, demons are on the outside, mentally pushing and shoving and tempting the victim relentlessly, never leaving him alone. That is, until those demons are driven away-or out, depending on the given scenario."

"So," Nancy said, "what you're saying, or at least what I think you're saying, is that demons are either possessing or oppressing those thieves, murderers, rapists and whatever?"

"In short, yes," Pastor Hart agreed. "You see, if God is not strong in your heart, and I didn't say way of life, although it is better if you do live as perfect a Christian life as possible. If He, God, is strong in your thinking and actions and decision-making, then the possibility of a harmful demon oppression is unlikely."

Clay cut in immediately. "I understand it now! Earlier this evening, when you said, 'We do it to ourselves,' by that you meant because of all the dishonesty, and hate and selfishness caused by demon possession or oppression, our decisions, especially by those with influence over others, are often harmful and create a negative impact on individuals or our society as a whole."

Pastor Hart smiled. "Exactly. Negative impact one on one. On families, on the job, on states, countries...even the world." He paused, then added, "You know, you two are getting a month's worth of sermons in one setting." His smile widened and he looked at Nancy. "But that spaghetti was worth it." She grinned back, and he continued. "Not wanting to get away from the subject, let me add, unlike the angels, God made us in his image. He did not wish for us to be robots of bone and flesh, but rather a creation of self-willed people who love him because we choose to do so. Just as it is important for us to want our children to love and appreciate us as parents, he too lives for the joy of his children loving him, and we are all his children. To put it simply, that is why He allows Satan to be the ruler of this world. Without that, there would be no choice and our love for God would cease being the beautiful, free thing that it is, and would become little more than an empty and shallow penance. And there is nothing as beautiful and precious in this world as true and honest love."

Clay looked at Nancy and gave her a warm smile. Then, looking back to Pastor Hart, he asked, "So now we know why demons are here, how they operate, and why the world is in such turmoil. But how do I fight the damn things?"

Sighing, Hart put down the Bible he held and picked up the other one again, opening it once more to the book of Ephesians.

Following a quick glance over the rim of his glasses, he began to read:

"Ephesians six, verses thirteen through eighteen. 'Wherefore take unto you the whole Armour of God, that ye may be able to withstand in the evil day, and having done all, to stand. Stand therefore, having your loins girt about with truth, and having on the breastplate of righteousness; and your feet shod with the preparation of the gospel of peace; above all, taking the shield of faith, wherewith ye shall be able to quench all the fiery darts of the wicked. And take the helmet of salvation, and the sword of the Spirit, which is the word of God, praying always with all prayer and supplication in the Spirit and watching thereunto with all perseverance and supplication for all saints."

Not looking up, Hart closed the Bible, placed it beside him and picked up the paraphrased version. "Now listen closely to the interpretation in paraphrase."

"Again, verses thirteen through eighteen: 'So use every piece of God's armor to resist the enemy whenever he attacks, and when it is all over, you will still be standing up. But to do this, you will need the strong belt of truth and the breastplate of God's approval. Wear shoes that are able to speed you on as you preach the Good News of peace with God. In every battle you will need faith as your shield to stop the fiery arrows aimed at you by Satan. And you will need the helmet of salvation and the sword of the Spirit-which is the Word of God.

Pray all the time. Ask God for anything in line with the Holy Spirit's wishes.

Plead with him, reminding him of your needs, and keep praying earnestly for all Christians everywhere.'"

Closing the book, Hart puffed out his cheeks, then exhaled and looked up.

"Well, what do you think?"

Clay and Nancy looked at one another, each wondering how much the other understood. Then they both turned to Pastor Hart. "I think we've got a pretty good grip, but can you put all that in a nutshell for us?" Clay asked.

Hart bobbed his head. "You bet I can. Together, you two have sixty years of experience dealing with life. You've learned a lot, and you make a hard-to-beat team when your heads are together. But, bottom line, Satan has been around a whole lot longer than you two, literally thousands of years. He has learned a lot, too, much more than you guys have. Imagine two tiny ants side by side up on their hind legs straining to push over the Empire State Building-well, that would be a fair comparison of you two trying to stand against Satan and his demons all by yourselves."

"So," Nancy said, feeling a sense of hopelessness, "you're telling us that we-and not just Clay and I, but the world in general-don't have a chance against Satan?"

"By yourselves as flesh and blood, no. But as flesh and blood with God, yes. As the scriptures just told us, so long as you wear the armor and pray, you can be the victor. But you must believe in God, have faith, and remember that your strength must come from the Lord's power within you. Demons must obey God. If you have faith and God is within you, then they must do as ordered. But remember, the quantity and quality of faith varies from person to person. That is why there are only a few out of millions who possess the capability of driving out demons from those possessed. You've got to have faith and you've got to trust. Sometimes that is quite difficult, especially in the face of adversity."

Hart closed his Bible and let it rest on his lap. "I promised myself I would not sit here and preach at you tonight. But I will tell you that everything hinges on faith and trust. Without faith you cannot trust. Without trust you cannot have faith. If you will allow me to read one more thing, I promise I will stop my preaching."

Clay and Nancy said it at the exact same time. "No, go ahead." The three smiled and Pastor Hart was secretly pleased they were eager for more.

Not bothering to switch Bibles this time, he opened the paraphrased version to the book of Matthew. One last time he glanced over the rim of his glasses. "I'm reading from the book of Matthew, chapter seventeen, verses fourteen through twenty-one. It will give you a good idea of the paramount importance of having faith."

His eyes lowered and he began reading.

"When they arrived at the bottom of the hill, a huge crowd was waiting for them.

A man came and knelt before Jesus and said, 'Sir, have mercy on my son, for he is mentally deranged, and in great trouble, for he often falls into the fire or into the water: so, I brought him to your disciples, but they couldn't cure him.' Jesus replied, 'Oh, you stubborn, faithless people! How long shall I bear with you?

Bring him here to me.' Then Jesus rebuked the demon in the boy, and it left him, and from that moment the boy was well. Afterwards the disciples asked Jesus privately, 'Why couldn't we cast that demon out?' 'Because of your little faith,' Jesus told them. 'For if you had faith even as small as a tiny mustard seed you could say to this mountain, 'Move!' and it would go far away. Nothing would be impossible. But this kind of demon won't leave unless you have prayed and gone without food'."

Hart closed the Bible then and pulled off his glasses. After stuffing them in his pocket he sat back and took a sip of coffee. The liquid had lost its warmth, and he made a face.

"That's turned cold, hasn't it?" Nancy asked.

He nodded. "I'm afraid so."

Rising from the couch, she went into the kitchen and returned with the coffee pot. Following the refill of everyone's cup, she took it back to the kitchen then returned and sat once again beside her husband.

"So, faith," Clay remarked the moment she was seated, "is like the nuclear weapon of Christianity?"

Pastor Hart took a small sip of the fresh hot coffee. 'Without it, Clay, demons will drag you screaming into Hell."

CHAPTER FORTY-ONE

SEAN PARK'S HOUSE ON Mullander Lane looked solemn when Michelle and Ron pulled onto the brick drive at exactly two minutes past noon. Shifting the teal green KIA van into park, Ron sat in silence, staring. He cursed fate's injustice and pressed his lips tightly to keep from shouting his anger.

Shutting off the engine, he glanced at his wife. "I'll go get it, Mic. You can wait here."

Reaching over, Michelle squeezed his hand. "No, I'll go in with you." He flashed a grateful smile, and they exited the van.

Holding hands, they walked to the front porch and up the cement steps. Ron removed a key from beneath one of the numerous flowerpots lining the stone porch-rail, turned, and paused, then walked to the door and inserted the key. When he opened the door, it squeaked with a cry of remorse; Ron's eyes grew wet. Even the old house shared his pain.

Inside, the empty place lay steeped in gray, striped shadows. The curtains were drawn, and the blinds were closed. The only light was that which filtered through the curtain material and the narrow slits between the blinds.

They crossed the shadowy living room past the new 52-inch TV, purchased primarily for Saturday afternoon football, or at least that had been the ploy his crafty mom had used to convince his dad to buy it. Ron smiled but it lasted only a second; depression quickly set in again.

They entered into the dining room and made their way across the highly polished hardwood floor, although for the most part deep shadows hid its gloss. They then passed through a wide-open archway and into the kitchen.

To their bewilderment, the table held only a round tray containing a half-filled napkin holder and a matching salt and pepper shaker. There was no envelope. Ron turned to Michelle. "Are you sure he said the kitchen?"

"Yes, very sure."

"Maybe he meant the dining room table."

Michelle nodded in agreement.

Exiting the kitchen, they returned to the dining room, and that's when Ron saw them. The sight of it brought him to a stop abrupt enough to cause Michelle to run into him. At first, she looked up at her husband, stunned and feeling foolish. Then she saw them, too, and exclaimed aloud, "Oh my dear God!"

Ron had missed their presence the first trip through. Both chairs had been placed close to the entranceway wall and would have been difficult to spot unless one was intentionally looking for them, especially since they sat steeped within the dark interior shadows.

His mom and dad were sitting side by side, bound and gagged. Standing behind them was a tall man with a pistol in each hand, the barrel of one pressed against his father's head, and the other his mother's. The stranger smiled and his teeth gleamed dimly in the gloomy diffuseness. "Surprise."

Surprised indeed was Ron Parks. He stood, momentarily confused. He glanced at his wife questioningly. But her expression told that she was at a loss as well.

Turning back to the gunman, four things flashed in the fast-whirling mind of Ron Parks. First, he wondered who this stranger was. Second, why was he holding a gun to his Mom and Dad's head? Third, why was his father here at home and not lying on his deathbed at the hospital? And lastly, Ron wondered, how could he get to the gunman safely to disarm him?

Whoever this guy was, he ordered Michelle to switch on the light. When she did, the room came alive, and Ron got a good look at the perpetrator.

He was six-two or three, dressed in a light blue short-sleeved shirt, faded blue jeans and white Boat Dockers with no socks. Blond hair fell to his shoulders and a pair of incredibly rich, blue eyes stared out from a perfectly square jawed face portraying trust and kindness. However, Ron knew better. Now that he had a good visual, it was clear the man was agent Lemus's Blue Eyes Killer.

Removing the gun pointed to the head of Mrs. Parks, the killer stuck it beneath his armpit and untied both gags. A warm smile came to his face. "There, now you can all talk."

But instead of conversation, there was an awkward silence as everyone stared, overwhelmed by what was happening, each trying to make sense of it.

After a moment, Blue Eyes shook his head and ended the quietness between them. "Look, not everyone in this room will be around to share in conversation by the time night arrives, so I suggest you talk while the opportunity remains."

Realizing by years of *savoir faire* that this madman meant what he said, Sean Parks broke the hush, hoping to keep him calm until an opportunity to disarm him arose. "Good to see you, son. You're looking beautiful, Michelle."

"Good to see you too, Dad," Ron said. Michelle tried to speak but couldn't. Instead, she flashed a forced smile as tears blurred her vision.

Looking at his mother, Ron asked, "How are you doing, Mom?"

"Doing okay, Ronnie. We're so sorry about this."

"That's alright. None of us expected it. No one had any idea."

Ron, like his father, understood the gravity of it all, even more so. He knew of the calculated coldness this madman was capable of. He also easily realized that if something was not done, death would come to one or all of them by nightfall.

Looking to the killer, Ron spoke calmly. "I know why you're here. And you know Clay Cooper is a friend. I'll tell you what. Let me give him a call, convince him to come down, to kill you just as you want. He will do it for me, guaranteed, especially if it means saving my wife and parents."

Blue Eyes stared at him, seemingly interested in his offer.

"I promise you," Ron continued, "he will come and not tell a soul if asked. Once it's done, and you're dead and happy and we're alive and happy, there will be no more problems. There is no need to harm any of us."

Ron's dad sat quiet in his chair, trying to make sense of the conversation. Ron had not talked to his father about the Blue Eyes Killer at all, so his father remained in the dark.

"Look," Ron said, "I have a cell phone right here on my belt. Let me get it out and call him."

Blue Eyes stared into Ron's eyes a long while, finally nodding. "Okay, get him on the phone."

Pulling his cellular from its case, Ron quickly dialed. At the other end, the phone rang and rang and rang. On the fourth ring, the answering machine kicked on, but just as it did, Clay picked up the receiver. There was a loud squealing while he disarmed the recorder. "Hello."

Ron sighed thankfully to himself. "Hey, it's me."

"Yeah. What's up?"

"I've got a problem, buddy."

"What do you need?"

"I'm in New Orleans."

"You didn't say anything about taking a vacation."

"I know. That's not why I'm here."

"What's wrong?"

"I'm at my parents'."

"They, okay?"

"They have a guest. Someone you know only too well."

There was a long pause before Clay answered. "Tell me...damn it. Tell me it's not him."

"Afraid so. He's going to kill us if you do not come down and finish what he wants you to do."

Blue Eyes interrupted. "Please slide the phone to me, Officer Parks. I would like very much to talk with Marshall Cooper myself." Ron started to take the phone to him, and Blue Eyes stopped him.

"No, please stay where you are and slide it across the floor to me."

Bending, Ron set it on the floor and booted it with his foot. It glided easily across the polished floor, ending up beneath his mother's chair. Removing the pistol from beneath his arm, the killer stuck it in his belt then squatted to pick up the phone. Standing back upright, he spoke into it. "Mr. Cooper, it's nice talking to you again. Here is the deal. This must all be coordinated quickly, so listen closely. I know Bob still has your phone tapped and will be dispatching the New Orleans Police to this address. You have a cellular at your end, I know. In five minutes, go outside and call me back on this phone. I'm sure you have the number, since Officer Parks happens to be your best friend. Trust me, do not call me a second late, and make sure you use the cellular. Now listen closely."

Blue Eyes removed the phone from his ear and extended it out toward Ron. Then, he lifted the gun from Ron's father's head, pointing it at Ron and pulling the trigger. He then moved it to Michelle and fired again. Both of the little feathered darts struck them high in the chest, Ron just below and an inch to the left of his neck, and Michelle slightly above her left breast. Both felt the tranquilizing agent begin to work immediately.

Michelle was first to drop to her knees. Ron quickly followed, his head spinning dizzily. Blues Eyes spoke loudly so Ron's fast-fading consciousness would make note, as well as to allow Clay to hear what was being said through the cellular. "Officer Parks, just so your emergency leave is not wasted, this is for you." Blue Eyes pulled a navy-blue straight razor from his pocket and opened it. He brushed his thumb against the blade and playfully said, "Oh, my blade, she is a sharp one." Then he pulled Sean Parks' head back and slit his throat. Moving to his wife, he smiled and did the same.

Michelle collapsed flaccidly into unconsciousness, falling hard against the floor. Ron dropped forward onto his hands and then fell to his elbows. With effort he struggled to crawl to his dying parents, but he too collapsed after only a few feet. Moving to Ron's side, Blue Eyes placed the phone to his mouth and said, "Now tell the nice Marshall what I just did for you. and do it quickly. Soon you will be incapable."

Ron Parks spoke slowly, his words slightly slurred and his body now nearly paralyzed. He managed to say, "Their throats. Clay, he cut their throats."

He broke into tears then, sobbing into the receiver, but his crying lasted only a few seconds. Just as Blue Eyes pulled the phone away, Ron Parks slipped into the benevolence of unconsciousness.

Blue Eyes raised the phone to his ear. "Isn't it a sad thing, hearing a grown man cry? Call me, buddy." He pushed the end-call button and smiled.

CHAPTER FORTY-TWO

CLAY SLAMMED DOWN THE phone and spun around on his heels shouting, "Son-of-a-bitch, son-of-a-bitch, son-of-a-bitch!" His yelling brought Nancy bounding down the stairs with her heart pounding.

"What's wrong?"

Just then the phone rang. Ignoring it, Nancy asked again, "Clay, what's wrong?"

He could not answer her. Anger raged in his head, destroying all control. The phone continued to ring. Clay stormed about the living room in small symmetrical circles with fists clenched and teeth gritted to the point that he was lucky his lower jaw did not break.

The phone would not stop ringing, so Nancy snatched it up, following her husband with her eyes.

"Yes, hello." The snap in her voice made Bob Lemus pause a second before answering.

"It's Lemus. I need to talk with Clay."

"I don't think he's in the mood right now, Bob."

Lemus acknowledged with a nod but insisted. "I know, and I understand, but he has to talk to me."

Nancy asked, "Were you just listening in on the conversation? What is going on?"

Ignoring her, Lemus pleaded, "Please, Nancy, put him on."

A minute more passed before Clay had calmed down enough to talk. Ending his pacing, he finally placed a hand on Nancy's shoulder and followed with a nod telling her it was okay. He took the phone. "Yeah, it's me."

There was caring in the voice of Bob Lemus, but also business. "I'm sorry, Clay." The agent let a few moments pass while searching for appropriate words. "You have to be strong," Lemus told him, "especially now. We have to get this cock-sucker, but we have to do it together. No matter how angry you are, or how much you want to save your friends, you can't do it alone. When you call him, you've got to let us in on it. You have about one minute before it's time. We are on our way to your place right now and will be there in ten to twelve minutes. For God's sake, wait on us, okay?"

Cooper told him "Got to go" and hung up.

Concerned, and now upset about being in the dark, Nancy asked her husband in no uncertain terms, "Will you please tell me what the hell is going on?"

Clay took her in his arms and began to cry. She held him tight rubbing his back affectionately. Finally, he let her go and wiped his eyes. It was difficult, but he managed to tell her. "That was Ron on the phone a minute ago. He and Michelle are in New Orleans, at his mom and dad's."

"Is something wrong down there?" Nancy asked.

Clay took a deep breath and wiped at a tear that broke free from his blurry eyes.

"It's Blue Eyes. He is there with them."

"Oh, no!" Nancy exclaimed. "So, what's going on? What has he done?"

Clay swallowed and looked her straight in the eyes. "He cut Sean and Evelyn's throats."

Nancy's legs grew weak, and she lowered herself to the couch. Pale, she looked up at her husband.

"What about Ron and Mic?"

"I don't know I have to call Blue Eyes back in..." he looked at his watch, but the hands were blurry, so he wiped his eyes with his sleeve, "about thirty seconds."

"Clay, I'm so frightened for them."

Clay kneeled in front of her and took her hands. "Me too, Nance. Very much so."

When Blue Eyes answered the cell phone, he was cheerful and upbeat; "Hey, Clay. So happy you called me back. How did Nance take the news about Sean and Evelyn? Bet it was hard on her. But then she's a woman, so she's used to hard things, right? And what the heck, Sean and Evelyn were old anyway, far beyond their prime. Whoa," Blue eyes paused the conversation a moment, then came back on. "Sorry, had to slow down, don't want to get stopped with this precious cargo I'm carrying. Anyway, the Parks, the senior couple, are old news-or should I say, dead news?" He laughed at his sick joke, then said, "In any event, what say we get down to what really matters, the bottom line, the hook, the last dollar, the grand finale, the final hullabaloo, and all those other stupid fucking clichés?"

Clay didn't answer, so Blue Eyes made a short whistling noise into the receiver "You there, Clay?"

"Yeah, you son of a bitch, I'm here."

Slight irritation showed in the killer's voice. "Hey, no need to get huffy with me, *buddy*. None of this would have happened in the first pace had you cooperated. Because of you, that poor skinned woman you found in your garage, my partner, and Sean and Evelyn are all dead. Bodies are just piling up, and all because you have this insatiable need to be a Town-Clown hero."

"Just cut the psychological bullshit and get on with it," Clay told him coldly. "And don't call me buddy. That's a privilege, not a right."

Okay then, here goes. In the middle of the state of Louisiana, there sits the city of Alexandria. You will get into your car and drive there. Be there by four o'clock tomorrow evening. When you get into town, call me on this cellular for further instructions. At this point in time, your friends are still alive; however, if you bring Agent Lemus and his band of worthless men, I will kill both of your friends, mail their heads to you, and move on. then I'll contact you another time, maybe in a month, maybe a year. Is that clear?"

"Yeah."

"Okay," Blue Eyes said cheerfully, "that said, just one last thing: have Nancy tell Bob to drive out to the old elevator. A.J. is there in the basement, in need of help. And when my favorite agent recues him, have him ask the counselor if he still likes me…or just considers me one big pain in the ass."

Blue Eyes laughed into the phone and then it went silent.

CHAPTER
FORTY-THREE

QUICKLY CLAY PACKED, TAKING with him not only his 9-millimeter and ankle weapon, but also a Remington twelve gauge and a box of slugs. Because he did not want to risk meeting up with Lemus, he practically ran out to the car the moment he'd finished. Nancy followed him out, wanting to go with him, but he was firm in telling her no. This would be the final confrontation one way or another, and he did not want her there. Upon his arrival in Alexandria, he would call her and tell her what information to pass on to Lemus.

Once away from the house, Clay got on the phone and called a small private detective agency in Lafayette. The phone rang only once. "A and J Security, Joe Hardon."

"Joe, Clayton Cooper."

"Hey, Clay! Long-time no hear. How's the Marshall business?"

"Not good, Joe. I'm on my way to Alexandria, Louisiana, on some serious shit. I need a contact down there, good help. Don't want police or feds. It's guaranteed to get rough and bloody. I'd like someone like yourself-a shoot first and ask dumb questions later kind of private investigator. And it has to be someone who knows the area really well and is totally trustworthy. It's a tall order. Anybody you can plug in?"

"Hold on a sec."

Clay heard him flip through a Rolodex, then come back on.

"Yeah, got it right here, one hell of a private eye. Alfie and I worked with her a couple years ago in New Orleans. She's a spitfire. I wouldn't want to cross her."

"Did you say, she?"

"Hey, don't let the gender mislead you. She can be meaner than a skinned rabid dog with boiling turpentine poured down its butt. If you're talking serious shit, she's your man."

Clay thought it over a second, then said, "Don't think me crazy, Joe, but blood and guts are only the half of it. There's some serious evil, demon shit involved. I mean it frightens even me. And like you, I'm fearless."

Joe laughed lightly. "Trust me on this Clay, if the gig's down and dirty, this girl is the one you want by your side."

"Okay," Clay said finally, "I'll trust you. Got her number?"

"Sure do. Her name is Janis Barr. Tell you what, I'll give her a call after we hang up, refresh her memory, and warn her you're coming down. If she's out of town or something, I'll call you back. What's your number?"

Clay gave it to him then wrote down Barr's cell. "Tell her I'll call her later today. Thanks, Joe."

Clay hung up. "Woman," he said into the emptiness of the car, "I hope you're everything the man says you are."

CHAPTER FORTY-FOUR

UPON ARRIVING AT THE Cooper house, Agent Lemus jumped out of the car before Jones brought it to a complete stop. Rushing into the house, the first words out of his mouth were, "Where the hell is he?"

Nancy felt both guilt and uneasiness at not telling the FBI where her husband was heading, but the lives of their best friends were at stake. All she would say was, "Sorry, Bob, I can only tell you that he's gone."

Lemus's jaw tightened, then relaxed slowly. "Where has he gone to?"

"I can't tell you that." She cringed, knowing he was going to explode, so to lighten the blow she added, "At least I can't tell you yet, not until he calls me."

"And when will that be?"

"Tomorrow," she said, cringing again.

Throwing up his hands, Lemus whirled around to face Clendes, Jones, and Spulder, who stood in a group behind him. "What the hell is this? Are we the frigging FBI, or a Ronald McDonald charter club?" Turning back, he told her sternly, "Damn it, Nancy, you know this maniac does not play fair. Clay cannot do this alone. For his sake, you have to tell us where he went. This guy will kill him, I'm telling you. He's already killed him once, and had it not been for me, your husband would be in the ground today"

Nancy mulled over his words. She knew Lemus was correct. Blue Eyes was more than just a man. He was an evil being in possession of unnatural powers. And he was heartless-perhaps literally, for all she knew. He was a cold-blooded murderer with no feelings or compassion. Yet her husband had been firm in that she should wait for his call.

Lemus grew more desperate, but he lowered his voice.

"Look, Nancy. I'm sure Clay has told you what happened in New Orleans. Right now, he is very, very angry…no, he's pissed, pardon my French. He has his mindset on saving your friends and revenging the parents. I am telling you; his anger will blind him to the point that he'll be incapable of thinking clearly at least not clearly enough to outwit the Blue Eyes Killer. He needs us. Trust me on this. I know you love him, but when it comes to things like this, we are the experts."

Lemus glanced back to the three men behind him, as if asking for confirmation. He looked back to Nancy. "Has he gone to New Orleans?"

Nancy stared thoughtfully into Lemus's eyes. She could see the frustration, but there was sincerity too. "No," She told him.

In her heart, she felt she owed Lemus that much. If for no other reason than for the fact that he truly cared. "Tell you what," she said, "Let me put on a pot of coffee and think on it. Then we can all sit down with a cup and talk more about it. I'm just not sure what I should do. Everything you've said is true, but I have to trust my husband, too. You know that. Now if you will excuse me." She turned and went to the kitchen.

Spulder, Jones, and Clendes seated themselves on the couch while Lemus remained standing. Lighting a cigarette, he began to pace, circling the couch like a nerve-wracked expectant father.

"Damn it," he mumbled, just loud enough for the three men to hear, although he was actually talking to himself. "What in hell is the matter with this woman?" Following a hard draw on his cigarette, he inhaled deeply and exhaled out his nose. His lips were far too tightly sealed to allow the smoke to exit.

CHAPTER FORTY-FIVE

THE TEAL GREEN VAN sped along Highway 10 past the Garyville exit sign. Ron Parks had begun to awaken. He shook his head, trying to clear his mind from the slowly fading effects of the tranquilizing agent.

He opened his eyes, his vision blurry at first. He realized he was lying on his back on the floor of the van. The seats had been removed and he lay looking at the driver. Ron's head was propped against something covered with blankets. Michelle was still unconscious, lying on her stomach with her face nestled in his crotch. It was Blue Eyes' idea of humor. Ron and Michelle were both chained to the seat-hooks.

Blue Eyes looked up into the rearview mirror and smiled. "Good morning, Officer Parks. Or perhaps more appropriately, good afternoon." Ron Parks did not reply. He pulled against the chains that bound him firmly and looked around. "No use," Blue Eyes told him, continuing to stare into the rearview mirror. "Chains are my specialty. There is no getting loose until I decide it's time." He pulled his eyes back to the road a second, then looked back into the mirror. "So, did you have a nice sleep?"

"Fuck you."

"My, Officer Parks, such hostility."

There was silence before Blue Eyes spoke again. "Do you know who I am?"

Ron nodded. "Yeah, I know who you are, you heartless son of a bitch."

Meeting Ron's eyes in the mirror, Blue Eyes told him, "I'm sorry for your parents. Their death was an unfortunate casualty. All because your supposed friend Clayton Cooper refused to cooperate."

Ron glared, assuring their gaze remained locked. "Blame who you will. I ask only one thing from you."

"And what might that be, Officer Parks?"

"When we get to where we're going, wherever in the hell that may be, I want just five minutes of your time, you and me, face-to-face, bare-hands. What do you say?"

Blue Eyes grinned thoughtfully, glanced at the road again, then back to the mirror. "Personally, I'd like that, but unfortunately, I have other plans for you and the misses as well. And by the way, you can call me Quinten."

Eyes fastened to the mirror, Ron told him in no uncertain terms, "Fuck you, asshole. I've got your Quinten hanging."

The grin on Blue Eyes' face turned into a broad smile. "Yes, I know. And I'm looking forward to seeing it."

Ron shook his head. "Man, you're one twisted sick freak."

"So, I've been told. Now if you will excuse me a moment, I've a call to make." Blue Eyes punched in the number and the voice at the other end answered.

"Yeah, hello."

"Clay. It's Blue Eyes. How's the trip? Bored yet?"

"No, too busy thinking about killing you."

"Oh, I hope so. Changes of plans. When you get to Alexandria, go directly to the downtown library. There will be a sealed envelope there for you. inside will be a riddle, one you must solve by 8:30 tomorrow evening or I'm afraid Ronnie and Mic will cease being your Euchre partners. I've decided I'm having fun with this game, so I'm raising the stakes. I will leave the envelope with the librarian. I have already called her and made the arrangements. Sounds like a very nice African-American woman. I can't wait to meet her. Her name is Lindie. When you get there, just ask for her. The clock is tick, tick, ticking! Any questions?"

"Just one. After I kill you, will you be coming back again?"

"Yes, in fact I will."

"Good, I'm looking forward to killing you more than once."

CHAPTER
FORTY-SIX

FROM HIS PANTS POCKET, Clay pulled a piece of paper with the number of the Alexandria contact. Punching in the digits, he listened while it rang. When Janis Barr answered, it came as a surprise for some reason. Perhaps he suspected she'd be out on a job and unable to answer her phone or taking a break from the rigors of private investigating, or even out of state on an extended vacation. Any one of those would have been in step with the way his luck was going. In any event, the female investigator had to repeat herself because of his hesitation.

"Barr here. Hello... Hello. Whoever you are, I'm hanging up in five. Five, Four, Three...."

"Yes," Clay injected quickly, "This is Marshall Clayton Cooper, Lafayette, Indiana. Joe Hardon called you."

Janis replied immediately, her voice accented with a soft southern drawl. "Yes, how y'all doing? Been expecting your call."

There was a lull in the conversation. Then Clay said, "To start things off on the right foot, I guess I should ask what you prefer to be called?"

He could almost hear her smile. "Well, my mother calls me Jannie, my father calls me baby girl, my bill collectors call me all the friggin' time, and my two cats don't give a rat's butt so long as I keep the litterbox changed. You can call me Janis or Barr. I prefer Janis."

Clay smiled to himself. "Janis it is. Call me Clay."

"Okay, Clay. Joe mentioned you're coming down to do some real serious business. What's up?"

"Without going into detail, Janis, I'm coming down to meet with a serial killer. A real twisted, evil man."

Janis half-laughed into the phone. "Well, I can't speak for the serial killer part, but I've dated a few of the others. So, I think I may be able to help. Have you ever been to Alexandria before?"

"No."

"How are you coming down?"

"Out of Indianapolis to 70, 70 to 55, 55 to Jackson, 20 to Monroe and 165 down to Alexandria."

"Outstanding. Just as you get into town, you'll pass a restaurant called Ragin' Cajun Cuisine. It will be on your left. They have the best damn cup of coffee in the south, and if you're hungry, their gumbo is to die for…but order water with it. Call me as soon as you reach the outskirts and I'll hightail it over and find a quiet table. You can't miss me. I'll be the small, cutesy strawberry blond with the big gun. Sound tough, don't I?"

"You sound like the right person for the job," Clay said. "I should be getting in around 6 or 7 tomorrow morning. I really appreciate your help on this. We can discuss your fee when I arrive."

Janis Barr laughed again. "Wouldn't hear of it. You can owe me one."

"Thanks. See you tomorrow." Clay hung up.

Janis sounded like a cool character. Also, the fact that Joe had recommended her made him feel a good deal better. There were lots of things he wanted to discuss with her, things like the fact that Blue Eyes was more than your typical serial killer, if serial killers could actually be called typical. He wanted-*no needed-* to explain that this man was literally evil, in the true sense of the word, and that he came with an army of demons.

He never once doubted that Janis Barr as a private investigator had seen it all, especially working in Louisiana, the state most famous for voodoo, psychics, witches, zombies, and even vampires. If these things were in fact real-he had no personal experience in such matters. As for the Devil, demons, and the frightful existence of Hell, that he could take to the bank.

CHAPTER FORTY-SEVEN

NANCY RETURNED TO THE living room. In her hand she held a serving tray on which sat the glass pot from the brewer, five spoons, a cup for everyone and a bowl filled with sugar packets and creamer. All men rose, out of politeness. Smiling warmly, Spulder took the tray from her hands and placed it on the coffee table.

Everyone sat again and grabbed a cup upon Nancy's request. She filled them, one by one, and then filled her own. Everyone but Jones drank it black. For a moment there was silence. Lemus took a sip then pulled his eyes to Nancy's face. "Nancy, I don't want to harp on this, and trust me, the last thing I want is to sound melodramatic, but if you do not tell us where Clay is heading, you may very well be the cause of your husband's death." He took another sip, set the cup down and leaned forward, resting his elbows on his knees. "Look, you two have already been through a hell of a lot and I don't want to see it end with a funeral. If nothing else, search your heart. It will convince you of the importance of telling us where he has gone."

Nancy stared at Bob Lemus. The man was an FBI agent, and she understood his unyielding drive to get Blue Eyes off the street. But there were other things in need of consideration. Clay was her husband, the man she had learned to trust in every circumstance. Lemus could very well be right, she reasoned; by not telling them the destination, she could cost her husband his life. Yet if she did give up the location, one single mistake by any one of the four men sitting in front of her now could bring about the same end. She bit her lip thoughtfully. Her husband was a resilient man, a self-reliant thinker. He mostly worked alone, and many times he had stated that he preferred it that way. But here they were dealing with the Blue Eyes Killer.

Breaking her gaze, Nancy took another sip of coffee, then set her cup down beside Lemus's. She looked soberly into his eyes. "If I tell you where he's s going, what assurance do I have you will keep him safe?"

Holding her gaze a long while, Lemus considered the question thoughtfully. He wanted so much to reassure her but knew he couldn't. "None," he told her. Nancy went pale, as if she had just lost all hope. Lemus added quickly, "Look, we have no guarantees either way. But I swear to you by the holiness of Jesus Christ and J. Edger Hoover, his chances are far better with us than doing this alone." Lemus took her hands. "Nancy, listen to me. We want Clay to be safe as much as you do. He's a smart man, and I have all confidence in him. But Blue Eyes is smarter than any one of us." He squeezed her hands gently for reassurance. "But as a team, the odds mount highly in our favor. Together we can do this. But you have to tell us where he's headed, and it has to be now."

Pressing her lips together and nodding, Nancy slipped her hands free of Lemus's and picked up her coffee cup. She sat back, tapping the cup contemplatively with her fingers.

"Okay," she said finally, "I'll tell you. But you take me with you."

Lemus's eyes widened. "No. No way. Not only would it be far too dangerous, but your husband would also kill me."

Nancy's voice was calm, but firm. "Bob, I already know where he's going. If I wanted, I could have already been on my way there. Wouldn't I be safer with the FBI than going alone?"

Lemus looked at the others and sighed with exasperation, then picked up his cup and rose to his feet. Taking a swallow, he stepped away, turned to look back at Nancy, began to speak, and then decided against it. Instead, he turned and silently walked away mumbling. Every eye watched him. The others sipped their coffee waiting, secretly amused that their boss had been cornered and would more than likely not have the last word, something they had never seen before.

A minute of pacing passed before Lemus returned and looked directly at Nancy. "If you go, you do exactly as told and stay where we say to stay. Agreed?"

Nancy thought on it, biting at her bottom lip. She took a sip of coffee without removing her eyes from his, swallowed, then told him coolly, "No deal. I stay at your side day and night. I go with you to wherever Clay is, and you keep nothing from me. That's the deal."

Drawing a deep breath, Bob Lemus smoothed the horseshoe hair on the back of his head. His jaw tightened, then loosened as he moaned in annoyance. The others waited for him to start yelling, but he fooled them. The reaction caused all three to pause as if frozen in place, some with their cups at their mouths.

"Okay," Lemus said, pointing a finger. "But always, and I mean *always*, you do as I say. Understand?"

Nancy smiled, ever so tightly. "I do, Bob."

CHAPTER
FORTY-EIGHT

L INDIE WOODHALL OBSERVED THE tall, handsome stranger enter through the library door and walk straight toward her desk, located in the center of the one-story public building. She knew he was the one who had called nearly four hours ago asking permission to leave a sealed envelope in her possession-not because he had told her what he would be wearing, or that he would arrive at a certain time but because she knew because she just knew.

He was tall, incredibly good-looking, and dressed in beltless blue jeans, a dark blue T-shirt beneath a light blue sport coat, and shoulder-length blond hair. But it was his eyes, his beautiful blue eyes, that caught her attention. He wasn't smiling yet, but she knew he would. When he did, it would be one of those gorgeous smiles' women had to fight to resist. Lindie also knew he would possess great charm, wit, and be the kind of man easy to talk to...and she also knew he was evil.

How it was Lindie knew of his dark character was unexplainable. It was just an ability that had been with her since her earliest memories. Her grandmother had said it was a gift given to her by God himself, the discernment of spirits, she had called it. She had even shown her in the Bible that the God-given gift actually existed. While she did see it as a gift, it also, from time to time, frightened her.

Whether it was connected or unconnected, she also possessed the ability of both speaking and interpreting the incomprehensible language of the angels, and, frightening to her, demons as well; this gift allowed her to speak in tongues, as she often did during church services, translating aloud God's personal message for her congregation. For the most part, someone else usually spoke the strange language initially and she interpreted, but it was sometimes the other way around. On rare occasions, she did both.

It was on her eleventh birthday, Sunday, December 25, that her grandmother had pulled her aside at church and told her sternly, "Girl, you have been given the gift. You are going to make the Good Lord mad if you don't start speaking his language. And oh, let me tell you child, you don't even want to get the Lord riled up." So it was on that day, nearly three decades ago, more afraid of her grandmother's wrath than the wrath of God, that she'd begun speaking and interpreting the heavenly language. Now, at the age of thirty-eight, it had become second nature.

The good-looking man with the beautiful blue eyes reached Lindie's desk and smiled, offering his hand. Lindie slowly rose and took it with apprehension. The moment she touched it, an icy coldness jolted her body, as though she had received a near-fatal shock from high voltage wire. The room vanished, and she stood on a ledge overlooking a world of burning souls that stretched forever. There was unbearable wailing, pain, and fear, and she could feel the radiating heat from the immense flames lapping high above the naked bodies of the damned. Then the blue-eyed stranger released her hand, and she was back. He was still smiling. "You are Lindie, I presume, since you look just as you sound on the phone, a beautiful African-American woman with the most beautiful colored skin I've seen in a long time." His voice was warm, and his smile widened.

Lindie nodded. "Thank you. And yes, I am Lindie." But her face remained sober.

"I spoke with you on the phone earlier today," the man with the deep blue eyes said. "You agreed to hold an envelope for me, until a friend comes to pick it up."

She gave a nod. "Yes, I will do that for you."

He pulled the envelope from his jacket pocket and handed it to her. When she took hold of her end they paused, both holding and staring, she is looking into the face of immorality and evil, and he into the eyes of goodness. He clearly sensed the love she possessed for her God, and he wondered what people saw in Him. They were down here alone, on their own, deserted by Him, left to struggle, and painfully feel their way through this boring, pitiless, every-man-for-himself world. All this only to die, following years of hardship and struggle. To breathe their last, usually painfully or doped up to the point that they were oblivious to those around them, all in a useless, worn-out body of flesh and blood. He abhorred their weakness and mindless dependency upon Him.

Lindie's eyes fluttered, then closed. While it did not shock her, it somewhat surprised her to discover she possessed yet another gift. In her head she had heard the very thoughts of this evil being, as if he had spoken aloud. Now, with her own mind, she rebutted him, her thoughts seeping into the spiritual realm and entering the consciousness of the man who appeared perfect but possessed a soul darker and colder than the deep, lightless depths of an unexplored ocean.

Her eyes opened; she spoke in her thoughts. "You, evil one, have no power but what my God allows you to have. This world is your master's world, and so we struggle. The world in which I wait to walk, is God's. And you know you shall never taste of its fruits or share in His magnificent glory. For in the end, you and all like you will be thrown into the Lake of Fire and be forever tormented, never again to be free. It is not my God who causes us to struggle here. It is your god, Satan. This is his domain, but only until my Lord returns, at which time we will know the delight of perfect peace and you in return will then experience the greatest of fear and pain. You, stealer of souls, are doomed, and your days are numbered. Now, in the name of Jesus Christ, the Son of God, I order you be gone from this place and never return."

As if awakening from a deep sleep, Lindie came back to reality. She was still standing behind her desk and the man with the deep blue eyes still stood before her. Saying nothing, he turned and started for the door. Halfway there he stopped and glanced back. Lindie drew in a sudden breath-his beautiful blue eyes had turned black, and he spoke in the tongue of demons ... "Nieshola, coreespeel diepieps ontue less ouut pes liank. Doo mont dell vee Coooooooper. Peesmoe sta ba forsh."

He turned then and walked to the door. Lindie sat heavily in her chair, feeling strangely weak and tired. Her eyes followed him. Softly, just under her breath, she interpreted the words he had spoken. "Librarian, the time is here for you to rise above your trivial work and perform a task of paramount importance. Make sure you give the envelope to the man called Cooper. There can be no mistakes."

Lindie Woodhall frowned, her strength slowly returning, and even though he was now outside and beyond the doors, she rose, shouting after him. "I'll see that he gets it, but only because my God wants me to. And let me tell you something else, you pompous black-eyed, evil ass! My work here is not trivial! I'm more than a librarian, as are all who work in this field! We're historians."

CHAPTER FORTY-NINE

URDUE AIRPORT APPEARED DESERTED when Clendes pulled into one of the diagonal parking places in front of the two-story brick terminal building. Lemus climbed out of the car and opened the back door for Nancy. She hurriedly got out, followed by Jones and Spulder. All went to the trunk to retrieve baggage, a single suitcase each, with Lemus and Spulder also grabbing briefcases.

Single file, they entered through the electronic door and proceeded to the terminal counter where Jones identified himself as pilot of the department's Lear jet. Within ten minutes they were boarded and, in the air, flying toward Alexandria.

Lemus put on a pot of coffee. After pushing the on button, he sat in one of the eight leather-bound chairs and made a call to the New York Field Office. Even the great Bob Lemus had a boss. The call lasted nearly five minutes, and Nancy listened to all that was said. The tone was positive and upbeat, Lemus was confident that this time the killer would be apprehended and held.

Agent Lemus knew full well that Nancy Cooper had been listening, but he really didn't care. Hanging up, he looked out of the small window and into the clouds. He believed everything he had told his supervisor to be true. This was going to be it. The time for capturing or killing Blue Eyes had come. The madman's days of elusiveness had come to an end. The FBI now had fingerprints and positive I.D, right on down to a photograph. It would no longer be that difficult to track him. And Blue Eyes, Lemus was confident, realized the same thing.

It was a beautiful afternoon. The sky through which they flew was a rich blue, with white clouds that took turns hiding the shimmering aircraft. Lemus sighed. The fight to apprehend the Blue Eyes Killer had been a long one, too long. The son of a bitch had killed far too many people. Pressing his lips together, Lemus glanced over at Nancy then again looked out the window.

Clayton Coop had no idea how much he had aided the department. The poor fellow had already been through hell, yet his assistance remained invaluable. Because of him and his wife, the agency now knew who the killer was, or at least possessed the necessary information to hunt him down. And for Cooper, it was still not over. What he would face in Alexandria was going to be far more than could be comprehended.

Lemus lit a cigarette. The FBI maintained files that could never be shared with the public, information pertaining to things paranormal and extra-terrestrial that would terrify not only the nation but the world as well. Clayton Cooper had just become one of those unfortunate citizens caught in the web of its top-secret existence.

Top-secret. Lemus said the word to himself while taking a long draw from his cigarette. Actually, in these circumstances, a more appropriate word for top-secret might be *unspeakable*.

Clendes disturbed Lemus's thought long enough to hand him a cup of coffee. Lemus nodded his thanks, then looked back out the window. He just wanted this to be over. Retirement was looking more and more inviting. Through his years with the department, he had done more than his share of tracking down the insane, jerking them out of society and sending them to prison or the chair. Yet he saw himself as little more than just another agent doing his job and expecting no special recognition…or did he?"

If it had not been for his natural, God-given talent of tracking these mental cases down, thousands of citizens now walking the streets living normal lives would already be dead, having died in terrible ways.

Bob Lemus took another draw from his cigarette. Humility, "Yeah," he said to himself, "You're loaded with it, Bob."

CHAPTER FIFTY

HARCLOUE PLANTATION SAT AT the end of a long, narrow drive lined with droopy-limbed oak trees draped in Spanish moss. Once colorful and filled with life, the old mansion now loomed dark and deserted. It looked just as it had one hundred and thirty-eight years ago, when it had been hastily abandoned because of invading Yankee soldiers.

The years had taken their toll, but the building remained proud and strong, enduring decades of southern rain, snow, and storms. The interior sat draped in cobwebs and layers of undisturbed dust. Dark stains of mildew covered the walls and flooring, giving the interior a pungent, musky odor. Original furniture ornamented every room, only now the once elaborate pieces sat rotting.

The estate, including 600 of its original 1300 acres, was now owned by descendants of the founding Charcloue family. Although thought eccentric by many, the inheritors chose to let the old mansion stand untouched over the decades, a humbling remembrance to the atrocities of a terrible war.

Through the years, a handful of tourists had stumbled upon the house. Nearly all who had laid eyes upon it either made an offer to buy it or dreamed of doing so. But the Charcloues always politely declined. It was because of the mansion's isolated location that Blue Eyes chose it to be the final meeting place.

With the Park's van located at the rear of the old building, he set about preparing for the encounter. The plantation house consisted of two stories and an attic. There were, ironically, exactly thirteen rooms-his favorite number. In the master bedroom, located at the front of the upstairs level, he cleared out all furniture, stacking it on the outside landing, then painstakingly painted a pentagram on the floor so large it touched all four walls.

When the paint dried, he carried the bed back in and centered it on the pentagram. When finished, Blues Eyes took in a deep breath, savoring the musky odor. From this very room, once eloquent French doors opened to the balcony that would serve him perfectly during the departure. Following Cooper's s thrust of the knife, when his soul left his body, he would float out through the doors and sail gracefully through the long-reaching limbs of the beautiful, moss-covered oak. Then he'd fly into the heavens amid the stars and moon, reveling in the freedom of being loosened from his worldly body. It would be perfect utopia. But the best would come last. He would receive a grandiose welcome as he flew in through the gates of Hell.

It was 5:06 pm when an old Ford Pinto rolled down the long drive to the abandoned mansion. A fading sun spotted the oak covered lane with deep swells of shadows. The car pulled to a stop in front of the big house and remained there for some time. Blue Eyes walked out on the second-floor balcony and shouted down to the driver of the car. "Well, old woman, are you coming in? Or does my presence frighten you?"

The car door opened, and a frail woman of color stepped out; slowly she turned her 82-year-old eyes upon the man smiling down from the balcony. The wrinkles on her face tightened. Despite the strong voodoo power, she possessed, he did frighten her. She was dressed in a black gypsy-style dress and wore six rings, five with different colored stones and the sixth displaying the face of a skull. Four strings of beads, also of different colors, hung around her neck. Bending slowly, she reached into the car and pulled a straw basket draped with a burlap cover.

With it in hand, she stood and hesitated, staring at the front door of the big house and considering whether or not she should even enter. The old woman's hair was thin and stringy, and quite gray, a result brought on not merely through heredity. It was also a result of intense voodoo rituals that had, little by little, robbed her soul of energy and life. But being a Voodoun had always been her destiny, and she had never regretted it.

Leaving the car, she entered into the old house. The man who frightened her stood waiting, grinning. Even here, within the dark confines of the house, his beautiful blue eyes glittered. In silence the old woman followed him into the downstairs dining room, where she placed her basket on the dust-laden table.

Blues Eyes looked from the basket and into her face. "You know what I want?"

The old woman nodded in silence. She pulled the burlap covering from the basket and pulled out two thick, round candles. After lighting them, she removed a box and dumped its contents on the table: a chicken head, a live baby snake, a gathering of small bones and a dead bat. She looked at Blue Eyes. "Do you have it?"

"Yes."

He pulled the picture of an FBI Lear Jet parked at an airport from his pocket. The Voodoun took it from his hand and looked at it, then grunted and laid it down with the other things lying on the table.

Reaching into the basket, she removed two more items: a crudely sown piece of burlap shaped like an airplane and a long needle. She looked at Blue Eyes a second time. "I will not kill them, only delay them. They will be forced to land and wait for repairs to the fuel line."

Blue Eyes nodded. "Just get on with it."

The old lady put down the pin and picked up the live snake now crawling over the pile of bone fragments. With the snake in her hand, she placed its head between her teeth and bit down. Its head crunched, severing from its body. Blood began to spurt, and she positioned the reptile so that the spraying blood spilled onto the burlap airplane. Leaning forward, she spit the head into the pile of paraphernalia on the table, picked up the long pin, and began to chant. "Pala, Pala, Papa

Legbo Lee a Gee!" She then drove the long pin through the airplane doll. "There," she said softly. "It is done. They will now begin to leak fuel slowly."

Blue Eyes pulled the bottle of chloroform from his pocket and quickly poured some on the cloth in his hand. The old lady had barely enough time to smell it before he forcibly placed it over her nose and mouth and pulled her tightly against him. She struggled but a short time. In less than ten seconds, the Voodoun lay in an unconscious heap on the floor.

The burlap airplane had fallen from her hand and lay beside her body. Blue Eyes picked it up and removed the long pin still impaling it. Grinning, he began running around the room, holding the plane above his head, and making motor sounds like a young child at play.

Then he stopped and began to giggle. He plunged the long needle once again through the burlap. His giggling grew louder, turning into laughter. And he stabbed the airplane, again and again and again.

CHAPTER
FIFTY-ONE

AGENT JONES TURNED IN his seat and yelled with urgency for his boss to come to the cockpit. Lemus left the leather chair and stuck his head through the narrow doorway. "What's up?"

Jones nodded his head toward the instrument panel. "We got a serious problem. We're losing fuel!"

"How bad?"

"Bad. At the rate the gauge is dropping, we have about a minute till we're empty. Either we completely severed the main fuel line, or we sprung a hundred leaks simultaneously. I've never seen anything like it."

"How long to reach ground and land?"

"Well, we're fifteen-thousand feet up. Longer than it will take the fuel to run out. In about forty seconds we'll be spiraling to our deaths."

Lemus looked back at Nancy Cooper; she was resting in her seat with eyes closed. Clendes and Spulder were chatting. He looked back to Jones. "Well, we have one choice. Get out the chutes. We're jumping."

Jones switched to autopilot and climbed out of his seat. Lemus walked quickly ahead of him back to the others. "Everybody up. We're jumping out of this crate."

Nancy opened her eyes wide. "We're WHAT?"

"You heard me," Lemus said. "We've ruptured a fuel line and the plane's going to crash. Everyone grab a chute and strap it on."

Jones had begun handing them out. Clendes and Spulder knew the procedure and were already snapping buckles. While Lemus did the same, Jones assisted Nancy with hers. Her hands were shaking. "I can't do this."

Jones smiled, respecting her fear. "Yes, you can. You can do anything you put your mind to. You've already proven that. Now listen to me, when you leave the aircraft," he placed her hand on the D-ring located on the left shoulder, "keep hold of this ring. As you fall, count to ten and then pull hard. That's all there is to it. Just count to ten and pull. The chute will do the rest. It will be a fun ride, I promise." He patted her shoulder thoughtfully "And it's okay to keep your eyes closed."

Clendes opened the boarding door. Instantly wind and sunlight rushed in, the wind howling fiercely around them. Clendes was first to jump, followed by Spulder. Both Jones and Lemus moved Nancy toward the open doorway. Jones put his mouth close to Nancy's ear, shouting to be heard above the wind. "Mrs. Cooper, if the ring you're holding fails," he pried her hand away from it and placed it on another near the bottom of the pack, "if it should fail, then pull this one. It's your backup chute. So, see, you're doubly safe." Placing her hand back on the main ring, he and Lemus inched her toes to the edge of the open door. Her eyes we closed tight.

Lemus took a turn shouting in her ear. "Remember Nancy. You have to pull the cord, or the chute will not open." She nodded without opening her eyes. Lemus glanced at Jones and shoved her out in the nothingness of the open sky. She was still screaming when they jumped.

CHAPTER FIFTY-TWO

CLAY CALLED JANIS BARR at three minutes past nine. He was less than an hour out of Alexandria. Her phone rang a total of five times. She had been blow-drying her hair, so had nearly missed it. A meeting time of ten o'clock was set for the Ragin' Cajun. If he were late, Janis assured Marshall Cooper that she would wait as long as necessary.

Hurriedly she finished drying, dressing in white slacks, a black silk blouse and a brown sport coat. Foregoing her shoulder rig, she chose a small-of-the-back clip holster for the 9-millimeter. Standing at the bathroom mirror, she put on her makeup-not much, peach eyeliner and light pink lipstick. She sprayed herself with two squeezes of Red Door and left the house.

Except for a large Caucasian woman in a brown and white plaid mumu, the restaurant was empty of customers. Janis slid into her favorite booth and ordered a cup of coffee with whole-wheat toast. She was not a big breakfast person. A young girl waited on her; one she had not seen before. Halfway through the toast and a second cup of coffee, the front door opened.

She knew instantly it was Clayton Cooper. The broad shoulders and crew-cut hair were a giveaway. He was handsome, as men go, and there was something in his face, an honesty that said he was a truly good person. She watched him talk with the young waitress, then smile and walk to her booth.

His smile was real and his handshake firm; she liked that. Too many people shook her hand as if she might break. Clay slid in the booth opposite her just as the waitress arrived.

"Can I get you something, sir?"

He looked up. "Just coffee, please."

The young waitress wrote on her ticket and left.

"I want you to know," Clay said, "that I truly appreciate your help.

Janis nodded. "Not a problem."

"Look, if you don't want to be part of this, I'll understand."

Janis grinned. "Are you kidding? I'm in this business for the same reason you are. Guys like him need a good 'wake up and smell the coffee, then proceed to a good old fashioned ass-whipping." "And I'm deffinately in."

Clay grinned. He liked this woman. "Great," he told her. "I was hoping you'd say that, since I really do need your help."

The waitress returned with Clay's coffee and refilled Janis's cup. They smiled and she left.

"So, what's up first?" Janis asked.

"Library. He left a note, or riddle, or something for me, something in an envelope."

Janis nodded. "As soon as you're finished with the coffee, we'll head that way."

Clay gulped down the contents of the cup.

"Finished."

CHAPTER FIFTY-THREE

WHEN CLAY ENTERED THE Alexandria library, he felt a fluttering in the pit of his stomach. He wanted the envelope yet feared what he'd find written in it. Janis followed him through the door and to the front desk.

Lindie Woodhall was sitting and smiled when they approached. Janis had known Lindie for nearly twenty years, having herself used the library and the woman's mastery of retrieving information many times while on cases. Clay took a deep breath and looked at Janis, then to the librarian.

"Hello," he said with ambivalence, "I'm Clayton Cooper. I believe you're holding an envelope for me."

Lindie rose slowly to her feet and bobbed her head. "Yes, I am," she reached beneath the desk, "I have it right here." Lindie glanced at Janis as if asking for verification, then handed the envelope over.

Cooper took it and let out a long breath. Turning to Janis, he said, "Let's find a table."

It was a white security envelope with printed lining for privacy. With nervous hands, Clay opened it with his pocketknife. Inside was a plain piece of notebook paper with three folds. He opened the paper slowly and read the handwritten note, then passed it to Janis. She took her time reading it.

Clay - this is it, the beginning of the end and the end of the beginning.

Decipher by eight tonight or poor Mic and Ronnie will be no more...or at least

living no more. There will still be skin and bones, of course, at least until it has

all rotted from their dead bodies and only their skeleton remains. So, if you wish

to save them, best get to work. Here it is:

A mansion old that should have glowed

Beneath the torch of war

Remains untouched just as it was

To this place at dark, you'll go

At ten tonight—when stars are bright

Walk down the road of oaks

I'll be upstairs so meet me there

Where this time you'll do it right

When you do arrive—to stay alive

Look in no other rooms

Come straight to me—because should you look

you'll find that Death in darkness looms.

Blue Eyes

P.S. Don't be late and don't be early!

Finished, Janis sat back in the chair and tapped the table thoughtfully with her fingers. Clay looked at her.

"What do you think?"

"He's talking about an old mansion, that's for certain. And he says it's untouched, meaning no one is living in it. I know of two around here like that. It's the line about the road of oaks that's throwing me. The two I know of have a few oaks, but they're scattered sporadically about the property, and both have close neighbors. I would think he'd pick a spot more isolated."

"What about surrounding towns?"

"Could be. He's given you till eight, then says be at the mansion by ten. I'd say he's allowed two hours' drive time."

Janis expressed deep concern. "You know, if it's okay, I think we could use a little help here. Do you mind if I call the librarian over?"

Clay shrugged. "No, but I don't want to put her in harm's way."

Janis understood and appreciated his concern for someone he didn't even know.

"Let's give her the choice." She caught Lindie's attention and motioned her over. There had been only two chairs at the table, so Clay retrieved a third for Lindie.

When Lindie sat, Janis said, "We need your help."

"Does it have something to do with the envelope?" She asked. Janis was holding it and Lindie glanced at it then into Clay's face and back to Janis. "Because if it does, I'm more than happy to help. I didn't like the man who left it. He's the epitome of wickedness."

Janis and Clay exchanged glances. Janis slid the note across the table to her. "Here, read this and tell us the place he's talking about."

Picking it up, she read with serious concentration. Clay and Janis watched her face, anxious for the answer. When finished Lindie refolded the note and sat silent, rummaging through her memories. Then she looked at them and commented confidently.

"I think I know the place. About three years ago, we clipped out an article on it and filed it away. I'll be right back."

She excused herself and returned to her desk, where six tan filing cabinets stood. They watched her pull open a drawer and remove a plain manila folder filled with newspaper clippings. When she found what she was searching for, she returned to the table and handed it to Janis.

"This is it."

Janis took it from her hand. In the center of the clipping was a photo of an old mansion with a long drive lined on both sides with towering oak trees. Below was a caption that read: **Charcloues of Baton Rouge leave family history untouched.**

The article told of the Charcloue family of 1864 who had abandoned their beautiful home during the civil war when the Union Army advanced on their land. But unlike many of the old southern mansions, theirs was spared from the customary torching of the house and the surrounding fields. Passed from generation to generation, the tradition of leaving the house just as it was the night of the invasion became the family custom, so everything inside and out remained original and untouched.

Because the mansion sat in the heart of six hundred acres, once over 1300, it remained virtually unknown to tourists and even many of the Baton Rouge residents. Several organizations had approached the Charcloues in hope of convincing them to transform the place into a tourist stop, but suggestions were always declined. And so, now well over a hundred years old, the place sat alone, virtually hidden in the middle of prime Louisiana woods.

When Clay finished reading the article, he handed it back to Lindie. The three returned to Lindie's desk, where she wrote down the address. They thanked her and upon leaving, Lindie gave warning: "I don't want to sound like some religious nut, but you two are going up against pure evil. This man is of the Devil. You can't fight him using guns. He has got to be dealt with using the Lord's word and lots of prayer. And I'll be putting you in my own. You all be careful."

They left the library and stepped out into bright sunshine. The sky was as blue as the eyes of the man they hunted. It was nearly 11:45 and Janis suggested they grab some lunch and form a plan while eating. Since they had gone to the library in Janis's Jeep, having left Clay's car at the Ragin' Cajun, they returned there to eat.

Back at the booth, Clay looked over the menu and asked Janis what she would recommend. Smiling to herself, she suggested the gumbo. That was what he ordered, along with a Diet Coke and two slices of rye bread.

Their conversation while waiting consisted of bringing Janis up to date on what had been happening in Indiana. They were both at a loss as to why the Blue Eyes killer had brought the fight to Louisiana, other than connecting him with Ron's mom and dad. Clay told of the creature that had caused him to wreck his truck and of his visit to Hell, but he omitted the part about the woman coming out of the crimson doors. In return, Janis told of her incident with the Pardaux boy and the demon creature warning her not to help.

The waitress came round and refilled their drinks. Clay decided to phone home. On the third ring a recorded message came through. It was from Nancy. *Clay. I don't want you to be angry, but I am on my way down there with Bob Lemus and the others. We are flying down in their jet. Should be there late afternoon. Bob said to tell you we are checking in at the Holiday Inn. Please, please, please, contact us. I love you.*

Clay shut off the cell phone and sat thinking to himself. Janis watched him quietly, waiting for him to come back to the present and hopefully fill her in. Eventually he looked at her and explained, "My wife is here staying at the Holiday Inn with a team of FBI agents. They are good men, but Blue Eyes told me explicitly if they showed up, he would kill my friends no questions asked."

Janis shrugged. "Really doesn't matter that they are in town. Baton Rouge is a good distance away. Blue Eyes will never know they are here in Alexandria. We'll have gone in and kicked his ass, gotten your friends back, and disappeared long before the FBI even begins to figure things out."

Clay considered her words and let a small grin show at the corners of his mouth. He really did like this Janis Barr.

When lunch arrived, they ate heartily. The spicy gumbo caused Clay to break out in a cold sweat, so he downed three glasses of water with it. Janis smiled, wondering if he finished it all because he loved it or because his masculinity was on the line. She guessed it was both.

When Janis and Clay left the restaurant, they drove to her house and she stocked up on a few personal items: a Browning twelve-gage with ten slugs, a small frame .45 (which she slipped in the pocket of her suit coat) and two black cases, one holding binoculars and the other a pair of night vision goggles. They threw the items into her jeep and left for Baton Rouge. Once there, they would drive out to the country and study the exterior layout of the Charcloue Mansion, then return to town and plan their strategy over dinner.

CHAPTER FIFTY-FOUR

THE DIRECTIONS LINDIE WOODHALL had written down were easy to follow for the most part, but the address eluded them. The edge of the six hundred acres was located five miles west of the outskirts of Baton Rouge. The search became difficult. There were no specific roads or signs to lead them to the Charcloue Mansion, and they dared not ask for information.

Finally, after taking several incorrect side roads, they turned onto a field with a tire-track lane running off toward a distant patch of woods. After coming upon the remains of what had once been field fence, they parked the Jeep and traveled on foot.

The old mansion sat less than a mile from where they had left the vehicle. It stood alone in the middle of a clearing, surrounded on three sides by fields overgrown with weeds. Just as had appeared in the newspaper clipping, beautiful, long-limbed oak trees draped in Spanish moss lined both sides of a narrow lane. Their intermingling branches formed a perfectly shaded quarter mile canopy stretching all the way to a circular drive at the front of the house. Five massive, round pillars towered to the second-floor balcony.

Concealed within the distant tree line, Janis pulled her binoculars from the case and lay down, resting her elbows on the ground for stability. Carefully, she focused the binoculars. It was obvious the place was deserted. She swept the ground floor first, concentrating on rooms beyond the six front porch windows. Only one contained even a remote resemblance of a curtain, so visibility was limited only by the afternoon shadows shrouding the interior.

She could make out fireplaces, pieces of furniture, and cabinets. Cobwebs covered everything, including what had once been a bright and beautiful crystal chandelier. She saw a long table encircled with twelve chairs and large candelabra in the center, noting that this must be the dining room. Though unrecognizable, portraits and oil paintings still hung on the walls. Through the window to the left of the entryway, she made out the shaded footing of a winding stairway. However, that was it; there were no indications that someone was In the house.

Refocusing the binoculars, Janis moved to the upstairs balcony. On the north end, it appeared that someone had removed furniture from one of the rooms and left it stacked outside. Because of the angle and balcony railing, it was nearly impossible to see in through the windows. Satisfied, Janis rose and handed the binoculars to Clay.

Remaining standing, he took a turn while Janis concentrated on the area surrounding the house. In the field to the right lay the remains of what had once been a large barn, probably a stable. Various lengths of split-rail fence that had once kept grazing cattle and horses away from the house stood scattered in no recognizable pattern. There were no other outreach buildings still standing. She was sure there had once been several, but they had long ago fallen, buried beneath decades of grass and weeds.

"Shit." Clay said suddenly and pulled the binoculars from his eyes.

"Get down!" Both dropped to the ground. Blue Eyes had stepped out onto the balcony. He pulled a cigarette from a familiar gold case and lit it with the matching lighter, then inhaled deeply. He stood for some time, blowing smoke rings into the air.

Clay was not sure if they had been spotted, so he and Janis remained motionless for a time. The late afternoon sun was warm, even in the shade of the trees. A soft breeze swirled, then was gone. Blue Eyes tossed his cigarette from the balcony but remained.

Finally, satisfied the man had no clue they were there, Clay once again raised the binoculars to his eyes. The killer was leaning on the rail and staring intently at something in the distance to their right. Then his head turned leisurely, coming around to stare into the exact spot where he and Janis lay. Clay felt a cold chill run down his spine. Blue Eyes let a long, drawn-out smile play at the corners of his lips, then turned and walked casually back into the house.

Alarmed that he knew they were there, Clay told Janis what had happened, and she bit at her lip thoughtfully for a moment. "Even if he does know, it really don't matter. Remember the note? We were warned not to be early or late. As long as we leave now and do not approach the house until 10:00, we will be doing exactly as told. Besides," she shrugged, "I have this feeling he knew we'd be by. Now come on, he won't hurt your friends. Let's get back and grab a bite. It may be a long night."

Although filled with a sense of uneasiness, Clay agreed. They returned to the Jeep and headed back to Baton Rouge. The sun was close to setting and had already begun to cover the countryside with shadows.

Blue Eyes walked casually down the winding staircase and into the parlor. He unzipped a long black bag sitting on the dust-covered sofa and pulled out a rifle with a scope. With it in hand, he climbed back up the stairs and took up a prone position on the balcony deck, resting the rifle barrel against the bottom section of the railing.

Carefully he adjusted the scope, focusing on one of the three persons hastily making their way across the field on the south side of the house; in this case it was FBI agent Clendes. He was in the center, Lemus to his right, and Nancy Cooper to the left. Blue Eyes shook his head, grinning. Scope set and centered on the agent's right shoulder; he gently squeezed the trigger. The rifle kicked lightly, making a brief ticking sound. The feathered dart went straight to its target and Clendes dropped within three steps.

"Say goodnight, Gracie," Blue Eyes said, smiling.

Quickly he worked the bolt and sent another at Nancy. She dropped only a foot ahead of the agent. By the time he had the bolt worked for the third shot, Lemus had dived to the right and lay motionless, concealed in the high grass. His weapon was in his hand. Moving his head ever so slowly, he glanced up into the sky. The sun was nearly down now, and the field was filling with deep shadows. Half an hour and darkness would come.

Blue Eyes knew what Lemus would do. When night arrived, he would move the agent and Mrs. Cooper to safety. That could not be. So carefully, the killer crawled off the balcony and back into the house. Once inside, he rose to his feet, walked to the center of the upstairs hall, and pulled down a narrow folding stairway from the fifteen-foot ceiling. He climbed the steep steps into the attic, walked to the center, and climbed yet another narrow stairway; this one leading to the highest point of the mansion, a small cupola. Staying low, he raised a window, resting the barrel of the rifle on the sill. He adjusted the scope. The grass and weeds hid Lemus very well, but not good enough.

The killer's rifle kicked once again, and Lemus felt the sting of the dart. He looked at it and said, "Shit." Just to be safe, Blue Eyes fired twice more. He really did not wish to overdose his favorite agent; however, should the tranquilizing ingredient stop his heart-well, that would be most unfortunate.

CHAPTER FIFTY-FIVE

THE HEADLIGHTS OF JANIS Barr's Jeep Liberty cut sharply through the dark Louisiana night. Lightning bugs glowed in the fields and the nocturnal air lingered hot and sticky. They ran with windows down, appreciative of the cooler air caused by the speed of the vehicle. Conversation between them was all but nonexistent. Each, although neither wanted to admit it, knew the gravity of the situation.

At 9:42 pm they pulled onto the lane leading to the old field fence where they had parked earlier. Bringing the Jeep to a stop, Janis killed the headlights and then turned off the engine. The sound of chirping crickets flooded the open windows. Directly over the Jeep, the moon sat perfectly round and bright, surrounded by stars that twinkled with amazing clarity. Glancing through the Jeep's dimly lit interior, the two nodded, then climbed out of the vehicle.

Fireflies speckled the meadow behind them, and there was no other sound apart from the chirping of crickets. It would have appeared a beautiful Louisiana night, but ahead the woods stood dark and foreboding. Moving to the rear of the vehicle, Janis opened the hatch, and both retrieved their shotguns and other items. Clay chose not to wear the ankle holster and instead tucked the small .380 behind his belt in the small of his back. Janis slung the strap of the night-vision case over her shoulder, then both loaded their shotguns. When finished, Janis closed the hatch quietly and they headed for the dark woods.

Sweat beaded their faces and their clothes clung to their bodies. No breeze existed and Clay likened it to the hot iron mills of Chicago. In the woods, the moon's light was limited to near total darkness, so Clay turned on a small flashlight. Because he was expected, there was no need in trying to remain unseen. Janis too carried a light but did not turn hers on. Although convinced Blue Eyes knew of her presence, by not using her light she might at least maintain a small element of surprise.

Once through the woods, standing at the edge where they had hidden earlier in the day, Janis wished Clay the best and darted away toward the back of the house. For a long while, Clay stood staring at the distant mansion. In a room upstairs, a dim light glowed; that would be his destination. Closing his eyes, he sighed and did something he had not done in a very long time. He prayed.

CHAPTER FIFTY-SIX

BOB LEMUS OPENED HIS eyes. He lay naked on his back and staring into thick blackness. Taking a deep breath, he coughed as stale musty air filled his lungs. Vigorously the agent blinked, attempting to see even a pinch of light, but the darkness around him remained absolute.

His right hand gripped his service weapon, and he knew someone had placed it there intentionally. Through reflex, he pushed the clip release, catching it with his free hand. Feeling with his fingers he discovered someone had left him with only one round. He slid the clip back into position.

With his left-hand Lemus reached through the darkness above him. Only inches from his face, his hand pressed against smooth wooden boards. Slowly he inched his fingers along their surface in the direction of his feet; they appeared to run the length of his body. Lemus's heart began to race. Lifting both arms, bent at the elbows, he pushed outward. Almost immediately, he struck a wall.

For the first time in his life, Bob Lemus felt the pure pangs of fear. He knew what Blue Eyes had done. For the three years the agent had been pursuing the killer, gathering a psychological profile on him, the madman had been doing the same in return. And now it was obvious the killer had done his job well.

Lemus began hyperventilating. Panic was rapidly overwhelming even the smallest remnant of self-control. His once brilliant and analytical mind was exploding, breaking away into fragmented pieces. He screamed into the tight lightless confines that imprisoned him. *"OH DEAR GOD, he's buried me alive!"*

CHAPTER FIFTY-SEVEN

CLAY, CLOAKED IN MOONLIGHT, walked unwaveringly down the oak drive. Like Janis, he was scared, but he was also determined it would all end here tonight. This sick, morbid killer was going to die, either by a ceremonial knife, a bullet, or his own bare hands. And given the choice, it would be his bare hands.

As he grew closer, he observed someone lighting candles in one of the rooms downstairs to his left, but he could not see who it was because of the angle. It took just under two minutes to reach the house, and when Clay was just a few feet from the front door Blue Eyes called down from the balcony. Clay stopped and looked up. The killer was leaning on the rail. Even in the moonlight Clay could see him smiling.

"Marshall, so nice to see you again. Do join me. But please, before coming up, stop by the parlor and say hello to your friends. They are in possession of a note you must read and agree to prior to coming up. If you refuse...well, it's one of those offers in which you have no choice." Blue Eyes turned then, disappearing somewhere into the upstairs.

Clay stared after him a few moments, then shook his head and walked to the front door. Pausing, he took a deep breath and pushed it open. With admitted trepidation he stepped inside. It was in the dining room that someone had lit the candles. Turning left, he walked to the room's doorway, halting abruptly beneath its open archway.

In the center of a dark, oak table, a large candelabra burned brightly. Shadowy light flickered. At each end of the table, tied upright in high back chairs so as to not fall forward, were the bodies of Sean and Evelyn Parks. Evelyn's back was to him, and Sean sat at the far end, facing the arched doorway. Sean's eyes were open, as if staring at him. Clay could not help himself. He began to cry. Wiping at his eyes, he entered with reluctance, moving slowly to the table. The blood in his veins boiled with hatred for the man waiting upstairs.

In front of their bodies sat a place-setting consisting of a tarnished silver goblet, neatly placed silverware, and a plate obviously filled with food but covered with a cloth napkin. It was all as if they were waiting for him to arrive so they could begin eating.

Clay could see a piece of paper rolled and stuffed into Sean's shirt pocket. Moving to Sean's side, he wiped at his eyes again and pulled it free. It was a note. Moving to the light of the candelabra, he read it.

Clay, wish I could see you, but as you can tell, Evelyn and I are dead. I want you to know that had you killed him as originally planned, we would still be alive. But hey, who knew? So here you are, with one last chance before any more of us must die. I want you to know, regardless, as far as Evelyn and I are concerned, our hearts are yours. The nice Mr. Blue Eyes has left special instructions for you to follow; look beneath my napkin for another note. And should you be hungry, bon appetite.

Clay crumpled the note. Hand shaking, he reached out for the end of the napkin, fearing what lay beneath it. If it were what he thought, he would not be able to handle it. Blue Eyes was sick and psychopathic, yes, but that would be going far beyond cruel and inhumane. It would surpass the unforgivable.

He snapped the napkin free; vomit rushed up from his stomach, exploding from his mouth. Dropping to his knees, Clay retched painfully. The human heart sat atop the piece of paper lying flat beneath it. He vomited twice more, and then began to cry.

For several minutes, he kneeled there. Even as he wept, his mind wondered if he would ever be able to forgive himself. Time elapsed, filled with memories. Great was his hurt, and amid it all, an agonizing fear seared his consciousness. Would his best friend blame him for this insane and senseless atrocity?

And there was one other thought, fusing itself amid the tears and pain and fear, but this one gave satisfaction. With closed fists, he vowed to fulfill it. Blue Eyes would never leave this house alive. Somewhere in the sadness and anger Clay's tears dried, and he found the strength to pull himself to his feet. With a deep breath, he summoned the courage to work the note gingerly from beneath the human heart. Ten words were written on it.

OOPS, the note you want is on the other plate.

Lifting his head, Clay screamed to the cold-blooded, bastard waiting upstairs, his words slicing through the musty stillness: *"You rotten bastard."*

Telling Sean, he was sorry, Clay moved down the edge of the table to where Evelyn's corpse sat tied. Pulling the napkin from atop her heart, he worked the note free with as little movement of the heart as possible. Again, he moved to the candelabra and read.

Okay remember, if you want your other friends to live, do exactly as told. Remove your clothes, all of them. Tuck your socks and underwear in your boots and set them in the middle of the table near the candelabra, then neatly fold your pants and shirt and place them next to your boots. You will have no need for weapons, so leave them lying on the table as well. Besides, where would you hide them? Next, strip both Evelyn and Sean of their clothing, neatly fold it and place it next to yours. If you do not do these things-and I will know-do not bother coming up for your friends. For I will see to it they too will be dead, and I gone by the time you reach us. When you've completed your assignment, come up the stairs to the second floor and walk to the bedroom at the far end overlooking the oak tree lane. What you see in the upstairs hallway will no doubt unnerve you, but providing you do exactly as instructed, it will all work out. Come directly to the front bedroom where I will be waiting. I have decided that this time the ceremony will take place in the nude, for you and I, and all present. Now hurry, my destiny waits.

Clay laid the note calmly on the table, closing his eyes. His heart pounded. He wanted to rush straight upstairs to this son of a bitch and kill him right now. If only there were no others involved! But there were, and he had them to think about.

So, with great enmity he laid his weapons on the table and removed his clothing, placing them neatly folded near the candelabra just as instructed. Naked, he approached the body of Sean Parks, slowly untying the rope holding his corpse. His eyes remained wet. Grabbing the body so as not to allow it to fall forward, he struggled to lay it on the floor. It was beginning to stiffen, and the smell of dried blood and stagnant body fluids made him sick to his stomach.

With the remains on the floor, he attempted to remove the clothing but found the limbs too stiff. Retrieving a knife from Sean's table setting, he cut the clothing free, then folded it and placed it on the table next to his. Sean's chest lay widely gapped, and he guessed it had been pulled apart following the slice of the killer's knife to allow easy access to the heart.

Clay took a moment to move away and breathe in fresh air. When rejuvenated, he went to Evelyn. Using the knife, he again began cutting off the clothing, then folded it and placed the items on the table with the others.

Reverently, he positioned the couple side by side, cried a moment while standing at their feet, then turned and headed for the stairs leading to the friends that were still alive, and the bastard he could not wait to kill.

CHAPTER FIFTY-EIGHT

JANIS BARR MOVED SUMMARILY through the moon's silvery shadows. She crossed through an open field, into the backyard, then between an old Pinto and dark van sitting at the backside of the house. She wondered who the vehicles belonged to and how many of their passengers were waiting inside the building.

At the back door of the old mansion she paused, pressing tightly against the wall. Her twelve-gauge shotgun was clutched in her hands. Straining, she listened. There was no sound, and darkness filled the interior. She reached out and gently turned the door handle. It opened with an eerie squeak. She didn't like this at all.

Swiftly, following three deep breaths to calm her nerves, she darted into the dark confines and dropping to one knee, ready to fire. But no one was there. Moonlight filtering through two tall, rectangular windows enabled her to see she was in a kitchen. She could make out, although vaguely, a table and chairs, a long counter, floor to ceiling cupboards, and a dark entranceway leading to the interior of the house. The place smelled strongly of mildew and rotting wood.

Rising quickly to her feet, she removed her night vision goggles from the case and set the case on the floor. She placed the goggles over her eyes, then blinked three times, adjusting to the green light.

Janis could see well into the hallway now, a good distance beyond the entranceway. It appeared safe-free of furniture, rugs, carpets, or any other paraphernalia. Pictures hung in wraithlike shadows tinted by the light of her goggles. Carefully, with prudence, she entered in. It was hotter inside the house, sweat trickled down her face. Clothing stuck irritatingly to new portions of her body, and she imagined the refreshing coolness of a cold shower.

Midway down the hallway, Janis came upon a piece of paper dangling at the end of a string. Halting, she listened intently...nothing. Nothing. The paper spun quietly at the end of the string, and she frowned, for there was no movement of air to cause it to spin, not even from her.

Cradling the barrel of the shotgun in the crook of her left arm, she took hold of the bottom edge of the paper and stopped the spinning. There was writing, and she moved her eyes closer. It had been hung there for her benefit. She read the words in somber silence.

Welcome Ms. Barr,

I have a surprise for you. At the end of the hallway, last room on the left, you will find an FBI agent by the name of Clendes. Yes, he is alive-so far. Your job is to simply enter the room and untie him. He possess important information. For you see, I have yet another FBI agent buried alive and very quickly running out of air. Clendes knows where he is. If you waste time looking for me, or for Marshall Cooper, the buried agent will most certainly die. You must ask yourself: is capturing me worth the death of a good man? Hurry now, a human life is hanging in the balance. And one more thing. We cannot be a hero without a challenge, now, can we? In the room you will meet someone who wants agent Clendes for himself and is waiting to kill you for trying to take him away.

Have fun!

Q.C.

"Asshole." Janis whispered the word softly to herself. Resting the shotgun against the wall, she removed the .45 auto from her jacket pocket and pulled the slide. With the weapon loaded, she placed it back into her pocket. She then pulled the nine-millimeter from its holster and did the same. With both weapons ready, she grabbed the shotgun and moved on.

At the door of the room in question she paused, observing two very important things. First, light was filtering out beneath the door. And second, somewhere behind it someone was rambling endlessly to himself.

CHAPTER FIFTY-NINE

CLAY SLOWLY CLIMBED THE stairway. He wanted to hurry, to charge the aging steps and reach Blue Eyes and choke the life out of him, but he understood the importance of allowing time for Janis to get into the house.

When he stepped onto the second floor and turned to walk where Blue Eyes waited, he froze. What he saw was impossible. It surpassed the sum of all his fears. His beloved Lifesaver was there in the hallway with Ron and Michelle. And that was but half the shock. The three were naked, with Nancy and Michelle standing balanced atop each of Ron's shoulders, Michelle on his left and Nancy on his right. Ron's hands were free, and he gripped both women by an ankle, attempting to keep them balanced. The women's hands had been tied behind their backs and they wobbled perilously. The three stood circled within a ring of burning candles.

To discourage Clay from lagging, the killer had placed a noose around the neck of each girl, with the running end of the rope disappearing through a rectangular hole in the vaulted ceiling. Clay guessed the opening to be the access to the attic. The ends of the ropes had been tied to rafters somewhere up there in the darkness. Blue Eyes had adjusted the rope to the perfect length and distance, placing the knot just below their ears so as to ensure the snapping of their necks should one of them slip.

Beyond them, he could see into the doorway of a room, a bedroom. Candles burned brightly and a bed was centered on the doorway so one could easily observe the hallway when lying on it. Blue Eyes was doing just that, lying comfortably, and watching Clay's every move.

Enjoying the anguish on Clay's face, the deranged madman smiled and called out to him. "Please Marshall, do not hesitate. As you can see, the ladies are having a difficult time balancing. I know you do not wish to see their vertebrae snapped and spinal cords severed, all because you took too long, and they grew tired and fell. So come down here and let us quickly finish what you should have done in the first place."

Clay followed his prompting and moved forward but paused when he reached Ron's side. Looking up into the shadowed faces of the two women fighting to stay balanced, he saw the fear in their eyes. They could not express it, however, nor encourage him to move quickly, for Blue Eyes had sealed their mouths with duct tape.

Ron' mouth had not been covered and with convincing urgency, he informed Clay of his waning strength. "I can't hold them forever, pal. Go kill the son-of-a-bitch and get back here."

Clay shook his head. "No time. The girls will never last. The bastard can...."

Blue Eyes called out again from the bed.

"Marshall. Your friend grows weaker with each second you waste. Come here, *now*. When you've finished with me, then you may rescue them."

Clay snapped his head, staring into the eyes of the man he so hated. "Fuck you. I'll kill you, but only after my friends are safe from harm."

"No. You will perform the ceremony first."

Blue Eyes pulled a pistol from beneath a small pillow at his head. Sitting up, he waved the weapon playfully. "This, Marshall, is a .22 caliber. A small piece of lead, yes, but fired into the hearts of those you so dearly love, well, it will make them just as dead as the old couple downstairs. If that is what you wish, then so be it. Let me show you, although I'm sure you are familiar with the potential damage of all loaded guns, what is in store if you do not come here to me this moment."

Blue Eyes leveled the gun on Ron and fired. Clay's mouth opened to yell, but the bullet left the muzzle, tearing into Ron's left thigh even before Clay uttered a sound. The searing pain was intense, virtually unbearable. Ron screamed over the fading report of the shot. He fought the impact of the tumbling lead, knowing it could knock him backward and cause the women to fall. With great effort and concentration, he gritted his teeth, sucking in a deep breath and enduring the pain.

Clay cried out, RON!" He turned his head to Blue Eyes, yelling so angrily he spit with his words. "What in hell are you doing? He can barely hold the girls now!" Whirling back to Ron and ensuring his back was to the killer, Clay told him quickly, "Hang in there. On three I'll rush him, blocking his view. When I tackle him and the fight starts, try and free the girls."

Ron, teeth gritted in agony and thigh now bleeding noticeably, shook his head.

"No, Clay. I can't. My feet are superglued to the floor. I can't move and I can't reach the girl's hands."

Blue Eyes called out once again, "Please Marshall, do stop plotting and come here. My next shot will be Trooper Park's other thigh, then each of his arms and finally his abdomen. You cannot win. Only ten seconds remain before I fire again. I suggest you begin walking my way."

Ron screamed at his friend. "Go, damn it! Do it and get back here!"

Blue Eyes settled back on the bed, haughty. "Yes, Marshal Cooper," he said, smiling into the candle-lit room. "Do it."

CHAPTER SIXTY

ANIS BARR STOOD OUTSIDE the door, trying to make sense of what was being said. Whoever the person was, they were angry about something; their mumbling was non-stop and littered with four-lettered words.

Procrastination to Janis Barr was a synonym for weakness and laziness. The practice of it, she believed, had a tendency to steal away confidence. Therefore, removing her night vision goggles, she set them on the floor, then reached for the door handle and pushed. The door opened with a soft squeal, coming to rest gently against the wall and remaining there, as if some invisible being had grabbed it and held it open for her.

Pulling the shotgun to her shoulder, she moved readily into the room. It was well-lit. A naked man, tied and gagged, sat huddled in the far corner. His head turned with surprise when she entered. Obviously, she reasoned, he was not the one doing the mumbling. Because of the gag he could not speak, but his head began nodding frantically, as if trying to warn her of something she did not know.

Halting, the shotgun still tight to her shoulder, she quickly scanned the room. It was a large study with three walls of shelving still filled with books. A large roll-top desk stood just to the right of the bound agent. It was from behind here the one who had been mumbling rose from an old chair and moved around to face her.

Swiftly, she looked him over, taking in what she saw and calculating. She wasn't sure what she was expecting, but this person was human, a man. Janis's immediate conclusion was simple: this fellow was flesh and blood. If he so much as crossed his eyes in a threatening way, the twelve-gauge she held would ruin his day.

While she had seen his kind before, his being here now, in the heart of Louisiana farmland, was out of place. This person was dirty, dressed as if he had been kidnapped from Chicago's skid row. His clothes were filthy, well-worn, and filled with holes, like those of the big city homeless. He stunk of wine and body odor and was in dire need of a shave and shower.

The dirty man took three steps toward Janis and then stopped, cocking his head. The grimy face expressed elation, and though she could not explain it, she felt as if it were not him looking her over, but rather there was someone else, or something else. A shiver went up her spine.

Then he grinned. His teeth were rotted. When he spoke it spooked her, causing her to grip the shotgun so tight that her fingers began to turn white. The tone was deep and authoritative; it did not fit the person standing before her. "Sooooo. You are the one who has come for him. Well, he is ours."

Janis looked quickly around the room. No one else was there. Glancing once again down the barrel of the shotgun, she asked, "What do you mean, ours? Who else is here?"

"This meat has been given by promise. But he who gave it did not say to us the one coming would be female."

"Who didn't say I'd be female?"

The man smelling of wine and soured clothes ignored her once again. "At first we were just going to kill you, but now seeing you are woman flesh, we have decided to do other things to you first."

Janis frowned. "You're disgusting. But you know, there is a part of me you can do something with. So, from me to *all* of you, whoever the hell all of you are, here's a nice hot, burning ball of lead. Now make sure you share it."

The shotgun blast jolted her shoulder, but the slug impacted him so hard he flew through the air, slamming into the wall and crashing in a mass on the floor next to the tied agent. Quickly Janis moved to Clendes' s side. Setting the shotgun beside her on the floor, she began untying his hands.

"Agent Clendes, I presume?"

"Yes, that would be me. And who are you, may I ask?"

"Janis Barr, PI. I'm here with Clayton Cooper."

"Do you know where he is?"

"No."

Finished with the untying of his hands, Janis asked. "I understand there is another agent buried alive somewhere?"

Clendes nodded. "Yes, and he's probably close to being out of air. We need to get to him fast." Clendes began untying the bonds about his feet.

"And by the way," he added apologetically, "sorry I'm not wearing any clothes. I woke up this way."

Janis smiled. "That's alright. You look handsomely natural."

Janis did not see the hand come up to grab her shoulder. Gripping the material of her jacket, he tossed her like a rag doll almost the length of the room. His strength was astonishing.

Quickly recovering from the shock of it, Janis rose to her feet. Surprise registered on her face. She had just shot this son of a bitch at almost point-blank range in the heart. Now he was climbing to his feet and moving toward her. Even the smelly shirt he wore was still smoldering where the hot slug had struck. Both of his arms rose, reaching out for her.

To gain a few more precious seconds, Janis moved backward, pulling the 9-millimeter rapidly from its holster. She emptied the clip into his chest. The gun echoed loudly in the room and the target skirted backward with the strike of each bullet, but he did not fall.

When the gun was empty, he rushed her, gripping her neck with a sudden firm grasp. His hand was not big, but it possessed power like none she had ever felt. Janis clutched his wrist with both hands. Her face turned blue. Desperately, she tried breaking the hold, but it proved useless. He lifted her easily with one hand, her feet dangling above the floor. In slow, controlled stages, his hand began to tighten, crushing her neck. Janis's eyes began to flutter, and one thought flashed as death rushed in to claim her: this one man possessed the power of ten.

Clendes pumped the shotgun and fired from the floor. The slug struck Janis's would be killer in the back, and the two tumbled forward. Falling hard, he lost his grip. Janis rolled free and choked as she fought to catch her breath. The skid row bum climbed back to his feet, turning to Clendes. Again, Clendes pumped the shotgun and fired, doing so until the only sound left was the empty click of the slide. So powerful were the repeated shots, the impact had literally walked the killer backward through the door and out of the room.

Recovered now, Janis climbed to her feet and pulled the .45 from her pocket. She was as much pissed as frightened. The man with the strength of ten reentered the room storming angrily toward Clendes. Janis raised the .45 at the ready and walked steadily behind him, shouting to the FBI agent.

"What the hell is this thing, that he won't die?"

Clendes shook his head, working desperately to finish untying his feet.

"I've seen it before. He's possessed by demons, and I think he's wearing a vest."

"How do we stop it?"

"Only two ways. Exorcize him or shoot him in the head!"

Clendes never finished untying. The crazed wino reached him taking hold of his hair, lifting him to his feet as if he were weightless. Clendes cried out from the pain.

Then Janis was there. "Hey!"

When the possessed man turned, she pressed the barrel of the .45 to his temple. "Sorry, no time to exorcise." She fired. The opposite side of his head exploded outward in a vortex of bone, blood, and tissue. Instantly flaccid, his body dropped to the floor where it stayed this time. He was dead.

Immediately, three dozen little black beings like the ones she had seen standing by the corpse of Lonzo Pardaux materialized, as if climbing out of the body. They walked to the open doorway then stopped as a group, turning to look at her. One of them stepped forward and in the same voice that had been talking through the wino said, "You're a fucking bitch."

Doing an about face, they then turned and walked out.

Janis shouted after them, "Yeah, the fucking bitch who kicked your little evil asses."

CHAPTER SIXTY-ONE

BOB LEMUS HAD QUIETED somewhat but remained constantly focused. It was the only thing that brought his fear of being buried alive even remotely under control. It was clear that Blue Eyes understood him well. Gripping his weapon tightly, he placed the barrel in his mouth, his hand shaking. One shot, one opportunity. The last thing he would ever do. His eyes closed and he whispered softly. To him, it was prayer: "Sweet Jesus, what else can I do?"

FBI agent Bob Lemus, internationally recognized, both feared and respected, stopper of a hundred killers, divorced father of two and grandfather of four, began to cry.

The world was filled with brave men and women, those who had gone far beyond the call of duty for the sake of others. He had always believed, and not the least bit arrogantly, that he was one of them. Until now. For here alone, buried beneath the earth, death inevitable, he dwelled on his successes and on his failures, and on those things he would miss most. He did not wish to die, especially this way. Perhaps Blue Eyes was the better man, for not only had he arranged the facing of his most feared phobia, but worse, in the end, he had seen to it the great Bob Lemus confronted the worst monster of them all: himself.

Sweat covered Lemus's naked body, rolling down his face and trunk and limbs in streams. The tight confines in which he lay were without a breeze, and sweating was the only mechanism his body possessed in keeping itself cool. But even the million beads of glistening sweat required at least a tiny element of wind or breeze or air for cooling and preventing impending heatstroke. Lemus knew how it worked. Once the sweating stopped, and it would, the body's core temperature would climb, and his brain would literally begin to cook. A stroke would ensue, with death right behind it. That is, if he did not run out of oxygen first.

Four pounds of pressure on the trigger. That was all he needed to end it. One pull, one loud bang, one single instant twinge of pain and no more worries. Blue Eyes would have the last laugh. In retrospect, that was what he truly hated most, the idea of evil winning out over good. He had dedicated the better part of his life to preventing that very thing.

Frowning, Lemus pulled the barrel of the gun from his mouth and whispered aloud into the dark grave, "*shit.*"

He took a breath. Panic exploded like a landmine, its psychological shrapnel shredding what little composure he had left. *He had run out of air.* Wildly he began to struggle, filling the dark confines with soundless screams and pounding against the boards sealing him in. Out of desperation, he fought to lift his legs and roll on his side to use his shoulders, but there was no room. Dear God, he wanted air, wanted to be free, but everything he had tried failed. The Blue Eyes killer, his greatest nemesis ever, the very definition of evil, had unconditionally sealed his fate.

With one last effort, fist weak, he struck out at the unyielding boards only inches above his face. They did not give, his arms fell to his side and he laid back into the deep darkness, gasping in silence.

Then strangely, inexplicably, the gasping stopped, and he began feeling warm and at peace. He began to understand, to accept, that this was his time and death had arrived on scene to take custody of his soul. With a tranquil calm, Bob Lemus closed his eyes. He smiled, satisfied, feeling that now, in the end, he was the one who had won, triumphing over the evil devices of the Blue Eyes Killer, for they would find him having died like a man, with courage and honor, and with a single bullet in his weapon, unused. Then he saw the bright light and was pulled into it.

CHAPTER SIXTY-TWO

AS FAST AS THEY could move without the candles blowing out, Janis Barr and agent Clendes made their way through the dark house to the basement doorway, the place Blue Eyes had told Clendes he had buried Lemus.

Together they clambered down the rickety stairs into a large open area. The floor was dirt, and it took only a short time to locate the freshly dug grave. Setting down his candle, Clendes began digging hurriedly with his bare hands, looking at Janis.

"See if you can find a shovel. I'm sure one was used."

She nodded and began her search. With only candlelight, the hunt was difficult. Seconds passed painfully with both knowing the terrible end should they be too late. At the wall opposite Clendes's head, Janis was suddenly startled and screamed a short yell. An old woman, hidden within the shadows, stood tied to a floor joist, her mouth gagged. Bringing the candle closer to her face, Janis saw she was both alive and awake. The woman's dark eyes stared out anxiously; she wanted to say something but was unable. Janis removed the gag and the old woman blurted out, "You must hurry! He put the shovel behind me. Grab it and dig like you are mad. Your friend is already in the light and may not want to return!"

Janis pulled the shovel out from behind her and threw it to Clendes, then turned and freed the old woman from her bonds, talking as she worked. "So, you're telling me he's already dead?"

The old woman nodded. "Yes, and I fear his wish will be that he does not return. The light he travels in is the good light, His light."

Janis felt sadness they had arrived too late yet wondered at the old lady's words. She asked, "His light? What do you mean?"

Your friend travels on his way to God."

Untying the last knot and freeing the woman, Janis turned to Clendes. "She says he's already dead."

The old woman rebuked Janis while making her way to the graveside. "Yes, I said he was dead, and in the light, but I did not say I could not bring him back. If you hurry, we may be able to turn him around. But you must do exactly as I say. Quickly now, uncover the body."

Clendes glanced at Janis, and she shrugged. He frowned then lowered his head and began working the shovel with frantic speed. Fortunately, the grave was shallow, just deep enough to bury the old wooden coffin in which Lemus lay.

Dirt removed, Clendes used the shovel's spade to pry the coffin lid free. Blue Eyes had nailed it closed, to ensure there would be no escape. Tossing the top quickly aside, they moved their candles close to Lemus's face. The old lady was right: he was dead, deep blue in color.

Clendes' s voice was urgent. "Help me get him out and I'll start CPR."

Together they pulled Lemus's body from the box, placing him on the hard dirt floor. Clendes began resuscitation efforts.

The old lady now kneeling beside the body looked up at Janis. "I am a Voudoun; my bag sits where I was tied. Get it quickly." Janis retrieved it and handed it to her. The old woman pulled a knife from the bag and, taking one of Lemus's fingers, made a slice, milking a small drop of his blood into the palm of her hand. She then pulled a strand of hair from his head and placed it with the blood, then with her fingers added a pinch of dirt from the grave. Those things done, she made a fist, touched her heart, then leaned forward and spread the mixture across Lemus's forehead.

Her dark eyes looked at Janis, then Clendes. "Go now and pray, one to the east corner and one to the west. Tell God this person is a good man and is needed, to send him back and help this world be a better place." Touching Clendes' s arm, the old woman told him, "You can stop your pumping and blowing, it will do him no good. He has traveled too far into the tunnel. I have placed the first breath of life on his forehead, now it is up to him and God to decide if he should come back for it. Quickly now, go and pray."

They rose to their feet and began moving to the corners, but Janis paused, looking down at the old Voudoun. "I mean no disrespect to you, but when, if, he comes back, will he be...normal?"

The old woman smiled ever so slightly. "Yes, he will be normal. This is not *Pet Cemetery.*"

Nodding, Janis and Clendes moved to the corners and kneeled. A soft chanting was coming from the Voudoun. Both crossed themselves, and there in the near total darkness, in the voices of whispers, they began praying for the return of Bob Lemus.

CHAPTER SIXTY-THREE

FOLLOWING ONE LAST GLANCE into the face of his wife and friends, Clay turned, determined. He walked toward Quinten Christenson, the Blue Eyes Killer. This time it would end. If killing him meant his coming back as an Incubus, the King of Demons, or pile of Dog Shit, he did not care. This bastard was going to die-in that bed and covered in his own blood.

Face stern, sober and cold, he yearned for the feel of the demon-handled knife in his hand once more. He could not wait to stand at the edge of the bed and raise the blade high above the bastard's chest. He would bury it deep.

Just short of the doorway, Blue Eyes stopped him. "When you step through the door, Marshall, you will find a small, round stand to your right. The ceremonial dagger lies upon it; pick it up and come here by my side. Remember, one well-placed thrust deep into my heart. You may leave the knife in place or remove it. It matters not."

There was a pause as Blue Eyes watched Clay look back at his friends and wife. Both women were teetering, fighting to maintain balance. They were rapidly losing strength in their legs, and he feared for them. Ron's face was flushed with agony, and he knew his best friend's strength was waning just as quickly. Turning back to the room, he entered, grabbed the knife, and marched straight to the bedside. "Let's do it."

Blue Eyes looked up ponderingly. "Clay, before we do, before we write this final chapter, so to speak, I have to ask: do you not wonder why you were the one chosen? Out of all the people on earth, why was it you? Why Clayton Cooper out of billions? Surely, you're a little curious?"

Clay shook his head. "I don't give a shit why. Let's get on with it."

Blue Eyes let a smile play at the corners of his mouth. "You're concerned for your friends, aren't you? Putting them ahead of yourself. How noble. Personally, I think you want to know, but the fear of my prolonging it may cause Trooper Parks to grow too weak and one or both of the girls may slip. So, just in case I am correct, allow me to put your trepidation to rest. Look, if you will, through the door behind you."

Clay glanced over his shoulder. Crowded in the hallway now, an army of the small black demons had gathered and stood quietly watching them. It was impossible to guess their number, but there were hundreds. Clay expected them to begin chanting but they remained still and noiseless. Their presence did alarm him, but what stood behind Ron and the girls put fear in his heart. Folded once again within itself was the beast that had chased his truck into the field the night he wrecked.

Blue Eyes called out to it, in words Clay did not understand. "Visia, pluus en topet."

The beast began unfolding until it stood totally erect, equal to the height of the top of the girls' heads. The same stink Clay had smelled before began filling the room. The creature's snakelike arms slithered around the waist of both women, pulling them together and lifting them free of Ron's shoulders. Clay could not hear them, but he was sure the girls were screaming. Despite the odor, Ron gave a sigh, thankful for the relief of the weight. The beast held both women suspended in air.

"Rest assured, Marshall," Blue Eyes told him, "he will not harm a hair on their heads and will hold them until I tell him otherwise. Now tell me the truth. Are you curious to know?"

Turning back to the killer, Clay nodded. "Okay, tell me."

"Wonderful. Then I must ask. Do you believe in reincarnation?"

"No"

"You should. Do you believe in God?"

"Yes, of course."

"Then you also believe in Biblical stories?"

Clay's forehead wrinkled. "Yeah. So where is all this going?"

Blue Eyes pressed his lips together. "Patience, if you please."

Clay shook his head. "Man, this is such shit. Let's just get on with it."

Blue Eyes remained calm. "Not until I've told you. It is important to me."

Blue Eyes, lying on his back, laced his fingers and let them rest on his abdomen. Staring into the shadowed ceiling, he began his story. "Many thousands of years ago, two brothers were born, both from the same womb. One grew to be a tiller of the land, and the other made his living tending herds of sheep. One of the two brothers your God loved, and one He did not.

"The one whom He loved was killed by the hand of the one whom He did not. It was a murder born out of jealousy and rage. God was angry and tossed the one who had slain his brother out into the cold, as it were, making his life miserable and tormenting. The slayer became a fugitive. To ensure his unhappiness-that is, eternal separation from God-He put a certain mark upon him, one very noticeable, so all would know not to kill him in the many lives that would follow. And so, for millennia, as it is with all souls, these two brothers kept returning to this plane, being reborn again and again, always into a new body, becoming different people, different personalities, one always good and one always bad, and the bad one always with the mark. The bad brother would perpetually reincarnate on the heels of the good brother, trying to connect, wanting to press the good brother into killing the bad, but fate- that is, God-would always prevent it. Countless times over the centuries, the two have served as world leaders in opposing countries, often waging war one nation against the other."

Clay scowled. "And why is it the bad brother wants the good brother to kill him?"

"Because, Marshall, in the end, when final Judgment Day arrives, the bad brother, along with Satan and all his following, will be cast into the Lake of Fire for all eternity. That event is undoubtedly another millennium away...a very long time to continue the tedious process of dying and being reborn again and again in the flesh. And I, unlike Christians, am not returning with the idea of working toward perfection. So, until the day of judgment arrives, the bad brother wishes to spend the remaining time flourishing in the power of darkness as an Incubus. And only the hand of the good brother, that being you, can make it happen."

Clay took a deep breath and let it out. "So, you're telling me that the characters in this Biblical story are you and I? That we're brothers, and this is the first time in thousands of years that we've been able to meet?"

Blue Eyes nodded. "Yes, Clay, we are brothers, and it has taken this long. So now if for no other reason, you can kill me out of brotherly love. Or revenge. Whichever you choose."

Clayton Cooper began to laugh. He walked to the door, whirled about, and then walked back to the bed. "This is a joke, isn't it? I mean, you are mentally ill. Supposing, just supposing, I gave it legitimate thought. To begin with-and I'm no Biblical scholar mind you, I haven't gone to church in over ten years-but I know what you say can't be true. Reincarnation doesn't exist in the Bible."

Blue Eyes pressed his lips together, then said. "The first time you have access to one of *His* books, open it to Revelations Chapter 3 and read."

Clay spoke without hesitation. "Bullshit. The devil is a liar and you're a liar. I tell you reincarnation doesn't exist. And we are not brothers, you piece of shit."

Blue Eyes unlaced his fingers, laying his arms at his side. He looked at Clay and grinned. "As much as Master Satan is against it, you should read your Bible more often. You would be amazed at what you would learn. Ignorance of God's word, my dear brother, is the net by which we catch all our fish. Now, enough said. To quote you, 'Let's do it.'"

Clay glanced quickly over his shoulder and into the hallway. Everyone and everything remained just as it was. The horde of black demons stared, and the foul-smelling beast still held the girls. Returning his gaze to Blue Eyes, Clay said, "Absolutely, let's do it. But first, have Mr. Stinky place the girls back on Ron's shoulders. And secondly, because when you're dead I have no idea what these things will do, I want them gone. I want it just you and I."

Blue Eyes protested, "No, Marshall, I cannot. Should I send them away, what guarantee would I have you would kill me?"

Clay tightened his jaws. "Guarantee! You want guarantee? Try Sean and Evelyn Parks, the woman in my garage, the two people you left glued together and hanging in the woods, the poor bastard at the motel with the milk jug, the two you shot at the elevator-of course *they* were no great loss-and then add to all that the trauma you've put my wife, myself, and my friends through! No, Blue Eyes, not this time. You said it yourself; it must be done by my hand. So, if you want me to grant your wish, this is where we come into agreement. Tell your cohorts to turn around and crawl back into Hell."

Blue Eyes studied Clay's eyes a long while. Finally, he nodded. "Okay. As you wish. But I warn you, if you do anything other than driving that blade deep into my heart, Hell will come against you with such wrath that 10,000 legions of *His* angels will be unable to turn the tide."

Clay's eyes grew cold. "Just send the freaks home."

Blue Eyes spoke once again in the strange tongue, and the creature that smelled placed the girls back upon Ron's shoulders; he and all the others turned. Resembling a cascade of flowing black water, they began an exodus down the stairs and out the front door into the hot Louisiana night.

CHAPTER SIXTY-FOUR

S THOUGH ROCKETED FROM the startling burst of a giant camera flash, the body of Bob Lemus without warning found itself standing at a gate, like none he had ever seen. It was open. Arched high above his head and bordered by two pearl towers, with high walls of glittering stone stretched far beyond his sight.

Just inside the gateway, came a man dressed in a white linen toga and open-toed sandals. Long, silver hair framed a face aglow with radiance, and the closer he came the more cheerful Bob Lemus became, elated with the greatest of joy. He could not explain it. He thought of the feeling as one of a small child experiencing the love and excitement of Daddy coming home from work.

Beyond the approaching man, within the walls were breathtaking mansions made of jasper, emerald, topaz, sapphire, and countless other hues he could not identify. The streets were pure gold and shined like glass. Music flowed from within, its melody gentle and soothing. Bob Lemus felt a peace and sense of belonging far beyond understanding. In his mind, he stood at the gate of true happiness.

The man in the white toga stopped just short of the gate. He smiled, then spoke with a voice whose tenderness matched the warmth and serenity of the music beyond. "You are seeing what no mere man has ever seen. Beyond this gate is that city where pain, sorrow, crying, and death no longer exist. There is no hunger or thirst; it is a place built not by man, but by God. Know that you do not approach the gate by which you should enter, but one through which you may, if you so choose. But know, there is much more left for you to do below, in the world run by the Prince of Darkness. There are many to be saved from his grasp. You have done much to make it a better place for the many who remain, yet much more remains to be done. Enter here if you wish and receive your crown of glory. But go back and continue your work, and when you return, that crown will be implanted with many jewels. Still, I tell you, returning will not be an easy choice. Elect to stay and He will receive you with joyous embrace. Go back and you will please Him greatly. The choice is for you to make. They below are calling for you, so decide and tell us your will."

Bob Lemus considered his words, weighed them in his mind and in his heart. Then a single tear ran down his cheek. He felt great sorrow at the thought of not staying, of going back. Never had he felt such lightness, such joyous perfection. There existed no feeling on earth that could compare to what lay beyond that gate. Going back would mean turmoil, struggle, and disappointment. Yes, there would be sporadic feelings of reward and moments of laughter, and even some joy, but going back would also mean having to die again. It was appointed unto every man once to die-he had known that for some time, but more importantly, he had just done that very thing-and because of this, he deserved to stay. But reaching far beyond the rewards of choosing to remain was the understanding that going back would please God. He realized, too, the importance of helping those still down there. They were in dire need of help from people like him, like the person he used to be... like the person he was going to be again.

Looking beyond the man standing within the gate, Bob Lemus viewed the beautiful city one last time...its golden streets and precious stoned mansions, its calm and tranquility. Wiping his eyes, he sniffled like a small child. "Send me back. Quickly."

The silver haired man nodded tenderly. "You will recall very little beyond traveling in the light. But in your heart, and you will not know why, there will live a verse, Psalms 121. It is yours to live by. Now return and fight the good fight."

In the cold darkness of the basement, lying prone upon the dirt floor, the body of agent Bob Lemus arched suddenly, sucking in a single deep breath. His body relaxed and he opened his eyes. It was dark, but not as dark as he remembered while buried in the box. Clendes and Janis Barr ended their prayer and rushed to his side, kneeling beside the old lady. Lemus looked into their eyes and asked the Voudoun, "Was bringing me back your doing?"

The old woman nodded firmly. "Some. It was mostly them." She moved her head to glance at Clendes and Barr, then back. "They prayed, but it was you who decided to return."

Lemus pulled himself into a sitting position. The candlelight cast their shadowy forms on the basement walls. Lemus looked at Clendes. "Where is Cooper?"

"Don't know."

"What about his wife?"

"Don't know that either."

Climbing to his feet, Lemus grabbed his weapon on the way up. The others rose with him. "Well, I'm back." He said. "Let's go find them. I have one round in this weapon, and I'll give you one guess whose freaking name is on it."

CHAPTER SIXTY-FIVE

FOLLOWED BY JANIS, THE Voudoun and Clendes, Lemus led the group single file out of the basement. Glancing over his shoulder, he spoke primarily to Janis but also included the old lady. "I apologize for our being naked. Truthfully it's embarrassing."

Janis swept Lemus's muscled back and perfectly rounded buttocks with her eyes. His movement beneath the soft candlelight highlighted a powerful physique.

"Oh, don't let it bother you, agent Lemus," she said coolly. "We're just a couple of women privileged enough to see a side of the FBI most only imagine."

Bob Lemus smiled. This woman was alright. He liked her wit, and she had salt. Being easy on the eyes didn't hurt, either.

Free of the basement, they moved cautiously down the same hallway in which Janis had traveled to find Clendes. The group checked out three rooms on the way before passing the one containing the body of the dead vagabond. The dim, candlelit area remained just as they had left it, the body lying exactly where it had fallen. None of them went in.

The hallway exited to a large foyer with the stairway leading up to Cooper and the others. The front door of the house stood open and was resting against the interior wall. Beyond the door lay a humidity-drenched darkness shimmering in moonlight with dark meadows filled with fireflies.

But inside, the four did not enter the foyer. Halting abruptly instead, they stood at the threshold as if they'd stepped onto the edge of the world. Spellbound, each stared on as a horde of small, black demons marched down the stairs passing only inches from their feet. Lemus guessed their numbers to be in the hundreds. The creatures moved past, oblivious to the humans watching them. In the middle of the herd, towering nearly to the ceiling, came the beast with the snakelike arms and yellowed, elliptical eyes. It too passed as if not noticing them, while at the same time emitting its terrible stench. The four covered their noses and mouths with their hands; fortunately, the odor followed the bizarre creature out the door and dissipated quickly.

Minutes inched by in curious silence before the end of the lengthy line came in view. When the last demon passed, it turned, glimpsing Lemus's naked body up and down. Not missing a step, the little being laughed lightly, "Better hope you grow before you sleep with her."

Lemus stared after him a moment, then looked down at himself and over to Janis. He was speechless.

Janis met his eyes and smiled.

CHAPTER SIXTY-SIX

CLAY STOOD STARING AT the three struggling forms in the hallway. Ron was at the base of it all, with the lives of both women once again dependent upon his stamina. Clay could see clearly his best friend was strained, weakened to point of exhaustion. He feared he might collapse at any moment, and to worsen the situation, the bullet wound in his thigh seeped blood continually.

For Clay himself, the end had arrived. There was no more time; he would be given no more chances. It had come down to the final moment-law or lawlessness. The choice rested with him. Plagued by the unbearable fear he could lose his beloved Lifesaver at any given second, he fought the urge to rush the maniac waiting so anxiously to die.

Turning back to face him, Clay watched with disgust as the sick bastard painted three long red stripes down his face. When finished he laid back, resting his head on a pillow enclosed within a black case with a white, embroidered pentagram. Nestling comfortably down into the sheet-covered bed, he sighed, shifting his eyes, looking first at the knife Clay held, then into the Marshall's face. With jubilance, he smiled. "Ready?"

Clay nodded without expression. "Are you?"

"Oh, indeed. I have been waiting a long time for this. I am most assuredly ready."

"Well," Clay said, "if the story you told is true and we are brothers, there is one last thing I want before I kill the brother who killed me, so long ago."

Blue Eye's brow furrowed. "And what might that be?"

"Privacy."

Clay glanced over his shoulder for one last look at those he loved, then closed the door, sealing the killer and himself in the room. "Now," he said, "I can with clear conscious send you to the Hell you so deserve." Clay raised the knife, slowly. This was it, he thought. He wanted nothing more than to plunge the blade deep into the killer's heart, to watch him die. Nobody deserved it more than Blue Eyes did. Yet to do so would be granting him his wish, and the deaths of Sean and Evelyn would be for nothing. One strong powerful stab and it would be over-yet if what Blue Eyes was saying were true, his death would mean the beginning of something just as horrible, if not worse than what he was currently doing. The very thought of aiding this psychopath in becoming a satanic Incubus disturbed him greatly.

Clay breathed in deeply, and at the same time closed his eyes. In the silence of his personal thoughts, he formed a plan, one involving something he was not truly good at...praying. Since that night talking with Pastor Hart, he had been attempting to pray, to communicate with God in his own way. But always he felt inadequate. Now, however, the chips were on the table, and it was time to play the final hand. Memories rushed through Clay's head. He recalled his corrupt, shameful behavior in Hell; until all of this had begun, his primary focus in life had been on the things of this world, and very little in the way of spirituality. In the broad spectrum of his life, God had been little more than an afterthought. Now, however, he saw and understood things in a much different way. Because only seconds existed before Blue Eyes interrupted, Clay took a deep breath and began the best he could with a prayer born not from logic or an educated mind, but rather from his heart.

"God, I'm no good at this and I hate to, but I've got to rush you. I know I have not gone to church in a long time, I haven't talked to you in a while. In fact, it seems the only time we do talk is when I'm asking for something. I'm sorry for that, but I have to ask for something one more time, something important. I have learned a lot these past few weeks-about you, about me, about dark things that happen, and about the importance of faith. I have learned that there is so much more involved in the fight of good and evil than I can possibly understand that we live in a world much more complicated than good guys versus bad guys. Life here is not just a game, and evil goes far beyond the thief, the rapist, and the murderer. I know now that evil isn't just another preacher's talk designed to scare people into filling the offering plate. I have seen Hell and its demons. I know of your angels and understand our helplessness against the power of the Devil. So please, I ask with all my heart, allow me to end this, as you would have it end. Because honestly, God, I don't have a clue what I should do."

Clay opened his eyes, hoping against hope, but nothing appeared to happen. Blue Eyes had not gone away. The knife in his hand remained raised above the killer's heart. A legion of angels had not flown down from Heaven to surround the bed and take over. It appeared that his attempt at prayer had failed miserably.

However, could he have seen beyond the closed door, and into the quiet of the hallway shadows, Clayton Cooper would have felt differently. He would have cheered aloud and smiled defiantly in the face of the Blue Eyes killer, raising his eyes to Heaven and shouting thank you. For Lemus and the others had climbed the stairway and moved silently to the three distressed figures. He would have seen the senior agent place Janis Barr on his shoulders and cut free the hands of both women. He would have seen their great relief when they removed the gag and noose about their necks, and he would have seen how Clendes lowered them to the floor, where they sat weakly and rubbed their legs, allowing the strength to return. He would have watched as Lemus helped Ron into a sitting position and immediately began cutting away thin slivers of wood from beneath each of his glued feet. And lastly, he would have nodded with great satisfaction in seeing Clendes dressing the bullet wound in Ron Park's thigh using a silk scarf offered by the old Voodoun.

While Clay saw none of it, he did remember something Pastor Hart had told him and Nancy the night of his visit; that faith and trust go together, that you could not have one without the other. Never in his life had believing and trusting been so difficult. It would all be so easy if God would only come down and say, "plunge the knife into the killer's heart," or "do not plunge it into his heart."

Blue Eyes opened his eyes and stared coldly into Clay's face. "You see, brother, He is not here for you. You are alone, you waste your time with Him. So quit your sniffling and do it. The very life of your wife and developing child are dependent upon it!"

Clay looked down at the man waiting to breathe his last, so anxious to die by his very hand. He saw uneasiness in the killer's expression. His eyes were beginning to change. Strained with anger, the madman said again, "Do it! Do it now, damn you!"

Clay tightened his grip on the knife he held.

The Killer's eyes nearly complete in their alteration, the enraged man shouted this time, his voice reverberating through the house. "Damn your hesitation, Able! Kill me!"

Clay raised his face to the ceiling, "God I know you will not damn me. I do have faith. Help me."

Behind him the door opened suddenly, and Bob Lemus was there, weapon pointed, one round aimed at the killer's heart. He circled the bed, telling Clay sternly, "Go. Get out of here, I'll take care of it."

Clay hesitated, remaining with arm poised for the thrust.

"Let Me damn this evil thing, Cooper," Lemus shouted. "Get the hell out, now."

The last speck of black filled his eyes, now complete in their dark transformation. The killer turned his stare upon Lemus. In his head, Clay heard a voice. He recognized it, having heard it for the first time while in the very depths of Hell. It was the same gentle voice that had sent him home to his Lifesaver.

"He must not die."

Instantly Clay reacted. "This is for Sean." He brought the knife down hard, plunging it deep into Blue Eye's thigh. In painful anger the killer screamed, turning to look at the instrument causing him sudden, excruciating pain; it stood buried to the handle, Clay still gripping it. Cooper shouted to Lemus, "Whatever we do, we can't kill him."

Eyes empowered with evil, the killer snapped his head to look at Clay. "You were warned. Now the greatest powers of Hell will come against you. You will know only pain and loss in this world."

With a sucking sound, Clay pulled the knife free of Blue Eye's thigh.

"Screw you and your powers. They've already come against me."

Lemus yelled; weapon still pointed. "Hey, Blue or Black! What the hell ever you are right now!"

Blue Eyes turned his unholy gaze upon Bob Lemus, and in the same instant Clay shouted, "And this one's for Evelyn." He brought the ceremonial knife down one more time in a powerful arch, driving it deeply into the killer's other thigh.

Blue Eyes turned to look at it as he had on the other side, but he did not yell this time, instead he sat up looking at Clay, smiling.

"Your power is weak, but mine grows stronger." Blue Eyes grabbed the knife handle, pulling it free from his leg, licking his own blood from the blade. "You cannot stand against me. None of you can."

Bob Lemus rushed in, bringing the butt of his weapon crashing hard against the killer's head, but it had little impact. Disbelieving, Lemus stepped back, stunned. Turning his eyes to Lemus, the killer raised a pointed finger.

"You are a thorn for which I have no more use; I order you, be dead." Lemus's eyes were locked onto the killers; Lemus felt a sudden crushing pain in his chest. Dropping his weapon, he grasped at the devastating sensation with an open hand. Breathing became impossible.

Instinctively, Clay grabbed the pillow the killer had been laying on. Pulling the case free, he tossed the pillow to the floor. In one fluid motion he slung the pillowcase over Blue Eyes' head, severing his vision with Lemus. Immediately the pain in the agent's chest vanished. Clay climbed upon the bed, and he and the killer struggled. Blue Eyes gripped Clay's wrists with great force; he remained strong, but now only with power limited to that of a man made of flesh and blood. Clay struggled frantically-this was a fight he had to win. If Blue Eyes were to work free, his dark eyes would regain their power and he would use this to kill the lot of them.

Bob Lemus, recovered fully, joined the fight, and through the doorway Janis Barr rushed in, leaping upon the bed yelling, "I want part of this!"

Lemus yelled out to Clendes, "Bring us rope and don't linger your ass, or we're all done for."

Quinten Christenson, the notorious Blue Eyes Killer, was little match for the three of them. Upon Clendes' return, his added strength ensured triumph. Within seconds, the killer lay tied like a roped calf on the very bed he had hoped to die upon and be sent to the Hell he called Utopia. Now the only hell he would taste would be prison isolation, and ultimately that long walk to the chair. It was over.

The Coopers and Parks hugged, shedding tears of both joy and remorse. Blue Eyes lay upon the bed tied tightly, with the pillowcase secured snugly with duct tape. The old Voodoun circled the bed chanting a ritual to keep him weak and helpless, and Clendes was sent on a mission to gather clothing.

Having found the killer's gold cigarette case and lighter, Lemus invited Janis Barr to the balcony for a much-needed smoke. Although she declined the cigarette, she was delighted to accept the invitation.

The Louisiana night remained quiet, blanketed by a silvery stillness. Fireflies glowed to the sound of chirping crickets, and twinkling stars filled a velvety heaven. Out of nowhere, a gentle breeze had been born and now cooled the once sticky air.

Staring at the moon, Bob Lemus took a draw from his cigarette and wondered if God had placed the bright globe there to watch over the earth. Turning, he leaned against the rail and stared into the bedroom at the others, now sitting together at the foot of the bed.

"You know," he said softly, " if I've learned nothing else from all of this, it's that I'm not getting any younger, and it's time to retire. Or at least, semi-retire."

Turning to stare at the couples herself, Janis nodded. "I know what you mean. It seems I hardly have time for anything but work anymore."

Turning back, the two leaned on the rail and looked off into the moonlit fields.

"Actually," Janis added, "I've been considering taking on a partner. I think we'd get along pretty well if you've a mind to move south."

Bob Lemus glanced Janis's way. She looked beautiful in the moonlight. "I think a partnership could work out rather well," he said smiling, "providing you don't believe everything you hear…or see."